## THE SLAYER OF SO

It is the year 1920. A de
Yezidees are plotting to                                    f
the world. Led by the e
Slayer of Souls, their ul
evil. The only person who stands between their dark
design and world chaos is a young woman named
Tressa Norne. An American orphaned in Mongolia,
Tressa was trained in the magical arts as a temple girl
in fabled Yian. She escapes the Yezidee and comes to
New York where she is enlisted by Secret Service
agent Victor Cleves. Soon she is locked in a psychic
life-and-death battle with the Eight Towers of the
Assassins. The world begins to slide into madness.
Now Tressa must face the true test and defy the Slayer
of Souls himself.

## THE MAKER OF MOONS

Roy Cardenhe joins Col. Franklyn Barris and Billy
Pierpont in the Cardinal Woods for a thinly disguised
hunting trip. What they are really after is a group of
counterfeiters who seem to have figured out how to
make gold. Separated from the group, Roy stumbles
across a strange pond where me meets a mysterious
woman named Ysonde who claims to be from a place
called Yian. But danger and magic are afoot in the
woods—strange crab-like creatures begin to appear—
and Roy begins to wonder if he is in the midst of a
dream. But no! Yue-Laou, the Maker of Moons, has
returned! And the wailing Yeth-hounds are loose in
the forest....

# THE SLAYER OF SOULS

## THE MAKER OF MOONS

### ROBERT W. CHAMBERS

STARK
HOUSE

**Stark House Press • Eureka California**

THE SLAYER OF SOULS / THE MAKER OF MOONS

Published by Stark House Press
1315 H Street
Eureka, CA 95501, USA
griffinskye3@sbcglobal.net
www.starkhousepress.com

ISBN: 1-933586-48-6
ISBN-13: 978-1-933586-48-9

Cover design and layout by Mark Shepard
Cover illustration by Lanceld Speed
Proofreading by Rick Ollerman

*Editor's Note: In the interest of maintaining this as a collection of fantastic fiction, the publisher
has edited the following three stories from* The Maker of Moons: *"In the Name of the Most
High," "The Boy's Sister" and "The Crime." There has also been a light editing at the end of the
first two stories in this collection to remove the connecting links which trivialize the content of the
stories. All spellings have been left in their original form from the first hardback editions. And
finally, the publisher would like to thank Mike Chomko for all his great detective work!*

First Stark House Press Edition: May 2014

# TABLE OF CONTENTS

# ROBERT W. CHAMBERS: THE MAKER OF MOONS

## by Gregory Shepard

Robert W. Chambers published nearly a hundred novels, anthologies and children's books but is best remembered today for only one collection, *The King in Yellow*, a loosely-connected group of horror stories that greatly influenced such authors as H. P. Lovecraft and Clark Ashton Smith. Although best known for this seminal horror collection, throughout most of his career, Chambers turned out society stories, romances and historical novels, becoming tremendously popular after the turn of the century but finding little staying power past the 1930s. Unfortunately, his outmoded romances could barely keep apace with his own lifetime, and before his death in 1933 he had already fallen out of favor.

Today we read Chambers in appreciation of a handful of stories—weird stories of cosmic dread, delightful in their morbid decadence, tales that exude a deep, sometimes delicate love of the greater mysteries of life and nature.

Chambers was born in Brooklyn on May 26, 1865, into a family of lawyers, architects and society matrons. His mother, Caroline Chambers, was a direct descendent of Roger Williams, the founder of Rhode Island. His father was William P. Chambers, a famous lawyer. Expectations were always high for his success, and he began his serious education at the Brooklyn Polytechnic Institute. He also studied painting at the Art Students' League in New York, which is where he met Charles Dana Gibson, who went on to fame as a book and magazine illustrator, the creator of the Gibson Girl.

At 21, in 1886, Chambers left for Paris to study art. After seven years at the Ècole des Beaux Arts and Académie Julian, he eventually exhibited in the Paris *Salon* in 1889. And upon returning to New York, he began selling illustrations to *Life*, *Vogue* and other popular magazines of the time. His career as a commercial artist was set.

But his true talents, or perhaps his preeminent love, lay with the pen. Chambers' first book was published anonymously in 1894, a novel of Paris student life called *In the Quarter*. This was successful enough that he followed it with a second novel, *The Red Republic*, the success of which encouraged his publisher to reprint *In the Quarter*, this time with the author's name on it.

*The King in Yellow* followed in 1895. This book, too, was also based on Chambers' Paris art years, but also took inspiration from the stories of Edgar Allan Poe, Ambrose Bierce—particularly "An Inhabitant of Carcosa"—and the decadent French writers of the late 19th century, as well as the rise of spiritualism that was taking place at the end of the century. This remarkable collection revolves around an accursed play, "The King in Yellow," which drives its readers to madness. The first four stories are tragic, horrific tales of individuals who meet their fate after reading the banned play, but by the end of the collection, the stories revolve around the Paris art scene rather than the damnable drama. Still, Lovecraft himself, in his study "The Supernatural in Literature," stated that *The King in Yellow* "achieves notable heights of cosmic fear," and would take inspiration from some of Chambers' arcane names and allusions in his own work.

*The King in Yellow* has become Chambers' touchstone, being almost continuously in print since its turn-of-the-century premiere. It also pointed the way toward the future fantasy collections which soon followed—*The Maker of Moons, The Mystery of Choice, In Search of the Unknown, The Tracer of Lost Persons, The Tree of Heaven* and *Police!!!*—marvelous titles that sometimes promised more than they delivered. Like *The King in Yellow*, Chambers always seemed to mix the fantastic with the mundane in his story collections. He would introduce his readers to strange, exotic characters on the one hand, then abandon that approach and toss in stories of battling soldiers and innocent love, having nothing to do with the previous subject or tone.

*The Maker of Moons* is one such collection. It begins with its title story, a delightfully mysterious tale set in the forests of upstate New York, where a trio of sportsman are secretly trying to track down a group of "moonshiners" who have figured out how to create gold. One of the sportsmen discovers a hidden pool and meets a mysterious young lady named Ysolde. The climax is both wondrous and mystifying. The second tale, "The Silent Land," concerns a fisherman who meets another mysterious French woman, this time named Diane, who has been living on his hunting property without his knowledge. He is immediately attracted, and as they move further into the forest, the reader is gradually pulled into their shared world of nature:

"Over moss and dead leaves aglisten in the pale forest light I passed,—over crumbling logs, damp and lichen-covered, half submerged in little pools; and the musty fragrance of the forest mould set me dreaming of dryads, and fauns, and lost altars, whose marbles, stained with tender green, glimmer in ancient forests."

Scenes like this abound in Chambers' works. His love of nature, coupled with his artist's eye, provide a perfect combination, as demonstrated in this further description from *The Slayer of Souls*:

"It was a strange spot he chose for Tressa—strange but lovely in its own unreal and rather spectral fashion—where a pearl-tinted mist veiled the St. Johns, and made exquisite ghosts of the palmettos, and softened the sun to a silver-gilt wafer pasted on a nacre sky.

It was a still country, where giant water-oaks towered, fantastic under their misty camouflage of moss, and swarming with small birds.

Among the trees the wood-ibis stole; without on the placid glass of the stream the eared grebe floated. There was no wind, no stirring of leaves, no sound save the muffled splash of silver mullet, the breathless whirr of a humming-bird, or the hushed rustle of lizards in the woods."

This is perhaps Chambers' one unifying feature. Whether writing historical novels or weird fantasies, Chambers' true strength as a writer comes to the fore when describing nature. Forests, streams and pools, the sound of bird cries, a trout hiding beneath a mossy ledge–the very air come alive with a sense of Nature's magic and beauty.

Chambers follows "The Silent Land" with "The Black Water," the story of an artist who is blinded in one eye in a tennis accident, but can't bring himself to admit this to the woman he loves—also named Ysolde—until a night in the forest turns their expedition into a tragic rout. This strange tale leads the reader to three very ordinary stories which have no fantasy elements, and in fact, have very little in common with the rest of the book. Then we return at end of the collection back to familiar territory with "A Pleasant Evening," a story of an artist who helps fulfill a lost promise from beyond the grave; and "The Man at the Next Table," an hilarious tale of feline reincarnation.

Like *The King in Yellow*, *The Maker of Moons* is an uneven collection, but at its best it reveals both a keen sense of mystery and a fierce love of nature. After this, Chambers produced more story collections of the same uneven nature, always producing at least a few stories in each that struck a sound note of otherworldliness. But he really made his fortune—if fortune need be made with his wealthy background—writing historical novels such as *Cardigan*, *Maids of Paradise* and *The Hidden Children*, and romantic society books such as *The Younger Set*, *The Gay Rebellion* and *The Restless Sex*. *Life* magazine called his satiric social comedy *Iole* "the most amusing and delectable bit of nonsense that has come to light for a long time," and that frothiness is to be found in many of his romances.

However, by 1916, Chambers' well of fantasy inspiration had dried up and he stopped writing works of the supernatural altogether. But before giving over to the commercial gods entirely, he produced one final flight of fancy, one last work of horrific melodrama—*The Slayer of Souls*. This marvelously overdone novel, first published in magazine format in 1919, is replete with some of Chambers' finest moments of magical mayhem and cosmic horror. Perhaps inspired by the early Oriental occult thrillers of Sax Rohmer, it presents a battle between Western pluck and Eastern intrigue.

Like his story collections, *The Slayer of Souls* also presents Robert W. Chambers at his worst and at his best. Though ostensibly writing about the modern woman and societal dilemmas like love and class, adultery, alcoholism and divorce, at times Chambers' approach to male/female relationships could be mawkish and sentimental. He would sometimes turn out love scenes that grate with their Victorian primness. *The Slayer of Souls* displays a bit of this, as well as a Red-baiting streak a mile wide, indicative of the anti-Bolshevik times and Chambers' own jingoistic tendencies. (His anti-German stance in books like *In Secret* is incredibly harsh to read today.)

But at his best, Chambers dazzled with his imaginative skills, evoking exotic places, mysterious villains and shadowy, otherworldly dominions. And for all Chambers' faults, it is his strengths as a writer that makes *The Slayer of Souls* worth reprinting, and worth reading today. The tale of Tressa Norne and Victor Cleves—she an American raised as a temple girl in Mongolia and he the Secret Service agent entrusted to guard her—as they do battle against the Eight Towers of the Assassins, bent on world domination, is both delightfully absurd and strangely thrilling, as shown by this climactic psychic battle with one of the assassins:

> "Then a terrible thing occurred. The entire flask glowed red hot in his grasp; and the man screamed and strove convulsively to fling the bottle; but it stuck to his hand, melted into the smoking flesh.
>
> Then he screamed again—or tried to—but his entire lower jaw came off and he stood there with the awful orifice gaping in the moonlight—stood, reeled a moment—and then—and *then*—his whole face slid off, leaving nothing but a bony mask out of which burst shriek after shriek—"

*The Slayer of Souls* was first published in an 11-part serial by *Hearst's* magazine from July 1919 to June 1920, and unfortunately when Chambers turned it into book form, he (or the publisher) kept the transitioning paragraphs that brought the reader back to the story between issues. After much agonizing, we have decided to leave these sections in and present the book as George H. Doran Company did back in 1920. But we can't help but wish that someone at Doran had taken the time to edit out these rough sections before its hardback premiere.

Sadly, after *The Slayer of Souls*, Robert Chambers never again wrote another work of fantasy or horror. He knew where his true success lay, and continued to mine his mainstream success even as his audience began to wane. Many critics have bemoaned Chambers' decision to write popular fiction to the exclusion of his obvious talents as a writer of the supernatural. Perhaps it is our great loss that he succumbed to that temptation to the exclusion of all else. But that was his decision, and he definitely wrote about a world he knew—the upper crust of society. And he knew what sold—historical fiction, which he turned to exclusively after 1924. In fact, Chambers once exclaimed to a critic who claimed that *The Man They Hanged*, a story about Captain Kidd, wasn't literature: "Literature! The word makes me sick!" At heart, Robert Chambers was a born storyteller, with no patience or pretense toward loftier aims. He wrote what he wanted to write.

And during his lifetime, he wrote a tremendous amount of fiction, as well as children's nature stories, fishing guides and essays. After Chambers' death on December 16, 1933, following abdominal surgery, his widow, Elsie Chambers, was left with nine more novels of his which she published posthumously, even though his audience had by now dried up.

For a while, Chambers' works languished in obscurity. His estate was plundered and his own collection of books stolen or given away.

Then, gradually, Chambers' horror stories began to find their way back to the marketplace. First in pulp digests like *Famous Fantastic Mysteries* in the 1940s. Then Shroud Publishers reprinted the story "The Maker of Moons" in a staplebound paper edition in 1954. Robert A. W. Lowndes began to reprint Chambers' *King in Yellow* stories in his *Magazine of Horror and Strange Stories* in 1963, re-introducing them to a younger audience. Finally, Ace Books reprinted the entire *The King in Yellow* in paperback with a fine Jack Gaughan rendering of the original hardcover illustration in 1965, and kept it in print for years. Today, with the current publishing state of rendering every single early 20th century book into a poorly proofed paperback or a free ebook, practically every single Robert W. Chambers book and story collection has been made available again in one format or another.

We at Stark House Press honor the memory of Chambers, and his limited output of supernatural and fantasy tales. We hope that by presenting *The Slayer of Souls* in its entirety and *The Maker of Moons* with a bit of light editing and its three non-fantasy stories excised, that we can share with you everything that we love best about Chambers' writing. H. L.

Mencken called Chambers "the Boudoir Balzac" in reference to his main-stream output. We prefer to remember him as the Balladeer of Lost Carcosa, the Poet of the Deep Forest, the Maker of Moons himself.

–January 2014
Eureka, CA

# THE SLAYER OF SOULS

# OF SOULS

## BY ROBERT W. CHAMBERS

To My Friend
George Armsby

TO
GEORGE


I

Mirror of Fashion,
Admiral of Finance,
Don't, in a passion,
Denounce this poor Romance;
For, while I dare not hope it might
Enthuse you,
Perhaps it will, some rainy night,
Amuse you.

II

So, your attention,
In poetry polite,
To my invention
I bashfully invite.
Don't hurl the book at Eddie's head
Deep laden,
Or Messmore's; you might hit instead
Will Braden.

III

Kahn among Canners,
And Grand Vizier of style,
Emir of Manners,
Accept—and place on file
This tribute, which I proffer while
I grovel,
And honor with thy matchless Smile
My novel.

R. W. C.

# CHAPTER I
# THE YEZIDEE

Only when the *Nan-yang Maru* sailed from Yuen-San did her terrible sense of foreboding begin to subside. For four years, waking or sleeping, the awful subconsciousness of supreme evil had never left her.

But now, as the Korean shore, receding into darkness, grew dimmer and dimmer, fear subsided and grew vague as the half-forgotten memory of horror in a dream.

She stood near the steamer's stern apart from other passengers, a slender, lonely figure in her silver-fox furs, her ulster and smart little hat, watching the lights of Yuen-San grow paler and smaller along the horizon until they looked like a level row of stars.

Under her haunted eyes Asia was slowly dissolving to a streak of vapour in the misty lustre of the moon.

Suddenly the ancient continent disappeared, washed out by a wave against the sky; and with it vanished the last shreds of that accursed nightmare which had possessed her for four endless years. But whether during those unreal years her soul had only been held in bondage, or whether, as she had been taught, it had been irrevocably destroyed, she still remained uncertain, knowing nothing about the death of souls or how it was accomplished.

As she stood there, her sad eyes fixed on the misty East, a passenger passing—an Englishwoman—paused to say something kind to the young American; and added, "if there is anything my husband and I can do it would give us much pleasure." The girl had turned her head as though not comprehending. The other woman hesitated.

"This is Doctor Norne's daughter, is it not?" she inquired in a pleasant voice.

"Yes, I am Tressa Norne.... I ask your pardon.... Thank you, madam:—I am—I seem to be—a trifle dazed—"

"What wonder, you poor child! Come to us if you feel need of companionship."

"You are very kind.... I seem to wish to be alone, somehow."

"I understand.... Good-night, my dear."

Late the next morning Tressa Norne awoke, conscious for the first time in four years that it was at last her own familiar self stretched out there on the pillows where sunshine streamed through the porthole. All that day she lay in her bamboo steamer chair on deck. Sun and wind conspired to dry every tear that wet her closed lashes. Her dark, glossy hair blew about her face; scarlet tinted her full lips again; the tense hands relaxed. Peace came at sundown.

That evening she took her Yu-kin from her cabin and found a chair on the deserted hurricane deck.

And here, in the brilliant moonlight of the China Sea, she curled up cross-legged on the deck, all alone, and sounded the four futile strings of her moon-lute, and hummed to herself, in a still voice, old songs she had sung in Yian before the tragedy. She sang the tent-song called *Tchinguiz*. She sang *Camel Bells* and *The Blue Bazaar*,—children's songs of the Yiort. She sang the ancient Khiounnou song called "The Saghalien":

I

In the month of Saffar
Among the river-reeds
I saw two horsemen
Sitting on their steeds.
Tulugum!
Heitulum!
By the river-reeds.

II

In the month of Saffar
A demon guards the ford.
Tokhta, my Lover!
Draw your shining sword!
Tulugum!
Heitulum!
Slay him with your sword!

III

In the month of Saffar
Among the water-weeds
I saw two horsemen
Fighting on their steeds.
Tulugum!
Heitulum!
How my lover bleeds!

IV

In the month of Saffar,
The Year I should have wed—

The Year of The Panther—
My lover lay dead,—
Tulugum!
Heitulum!
Dead without a head.

And songs like these—the one called "Keuke Mongol," and an ancient air of the Tchortchas called "The Thirty Thousand Calamities," and some Chinese boatmen's songs which she had heard in Yian before the tragedy; these she hummed to herself there in the moonlight playing on her round-faced, short-necked lute of four strings.

Terror indeed seemed ended for her, and in her heart a great overwhelming joy was welling up which seemed to overflow across the entire moonlit world.

She had no longer any fear; no premonition of further evil. Among the few Americans and English aboard, something of her story was already known. People were kind; and they were also considerate enough to subdue their sympathetic curiosity when they discovered that this young American girl shrank from any mention of what had happened to her during the last four years of the Great World War.

It was evident, also, that she preferred to remain aloof; and this inclination, when finally understood, was respected by her fellow passengers. The clever, efficient and polite Japanese officers and crew of the *Nan-yang Maru* were invariably considerate and courteous to her, and they remained nicely reticent, although they also knew the main outline of her story and very much desired to know more. And so, surrounded now by the friendly security of civilised humanity, Tressa Norne, reborn to light out of hell's own shadows, awoke from four years of nightmare which, after all, perhaps, never had seemed entirely actual.

And now God's real sun warmed her by day; His real moon bathed her in creamy coolness by night; sky and wind and wave thrilled her with their blessed assurance that this was once more the real world which stretched illimitably on every side from horizon to horizon; and the fair faces and pleasant voices of her own countrymen made the past seem only a ghastly dream that never again could enmesh her soul with its web of sorcery.

And now the days at sea fled very swiftly; and when at last the Golden Gate was not far away she had finally managed to persuade herself that nothing really can harm the human soul; that the monstrous devil-years were ended, never again to return; that in this vast, clean Western Continent there could be no occult threat to dread, no gigantic menace to destroy her body, no secret power that could consign her soul to the dreadful abysm of spiritual annihilation.

Very early that morning she came on deck. The November day was delightfully warm, the air clear save for a belt of mist low on the water to
the southward.

She had been told that land would not be sighted for twenty-four
hours, but she went forward and stood beside the starboard rail, searching the horizon with the enchanted eyes of hope.

As she stood there a Japanese ship's officer crossing the deck, forward,
halted abruptly and stood staring at something to the southward.

At the same moment, above the belt of mist on the water, and perfectly
clear against the blue sky above, the girl saw a fountain of gold fire rise
from the fog, drift upward in the daylight, slowly assume the incandescent outline of a serpentine creature which leisurely uncoiled and hung
there floating, its lizard-tail undulating, its feet with their five stumpy
claws closing, relaxing, like those of a living reptile. For a full minute this
amazing shape of fire floated there in the sky, brilliant in the morning light,
then the reptilian form faded, died out, and the last spark vanished in the
sunshine.

When the Japanese officer at last turned to resume his promenade, he
noticed a white-faced girl gripping a stanchion behind him as though she
were on the point of swooning. He crossed the deck quickly. Tressa
Norne's eyes opened.

"Are you ill, Miss Norne?" he asked.

"The—the Dragon," she whispered.

The officer laughed. "Why, that was nothing but Chinese day-fireworks," he explained. "The crew of some fishing boat yonder in the fog is
amusing itself." He looked at her narrowly, then with a nice little bow and
smile he offered his arm: "If you are indisposed, perhaps you might wish
to go below to your stateroom, Miss Norne?"

She thanked him, managed to pull herself together and force a ghost of
a smile.

He lingered a moment, said something cheerful about being nearly home,
then made her a punctilious salute and went his way.

Tressa Norne leaned back against the stanchion and closed her eyes. Her
pallor became deathly. She bent over and laid her white face in her folded
arms.

After a while she lifted her head, and, turning very slowly, stared at the
fog-belt out of frightened eyes.

And saw, rising out of the fog, a pearl-tinted sphere which gradually
mounted into the clear daylight above like the full moon's phantom in the
sky.

Higher, higher rose the spectral moon until at last it swam in the very zenith. Then it slowly evaporated in the blue vault above.

A great wave of despair swept her; she clung to the stanchion, staring with half-blinded eyes at the flat fog-bank in the south.

But no more "Chinese day-fireworks" rose out of it. And at length she summoned sufficient strength to go below to her cabin and lie there, half senseless, huddled on her bed.

When land was sighted, the following morning, Tressa Norne had lived a century in twenty-four hours. And in that space of time her agonised soul had touched all depths.

But now as the Golden Gate loomed up in the morning light, rage, terror, despair had burned themselves out. From their ashes within her mind arose the cool wrath of desperation armed for anything, wary, alert, passionately determined to survive at whatever cost, recklessly ready to fight for bodily existence.

That was her sole instinct now, to go on living, to survive, no matter at what price. And if it were indeed true that her soul had been slain, she defied its murderers to slay her body also.

That night, at her hotel in San Francisco, she double-locked her door and lay down without undressing, leaving all lights burning and an automatic pistol underneath her pillow.

Toward morning she fell asleep, slept for an hour, started up in awful fear. And saw the double-locked door opposite the foot of her bed slowly opening of its own accord.

Into the brightly illuminated room stepped a graceful young man in full evening dress carrying over his left arm an overcoat, and in his other hand a top-hat and silver tipped walking-stick.

With one bound the girl swung herself from the bed to the carpet and clutched at the pistol under her pillow.

"Sanang!" she cried in a terrible voice.

"Keuke Mongol!" he said, smilingly.

For a moment they confronted each other in the brightly lighted bedroom, then, partly turning, he cast a calm glance at the open door behind him; and, as though moved by a wind, the door slowly closed. And she heard the key turn of itself in the lock, and saw the bolt slide smoothly into place again.

Her power of speech came back to her presently—only a broken whisper at first: "Do you think I am afraid of your accursed magic?" she managed to gasp. "Do you think I am afraid of you, Sanang?"

"You are afraid," he said serenely.

"You lie!"

"No, I do not lie. To one another the Yezidees never lie."

"You lie again, assassin! I am no Yezidee!"

He smiled gently. His features were pleasing, smooth, and regular; his cheek-bones high, his skin fine and of a pale and delicate ivory colour. Once his black, beautifully shaped eyes wandered to the levelled pistol which she now held clutched desperately close to her right hip, and a slightly ironical expression veiled his gaze for an instant.

"Bullets?" he murmured. "But you and I are of the Hassanis."

"The third lie, Sanang!" Her voice had regained its strength. Tense, alert, blue eyes ablaze, every faculty concentrated on the terrible business before her, the girl now seemed like some supple leopardess poised on the swift verge of murder.

"Tokhta!"* She spat the word. "Any movement toward a hidden weapon, any gesture suggesting recourse to magic—and I kill you, Sanang, exactly where you stand!"

"With a pistol?" He laughed. Then his smooth features altered subtly. He said: "Keuke Mongol, who call yourself Tressa Norne,—Keuke—heavenly azure-blue,—named so in the temple because of the colour of your eyes— listen attentively, for this is the Yarlig which I bring to you by word of mouth from Yian, as from Yezidee to Yezidee:

"Here, in this land called the United States of America, the Temple girl, Keuke Mongol, who has witnessed the mysteries of Erlik and who un-derstands the magic of the Sheiks-el-Djebel, and who has seen Mount Alamout and the eight castles and the fifty thousand Hassanis in white turbans and in robes of white;—*you*—Azure-blue eyes—heed the Yarlig!—or may thirty thousand calamities overtake you!"

There was a dead silence; then he went on seriously: "It is decreed: You shall cease to remember that you are a Yezidee, that you are of the Has-sanis, that you ever have laid eyes on Yian the Beautiful, that you ever set naked foot upon Mount Alamout. It is decreed that you remember noth-ing of what you have seen and heard, of what has been told and taught during the last four years reckoned as the Christians reckon from our Year of the Bull. Otherwise—my Master sends you this for your *convenience*."

Leisurely, from under his folded overcoat, the young man produced a roll of white cloth and dropped it at her feet and the girl shrank aside, shud-dering, knowing that the roll of white cloth was meant for her winding-sheet.

Then the colour came back to lip and cheek; and, glancing up from the soft white shroud, she smiled at the young man: "Have you ended your Ori-

---

*"Look out!" Nomad-Mongol dialect.

ental mummery?" she asked calmly. "Listen very seriously in your turn, Sanang, Sheik-el-Djebel, Prince of the Hassanis who, God knows when and how, have come out into the sunshine of this clean and decent country, out of a filthy darkness where devils and sorcerers make earth a hell.

"If you, or yours, threaten me, annoy me, interfere with me, I shall go to our civilised police and tell all I know concerning the Yezidees. I mean to live. Do you understand? You know what you have done to me and mine. I come back to my own country alone, without any living kin, poor, homeless, friendless,—and, perhaps, damned. I intend, nevertheless, to survive. I shall not relax my clutch on bodily existence whatever the Yezidees may pretend to have done to my soul. I am determined to live in the body, anyway."

He nodded gravely.

She said: "Out at sea, over the fog, I saw the sign of Yu-lao in fire floating in the day-sky. I saw his spectral moon rise and vanish in mid-heaven. I understood. But—" And here she suddenly showed an edge of teeth under the full scarlet upper lip: "Keep your signs and your shrouds to yourself, dog of a Yezidee!—toad!—tortoise-egg!—he-goat with three legs! Keep your threats and your messages to yourself! Keep your accursed magic to yourself! Do you think to frighten me with your sorcery by showing me the Moons of Yu-lao?—by opening a bolted door? I know more of such magic than do you, Sanang—Death Adder of Alamout!"

Suddenly she laughed aloud at him—laughed insultingly in his expressionless face:

"I saw you and Gutchlug Khan and your cowardly Tchortchas in red-lacquered jackets slink out of the Temple of Erlik where the bronze gong thundered and a cloud settled down raining little yellow snakes all over the marble steps—all over you, Prince Sanang! You were *afraid*, my Tougtchi!—you and Gutchlug and your red Tchortchas with their halberds all dripping with human entrails! And I saw you mount and gallop off into the woods while in the depths of the magic cloud which rained little yellow snakes all around you, we temple girls laughed and mocked at you— at you and your cowardly Tchortcha horsemen."

A slight tinge of pink came into the young man's pale face. Tressa Norne stepped nearer, her levelled pistol resting on her hip.

"Why did you not complain of us to your Master, the Old Man of the Mountain?" she asked jeeringly. "And where, also, was your Yezidee magic when it rained little snakes?—What frightened you away—who had boldly come to seize a temple girl—you who had screwed up your courage sufficiently to defy Erlik in his very shrine and snatch from his temple a young thing whose naked body wrapped in gold was worth the chance of death to you?"

The young man's top-hat dropped to the floor. He bent over to pick it up. His face was quite expressionless, quite colourless, now.

"I went on no such errand," he said with an effort. "I went with a thousand prayers on scarlet paper made in—"

"A lie, Yezidee! You came to seize *me!*"

He turned still paler. "By Abu, Omar, Otman, and Ali, it is not true!"

"You lie!—by the Lion of God, Hassini!"

She stepped closer. "And I'll tell you another thing you fear—you Yezidee of Alamout—you robber of Yian—you sorcerer of Sabbah Khan, and chief of his sect of Assassins! You fear this native land of mine, America; and its laws and customs, and its clear, clean sunshine; and its cities and people; and its police! Take that message back. We Americans fear nobody save the true God!—nobody—neither Yezidee nor Hassani nor Russ nor German nor that sexless monster born of hell and called the Bolshevik!"

"Tokhta!" he cried sharply.

"Damn you!" retorted the girl; "get out of my room! Get out of my sight! Get out of my path! Get out of my life! Take that to your Master of Mount Alamout! I do what I please; I go where I please; I live as I please. And if I please, *I turn against him!*"

"In that event," he said hoarsely, "there lies your winding-sheet on the floor at your feet! Take up your shroud; and make Erlik seize you!"

"Sanang," she said very seriously.

"I hear you, Keuke Mongol."

"Listen attentively. I wish to live. I have had enough of death in life. I desire to remain a living, breathing thing—even if it be true—as you Yezidees tell me, that you have caught my soul in a net and that your sorcerers really control its destiny.

"But damned or not, I passionately desire to live. And I am coward enough to hold my peace for the sake of living. So—I remain silent. I have no stomach to defy the Yezidees; because, if I do, sooner or later I shall be killed. I know it. I have no desire to die for others—to perish for the sake of the common good. I am young. I have suffered too much; I am determined to live—and let my soul take its chances between God and Erlik."

She came close to him, looked curiously into his pale face.

"I laughed at you out of the temple cloud," she said. "I know how to open bolted doors as well as you do. And I know *other things*. And if you ever again come to me in this life I shall first torture you, then slay you. Then I shall tell all!... and unroll my shroud."

"I keep your word of promise until you break it," he interrupted hastily. "Yarlig! It is decreed!" And then he slowly turned as though to glance over his shoulder at the locked and bolted door.

"Permit me to open it for you, Prince Sanang," said the girl scornfully. And she gazed steadily at the door.

Presently, all by itself, the key turned in the lock, the bolt slid back, the door gently opened.

Toward it, white as a corpse, his overcoat on his left arm, his stick and top-hat in the other hand, crept the young man in his faultless evening garb.

Then, as he reached the threshold, he suddenly sprang aside. A small yellow snake lay coiled there on the door sill. For a full throbbing minute the young man stared at the yellow reptile in unfeigned horror. Then, very cautiously, he moved his fascinated eyes sideways and gazed in silence at Tressa Norne.

The girl laughed.

"Sorceress!" he burst out hoarsely. "Take that accursed thing from my path!"

"What thing, Sanang?" At that his dark, frightened eyes stole toward the threshold again, seeking the little snake. But there was no snake there. And when he was certain of this he went, twitching and trembling all over.

Behind him the door closed softly, locking and bolting itself.

And behind the bolted door in the brightly lighted bedroom Tressa Norne fell on both knees, her pistol still clutched in her right hand, calling passionately upon Christ to forgive her for the dreadful ability she had dared to use, and begging Him to save her body from death and her soul from the snare of the Yezidee.

CHAPTER II
# THE YELLOW SNAKE

When the young man named Sanang left the bed-chamber of Tressa
Norne he turned to the right in the carpeted corridor outside and hurried
toward the hotel elevator. But he did not ring for the lift; instead he took
the spiral iron stairway which circled it, and mounted hastily to the floor
above.

Here was his own apartment and he entered it with a key bearing the
hotel tag. A dusky-skinned powerful old man wearing a grizzled beard and
a greasy broadcloth coat of old-fashioned cut known to provincials as a
"Prince Albert" looked up from where he was seated cross-legged upon the
sofa, sharpening a curved knife on a whetstone.

"Gutchlug," stammered Sanang, "I am afraid of her! What happened two
years ago at the temple happened again a moment since, there in her very
bedroom! She made a yellow death-adder out of nothing and placed it
upon the threshold, and mocked me with laughter. May Thirty Thousand
Calamities overtake her! May Erlik seize her! May her eyes rot out and her
limbs fester! May the seven score and three principal devils—"

"You chatter like a temple ape," said Gutchlug tranquilly. "Does Keuke
Mongol die or live? That alone interests me."

"Gutchlug," faltered the young man, "thou knowest that m-my heart is
inclined to mercy toward this young Yezidee—"

"I know that it is inclined to lust," said the other bluntly.

Sanang's pale face flamed.

"Listen," he said. "If I had not loved her better than life had I dared go
that day to the temple to take her for my own?"

"You loved life better," said Gutchlug. "You fled when it rained snakes on
the temple steps—you and your Tchortcha horsemen! Kai! I also ran. But
I gave every soldier thirty blows with a stick before I slept that night. And
you should have had your thirty, also, conforming to the Yarlig, my
Tougtchi."

Sanang, still holding his hat and cane and carrying his overcoat over his
left arm, looked down at the heavy, brutal features of Gutchlug Khan—
at the cruel mouth with its crooked smile under the grizzled beard; at the
huge hands—the powerful hands of a murderer—now deftly honing to
a razor-edge the Kalmuck knife held so firmly yet lightly in his great blunt
fingers.

"Listen attentively, Prince Sanang," growled Gutchlug, pausing in his monotonous task to test the blade's edge on his thumb—"Does the Yezidee

Keuke Mongol live? Yes or no?"

Sanang hesitated, moistened his pallid lips. "She dares not betray us."

"By what pledge?"

"Fear."

"That is no pledge. You also were afraid, yet you went to the temple!"

"She has listened to the Yarlig. She has looked upon her shroud. She has admitted that she desires to live. Therein lies her pledge to us."

"And she placed a yellow snake at your feet!" sneered Gutchlug. "Prince Sanang, tell me, what man or devil in all the chronicles of the past has ever tamed a Snow-Leopard?" And he continued to hone his yataghan.

"Gutchlug—"

"No, she dies," said the other tranquilly.

"Not yet!"

"When, then?"

"Gutchlug, thou knowest me. Hear my pledge! At her first gesture toward treachery—her first thought of betrayal—I myself will end it all."

"You promise to slay this young snow-leopardess?"

"By the four companions, I swear to kill her with my own hands!"

Gutchlug sneered. "Kill her—yes—with the kiss that has burned thy lips to ashes for all these months. I know thee, Sanang. Leave her to me. Dead she will no longer trouble thee."

"Gutchlug!"

"I hear, Prince Sanang."

"Strike when I nod. Not until then."

"I hear, Tougtchi. I understand thee, my Banneret. I whet my knife. Kai!"

Sanang looked at him, put on his top-hat and overcoat, pulled on a pair of white evening gloves.

"I go forth," he said more pleasantly.

"I remain here to talk to my seven ancestors and sharpen my knife," remarked Gutchlug.

"When the white world and the yellow world and the brown world and the black world finally fall before the Hassanis," said Sanang with a quick smile, "I shall bring thee to her. Gutchlug—once—before she is veiled, thou shalt behold what is lovelier than Eve."

The other stolidly whetted his knife.

Sanang pulled out a gold cigarette case, lighted a cigarette with an air.

"I go among Germans," he volunteered amiably. "The huns swam across two oceans, but, like the unclean swine, it is their own throats they cut when they swim! Well, there is only one God. And not very many angels. Erlik is greater. And there are many million devils to do his bidding. Adieu. There is rice and there is koumiss in the frozen closet. When I return you shall have been as asleep for hours."

When Sanang left the hotel one of two young men seated in the hotel lobby got up and strolled out after him.

A few minutes later the other man went to the elevator, ascended to the fourth floor, and entered an apartment next to the one occupied by Sanang.

There was another man there, lying on the lounge and smoking a cigar. Without a word, they both went leisurely about the matter of disrobing for the night.

When the shorter man who had been in the apartment when the other entered, and who was dark and curly-headed, had attired himself in pyjamas, he sat down on one of the twin beds to enjoy his cigar to the bitter end.

"Has Sanang gone out?" he inquired in a low voice.

"Yes. Benton went after him."

The other man nodded. "Cleves," he said, "I guess it looks as though this Norne girl is in it, too."

"What happened?"

"As soon as she arrived, Sanang made straight for her apartment. He remained inside for half an hour. Then he came out in a hurry and went to his own rooms, where that surly servant of his squats all day, shining up his arsenal, and drinking koumiss."

"Did you get their conversation?"

"I've got a record of the gibberish. It requires, an interpreter, of course."

"I suppose so. I'll take the records east with me to-morrow, and by the same token I'd better notify New York that I'm leaving."

He went, half-undressed, to the telephone, got the telegraph office, and sent the following message:

"RECKLOW, *New York*:
    "Leaving to-morrow for N.Y. with samples. Retain expert
    in Oriental fabrics.
                                        "VICTOR CLEVES."

"Report for me, too," said the dark young man, who was still enjoying his cigar on his pillows.

So Cleves sent another telegram, directed also to

"RECKLOW, *New York*:
    "Benton and I are watching the market. Chinese im-
    portations fluctuate. Recent consignment per *Nanyang
    Maru* will be carefully inspected and details forwarded.
                                        "ALEK SELDEN."

In the next room Gutchlug could hear the voice of Cleves at the telephone, but he merely shrugged his heavy shoulders in contempt. For he
had other things to do beside eavesdropping.

Also, for the last hour—in fact, ever since Sanang's departure—something had been happening to him—something that happens to a Hassani
only once in a lifetime. And now this unique thing had happened to him—
to him, Gutchlug Khan—to him before whose Khiounnou ancestors
eighty-one thousand nations had bowed the knee.

It had come to him at last, this dread thing, unheralded, totally unex-
pected, a few minutes after Sanang had departed.

And he suddenly knew he was going to die.

And, when, presently, he comprehended it, he bent his grizzled head and
listened seriously. And, after a little silence, he heard his soul bidding him
farewell.

So the chatter of white men at a telephone in the next apartment had
no longer any significance for him. Whether or not they had been spy-
ing on him; whether they were plotting, made no difference to him now.

He tested his knife's edge with his thumb and listened gravely to his soul
bidding him farewell.

But, for a Yezidee, there was still a little detail to attend to before his soul
departed;—two matters to regulate. One was to select his shroud. The
other was to cut the white throat of this young snow-leopardess called
Keuke Mongol, the Yezidee temple girl.

And he could steal down to her bedroom and finish that matter in five
minutes.

But first he must choose his shroud, as is the custom of the Yezidee.

That office, however, was quickly accomplished in a country where fine
white sheets of linen are to be found on every hotel bed.

So, on his way to the door, his naked knife in his right hand, he paused
to fumble under the bedcovers and draw out a white linen sheet.

Something hurt his hand like a needle. He moved it, felt the thing squirm
under his fingers and pierce his palm again and again. With a shriek, he
tore the bedclothes from the bed.

A little yellow snake lay coiled there.

He got as far as the telephone, but could not use it. And there he fell
heavily, shaking the room and dragging the instrument down with him.

There was some excitement. Cleves and Selden in their bathrobes went
in to look at the body. The hotel physician diagnosed it as heart-trouble.
Or, possibly, poison. Some gazed significantly at the naked knife still
clutched in the dead man's hands.

Around the wrist of the other hand was twisted a pliable gold bracelet representing a little snake. It had real emeralds for eyes.

It had not been there when Gutchlug died.

But nobody except Sanang could know that. And later when Sanang came back and found Gutchlug very dead on the bed and a policeman sitting outside, he offered no information concerning the new bracelet shaped like a snake with real emeralds for eyes, which adorned the dead man's left wrist.

Toward evening, however, after an autopsy had confirmed the house physician's diagnosis that heart-disease had finished Gutchlug, Sanang mustered enough courage to go to the desk in the lobby and send up his card to Miss Norne.

It appeared, however, that Miss Norne had left for Chicago about noon.

CHAPTER III
# GREY MAGIC

To Victor Cleves came the following telegram in code:

"Washington,
"April 14th, 1919.

"Investigation ordered by the State Department as the result of frequent mention in despatches of Chinese troops operating with the Russian Bolsheviki forces has disclosed that the Bolsheviki are actually raising a Chinese division of 30,000 men recruited in Central Asia. This division has been guilty of the greatest cruelties. A strange rumour prevails among the Allied forces at Archangel that this Chinese division is led by Yezidee and Hassani officers belonging to the sect of devil-worshipers and that they employ black arts and magic in battle.

"From information so far gathered by the several branches of the United States Secret Service operating throughout the world, it appears possible that the various revolutionary forces of disorder, in Europe and Asia, which now are violently threatening the peace and security, of all established civilisation on earth, may have had a common origin. This origin, it is now suspected, may date back to a very remote epoch; the wide-spread forces of violence and merciless destruction may have had their beginning among some ancient and predatory race whose existence was maintained solely by robbery and murder.

"Anarchists, terrorists, Bolshevists, Reds of all shades and degrees, are now believed to represent in modern times what perhaps once was a tribe of Assassins—a sect whose religion was founded upon a common predilection for crimes of violence.

"On this theory then, for the present, the United States Government will proceed with this investigation of Bolshevism; and the Secret Service will continue to pay particular attention to all Orientals in the United States and other countries. You personally are formally instructed to keep in touch with XLY-371 (Alek Selden) and ZB-303 (James Benton), and to employ every possible means to become friendly with the girl Tressa Norne, win her confidence, and, if possible, enlist her actively in the Government Service as your particular aide and comrade.

"It is equally important that the movements of the Oriental, called Sanang, be carefully observed in order to discover the identity and whereabouts of his companions. However, until further instructions he is not to be taken into custody. M. H. 2479.

"(Signed)
"(JOHN RECKLOW.)"

The long despatch from John Recklow made Cleves's duty plain enough.

For months, now, Selden and Benton had been watching Tressa Norne. And they had learned practically nothing about her.

And now the girl had come within Cleves's sphere of operation. She had been in New York for two weeks. Telegrams from Benton in Chicago, and from Selden in Buffalo, had prepared him for her arrival.

He had his men watching her boarding-house on West Twenty-eighth Street, men to follow her, men to keep their eyes on her at the theatre, where every evening, at 10:45, her *entr'acte* was staged. He knew where to get her. But he, himself, had been on the watch for the man Sanang; and had failed to find the slightest trace of him in New York, although warned that he had arrived.

So, for that evening, he left the hunt for Sanang to others, put on his evening clothes, and dined with fashionable friends at the Patroons' Club, who never for an instant suspected that young Victor Cleves was in the Service of the United States Government. About half-past nine he strolled around to the theatre, desiring to miss as much as possible of the popular show without being too late to see the curious little *entr'acte* in which this girl, Tressa Norne, appeared alone.

He had secured an aisle seat near the stage at an outrageous price; the main show was still thundering and fizzing and glittering as he entered the theatre; so he stood in the rear behind the orchestra until the descending curtain extinguished the outrageous glare and din.

Then he went down the aisle, and as he seated himself Tressa Norne stepped from the wings and stood before the lowered curtain facing an expectant but oddly undemonstrative audience.

The girl worked rapidly, seriously, and in silence. She seemed a mere child there behind the footlights, not more than sixteen anyway—her winsome eyes and wistful lips unspoiled by the world's wisdom.

Yet once or twice the mouth drooped for a second and the winning eyes darkened to a remoter blue—the brooding iris hue of far horizons.

She wore the characteristic tabard of stiff golden tissue and the gold pagoda-shaped headpiece of a Yezidee temple girl. Her flat, slipper-shaped footgear was of stiff gold, too, and curled upward at the toes.

All this accentuated her apparent youth. For in face and throat no firmer contours had as yet modified the soft fullness of immaturity; her limbs were boyish and frail, and her bosom more undecided still, so that the embroidered breadth of gold fell flat and straight from her chest to a few inches above the ankles.

She seemed to have no stock of paraphernalia with which to aid the performance; no assistant, no orchestral diversion, nor did she serve herself with any magician's patter. She did her work close to the footlights.

Behind her loomed a black curtain; the strip of stage in front was bare even of carpet; the orchestra remained mute.

But when she needed anything—a little table, for example—well, it was suddenly there where she required it—a tripod, for instance, evidently fitted to hold the big iridescent bubble of glass in which swarmed little tropical fishes—and which arrived neatly from nowhere. She merely placed her hands before her as though ready to support something weighty which she expected and—suddenly, the huge crystal bubble was visible, resting between her hands. And when she tired of holding it, she set it upon the empty air and let go of it; and instead of crashing to the stage with its finny rainbow swarm of swimmers, out of thin air appeared a tripod to support it.

Applause followed, not very enthusiastic, for the sort of audience which sustains the shows of which her performance was merely an *entr'acte* is an audience responsive only to the obvious.

Nobody ever before had seen that sort of magic in America. People scarcely knew whether or not they quite liked it. The lightning of innovation stupefies the dull; ignorance is always suspicious of innovation—always afraid to put itself on record until its mind is made up by somebody else.

So in this typical New York audience approbation was cautious, but every fascinated eye remained focused on this young girl who continued to do incredible things, which seemed to resemble "putting something over" on them; a thing which no uneducated American conglomeration ever quite forgives.

The girl's silence, too, perplexed them; they were accustomed to gabble, to noise, to jazz, vocal and instrumental, to that incessant metropolitan clamour which fills every second with sound in a city whose only distinction is its din. Stage, press, art, letters, social existence unless noisy mean nothing in Gotham; reticence, leisure, repose are the three lost arts. The megaphone is the city's symbol; its chiefest crime, silence.

The girl having finished with the big glass bubble full of tiny fish, picked it up and tossed it aside. For a moment it apparently floated there in space like a soap-bubble. Changing rainbow tints waxed and waned on the surface, growing deeper and more gorgeous until the floating globe glowed scarlet, then suddenly burst into flame and vanished. And only a strange, sweet perfume lingered in the air.

But she gave her perplexed audience no time to wonder; she had seated herself on the stage and was already swiftly busy unfolding a white veil with which she presently covered herself, draping it over her like a tent.

The veil seemed to be translucent; she was apparently visible seated beneath it. But the veil turned into smoke, rising into the air in a thin white cloud; and there, where she had been seated, was a statue of white stone the image of herself!—in all the frail springtide of early adolescence—a white statue, cold, opaque, exquisite in its sculptured immobility.

There came, the next moment, a sound of distant thunder; flashes lighted the blank curtain; and suddenly a vein of lightning and a sharper peal shattered the statue to fragments.

There they lay, broken bits of her own sculptured body, glistening in a heap behind the footlights. Then each fragment began to shimmer with a rosy internal light of its own, until the pile of broken marble glowed like living coals under thickening and reddening vapours. And, presently, dimly perceptible, there she was in the flesh again, seated in the fiery centre of the conflagration, stretching her arms luxuriously, yawning, seemingly awakening from refreshing slumber, her eyes unclosing to rest with a sort of confused apology upon her astounded audience.

As she rose to her feet nothing except herself remained on the stage— no debris, not a shred of smoke, not a spark.

She came down, then, across an inclined plank into the orchestra among the audience.

In the aisle seat nearest her sat Victor Cleves. His business was to be there that evening. But she didn't know that, knew nothing about him—had never before set eyes on him.

At her gesture of invitation he made a cup of both his hands. Into these she poured a double handful of unset diamonds—or what appeared to be diamonds—pressed her own hands above his for a second—and the diamonds in his palms had become pearls.

These were passed around to people in the vicinity, and finally returned to Mr. Cleves, who, at her request, covered the heap of pearls with both his hands, hiding them entirely from view.

At her nod he uncovered them. The pearls had become emeralds. Again, while he held them, and without even touching him, she changed them into rubies. Then she turned away from him, apparently forgetting that he still held the gems, and he sat very still, one cupped hand over the other, while she poured silver coins into a woman's gloved hands, turned them into gold coins, then flung each coin into the air, where it changed to a living, fragrant rose and fell among the audience.

Presently she seemed to remember Cleves, came back down the aisle, and under his close and intent gaze drew from his cupped hands, one by one, a score of brilliant little living birds, which continually flew about her and finally perched, twittering, on her golden headdress—a rainbow-crest of living jewels.

As she drew the last warm, breathing little feathered miracle from

Cleves's hands and released it, he said rapidly under his breath: "I want a word with you later. Where?"

She let her clear eyes rest on him for a moment, then with a shrug so slight that it was perceptible, perhaps, only to him, she moved on along the inclined way, stepped daintily over the footlights, caught fire, apparently, nodded to a badly rattled audience, and sauntered off, burning from head to foot.

What applause there was became merged in a dissonant instrumental outburst from the orchestra; the great god Jazz resumed direction, the mindless audience breathed freely again as the curtain rose upon a familiar, yelling turbulence, including all that Gotham really understands and cares for—legs and noise.

Victor Cleves glanced up at the stage, then continued to study the name of the girl on the programme. It was featured in rather pathetic solitude under *"Entr'acte."* And he read further: "During the *entr'acte* Miss Tressa Norne will entertain you with several phases of Black Magic. This strange knowledge was acquired by Miss Norne from the Yezidees, among which almost unknown people still remain descendants of that notorious and formidable historic personage known in the twelfth century as The Old Man of the Mountain—or The Old Man of Mount Alamout.

"The pleasant profession of this historic individual was assassination; and some historians now believe that genuine occult power played a part in his dreadful record—a record which terminated only when the infantry of Genghis Khan took Mount Alamout by storm and hanged the Old Man of the Mountain and burned his body under a boulder of You-Stone.

"For Miss Norne's performance there appears to be no plausible, practical or scientific explanation.

"During her performance the curtain will remain lowered for fifteen minutes and will then rise on the last act of 'You Betcha Life.'"

The noisy show continued while Cleves, paying it scant attention, brooded over the programme. And ever his keen, grey eyes reverted to her name, Tressa Norne.

Then, for a little while, he settled back and let his absent gaze wander over the galloping battalions of painted girls and the slapstick principals whose perpetual motion evoked screams of approbation from the audience amid the din of the great god Jazz.

He had an aisle seat; he disturbed nobody when he went out and around to the stage door.

The aged man on duty took his card, called a boy and sent it off. The boy returned with the card, saying that Miss Norne had already dressed and departed.

Cleves tipped him and then tipped the doorman heavily.

"Where does she live?" he asked.

"Say," said the old man, "I dunno, and that's straight. But them ladies mostly goes up to the roof for a look in at the 'Moonlight Masque' and a dance afterward. Was you ever up there?"

"Yes."

"Seen the new show?"

"No."

"Well, g'wan up while you can get a table. And I bet the little girl will be somewheres around."

"The little girl" *was* "somewheres around." He secured a table, turned and looked about at the vast cabaret into which only a few people had yet filtered, and saw her at a distance in the carpeted corridor buying violets from one of the flower-girls.

A waiter placed a reserve card on his table; he continued on around the outer edge of the auditorium.

Miss Norne had already seated herself at a small table in the rear, and a waiter was serving her with iced orange juice and little French cakes.

When the waiter returned Cleves went up and took off his hat.

"May I talk with you for a moment, Miss Norne?" he said.

The girl looked up, the wheat-straw still between her scarlet lips. Then, apparently recognising in him the young man in the audience who had spoken to her, she resumed her business of imbibing orange juice.

The girl seemed even frailer and younger in her hat and street gown. A silver-fox stole hung from her shoulders; a gold bag lay on the table under the bunch of violets.

She paid no attention whatever to him. Presently her wheat-straw buckled, and she selected a better one.

He said: "There's something rather serious I'd like to speak to you about if you'll let me. I'm not the sort you evidently suppose. I'm not trying to annoy you."

At that she looked around and upward once more. Very, very young, but already spoiled, he thought, for the dark-blue eyes were coolly appraising him, and the droop of the mouth had become almost sullen. Besides, traces of paint still remained to incarnadine lip and cheek and there was a hint of hardness in the youthful plumpness of the features.

"Are you a professional?" she asked without curiosity.

"A theatrical man? No."

"Then if you haven't anything to offer me, what is it you wish?"

"I have a job to offer if you care for it and if you are up to it," he said.

Her eyes became slightly hostile:

"What kind of job do you mean?"

"I want to learn something about you first. Will you come over to my table and talk it over?"

"No."

"What sort do you suppose me to be?" he inquired, amused.

"The usual sort, I suppose."

"You mean a Johnny?"

"Yes—of sorts."

She let her insolent eyes sweep him once more, from head to foot.

He was a well-built young man and in his evening dress he had that something about him which placed him very definitely where he really belonged.

"Would you mind looking at my card?" he asked.

He drew it out and laid it beside her, and without stirring she scanned it sideways.

"That's my name and address," he continued. "I'm not contemplating mischief. I've enough excitement in life without seeking adventure. Besides, I'm not the sort who goes about annoying women."

She glanced up at him again:

"You are annoying me!"

"I'm sorry. I was quite honest. Good-night." He took his *congé* with unhurried amiability; had already turned away when she said:

"Please... what do you desire to say to me?" He came back to her table:

"I couldn't tell you until I know a little more about you."

"What—do you wish to know?"

"Several things. I could scarcely ask you—go over such matters with you—standing here."

There was a pause; the girl juggled with the straw on the table for a few moments, then, partly turning, she summoned a waiter, paid him, adjusted her stole, picked up her gold bag and her violets and stood up. Then she turned to Cleves and gave him a direct look, which had in it the impersonal and searching gaze of a child.

When they were seated at the table reserved for him the place already was filling rapidly—backwash from the theatres slopped through every aisle—people not yet surfeited with noise, not yet sufficiently sodden by their worship of the great god Jazz.

"Jazz," said Cleves, glancing across his dinner-card at Tressa Norne— "what's the meaning of the word? Do you happen to know?"

"Doesn't it come from the French 'jaser'?"

He smiled. "Possibly. I'm rather hungry. Are you?"

"Yes."

"Will you indicate your preferences?"

She studied her card, and presently he gave the order.

"I'd like some champagne," she said, "unless you think it's too expensive."

He smiled at that, too, and gave the order.

"I didn't suggest any wine because you seem so young," he said.

"How old do I seem?"

"Sixteen perhaps."

"I am twenty-one."

"Then you've had no troubles."

"I don't know what you call trouble," she remarked, indifferently, watching the arriving throngs.

The orchestra, too, had taken its place.

"Well," she said, "now that you've picked me up, what do you really want of me?" There was no mitigating smile to soften what she said. She dropped her elbows on the table, rested her chin between her palms and looked at him with the same searching, undisturbed expression that is so disconcerting in children. As he made no reply: "May I have a cocktail?" she inquired.

He gave the order. And his mind registered pessimism. "There is nothing doing with this girl," he thought. "She's already on the toboggan." But he said aloud: "That was beautiful work you did down in the theatre, Miss Norne."

"Did you think so?"

"Of course. It was astounding work."

"Thank you. But managers and audiences differ with you."

"Then they are very stupid," he said.

"Possibly. But that does not help me pay my board."

"Do you mean you have trouble in securing theatrical engagements?"

"Yes, I am through here to-night, and there's nothing else in view, so far."

"That's incredible!" he exclaimed.

She lifted her glass, slowly drained it.

For a few moments she caressed the stem of the empty glass, her gaze remote.

"Yes, it's that way," she said. "From the beginning I felt that my audiences were not in sympathy with me. Sometimes it even amounts to hostility. Americans do not like what I do, even if it holds their attention. I don't quite understand why they don't like it, but I'm always conscious they don't. And of course that settles it—to-night has settled the whole thing, once and for all."

"What are you going to do?"

"What others do, I presume."

"What do others do?" he inquired, watching the lovely sullen eyes.

"Oh, they do what I'm doing now, don't they?—let some man pick them up and feed them." She lifted her indifferent eyes. "I'm not criticising you. I meant to do it some day—when I had courage. That's why I just asked you if I might have some champagne—finding myself a little scared at my first step.... But you *did* say you might have a job for me. Didn't you?"

"Suppose I haven't. What are you going to do?"

The curtain was rising. She nodded toward the bespangled chorus. "Probably that sort of thing. They've asked me."

Supper was served. They both were hungry and thirsty; the music made conversation difficult, so they supped in silence and watched the imbecile show conceived by vulgarians, produced by vulgarians and served up to mental degenerates of the same species—the average metropolitan audience.

For ten minutes a pair of comedians fell up and down a flight of steps, and the audience shrieked approval.

"Miss Norne?"

The girl who had been watching the show turned in her chair and looked back at him.

"Your magic is by far the most wonderful I have ever seen or heard of. Even in India such things are not done."

"No, not in India," she said, indifferently.

"Where then?"

"In China."

"You learned to do such things there?"

"Yes."

"Where, in China, did you learn such amazing magic?"

"In Yian."

"I never heard of it. Is it a province?"

"A city."

"And you lived there?"

"Fourteen years."

"When?"

"From 1904 to 1918."

"During the great war," he remarked, "you were in China?"

"Yes."

"Then you arrived here very recently."

"In November, from the Coast."

"I see. You played the theatres from the Coast eastward."

"And went to pieces in New York," she added calmly, finishing her glass of champagne.

"Have you any family?" he asked.

"No."

"Do you care to say anything further?" he inquired, pleasantly.

"About my family? Yes, if you wish. My father was in the spice trade in Yian. The Yezidees took Yian in 1910, threw him into a well in his own compound and filled it up with dead imperial troops. I was thirteen years old.... The Hassani did that. They held Yian nearly eight years, and I lived with my mother, in a garden pagoda, until 1914. In January of that year Germans got through from Kiaou-Chou. They had been six months on the way. I think they were Hassanis. Anyway, they persuaded the Hassanis to massacre every English-speaking prisoner. And so—my mother died in the garden pagoda of Yian.... I was not told for four years."

"Why did they spare you?" he asked, astonished at her story so quietly told, so utterly destitute of emotion.

"I was seventeen. A certain person had placed me among the temple girls in the temple of Erlik. It pleased this person to make of me a Mongol temple girl as a mockery at Christ. They gave me the name Keuke Mongol. I asked to serve the shrine of Kwann-an—she being like to our Madonna. But this person gave me the choice between the halberds of the Tchortchas and the sorcery of Erlik."

She lifted her sombre eyes. "So I learned how to do the things you saw. But—what I did there on the stage is not—respectable."

An odd shiver passed over him. For a second he took her literally, suddenly convinced that her magic was not white but black as the demon at whose shrine she had learned it. Then he smiled and asked her pleasantly, whether indeed she employed hypnosis in her miraculous exhibitions.

But her eyes became more sombre still, and, "I don't care to talk about it," she said. "I have already said too much."

"I'm sorry. I didn't mean to pry into professional secrets—"

"I can't talk about it," she repeated. "...Please—my glass is quite empty." When he had refilled it:

"How did you get away from Yian?" he asked.

"The Japanese."

"What luck!"

"Yes. One battle was fought at Buldak. The Hassanis and Blue Flags were terribly cut up. Then, outside the walls of Yian, Prince Sanang's Tchortcha infantry made a stand. He was there with his Yezidee horsemen, all in leather and silk armour with casques and corselets of black Indian steel.

"I could see them from the temple—saw the Japanese gunners open fire. The Tchortchas were blown to shreds in the blast of the Japanese guns.... Sanang got away with some of his Yezidee horsemen."

"Where was that battle?"

"I told you, outside the walls of Yian."

"The newspapers never mentioned any such trouble in China," he said, suspiciously.

"Nobody knows about it except the Germans and the Japanese."

"Who is this Sanang?" he demanded.

"A Yezidee-Mongol. He is one of the Sheiks-el-Djebel—a servant of The Old Man of Mount Alamout."

"What is *he?*"

"A sorcerer—assassin."

"What!" exclaimed Cleves incredulously.

"Why, yes," she said, calmly. "Have you never heard of The Old Man of Mount Alamout?"

"Well, yes—"

"The succession has been unbroken since 1090 B.C. A Hassan Sabbah is still the present Old Man of the Mountain. His Yezidees worship Erlik. They are sorcerers. But you would not believe that."

Cleves said with a smile, "Who is Erlik?"

"The Mongols' Satan."

"Oh! So these Yezidees are devil-worshipers!"

"They are more. They *are* actually devils."

"You don't really believe that even in unexplored China there exists such a creature as a real sorcerer, do you?" he inquired, smilingly.

"I don't wish to talk of it."

To his surprise her face had flushed, and he thought her sensitive mouth quivered a little.

He watched her in silence for a moment; then, leaning a little way across the table:

"Where are you going when the show here closes?"

"To my boarding-house."

"And then?"

"To bed," she said, sullenly.

"And to-morrow what do you mean to do?"

"Go out to the agencies and ask for work."

"And if there is none?"

"The chorus," she said, indifferently.

"What salary have you been getting?" She told him.

"Will you take three times that amount and work with me?"

CHAPTER IV

# BODY AND SOUL

The girl's direct gaze met his with that merciless searching intentness he already knew. "What do you wish me to do?"

"Enter the service of the United States."

"Wh-what?"

"Work for the Government."

She was too taken aback to answer.

"Where were you born?" he demanded abruptly.

"In Albany, New York," she replied in a dazed way.

"You are loyal to your country?"

"Yes—certainly."

"You would not betray her?"

"No."

"I don't mean for money; I mean from fear."

After a moment, and, avoiding his gaze: "I am afraid of death," she said very simply.

He waited.

"I—I don't know what I might do—being afraid," she added in a troubled voice. "I desire to—live."

He still waited.

She lifted her eyes: "I'd try not to betray my country," she murmured.

"Try to face death for your country's honour?"

"Yes."

"And for your own?"

"Yes; and for my own."

He leaned nearer: "Yet you're taking a chance on your own honour to-night."

She blushed brightly: "I didn't think I was taking a very great chance with you."

He said: "You have found life too hard. And when you faced failure in New York you began to let go of life—real life, I mean. And you came up here to-night wondering whether you had courage to let yourself go. When I spoke to you it scared you. You found you hadn't the courage. But perhaps to-morrow you might find it—or next week—if sufficiently scared by hunger—you might venture to take the first step along the path that you say others usually take sooner or later."

The girl flushed scarlet, sat looking at him out of eyes grown dark with anger.

He said: "You told me an untruth. You *have* been tempted to betray your country. You have resisted. You *have* been threatened with death. You *have* had courage to defy threats and temptations where your country's honour was concerned!"

"How do you know?" she demanded.

He continued, ignoring the question: "From the time you landed in San Francisco you have been threatened. You tried to earn a living by your magician's tricks, but in city after city, as you came East, your uneasiness grew into fear, and your fear into terror, because every day more terribly confirmed your belief that people were following you determined either to use you to their own purposes or to murder you—"

The girl turned quite white and half rose in her chair, then sank back, staring at him out of dilated eyes. Then Cleves smiled: "So you've got the nerve to do Government work," he said, "and you've got the intelligence, and the knowledge, and something else—I don't know exactly what to call it—Skill? Dexterity? Sorcery?" he smiled—"I mean your professional ability. That's what I want—that bewildering dexterity of yours, to help your own country in the fight of its life. Will you enlist for service?"

"W-what fight?" she asked faintly.

"The fight with the Red Spectre."

"Anarchy?"

"Yes.... Are you ready to leave this place? I want to talk to you."

"Where?"

"In my own rooms."

After a moment she rose.

"I'll go to your rooms with you," she said. She added very calmly that she was glad it was to be his rooms and not some other man's.

Out of countenance, he demanded what she meant, and she said quite candidly that she'd made up her mind to live at any cost, and that if she couldn't make an honest living she'd make a living anyway.

He offered no reply to this until they had reached the street and he had called a taxi.

On their way to his apartment he re-opened the subject rather bluntly, remarking that life was not worth living at the price she had mentioned.

"That is the accepted Christian theory," she replied coolly, "but circumstances alter things."

"Not such things."

"Oh, yes, they do. If one is already damned, what difference does anything else make?"

He asked, sarcastically, whether she considered herself already damned.

She did not reply for a few moments, then she said, in a quick, breathless way, that souls have been entrapped through ignorance of evil. And asked him if he did not believe it.

"No," he said, "I don't."

She shook her head. "You couldn't understand," she said. "But I've made up my mind to one thing; even if my soul has perished, my body shall not die for a long, long time. I mean to live," she added. "I shall not let my body be slain! They shall not steal life from me, whatever they have done to my soul—"

"What in heaven's name are you talking about?" he exclaimed. "Do you actually believe in soul-snatchers and life-stealers?"

She seemed sullen, her profile turned to him, her eyes on the brilliantly lighted avenue up which they were speeding. After a while: "I'd rather live decently and respectably if I can," she said. "That is the natural desire of any girl, I suppose. But if I can't, nevertheless I shall beat off death at any cost. And whatever the price of life is, I shall pay it. Because I am absolutely determined to go on living. And if I can't provide the means I'll have to let some man do it, I suppose."

"It's a good thing it was I who found you when you were out of a job," he remarked coldly.

"I hope so," she said. "Even in the beginning I didn't really believe you meant to be impertinent"—a tragic smile touched her lips—"and I was almost sorry—"

"Are you quite crazy?" he demanded.

"No, my mind is untouched. It's my soul that's gone.... Do you know I was very hungry when you spoke to me? The management wouldn't advance anything, and my last money went for my room.... Last Monday I had three dollars to face the future—and no job. I spent the last of it to-night on violets, orange juice and cakes. My furs and my gold bag remain. I can go two months more on them. Then it's a job or—" She shrugged and buried her nose in her violets.

"Suppose I advance you a month's salary?" he said.

"What am I to do for it?"

The taxi stopped at a florist's on the corner of Madison Avenue and 58th Street. Overhead were apartments. There was no elevator—merely the street door to unlock and four dim flights of stairs rising steeply to the top.

He lived on the top floor. As they paused before his door in the dim corridor:

"Are you afraid?" he asked.

She came nearer, laid a hand on his arm:

"Are *you* afraid?"

He stood silent, the latch-key in his hand.

"I'm not afraid of myself—if that is what you mean," he said.

"That is partly what I mean... you'll have to mount guard over your soul."

"I'll look out for my soul," he retorted dryly.

"Do so. I lost mine. I—I would not wish any harm to yours through our companionship."

"Don't you worry about my soul," he remarked, fitting the key to the lock. But again her hand fell on his wrist:

"Wait. I can't—can't help warning you. Neither your soul nor your body are safe if—if you ever do make of me a companion. I've *got* to tell you this!"

"What are you talking about?" he demanded bluntly.

"Because you have been courteous—considerate—and you *don't* know— oh, you don't realise what spiritual peril is!—What your soul and body have to fear if you—if you win me over—if you ever manage to make of me a friend!"

He said: "People follow and threaten you. We know that. I understand also that association with you involves me, and that I shall no doubt be menaced with bodily harm."

He laid his hand on hers where it still rested on his sleeves:

"But that's my business, Miss Norne," he added with a smile. "So, otherwise, it being merely a plain business affair between you and me, I think I may also venture my immortal soul alone with you in my room."

The girl flushed darkly.

"You have misunderstood," she said.

He looked at her coolly, intently; and arrived at no conclusion. Young, very lovely, confessedly without moral principle, he still could not believe her actually depraved. "What did you mean?" he said bluntly.

"In companionship with the lost, one might lose one's way—unawares.... Do you know that there is an Evil loose in the world which is bent upon conquest by *obtaining control of men's minds?*"

"No," he replied, amused.

"And that, through the capture of men's minds and souls the destruction of civilisation is being planned?"

"Is that what you learned in your captivity, Miss Norne?"

"You do not believe me."

"I believe your terrible experiences in China have shaken you to your tragic little soul. Horror and grief and loneliness have left scars on tender, impressionable youth. They would have slain maturity—broken it, crushed it. But youth is flexible, pliable, and bends—gives way under pressure. Scars become slowly effaced. It shall be so with you. You will learn to understand that nothing really can harm the soul."

For a few moments' silence they stood facing each other on the dim landing outside his locked door.

"Nothing can slay our souls," he repeated in a grave voice. "I do not be-

lieve you really ever have done anything to wound even your self-respect.
I do not believe you are capable of it, or ever have been, or ever will be.
But somebody has deeply wounded you, spiritually, and has wounded your
mind to persuade you that your soul is no longer in God's keeping. For that
is a lie!"

He saw her features working with poignant emotions as though struggling to believe him.

"Souls are never lost," he said. "Ungoverned passions of every sort
merely cripple them for a space. God always heals them in the end."

He laid his hand on the door-knob once more and lifted the latch-key.

"Don't!" she whispered, catching his hand again, "if there should be somebody in there waiting for us!"

"There is not a soul in my rooms. My servant sleeps out."

"There *is* somebody there!" she said, trembling.

"Nobody, Miss Norne. Will you come in with me?"

"I don't dare—"

"Why?"

"You and I alone together—no! oh, please—please! I am afraid!"

"Of what?"

"Of—giving you—my c-confidence—and trust—and—and f-friend-
ship."

"I want you to."

"I must not! It would destroy us both, soul and body!"

"I tell you," he said, impatiently, "that there is no destruction of the soul—
and it's a clean comradeship anyway—a fighting friendship I ask of
you—all I ask; all I offer! Wherein, then, lies this peril in being alone together?"

"Because I am finding it in my heart to believe in you, trust you, hold fast
to your strength and protection. And if I give way—yield—and if I make
you a promise—and *if there is anybody in that room to see us and hear us*—
then we shall be destroyed, both of us, soul and body—"

He took her hands, held them until their trembling ceased.

"I'll answer for our bodies. Let God look after the rest. Will you trust
Him?"

She nodded.

"And me?"

"Yes."

But her face blanched as he turned the latch-key, switched on the electric light, and preceded her into the room beyond.

The place was one of those accentless, typical bachelor apartments
made comfortable for anything masculine, but quite unlivable otherwise.

Live coals still glowed in the hob grate; he placed a lump of cannel coal on the embers, used a bellows vigorously and the flame caught with a greasy crackle.

The girl stood motionless until he pulled up an easy chair for her, then he found another for himself. She let slip her furs, folded her hands around the bunch of violets and waited.

"Now," he said, "I'll come to the point. In 1916 I was at Plattsburg, expecting a commission. The Department of Justice sent for me. I went to Washington where I was made to understand that I had been selected to serve my country in what is vaguely known as the Secret Service—and which includes government agents attached to several departments.

"The great war is over; but I am still retained in the service. Because something more sinister than a hun victory over civilisation threatens this Republic. And threatens the civilised world."

"Anarchy," she said.

"Bolshevism."

She did not stir in her chair.

She had become very white. She said nothing. He looked at her with his quiet, reassuring smile.

"That's what I want of you," he repeated.

"I want your help," he went on, "I want your valuable knowledge of the Orient. I want whatever secret information you possess. I want your rather amazing gifts, your unprecedented experience among almost unknown people, your familiarity with occult things, your astounding powers—whatever they are—hypnotic, psychic, material.

"Because, to-day, civilisation is engaged in a secret battle for existence against gathering powers of violence, the force and limit of which are still unguessed.

"It is a battle between righteousness and evil, between sanity and insanity, light and darkness, God and Satan! And if civilisation does not win, then the world perishes."

She raised her still eyes to his, but made no other movement.

"Miss Norne," he said, "we in the International Service know enough about you to desire to know more.

"We already knew the story you have told to me. Agents in the International Secret Service kept in touch with you from the time that the Japanese escorted you out of China.

"From the day you landed, and all across the Continent to New York, you have been kept in view by agents of this government.

"Here, in New York, my men have kept in touch with you. And now, to-night, the moment has come for a personal understanding between you and me."

The girl's pale lips moved—became stiffly articulate: "I—I wish to live," she stammered, "I fear death."

"I know it. I know what I ask when I ask your help."

She said in the ghost of a voice: "If I turn against *them*—they will kill me."

"They'll try," he said quietly.

"They will not fail, Mr. Cleves."

"That is in God's hands."

She became deathly white at that.

"No," she burst out in an agonised voice, "it is not in God's hands! If it were, I should not be afraid! It is in the hands of those who stole my soul!"

She covered her face with both arms, fairly writhing on her chair.

"If the Yezidees have actually made you believe any such nonsense"— he began; but she dropped her arms and stared at him out of terrible blue eyes:

"I don't want to die, I tell you! I am afraid! *afraid!* If I reveal to you what I know they'll kill me. If I turn against them and aid you, they'll slay my body, and send it after my soul!"

She was trembling so violently that he sprang up and went to her. After a moment he passed one arm around her shoulders and held her firmly, close to him.

"Come," he said, "do your duty. Those who enlist under the banner of Christ have nothing to dread in this world or the next."

"If—if I could believe I were safe there."

"I tell you that you are. So is every human soul! What mad nonsense have the Yezidees made you believe? Is there any surer salvation for the soul than to die in Christ's service?"

He slipped his arm from her quivering shoulders and grasped both her hands, crushing them as though to steady every fibre in her tortured body.

"I want you to live. I want to live, too. But I tell you it's in God's hands, and we soldiers of civilisation have nothing to fear except failure to do our duty. Now, then, are we comrades under the United States Government?"

"O God—I—dare not!"

"*Are* we?"

Perhaps she felt the physical pain of his crushing grip for she turned and looked him in the eyes.

"I don't want to die," she whispered. "Don't make me!"

"Will you help your country?"

The terrible directness of her child's gaze became almost unendurable to him.

"Will you offer your country your soul and body?" he insisted in a low, tense voice.

Her stiff lips formed a word.

"Yes!" he exclaimed.

"Yes."

For a moment she rested against his shoulder, deathly white, then in a flash she had straightened, was on her feet in one bound and so swiftly that he scarcely followed her movement—was unaware that she had risen until he saw her standing there with a pistol glittering in her hand, her eyes fixed on the portieres that hung across the corridor leading to his bedroom.

"What on earth," he began, but she interrupted him, keeping her gaze focused on the curtains, and, the pistol resting level on her hip.

"I'll answer you if I die for it!" she cried. "I'll tell you everything I know! You wish to learn what is this monstrous evil that threatens the world with destruction—what you call anarchy and Bolshevism? It is an Evil that was born before Christ came! It is an Evil which not only destroys cities and empires and men but which is more terrible still for it obtains control of the human mind, and uses it at will; and it obtains sovereignty over the soul, and makes it prisoner. Its aim is to dominate first, then to destroy. It was conceived in the beginning by Erlik and by Sorcerers and devils.... Always, from the first, there have been sorcerers and living devils.

"And when human history began to be remembered and chronicled, devils were living who worshiped Erlik and practised sorcery.

"They have been called by many names. A thousand years before Christ Hassan Sabbah founded his sect called Hassanis or Assassins. The Yezidees are of them. Their Chief is still called Sabbah; their creed is the annihilation of civilisation!"

Cleves had risen. The girl spoke in a clear, accentless monotone, not looking at him, her eyes and pistol centred on the motionless curtains.

"Look out!" she cried sharply.

"What is the matter?" he demanded. "Do you suppose anybody is hidden behind that curtain in the passageway?"

"If there is," she replied in her excited but distinct voice, "here is a tale to entertain him:

"The Hassanis are a sect of assassins which has spread out of Asia all over the world, and they are determined upon the annihilation of everything and everybody in it except themselves!

"In Germany is a branch of the sect. The hun is the lineal descendant of the ancient Yezidee; the gods of the hun are the old demons under other names; the desire and object of the hun is the same desire—to rule the minds and bodies and souls of men and use them to their own purposes!"

She lifted her pistol a little, came a pace forward:

"Anarchist, Yezidee, Hassani, Boche, Bolshevik—all are the same—all are secretly swarming in the hidden places for the same purpose!"

The girl's blue eyes were aflame, now, and the pistol was lifting slowly in her hand to a deadly level.

"Sanang!" she cried in a terrible voice.

"Sanang!" she cried again in her terrifying young voice—"Toad! Tortoise egg! Spittle of Erlik! May the Thirty Thousand Calamities overtake you! Sheik-el-Djebel!—cowardly Khan whom I laughed at from the temple when it rained yellow snakes on the marble steps when all the gongs in Yian sounded in your frightened ears!"

She waited.

"What! You won't step out? *Tokhta!*" she exclaimed in a ringing tone, and made a swift motion with her left hand. Apparently out of her empty open palm, like a missile hurled, a thin, blinding beam of light struck the curtains, making them suddenly transparent.

*A man stood there.*

He came out, moving very slowly as though partly stupefied. He wore evening dress under his overcoat, and had a long knife in his right hand.

Nobody spoke.

"So—I really was to die then, if I came here," said the girl in a wondering way.

Sanang's stealthy gaze rested on her, stole toward Cleves. He moistened his lips with his tongue. "You deliver me to this government agent?" he asked hoarsely.

"I deliver nobody by treachery. You may go, Sanang."

He hesitated, a graceful, faultless, metropolitan figure in top-hat and evening attire. Then, as he started to move, Cleves covered him with his weapon.

"I can't let that man go free!" cried Cleves angrily.

"Very well!" she retorted in a passionate voice—"then take him if you are able! *Tokhta!* Look out for yourself!"

Something swift as lightning struck the pistol from his grasp,—blinded him, half stunned him, set him reeling in a drenching blaze of light that blotted out all else.

He heard the door slam; he stumbled, caught at the back of a chair while his senses and sight were clearing.

"By heavens!" he whispered with ashen lips, "you—you *are* a sorceress— or something. What—what are you doing to me?"

There was no answer. And when his vision cleared a little more he saw her crouched on the floor, her head against the locked door, listening, perhaps—or sobbing—he scarcely understood which until the quiver of her shoulders made it plainer.

When at last Cleves went to her and bent over and touched her she looked up at him out of wet eyes, and her grief-drawn mouth quivered.

"I—I don't know," she sobbed, "if he truly stole away my soul—there—

there in the temple dusk of Yian. But he—he stole my heart—for all his wickedness—Sanang, Prince of the Yezidees—and I have been fighting him for it all these years—all these long years—fighting for what he stole in the temple dusk!... And now—now I have it back—my heart—all broken to pieces—here on the floor behind your—your bolted door."

CHAPTER V
# THE ASSASSINS

On the wall hung a map of Mongolia, that indefinite region a million and a half square miles in area, vast sections of which have never been explored.

Turkestan and China border it on the south, and Tibet almost touches it, not quite.

Even in the twelfth century, when the wild Mongols broke loose and nearly overran the world, the Tibet infantry under Genghis, the Tchortcha horsemen drafted out of Black China, and a great cloud of Mongol cavalry under the Prince of the Vanguard commanding half a hundred Hezars, never penetrated that grisly and unknown waste. The "Eight Towers of the Assassins" guarded it—still guard it, possibly.

The vice-regent of Erlik, Prince of Darkness, dwelt within this unknown land. And dwells there still, perhaps.

In front of this wall-map stood Tressa Norne.

Behind her, facing the map, four men were seated—three of them under thirty.

These three were volunteers in the service of the United States Government—men of independent means, of position, who had volunteered for military duty at the outbreak of the great war. However, they had been assigned by the Government to a very different sort of duty no less exciting than service on the fighting line, but far less conspicuous, for they had been drafted into the United States Department of Justice.

The names of these three were Victor Cleves, a professor of ornithology at Harvard University before the war; Alexander Selden, junior partner in the banking firm of Milwyn, Selden, and Co., and James Benton, a New York architect.

The fourth man's name was John Recklow. He might have been over fifty, or under. He was well-built, in a square, athletic way, clear-skinned and ruddy, grey-eyed, quiet in voice and manner. His hair and moustache had turned silvery. He had been employed by the Government for many years. He seemed to be enormously interested in what Miss Norne was saying.

Also he was the only man who interrupted her narrative to ask questions. And his questions revealed a knowledge which was making the girl more sensitive and uneasy every moment.

Finally, when she spoke of the Scarlet Desert, he asked if the Scarlet Lake were there and if the Xin was still supposed to inhabit its vermilion depths. And at that she turned and looked at him, her forefinger still resting on the map.

"Where have you ever heard of the Scarlet Lake and the Xin?" she asked as though frightened.

Recklow said quietly that as a boy he had served under Gordon and Sir Robert.

"If, as a boy, you served under Chinese Gordon, you already know much of what I have told you, Mr. Recklow. Is it not true?" she demanded nervously.

"That makes no difference," he replied with a smile. "It is all very new to these three young gentlemen. And as for myself, I am checking up what you say and comparing it with what I heard many, many years ago when my comrade Barres and I were in Yian."

"Did you really know Sir Robert Hart?"

"Yes."

"Then why do you not explain to these gentlemen?"

"Dear child," he interrupted gently, "what did Chinese Gordon or Sir Robert Hart, or even my comrade Barres, or I myself know about occult Asia in comparison to what you know?—a girl who has actually served the mysteries of Erlik for four amazing years!"

She paled a trifle, came slowly across the room to where Recklow was seated, laid a timid hand on his sleeve.

"Do you believe there are sorcerers in Asia?" she asked with that child-like directness which her wonderful blue eyes corroborated.

Recklow remained silent.

"Because," she went on, "if, in your heart, you do not believe this to be an accursed fact, then what I have to say will mean nothing to any of you."

Recklow touched his short, silvery moustache, hesitating. Then:

"The worship of Erlik is devil worship," he said. "Also I am entirely prepared to believe that there are, among the Yezidees, adepts who employ scientific weapons against civilisation—who have probably obtained a rather terrifying knowledge of psychic laws which they use scientifically, and which to ordinary, God-fearing folk appear to be the black magic of sorcerers."

Cleves said: "The employment by the huns of poison gases and long-range cannon is a parallel case. Before the war we could not believe in the possibility of a cannon that threw shells a distance of seventy miles."

The girl still addressed herself to Recklow: "Then you do not believe there are real sorcerers in Asia, Mr. Recklow?"

"Not sorcerers with supernatural powers for evil. Only degenerate human beings who, somehow, have managed to tap invisible psychic currents, and have learned how to use terrific forces about which, so far, we know practically nothing."

She spoke again in the same uneasy voice: "Then you do not believe that either God or Satan is involved?"

"No," he replied smilingly, "and you must not so believe."

"Nor the—the destruction of human souls," she persisted; "you do not believe it is being accomplished to-day?"

"Not in the slightest, dear young lady," he said cheerfully.

"Do you not believe that to have been instructed in such unlawful knowledge is damning? Do you not believe that ability to employ unknown forces is forbidden of God, and that to disobey His law means death to the soul?"

"No!"

"That it is the price one pays to Satan for occult power over people's minds?" she insisted.

"Hypnotic suggestion is not one of the cardinal sins," explained Recklow, still smiling—"unless wickedly employed. The Yezidee priesthood is a band of so-called sorcerers only because of their wicked employment of whatever hypnotic and psychic knowledge they may have obtained.

"There was nothing intrinsically wicked in the huns' discovery of phosgene. But the use they made of it made devils out of them. My ability to manufacture phosgene gas is no crime. But if I manufacture it and use it to poison innocent human beings, then, in that sense, I am, perhaps, a sort of modern sorcerer."

Tressa Norne turned paler:

"I had better tell you that I *have* used—forbidden knowledge—which the Yezidees taught me in the temple of Erlik."

"Used it how?" demanded Cleves.

"To—to earn a living.... And once or twice to defend myself."

There was the slightest scepticism in Recklow's bland smile. "You did quite right, Miss Norne."

She had become very white now. She stood beside Recklow, her back toward the suspended map, and looked in a scared sort of way from one to the other of the men seated before her, turning finally to Cleves, and coming toward him.

"I—I once killed a man," she said with a catch in her breath.

Cleves reddened with astonishment. "Why did you do that?" he asked.

"He was already on his way to kill me in bed."

"You were perfectly right," remarked Recklow coolly.

"I don't know... I was in bed.... And then, on the edge of sleep, I felt his mind groping to get hold of mine—feeling about in the darkness to get hold of my brain and seize it and paralyse it."

All colour had left her face. Cleves gripped the arm of his chair and watched her intently.

"I—I had only a moment's mental freedom," she went on in a ghost of a voice. "I was just able to rouse myself, fight off those murderous brain-fingers—let loose a clear mental ray.... And then, O God! I saw him in his room with his Kalmuck knife—saw him already on his way to murder me—Gutchlug Khan, the Yezidee—looking about in his bedroom for a shroud.... And when—when he reached for the bed to draw forth a fine, white sheet for the shroud without which no Yezidee dares journey deathward—then—*then* I became frightened.... And I killed him—I slew him there in his hotel bedroom on the floor above mine!"

Selden moistened his lips: "That Oriental, Gutchlug, died from heart-failure in a San Francisco hotel," he said. "I was there at the time."

"He died by the fangs of a little yellow snake," whispered the girl.

"There was no snake in his room," retorted Cleves.

"And no wound on his body," added Selden. "I attended the autopsy."

She said, faintly: "There was no snake, and no wound, as you say.... Yet Gutchlug died of both there in his bedroom.... And before he died he heard his soul bidding him farewell; and he saw the death-adder coiled in the sheet he clutched—saw the thing strike him again and again—saw and felt the tiny wounds on his left hand; felt the fangs pricking deep, deep into the veins; died of it there within the minute—died of the swiftest poison known. And yet—"

She turned her dead-white face to Cleves—"And yet *there was no snake there!*... And never had been.... And so I—I ask you, gentlemen, if souls do not die when minds learn to fight death with death—and deal it so swiftly, so silently, while one's body lies, unstirring on a bed—in a locked room on the floor below—"

She swayed a little, put out one hand rather blindly.

Recklow rose and passed a muscular arm around her; Cleves, beside her, held her left hand, crushing it, without intention, until she opened her eyes with a cry of pain.

"Are you all right?" asked Recklow bluntly.

"Yes." She turned and looked at Cleves and he caressed her bruised hand as though dazed.

"Tell me," she said to Cleves—"you who know—know more about my mind than anybody living—" a painful colour surged into her face—but she went on steadily, forcing herself to meet his gaze: "tell me, Mr. Cleves—do you still believe that nothing can really destroy my soul? And that it shall yet win through to safety?"

He said: "Your soul is in God's keeping, and always shall be.... And if the Yezidees have made you believe otherwise, they lie."

Recklow added in a slow, perplexed way: "I have no personal knowledge of psychic power. I am not psychic, not susceptible. But if you actually possess such ability, Miss Norne, and if you have employed such knowledge to defend your life, then you have done absolutely right."

"No guilt touches you," added Selden with an involuntary shiver, "if by hypnosis or psychic ability you really did put an end to that would-be murderer, Gutchlug."

Selden said: "If Gutchlug died by the fangs of a yellow death-adder which existed only in his own mind, and if you actually had anything to do with it you acted purely in self-defence."

"You did your full duty," added Benton—"but—good God!—it seems incredible to me, that such power can actually be available in the world!"

Recklow spoke again in his pleasant, undisturbed voice: "Go back to the map, Miss Norne, and tell us a little more about this rather terrifying thing which you believe menaces the civilised world with destruction."

Tressa Norne laid a slim finger on the map. Her voice had become steady. She said:

"The devil-worship, of which one of the modern developments is Bolshevism, and another the terrorism of the hun, began in Asia long before Christ's advent: At least so it was taught us in the temple of Erlik.

"It has always existed, its aim always has been the annihilation of good and the elevation of evil; the subjection of right by might, and the world-wide triumph of wrong.

"Perhaps it is as old as the first battle between God and Satan. I have wondered about it, sometimes. There in the dusk of the temple when the Eight Assassins came—the eight Sheiks-el-Djebel, all in white—chanting the Yakase of Sabbah—always that dirge when they came and spread their eight white shrouds on the temple steps—"

Her voice caught; she waited to recover her composure. Then went on:

"The ambition of Genghis was to conquer the world by force of arms. It was merely of physical subjection that he dreamed. But the Slayer of Souls—"

"Who?" asked Recklow sharply.

"The Slayer of Souls—Erlik's vice-regent on earth—Hassan Sabbah. The Old Man of the Mountain. It is of him I am speaking," exclaimed Tressa Norne—with quiet resolution. "Genghis sought only physical conquest of man; the Yezidee's ambition is more awful, *for he is attempting to surprise and seize the very minds of men!*"

There was a dead silence. Tressa looked palely upon the four.

"The Yezidees—who you tell me are not sorcerers—are using power—which you tell me is not magic accursed by God—to waylay, capture, enslave, and destroy *the minds and souls of mankind.*

"It may be that what they employ is hypnotic ability and psychic power and can be, some day, explained on a scientific basis when we learn more about the occult laws which govern these phenomena.

"But could anything render the threat less awful? For there have existed for centuries—perhaps always—a sect of Satanists determined upon the destruction of everything that is pure and holy and good on earth; and they are resolved to substitute for righteousness the dreadful reign of hell.

"In the beginning there were comparatively few of these human demons. Gradually, through the eras, they have increased. In the twelfth century there were fifty thousand of the Sect of Assassins.

"Beside the castle of the Slayer of Souls on Mount Alamout—" she laid her finger on the map—"eight other towers were erected for the Eight Chief Assassins, called Sheiks-el-Djebel.

"In the temple we were taught where these eight towers stood." She picked up a pencil, and on eight blank spaces of unexplored and unmapped Mongolia she made eight crosses. Then she turned to the men behind her.

"It was taught to us in the temple that from these eight *foci* of infection the disease of evil has been spreading throughout the world; from these eight towers have gone forth every year the emissaries of evil—perverted missionaries—to spread the poisonous propaganda, to teach it, to tamper stealthily with the minds of men, dominate them, pervert them, instruct them in the creed of the Assassin of Souls.

"All over the world are people, already contaminated, whose minds are already enslaved and poisoned, and who are infecting the still healthy brains of others—stealthily possessing themselves of the minds of mankind—teaching them evil, inviting them to mock the precepts of Christ.

"Of such lost minds are the degraded brains of the Germans—the pastors and philosophers who teach that might is right.

"Of such crippled minds are the Bolsheviki, poisoned long, long ago by close contact with Asia which, before that, had infected and enslaved the minds of the ruling classes with ferocious philosophy.

"Of such minds are all anarchists of every shade and stripe—all terrorists, all disciples of violence,—the murderously envious, the slothful slinking brotherhood which prowls through the world taking every opportunity to set it afire; those mentally dulled by reason of excesses; those weak intellects become unsound through futile gabble,—parlour socialists, amateur revolutionists, theoretical incapables excited by discussion fit only for healthy minds."

She left the map and came over to where the four men were seated terribly intent upon her every word.

"In the temple of Erlik, where my girlhood was passed after the murder of my parents, I learned what I am repeating to you," she said.

"I learned this, also, that the Eight Towers still exist—still stand to-day,—at least theoretically—and that from the Eight Towers pours forth across the world a stream of poison.

"I was told that, to every country, eight Yezidees were allotted—eight sorcerers—or adepts in scientific psychology if you prefer it—whose mission is to teach the gospel of hell and gradually but surely to win the minds of men to the service of the Slayer of Souls.

"That is what was taught us in the temple. We were educated in the development of occult powers—for it seems all human beings possess this psychic power latent within them—only few, even when instructed, acquire any ability to control and use this force....

"I—I learned—rapidly. I even thought, sometimes, that the Yezidees were beginning to be a little afraid of me,—even the Hassani priests.... And the Sheiks-el-Djebel, spreading their shrouds on the temple steps, looked at me with unquiet eyes, where I stood like a corpse amid the incense clouds—"

She passed her fingers over her eyelids, then framed her face between both hands for a moment's thought lost in tragic retrospection.

"Kai!" she whispered dreamily as though to herself—"what Erlik awoke within my body that was asleep, God knows, but it was as though a twin comrade arose within me and looked out through my eyes upon a world which never before had been visible."

Utter silence reigned in the room: Cleves's breathing seemed almost painful to him so intently was he listening and watching this girl; Benton's hands whitened with his grip on the chair-arms; Selden, tense, absorbed, kept his keen gaze of a business man fastened on her face. Recklow slowly caressed the cold bowl of his pipe with both thumbs.

Tressa Norne's strange and remote eyes subtly altered, and she lifted her head and looked calmly at the men before her.

"I think that there is nothing more for me to add," she said. "The Red Spectre of Anarchy, called Bolshevism at present, threatens our country. Our Government is now awake to this menace and the Secret Service is moving everywhere.

"Great damage already has been done to the minds of many people in this Republic; poison has spread; is spreading. The Eight Towers still stand. The Eight Assassins are in America.

"But these eight Assassins know me to be their enemy.... They will surely attempt to kill me.... I don't believe I can avoid—death—very long.... But I want to serve my country and—and mankind."

"They'll have to get me first," said Cleves, bluntly. "I shall not permit you out of my sight."

Recklow said in a musing voice: "And these eight gentlemen, who are very likely to hurt us, also, are the first people we ought to hunt."

"To get them," added Selden, "we ought to choke the stream at its source."

"To find out who they are is what is going to worry us," added Benton. Cleves had stood holding a chair for Tressa Norne. Finally she noticed it and seated herself as though tired.

"Is Sanang one of these eight?" he asked her. The girl turned and looked up at him, and he saw the flush mounting in her face.

"Sometimes," she said steadily, "I have almost believed he was Erlik's own vice-regent on earth—the Slayer of Souls himself."

Benton and Selden had gone. Recklow left a little later. Cleves accompanied him out to the landing.

"Are you going to keep Miss Norne here with you for the present?" inquired the older man.

"Yes. I dare not let her out of my sight, Recklow. What else can I do?"

"I don't know. Is she prepared for the consequences?"

"Gossip? Slander?"

"Of course."

"I can get a housekeeper."

"That only makes it look worse."

Cleves reddened. "Well, do you want to find her in some hotel or apartment with her throat cut?"

"No," replied Recklow, gently, "I do not."

"Then what else is there to do but keep her here in my own apartment and never let her out of my sight until we can find and lock up the eight gentlemen who are undoubtedly bent on murdering her?"

"Isn't there some woman in the Service who could help out? I could mention several."

"I tell you I can't trust Tressa Norne to anybody except myself," insisted Cleves. "I got her into this; I am responsible if she is murdered; I dare not entrust her safety to anybody else. And, Recklow, it's a ghastly responsibility for a man to induce a young girl to face death, even in the service of her country."

"If she remains here alone with you she'll face social destruction," remarked Recklow.

Cleves was silent for a moment, then he burst out: "Well, what am I to do? What is there left for me to do except to watch over her and see her through this devilish business? What other way have I to protect her, Recklow?"

"You could offer her the protection of your name," suggested the other, carelessly.

"What? You mean—marry her?"

"Well, nobody else would be inclined to, Cleves, if it ever becomes known she has lived here quite alone with you."

Cleves stared at the elder man.

"This is nonsense," he said in a harsh voice. "That young girl doesn't want to marry anybody. Neither do I. She doesn't wish to have her throat cut, that's all. And I'm determined she shan't."

"There are stealthier assassins, Cleves,—the slayers of reputations. It goes badly with their victim. It does indeed."

"Well, hang it, what do you think I ought to do?"

"I think you ought to marry her if you're going to keep her here."

"Suppose she doesn't mind the unconventionality of it?"

"All women mind. No woman, at heart, is unconventional, Cleves."

"She—she seems to agree with me that she ought to stay here.... Besides, she has no money, no relatives, no friends in America—"

"All the more tragic. If you really believe it to be your duty to keep her here where you can look after her bodily safety, then the other obligation is still heavier. And there may come a day when Miss Norne will wish that you had been less conscientious concerning the safety of her pretty throat.... For the knife of the Yezidee is swifter and less cruel than the tongue that slays with a smile.... And this young girl has many years to live, after this business of Bolshevism is dead and forgotten in our Republic."

"Recklow!"

"Yes?"

"You think I might dare try to find a room somewhere else for her and let her take her chances? *Do* you?"

"It's your affair."

"I know—hang it! I know it's my affair. I've unintentionally made it so. But can't you tell me what I ought to do?"

"I can't."

"What would *you* do?"

"Don't ask me," returned Recklow, sharply. "If you're not man enough to come to a decision you may turn her over to me."

Cleves flushed brightly. "Do you think *you* are old enough to take my job and avoid scandal?"

Recklow's cold eyes rested on him: "If you like," he said, "I'll assume your various kinds of personal responsibility toward Miss Norne."

Cleve's visage burned. "I'll shoulder my own burdens," he retorted.

"Sure. I knew you would." And Recklow smiled and held out his hand. Cleves took it without cordiality. Standing so, Recklow, still smiling, said: "What a rotten deal that child has had—is having. Her father and mother were fine people. Did you ever hear of Dr. Norne?"

"She mentioned him once."

"They were up-State people of most excellent antecedents and no money.

"Dr. Norne was our Vice-Consul at Yarkand in the province of Sin Kiang. All he had was his salary, and he lost that and his post when the administration changed. Then he went into the spice trade.

"Some Jew syndicate here sent him up the Yarkand River to see what could be done about jade and gold concessions. He was on that business when the tragedy happened. The Kalmuks and Khirghiz were responsible, under Yezidee instigation. And there you are:—and here is his child, Cleves—back, by some miracle, from that flowering hell called Yian, believing in her heart that she really lost her soul there in the temple. And now, here in her own native land, she is exposed to actual and hourly danger of assassination.... Poor kid!... Did you ever hear of a rottener deal, Cleves?"

Their hands had remained clasped while Recklow was speaking. He spoke again, clearly, amiably: "To lay down one's life for a friend is fine. I'm not sure that it's finer to offer one's honour in behalf of a girl whose honour is at stake."

After a moment Cleves's grip tightened.

"All right," he said.

Recklow went downstairs.

CHAPTER VI

# IN BATTLE

Cleves went back into the apartment; he noticed that Miss Norne's door was ajar. To get to his own room he had to pass that way; and he saw her, seated before the mirror, partly undressed, her dark, lustrous hair being combed out and twisted up for the night.

Whether this carelessness was born of innocence or of indifference mattered little; he suddenly realised that these conditions wouldn't do. And his first feeling was of anger.

"If you'll put on your robe and slippers," he said in an unpleasant voice, "I'd like to talk to you for a few moments."

She turned her head on its charming neck and looked around and up at him over one naked shoulder.

"Shall I come into your room?" she inquired.

"No!... when you've got some clothes on, call me."

"I'm quite ready now," she said calmly, and drew the Chinese slippers over her bare feet and passed a silken loop over the silver bell buttons on her right shoulder. Then, undisturbed, she continued to twist up her hair, following his movements in the mirror with unconcerned blue eyes.

He entered and seated himself, the impatient expression still creasing his forehead and altering his rather agreeable features.

"Miss Norne," he said, "you're absolutely convinced that these people mean to do you harm. Isn't that true?"

"Of course," she said simply.

"Then, until we get them, you're running a serious risk. In fact, you live in hourly peril. That is your belief, isn't it?"

She put the last peg into her thick, curly hair, lowered her arms, turned, dropped one knee over the other, and let her candid gaze rest on him in silence.

"What I mean to explain," he said coldly, "is that as long as I induced you to go into this affair I'm responsible for you. If I let you out of my sight here in New York and if anything happens to you, I'll be as guilty as the dirty beast who takes your life. What is your opinion? It's up to me to stand by you now, isn't it?"

"I had rather be near you—for a while," she said timidly.

"Certainly. But, Miss Norne, our living here together, in my apartment—or living together anywhere else—is never going to be understood by other people. You know that, don't you?"

After a silence, still looking at him out of clear, unembarrassed eyes: "I know.... But... I don't want to die."

"I told you," he said sharply, "they'll have to kill me first. So that's all right. But how about what I am doing to your reputation?"

"I understand."

"I suppose you do. You're very young. Once out of this blooming mess, you will have all your life before you. But if I kill your reputation for you while saving your body from death, you'll find no happiness in living. Do you realise that?"

"Yes."

"Well, then? Have you any solution for this problem that confronts you?"

"No."

"Haven't you any idea to suggest?"

"I don't—don't want to die," she repeated in an unsteady voice.

He bit his lip; and after a moment's scowling silence under the merciless scrutiny of her eyes: "Then you had better marry me," he said.

It was some time before she spoke. For a second or two he sustained the searching quality of her gaze, but it became unendurable.

Presently she said: "I don't ask it of you. I can shoulder my own burdens." And he remembered what he had just said to Recklow.

"You've shouldered more than your share," he blurted out. "You are deliberately risking death to serve your country. I enlisted you. The least I can do is to say my affections are not engaged; so naturally the idea of— of marrying anybody never entered my head."

"Then you do not care for anybody else?"

Her candour amazed and disconcerted him.

"No." He looked at her, curiously. "Do you care for anybody in that way?"

A light blush tinted her face. She said gravely: "If we really are going to marry each other I had better tell you that I did care for Prince Sanang."

"What!" he cried, astounded.

"It seems incredible, doesn't it? Yet it is quite true. I fought him; I fought myself; I stood guard over my mind and senses there in the temple; I knew what he was and I detested him and I mocked him there in the temple.... And I loved him."

"Sanang!" he repeated, not only amazed but also oddly incensed at the naïve confession.

"Yes, Sanang.... If we are to marry, I thought I ought to tell you. Don't you think so?"

"Certainly," he replied in an absent-minded way, his mind still grasping at the thing. Then, looking up: "Do you still care for this fellow?"

She shook her head.

"Are you perfectly sure, Miss Norne?"

"As sure as that I am alive when I awake from a nightmare. My hatred for Sanang is very bitter," she added frankly, "and yet somehow it is not my wish to see him harmed."

"You still care for him a little?"

"Oh, no. But—can't you understand that it is not in me to wish him harm?... No girl feels that way—once having cared. To become indifferent to a familiar thing is perhaps natural; but to desire to harm it is not in my character."

"You have plenty of character," he said, staring at her.

"You don't think so. Do you?"

"Why not?"

"Because of what I said to you on the roof-garden that night. It was shameful, wasn't it?"

"You behaved like many a thoroughbred," he returned bluntly; "you were scared, bewildered, ready to bolt to any shelter offered."

"It's quite true I didn't know what to do to keep alive. And that was all that interested me—to keep on living—having lost my soul and being afraid to die and find myself in hell with Erlik."

He said: "Isn't that absurd notion out of your head yet?"

"I don't know.... I can't suddenly believe myself safe after all those years. It is not easy to root out what was planted in childhood and what grew to be part of one during the tender and formative period.... You can't understand, Mr. Cleves—you can't ever feel or visualise what became my daily life in a region which was half paradise and half hell—"

She bent her head and took her face between her fingers, and sat so, brooding.

After a little while: "Well," he said, "there's only one way to manage this affair—if you are willing, Miss Norne."

She merely lifted her eyes.

"I think," he said, "there's only that one way out of it. But you understand"—he turned pink—"it will be quite all right—your liberty—privacy—I shan't bother you—annoy—"

She merely looked at him.

"After this Bolshevistic flurry is settled—in a year or two—or three—then you can very easily get your freedom; and you'll have all life before you"... he rose: "—and a jolly good friend in me—a good comrade, Miss Norne. And that means you can count on me when you go into business—or whatever you decide to do."

She also had risen, standing slim and calm in her exquisite Chinese robe, the sleeves of which covered her finger tips.

"Are you going to marry me?" she asked.

"If you'll let me."

"Yes—I will... it's so generous and considerate of you. I—I don't ask it; I really don't—"

"But *I* do."

"—And I never dreamed of such a thing."

He forced a smile. "Nor I. It's rather a crazy thing to do. But I know of no saner alternative.... So we had better get our license to-morrow.... And that settles it."

He turned to go; and, on her threshold, his feet caught in something on the floor and he stumbled, trying to free his feet from a roll of soft white cloth lying there on the carpet. And when he picked it up, it unrolled, and a knife fell out of the folds of cloth and struck his foot.

Still perplexed, not comprehending, he stooped to recover the knife. Then, straightening up, he found himself looking into the colourless face of Tressa Norne.

"What's all this?" he asked—"this sheet and knife here on the floor outside your door?"

She answered with difficulty: "They have sent you your shroud, I think."

"Are not those things yours? Were they not already here in your baggage?" he demanded incredulously. Then, realising that they had not been there on the door-sill when he entered her room a few moments since, a rough chill passed over him—the icy caress of fear.

"Where did that thing come from?" he said hoarsely. "How could it get here when my door is locked and bolted? Unless there's somebody hidden here!"

Hot anger suddenly flooded him; he drew his pistol and sprang into the passageway.

"What the devil is all this!" he repeated furiously, flinging open his bedroom door and switching on the light.

He searched his room in a rage, went on and searched the dining-room, smoking-room, and kitchen, and every clothes-press and closet, always aware of Tressa's presence close behind him. And when there remained no tiniest nook or cranny in the place unsearched, he stood in the centre of the carpet glaring at the locked and bolted door.

He heard her say under her breath: "This is going to be a sleepless night. And a dangerous one." And, turning to stare at her, saw no fear in her face, only excitement.

He still held clutched in his left hand the sheet and the knife. Now he thrust these toward her.

"What's this damned foolery, anyway?" he demanded harshly. She took the knife with a slight shudder. "There is something engraved on the silver hilt," she said.

He bent over her shoulder.

"Eighur," she added calmly, "not Arabic. The Mongols had no written characters of their own."

She bent closer, studying the inscription. After a moment, still studying the Eighur characters, she rested her left hand on his shoulder—an impulsive, unstudied movement that might have meant either confidence or protection.

"Look," she said, "it is not addressed to you after all, but to a symbol—a series of numbers, 53-6-26."

"That is my designation in the Federal Service," he said, sharply.

"Oh!" she nodded slowly. "Then this is what is written in the Mongol-Yezidee dialect, traced out in Eighur characters: 'To 53-6-26! By one of the Eight Assassins the Slayer of Souls sends this shroud and this knife from Mount Alamout. Such a blade shall divide your heart. This sheet is for your corpse.'"

After a grim silence he flung the soft white cloth on the floor.

"There's no use my pretending I'm not surprised and worried," he said; "I don't know how that cloth got here. Do you?"

"It was sent."

"How?"

She shook her head and gave him a grave, confused look.

"There are ways. You could not understand.... This is going to be a sleepless night for us."

"You can go to bed, Tressa. I'll sit up and read and keep an eye on that door."

"I can't let you remain alone here. I'm afraid to do that."

He gave a laugh, not quite pleasant, as he suddenly comprehended that the girl now considered their roles to be reversed.

"Are *you* planning to sit up in order to protect *me?*" he asked, grimly amused.

"Do you mind?"

"Why, you blessed little thing, I can take care of myself. How funny of you, when I am trying to plan how best to look out for *you!*"

But her face remained pale and concerned, and she rested her left hand more firmly on his shoulder.

"I wish to remain awake with you," she said. "Because I myself don't fully understand this"—she looked at the knife in her palm, then down at the shroud. "It is going to be a strange night for us," she sighed. "Let us sit together here on the lounge where I can face *that bolted door.* And if you are willing, I am, going to turn out the lights—" She suddenly bent forward and switched them off—"because I must keep my mind on guard."

"Why do you do that?" he asked, "you can't see the door, now."

"Let me help you in my own way," she whispered. "I—I am very deeply disturbed, and very, very angry. I do not understand this new menace. Yezidee that I am, I do not understand what kind of danger threatens you through your loyalty to me."

She drew him forward, and he opened his mouth to remonstrate, to laugh; but as he turned, his foot touched the shroud, and an uncontrollable shiver passed over him.

They went close together, across the dim room to the lounge, and seated themselves. Enough light from Madison Avenue made objects in the room barely discernible.

Sounds from the street below became rarer as the hours wore away. The iron jar of trams, the rattle of vehicles, the harsh warning of taxicabs broke the stillness at longer and longer intervals, until, save only for that immense and ceaseless vibration of the monstrous iron city under the foggy stars, scarcely a sound stirred the silence.

The half-hour had struck long ago on the bell of the little clock. Now the clear bell sounded three times.

Cleves stirred on the lounge beside Tressa. Again and again he had thought that she was asleep for her head had fallen back against the cushions, and she lay very still. But always, when he leaned nearer to peer down at her, he saw her eyes open, and fixed intently upon the bolted door.

His pistol, which still rested on his knee, was pointed across the room, toward the door. Once he reminded her in a whisper that she was unarmed and that it might be as well for her to go and get her pistol. But she murmured that she was sufficiently equipped; and, in spite of himself, he shivered as he glanced down at her frail and empty hands.

It was some time between three and half-past, he judged, when a sudden movement of the girl brought him upright on his seat, quivering with excitement.

"Mr. Cleves!"

"Yes?"

"The Sorcerers!"

"Where? Outside the door?"

"Oh, my God," she murmured, *"they are after my mind again!* Their fingers are groping to seize my brain and get possession of it!"

"What!" he stammered, horrified.

"Here—in the dark," she whispered—"and I feel their fingers caressing me—searching—moving stealthily to surprise and grasp my thoughts.... I know what they are doing... I am resisting... I am fighting—fighting!"

She sat bolt upright with clenched hands at her breast, her face palely aglow in the dimness as though illumined by some vivid inward light— or, as he thought—from the azure blaze in her wide-open eyes.

"Is—is this what you call—what you believe to be magic?" he asked unsteadily. "Is there some hostile psychic influence threatening you?"

"Yes. I'm resisting. I'm fighting—fighting. They shall not trap me. They shall not harm you!... I know how to defend myself and you!... And *you!*"

Suddenly she flung her left arm around his neck and the delicate clenched hand brushed his cheek.

"They shall not have you," she breathed. "I am fighting. I am holding my own. There are eight of them—eight Assassins! My mind is in battle with theirs—fiercely in battle.... I hold my own! I am armed and waiting!"

With a convulsive movement she drew his head closer to her shoulder. "Eight of them!" she whispered,—"trying to entrap and seize my brain. But my thoughts are free! My mind is defending you—you, here in my arms!"

After a breathless silence: "Look out!" she whispered with terrible energy; "they are after *your* mind at last. Fix your thoughts on me! Keep your mind clear of their net! Don't let their ghostly fingers touch it. Look at me!" She drew him closer. "Look at *me!* Believe in *me!* I can resist. I can defend you. Does your head feel confused?"

"Yes—numb."

"*Don't sleep!* Don't close your eyes! Keep them open and look at me!"

"I can scarcely see you—"

"You *must* see me!"

"My eyes are heavy," he said drowsily. "I can't see you, Tressa—"

"Wake! Look at me! Keep your mind clear. Oh, I beg you—I beg you! They're after our minds and souls, I tell you! Oh, believe in me," she beseeched him in an agonised whisper—"Can't you believe in me for a moment,—as if you loved me!"

His heavy lids lifted and he tried to look at her.

"Can you see me? *Can* you?"

He muttered something in a confused voice.

"Victor!"

At the sound of his own name, he opened his eyes again and tried to straighten up, but his pistol fell to the carpet.

"Victor!" she gasped, "clear your mind in the name of God!"

"I can not—"

"I tell you hell is opening beyond that door!—outside your bolted door, there! Can't you believe me! Can't you hear me! Oh, what will hold you if the love of God can not!" she burst out. "I'd crucify myself for you if you'd look at me—if you'd only fight hard enough to believe in me—as though you loved me!"

His eyes unclosed but he sank back against her shoulder.

"Victor!" she cried in a terrible voice.

There was no answer.

"If the love of God could only hold you for a moment more!"—she stammered with her mouth against his ear, "just for a moment, Victor! Can't you hear me?"

"Yes—very far away."

"Fight for me! Try to care for me! Don't let Sanang have me!"

He shuddered in her arms, reached out and resting heavily on her shoulder, staggered to his feet and stood swaying like a drunken man.

"No, by God," he said thickly, "Sanang shall not touch you."

The girl was on her feet now, holding him upright with an arm around his shoulders.

"They can't—can't harm us together," she stammered. "Hark! Listen! Can you hear? Oh, can you hear?"

"Give me my pistol," he tried to say, but his tongue seemed twisted. "No—by God—Sanang shall not touch you."

She stooped lithely and recovered the weapon. "Hush," she said close to his burning face. "Listen. Our minds are safe! I can hear somebody's soul bidding its body farewell!"

White-lipped she burst out laughing, kicked the shroud out of the way, thrust the pistol into his right hand, went forward, forcing him along beside her, and drew the bolts from the door.

Suddenly he spoke distinctly:

"Is there anything outside that door on the landing?"

"Yes... I don't know what. Are you ready?" She laid her hand on lock and knob.

He nodded. At the same instant she jerked open the door; and a hunchback who had been picking at the lock fell headlong into the room, his pistol exploding on the carpet in a streak of fire.

It was a horrible struggle to secure the powerful misshapen creature, for he clawed and squealed and bounced about on the floor, striking blindly with apelike arms. But at last Cleves held him down, throttled and twitching, and Tressa ripped strips from the shroud to truss up the writhing thing.

Then Cleves switched on the light.

"Why—why—you rat!" he exclaimed in hysterical relief at seeing a living man whom he recognised there at his feet. "What are you doing here?"

The hunchback's red eyes blazed up at him from the floor.

"Who—who is he?" faltered the girl.

"He's a German tailor named Albert Feke—one of the Chicago Bolsheviki—the most dangerous sort we harbour—one of their vile leaders who preaches that might is right and tells his disciples to go ahead and take what they want."

He looked down at the malignant cripple. "You're wanted for the I.W.W. bomb murder, Albert. Did you know it?"

The hunchback licked his bloody lips. Then he kicked himself to a sitting position, squatted there like a toad and looked steadily at Tressa Norne out of small red-rimmed eyes. Blood dripped on his beard; his huge hairy fists, tied and crossed behind his back, made odd, spasmodic movements.

Cleves went to the telephone. Presently Tressa heard his voice, calm and distinct as usual:

"We've caught Albert Feke. He's here at my rooms. I'd like to have you come over, Recklow.... Oh, yes, he kicked and scuffled and scratched like a cat.... What?... No, I hadn't heard that he'd been in China.... Who?... Albert Feke? You say he was one of the Germans who escaped from Shantung four years ago?... You think he's a Yezidee! You mean one of the Eight Assassins?"

The hunchback, staring at Tressa out of red-rimmed eyes, suddenly snarled and lurched his misshapen body at her.

"Teufelstuck!" he screamed, "ain't I tell efferybody in Yian already it iss safer if we cut your throat! Devil-slut of Erlik—snow-leopardess!—cat of the Yezidees who has made of Sanang a fool!— it iss I who haf said always, always, that you know too damn much!... Kai!... I hear my soul bidding me farewell. Gif me my shroud!"

Cleves came back from the telephone. With the toe of his left foot he lifted the shroud and kicked it across the hunchback's knees.

"So you were one of the huns who instigated the massacre in Yian," he said, curiously. At that Tressa turned very white and a cry escaped her.

But the hunchback's features were all twisted into ferocious laughter, and he beat on the carpet with the heels of his great splay feet.

"Ja! Ja!" he shrieked, "in Yian it vas a goot hunting! English and Yankee men und vimmens ve haff dropped into dose deep wells down. Py Gott in Himmel, how dey schream up out of dose deep wells in Yian!" He began to cackle and shriek in his frenzy. "Ach Gott ja! It iss not you either— you there, Keuke Mongol, who shall escape from the Sheiks-el-Djebel! It iss dot Old Man of the Mountain who shall tell your soul it iss time to say farewell! Ja! Ja! Ach Gott!—it iss my only regret that I shall not see the world when it is all afire! Ja! Ja!—all on fire like hell! But you shall see it, slut-leopard of the snows! You shall see it und you shall burn! Kai! Kai! My soul it iss bidding my body farewell. Kai! May Erlik curse you, Keuke Mongol—Heavenly Azure—Sorceress of the temple!—"

He spat at her and rolled over in his shroud. The girl looking down on him closed her eyes for a moment, and Cleves saw her bloodless lips move, and bent nearer, listening. And he heard her whispering to herself:

"Preserve us all, O God, from the wrath of Satan who was stoned."

CHAPTER VII
# THE BRIDAL

Over the United States stretched an unseen network of secret intrigue woven tirelessly night and day by the busy enemies of civilisation—Reds, parlour-socialists, enemy-aliens, terrorists, Bolsheviki, pseudo-intellectuals, I.W.W.'s, social faddists, and amateur meddlers of every nuance—all the various varieties of the vicious, witless, and mentally unhinged— brought together through the "cohesive power of plunder" and the degeneration of cranial tissue.

All over the United States the various departmental divisions of the Secret Service were busily following up these threads of intrigue leading everywhere through the obscurity of this vast and secret maze.

To meet the constantly increasing danger of physical violence and to uncover secret plots threatening sabotage and revolution, there were capable agents in every branch of the Secret Service, both Federal and State.

But in the first months of 1919 something more terrifying than physical violence suddenly threatened civilised America,—a wild, grotesque, incredible threat of a *war on human minds!*

And, little by little, the United States Government became convinced that this ghastly menace was no dream of a disordered imagination, but that it was real: that among the enemies of civilisation there actually existed a few powerful but perverted minds capable of wielding psychic forces as terrific weapons: that by the sinister use of psychic knowledge controlling these mighty forces the very minds of mankind could be stealthily approached, seized, controlled and turned upon civilisation to aid in the world's destruction.

In terrible alarm the Government turned to England for advice. But Sir William Crookes was dead.

However, in England, Sir Conan Doyle immediately took up the matter, and in America Professor Hyslop was called into consultation.

And then, when the Government was beginning to realise what this awful menace meant, and that there were actually in the United States possibly half a dozen people who already had begun to carry on a diabolical warfare by means of psychic power, for the purpose of enslaving and controlling the very minds of men,—then, in the terrible moment of discovery, a young girl landed in America after fourteen years' absence in Asia.

And this was the amazing girl that Victor Cleves had just married, at Recklow's suggestion, and in the line of professional duty,—and moral duty, perhaps.

It had been a brief, matter-of-fact ceremony. John Recklow, of the Secret Service, was there; also Benton and Selden of the same service.

The bride's lips were unresponsive; cold as the touch of the groom's unsteady hand.

She looked down at her new ring in a blank sort of way, gave her hand listlessly to Recklow and to the others in turn, whispered a timidly comprehensive "Thank you," and walked away beside Cleves as though dazed.

There was a taxicab waiting. Tressa entered. Recklow came out and spoke to Cleves in a low voice.

"Don't worry," replied Cleves dryly. "That's why I married her."

"Where are you going now?" inquired Recklow.

"Back to my apartment."

"Why don't you take her away for a month?"

Cleves flushed with annoyance: "This is no occasion for a wedding trip. You understand that, Recklow."

"I understand. But we ought to give her a breathing space. She's had nothing but trouble. She's worn out."

Cleves hesitated: "I can guard her better in the apartment. Isn't it safer to go back there, where your people are always watching the street and house day and night?"

"In a way it might be safer, perhaps. But that girl is nearly exhausted. And her value to us is unlimited. She may be the vital factor in this fight with anarchy. Her weapon is her mind. And it's got to have a chance to rest."

Cleves, with one hand on the cab door, looked around impatiently.

"Do *you*, also, conclude that the psychic factor is actually part of this damned problem of Bolshevism?"

Recklow's cool eyes measured him: "Do *you?*"

"My God, Recklow, I don't know—after what my own eyes have seen."

"I don't know either," said the other calmly, "but I am taking no chances. I don't attempt to explain certain things that have occurred. But if it be true that a misuse of psychic ability by foreigners—Asiatics—among the anarchists is responsible for some of the devilish things being done in the United States, then your wife's unparalleled knowledge of the occult East is absolutely vital to us. And so I say, better take her away somewhere and give her mind a chance to recover from the incessant strain of these tragic years."

The two men stood silent for a moment, then Recklow went to the window of the taxicab.

"I have been suggesting a trip into the country, Mrs. Cleves," he said pleasantly, "—into the real country, somewhere,—a month's quiet in the woods, perhaps. Wouldn't it appeal to you?"

Cleves turned to catch her low-voiced answer.

"I should like it very much," she said in that odd, hushed way of speaking, which seemed to have altered her own voice and manner since the ceremony a little while before.

Driving back to his apartment beside her, he strove to realise that this girl was his wife.

One of her gloves lay across her lap, and on it rested a slender hand. And on one finger was his ring.

But Victor Cleves could not bring himself to believe that this brand-new ring really signified anything to him,—that it had altered his own life in any way. But always his incredulous eyes returned to that slim finger resting there, unstirring, banded with a narrow circlet of virgin gold.

In the apartment they did not seem to know exactly what to do or say— what attitude to assume—what effort to make.

Tressa went into her own room, removed her hat and furs, and came slowly back into the living-room, where Cleves still stood gazing absently out of the window.

A fine rain was falling.

They seated themselves. There seemed nothing better to do.

He said, politely: "In regard to going away for a rest, you wouldn't care for the North Woods, I fancy, unless you like winter sports. Do you?"

"I like sunlight and green leaves," she said in that odd, still voice.

"Then, if it would please you to go South for a few weeks' rest—"

"Would it inconvenience you?"

Her manner touched him.

"My dear Miss Norne," he began, and checked himself, flushing painfully. The girl blushed, too; then, when he began to laugh, her lovely, bashful smile glimmered for the first time.

"I really can't bring myself to realise that you and I are married," he explained, still embarrassed, though smiling.

Her smile became an endeavour. "I can't believe it either, Mr. Cleves," she said. "I feel rather stunned."

"Hadn't you better call me Victor—under the circumstances?" he suggested, striving to speak lightly.

"Yes.... It will not be very easy to say it—not for some time, I think."

"Tressa?"

"Yes."

"Yes—*what?*"

"Yes—Victor."

"That's the idea," he insisted with forced gaiety. "The thing to do is to face this rather funny situation and take it amiably and with good humour. You'll have your freedom some day, you know."

"Yes—I—know."

"And we're already on very good terms. We find each other interesting, don't we?"

"Yes."

"It even seems to me," he ventured, "it certainly seems to me, at times, as though we are approaching a common basis of—of mutual—er—esteem."

"Yes. I—I do esteem you, Mr. Cleves."

"In point of fact," he concluded, surprised, "we *are* friends—in a way. Wouldn't you call it—friendship?"

"I think so, I think I'd call it that," she admitted.

"I think so, too. And that is lucky for us. That makes this crazy situation more comfortable—less—well, perhaps less ponderous."

The girl assented with a vague smile, but her eyes remained lowered.

"You see," he went on, "when two people are as oddly situated as we are, they're likely to be afraid of being in each other's way. But they ought to get on without being unhappy as long as they are quite confident of each other's friendly consideration. Don't you think so, Tressa?"

Her lowered eyes rested steadily on her ring-finger. "Yes," she said. "And I am not—unhappy, or—afraid."

She lifted her blue gaze to his; and, somehow, he thought of her barbaric name, Keuke,—and its Yezidee significance, "heavenly—azure."

"Are we really going away together?" she asked timidly.

"Certainly, if you wish."

"If you, also, wish it, Mr. Cleves."

He found himself saying with emphasis that he always wished to do what she desired. And he added, more gently:

"You *are* tired, Tressa—tired and lonely and unhappy."

"Tired, but not the—others."

"Not unhappy?"

"No."

"Aren't you lonely?"

"Not with you."

The answer came so naturally, so calmly, that the slight sensation of pleasure it gave him arrived only as an agreeable afterglow.

"We'll go South," he said.... "I'm so glad that you don't feel lonely with me."

"Will it be warmer where we are going, Mr. Cleves?"

"Yes—you poor child! You need warmth and sunshine, don't you? Was it warm in Yian, where you lived so many years?"

"It was always June in Yian," she said under her breath.

She seemed to have fallen into a revery; he watched the sensitive face.

Almost imperceptibly it changed; became altered, younger, strangely lovely.

Presently she looked up—and it seemed to him that it was not Tressa Norne at all he saw, but little Keuke—Heavenly Azure—of the Yezidee temple, as she dropped one slim knee over the other and crossed her hands above it.

"It was very beautiful in Yian," she said, "—Yian of the thousand bridges and scented gardens so full of lilies. Even after they took me to the temple, and I thought the world was ending, God's skies still remained soft overhead, and His weather fair and golden.... And when, in the month of the Snake, the Eight Sheiks-el-Djebel came to the temple to spread their shrouds on the rose-marble steps, then, after they had departed, chanting the Prayers for the Dead, each to his Tower of Silence, we temple girls were free for a week.... And once I went with Tchagane—a girl—and with Yu-lun—another girl—and we took our keutch, which is our luggage, and we went to the yaïlak, or summer pavilion on the Lake of the Ghost. Oh, wonderful,—a silvery world of pale-gilt suns and of moons so frail that the cloud-fleece at high-noon has more substance!"

Her voice died out; she sat gazing down at her spread fingers, on one of which gleamed her wedding-ring.

After a little, she went on dreamily:

"On that week, each three months, we were free.... If a young man should please us...."

"Free?" he repeated.

"To love," she explained coolly.

"Oh." He nodded, but his face became rather grim.

"There came to me at the yaïlak," she went on carelessly, "one Khassar Noïane—Noïane means Prince—all in a surcoat of gold tissue with green vines embroidered, and wearing a green cap trimmed with dormouse, and green boots inlaid with stiff gold....

"He was so young... a boy. I laughed. I said: 'Is this a Yaçaoul? An Urdu-envoy of Prince Erlik?'—mocking him as young and thoughtless girls mock—not in unfriendly manner—though I would not endure the touch of any man at all.

"And when I laughed at him, this Eighur boy flew into such a rage! Kai! I was amazed.

"'Sou-sou! Squirrel!' he cried angrily at me. 'Learn the Yacaz, little chatterer! Little mocker of men, it is ten blows with a stick you require, not kisses!'

"At that I whistled my two dogs, Bars and Alaga, for I did not think what he said was funny.

"I said to him: 'You had better go home, Khassar Noïane, for if no man has ever pleased me where I am at liberty to please myself, here on the Lake of the Ghost, then be very certain that no boy can please Keuke Mongol here or anywhere!'

"And at that—kai! What did he say—that monkey?" She looked at her husband, her splendid eyes ablaze with wrathful laughter, and made a gesture full of angry grace:

"'Squirrel!' he cries—'little malignant sorceress of Yian! May everything high about you become a sandstorm, and everything long a serpent, and everything broad a toad, and everything—'

"But I had had enough, Victor," she added excitedly, "and I made a wild bee bite him on the lip! *What* do you think of such a courtship?" she cried, laughing. But Cleves's face was a study in emotions.

And then, suddenly, the laughing mask seemed to slip from the bewitching features of Keuke Mongol; and there was Tressa Norne—Tressa Cleves—disconcerted, paling a little as the memory of her impulsive confidence in this man beside her began to dawn on her more clearly.

"I—I'm sorry—" she faltered.... "You'll think me silly—think evil of me, perhaps—"

She looked into his troubled eyes, then suddenly she took her face into both hands and covered it, sitting very still.

"We'll go South together," he said in an uncertain voice.... "I hope you will try to think of me as a friend.... I'm just troubled because I am so anxious to understand you. That is all.... I'm—I'm troubled, too, because I am anxious that you should think well of me. Will you try, always?"

She nodded.

"I want to be your friend, always," he said.

"Thank you, Mr. Cleves."

It was a strange spot he chose for Tressa—strange but lovely in its own unreal and rather spectral fashion—where a pearl-tinted mist veiled the St. Johns, and made exquisite ghosts of the palmettos, and softened the sun to a silver-gilt wafer pasted on a nacre sky.

It was a still country, where giant water-oaks towered, fantastic under their misty camouflage of moss, and swarming with small birds.

Among the trees the wood-ibis stole; without on the placid glass of the stream the eared grebe floated. There was no wind, no stirring of leaves, no sound save the muffled splash of silver mullet, the breathless whirr of a humming-bird, or the hushed rustle of lizards in the woods.

For Tressa this was the blessed balm that heals,—the balm of silence. And, for the first week, she slept most of the time, or lay in her hammock watching the swarms of small birds creeping and flitting amid the moss-draped labyrinths of the live-oaks at her very door.

It had been a little club house before the war, this bungalow on the St. Johns at Orchid Hammock. Its members had been few and wealthy; but some were dead in France and Flanders, and some still remained overseas, and others continued busy in the North.

And these two young people were quite alone there, save for a negro cook and a maid, and an aged negro kennel-master who wore a scarlet waist-coat and cords too large for his shrunken body, and who pottered, pottered through the fields all day, with his whip clasped behind his bent back and the pointers ranging wide, or plodding in at heel with red tongues lolling.

Twice Cleves went a little way for quail, using Benton's dogs; but even here in this remote spot he dared not move out of view of the little house where Tressa lay asleep.

So he picked up only a few brace of birds, and confined his sport to impaling too-familiar scorpions on the blade of his knife.

And all the while life remained unreal for him; his marriage seemed utterly unbelievable; he could not realise it, could not reconcile himself to conditions so incomprehensible.

Also, ever latent in his mind, was knowledge that made him restless—the knowledge that the young girl he had married had been in love with another man: Sanang.

And there were other thoughts—thoughts which had scarcely even taken the shape of questions.

One morning he came from his room and found Tressa on the veranda in her hammock. She had her moon-lute in her lap.

"You feel better—much better!" he said gaily, saluting her extended hand.

"Yes. Isn't this heavenly? I begin to believe it is life to me, this pearl-tinted world, and the scent of orange bloom and the stillness of paradise itself."

She gazed out over the ghostly river. Not a wing stirred its glassy surface.

"Is this dull for you?" she asked in a low voice.

"Not if you are contented, Tressa."

"You're so nice about it. Don't you think you might venture a day's real shooting?"

"No, I think I won't," he replied.

"On my account?"

"Well—yes."

"I'm so sorry."

"It's all right as long as you're getting rested. What is that instrument?"

"My moon-lute."

"Oh, is that what it's called?"

She nodded, touched the strings. He watched her exquisite hands.

"Shall I?" she inquired a little shyly.

"Go ahead. I'd like to hear it!"

"I haven't touched it in months—not since I was on the steamer." She sat up in her hammock and began to swing there; and played and sang while swinging in the flecked shadow of the orange bloom:

> *"Little Isle of Cispangou,*
> *Isle of iris, isle of cherry,*
> *Tell your tiny maidens merry*
> *Clouds are looming over you!*
> > *La--la!*
> > *La--la!*
> *All your ocean's but a ferry;*
> *Ships are bringing death to you!*
> > *La--lou!*
> > *La--lou!*
>
> *"Little Isle of Cispangou,*
> *Half a thousand ships are sailing;*
> *Captain Death commands each crew;*
> *Lo! the ruddy moon is paling!*
> > *La--la!*
> > *La--la!*
> *Clouds the dying moon are veiling,*
> *Every cloud a shroud for you!*
> > *La--lou!*
> > *La--lou!"*

"Cispangou," she explained, "is the very, very ancient name, among the Mongols, for Japan."

"It's not exactly a gay song," he said. "What's it about?"

"Oh, it's a very ancient song about the Mongol invasion of Japan. I know scores and scores of such songs."

She sang some other songs. Afterward she descended from the hammock and came and sat down beside him on the veranda steps.

"I wish I could amuse you," she said wistfully.

"Why do you think I'm bored, Tressa? I'm not at all."

But she only sighed, lightly, and gathered her knees in both arms.

"I don't know how young men in the Western world are entertained," she remarked presently.

"You don't have to entertain me," he said, smiling.

"I should be happy to, if I knew how."

"How are young men entertained in the Orient?"

"Oh, they like songs and stories. But I don't think you do."

He laughed in spite of himself.

"Do you really wish to entertain me?"

"I do," she said seriously.

"Then please perform some of those tricks of magic which you can do so amazingly well."

Her dawning smile faded a trifle. "I don't—I haven't—" She hesitated.

"You haven't your professional paraphernalia with you," he suggested.

"Oh—as for that—"

"Don't you need it?"

"For some things—some kinds of things.... I *could* do—other things—"

He waited. She seemed disconcerted. "Don't do anything you don't wish to do, Tressa," he said.

"I was only—only afraid—that if I should do some little things to amuse you, I might stir—stir up—interfere—encounter some sinister current—and betray myself—betray my whereabouts—"

"Well, for heaven's sake don't venture then!" he said with emphasis. "Don't do anything to stir up any other wireless—any Yezidee—"

"I am wondering," she reflected, "just what I dare venture to do to amuse you."

"Don't bother about me. I wouldn't have you try any psychic stunt down here, and run the chance of stirring up some Asiatic devil somewhere!"

She nodded absently, occupied with her own thoughts, sitting there, chin on hand, her musing eyes intensely blue.

"I think I can amuse you," she concluded, "without bringing any harm to myself."

"Don't try it, Tressa!—"

"I'll be very careful. Now, sit quite still—closer to me, please."

He edged closer; and became conscious of an indefinable freshness in the air that enveloped him, like the scent of something young and growing. But it was no magic odour,—merely the virginal scent of her hair and skin that even clung to her summer gown.

He heard her singing under her breath to herself:

> "*La--la!*
> "*La--la!*"

and murmuring caressingly in an unknown tongue.

Then, suddenly in the pale sunshine, scores of little birds came hovering around them, alighting all over them. And he saw them swarming out of the mossy festoons of the water-oaks—scores and scores of tiny birds—Parula warblers, mostly—all flitting fearlessly down to alight upon his shoulders and knees, all keeping up their sweet, dreamy little twittering sound.

"This is wonderful," he whispered.

The girl laughed, took several birds on her forefinger.

"This is nothing," she said. "If I only dared—wait a moment!—" And, to the Parula warblers: "Go home, little friends of God!"

The air was filled with the musical whisper of wings. She passed her right arm around her husband's neck.

"Look at the river," she said.

"Good God!" he blurted out. And sat dumb.

For, over the St. Johns misty surface, there was the span of a bridge—a strange, marble bridge humped up high in the centre.

And over it were passing thousands of people—he could make them out vaguely—see them passing in two never-ending streams—tinted shapes on the marble bridge.

And now, on the farther shore of the river, he was aware of a city—a vast one, with spectral pagoda shapes against the sky—

Her arm tightened around his neck.

He saw boats on the river—like the grotesque shapes that decorate ancient lacquer.

She rested her face lightly against his cheek.

In his ears was a far confusion of voices—the stir and movement of multitudes—noises on ships, boatmen's cries, the creak of oars.

Then, far and sonorous, quavering across the water from the city, the din of a temple gong.

There were bells, too—very sweet and silvery—camel bells, bells from the Buddhist temples.

He strained his eyes, and thought, amid the pagodas, that there were minarets, also.

Suddenly, clear and ringing came the distant muezzin's cry: "There is no other god but God!... It is noon. Mussulmans, pray!"

The girl's arm slipped from his neck and she shuddered and pushed him from her.

There was nothing, now, on the river or beyond it but the curtain of hanging mist; no sound except the cry of a gull, sharp and querulous in the vapours overhead.

"Have—have you been amused?" she asked.

"What did you do to me!" he demanded harshly.

She smiled and drew a light breath like a sigh. "God knows what we living do to one another,—or to ourselves," she said. "I only tried to amuse you—after taking counsel with the birds."

"What was that bridge I saw!"

"The Bridge of Ten Thousand Felicities."

"And the city?"

"Yian."

"You lived there?"

"Yes."

He moistened his dry lips and stole another glance at this very common-place Florida river. Sky and water were blank and still, and the ghostly trees stood tall, reflected palely in the translucent tide.

"You merely made me visualise what you were thinking about," he concluded in a voice which still remained unsteady.

"Did you *hear* nothing?"

He was silent, remembering the bells and the enormous murmur of a living multitude.

"And—there were the birds, too." She added, with an uncertain smile: "I do not mean to worry you.... And you did ask me to amuse you."

"I don't know how you did it," he said harshly. "And the details—those thousands and thousands of people on the bridge!... And there was one, quite near this end of the bridge, who looked back.... A young girl who turned and laughed at us—"

"That was Yulun."

"Who?"

"Yulun. I taught her English."

"A temple girl?"

"Yes. From Black China."

"How could you make *me* see *her!*" he demanded.

"Why do you ask such things? I do not know how to tell you how I do it."

"It's a dangerous, uncanny knowledge!" he blurted out; and suddenly checked himself, for the girl's face went white.

"I don't mean uncanny," he hastened to add. "Because it seems to me that what you did by juggling with invisible currents to which, when attuned, our five senses respond, is on the same lines as the wireless telegraph and telephone."

She said nothing, but her colour slowly returned.

"You mustn't be so sensitive," he added. "I've no doubt that it's all quite normal—quite explicable on a perfectly scientific basis. Probably it's no more mysterious than a man in an airplane over midocean conversing with people ashore on two continents."

For the remainder of the day and evening Tressa seemed subdued—not restless, not nervous, but so quiet that, sometimes, glancing at her askance, Cleves involuntarily was reminded of some lithe young creature of the

wilds, intensely alert and still, immersed in fixed and dangerous meditation.

About five in the afternoon they took their golf sticks, went down to the
river, and embarked in the canoe.

The water was glassy and still. There was not a ripple ahead, save when
a sleeping gull awoke and leisurely steered out of their way.

Tressa's arms and throat were bare and she wore no hat. She sat forward,
wielding the bow paddle and singing to herself in a low voice.

"You feel all right, don't you?" he asked.

"Oh, I am so well, physically, now! It's really wonderful, Victor—like being a child again," she replied happily.

"You're not much more," he muttered.

She heard him: "Not very much more—in years," she said.... "Does
Scripture tell us how old Our Lord was when He descended into Hell?"

"I don't know," he replied, startled.

After a little while Tressa tranquilly resumed her paddling and singing:

> "—And eight tall towers
> Guard the route
> Of human life,
> Where at all hours
> Death looks out,
> Holding a knife
> Rolled in a shroud.
>
> For every man,
> Humble or proud,
> Mighty or bowed,
> Death has a shroud;—for every man,—
> Even for Tchingniz Khan!
> Behold them pass!—lancer,
> Baroulass,
> Temple dancer
> In tissue gold,
> Khiounnou,
> Karlik bold,
> Christian, Jew,—
> Nations swarm to the great Urdu.
> Yaçaoul, with your kettledrum,
> Warn your Khan that his hour is come!
> Shroud and knife at his spurred feet throw,
> And bid him stretch his neck for the blow!—"

"You know," remarked Cleves, "that some of those songs you sing are devilish creepy."

Tressa looked around at him over her shoulder, saw he was smiling, smiled faintly in return.

They were off Orchid Cove now. The hotel and cottages loomed dimly in the silver mist. Voices came distinctly across the water. There were people on the golf course paralleling the river; laughter sounded from the clubhouse veranda.

They went ashore.

CHAPTER VIII

# THE MAN IN WHITE

It was at the sixth hole that they passed the man ahead who was playing all alone—a courteous young fellow in white flannels, who smiled and bowed them "through" in silence.

They thanked him, drove from the tee, and left the polite and reticent young man still apparently hunting for a lost ball.

Like other things which depended upon dexterity and precision, Tressa had taken most naturally to golf. Her supple muscles helped.

At the ninth hole they looked back but did not see the young man in white flannels.

Hammock, set with pine and palmetto, and intervals of evil-looking swamp, flanked the course. Rank wire-grass, bayberry and scrub palmetto bounded the fairgreen.

On every blossoming bush hung butterflies—Palomedes swallowtails—drugged with sparkle-berry honey, their gold and black velvet wings conspicuous in the sunny mist.

"Like the ceremonial vestments of a Yezidee executioner," murmured the girl. "The Tchortchas wear red when they robe to do a man to death."

"I wish you could forget those things," said Cleves.

"I am trying.... I wonder where that young man in white went."

Cleves searched the links. "I don't see him. Perhaps he had to go back for another ball."

"I wonder who he was," she mused.

"I don't remember seeing him before," said Cleves.... "Shall we start back?"

They walked slowly across the course toward the tenth hole.

Tressa teed up, drove low and straight. Cleves sliced, and they walked together into the scrub and towards the woods, where his ball had bounded into a bunch of palm trees.

Far in among the trees something white moved and vanished.

"Probably a white egret," he remarked, knocking about in the scrub with his midiron.

"It was that young man in white flannels," said Tressa in a low voice.

"What would he be doing in there?" he asked incredulously. "That's merely a jungle, Tressa—swamp and cypress, thorn and creeper,—and no man would go into that mess if he could. There is no bottom to those swamps."

"But I saw him in there," she said in a troubled voice.

"But when I tell you that only a wild animal or a snake or a bird could move in that jungle! The bog is one vast black quicksand. There's death in those depths."

"Victor."

"Yes?" He looked around at her. She was pale. He came up and took her hand inquiringly.

"I don't feel—well," she murmured. "I'm not ill, you understand—"

"What's the matter, Tressa?"

She shook her head drearily: "I don't know.... I wonder whether I should have tried to amuse you this morning—"

"You don't think you've stirred up any of those Yezidee beasts, do you?" he asked sharply.

And as she did not answer, he asked again whether she was afraid that what she had done that morning might have had any occult consequences. And he reminded her that she had hesitated to venture anything on that account.

His voice, in spite of him, betrayed great nervousness now, and he saw apprehension in her eyes, also.

"Why should that man in white have followed us, keeping out of sight in the woods?" he went on. "Did you notice about him anything to disturb you, Tressa?"

"Not at the time. But—it's odd—I can't put him out of my mind. Since we passed him and left him apparently hunting a lost ball, I have not been able to put him out of my mind."

"He seemed civil and well bred. He was perfectly good-humoured—all courtesy and smiles."

"I think—perhaps—it was the way he smiled at us," murmured the girl. "Everybody in the East smiles when they draw a knife...."

He placed his arm through hers. "Aren't you a trifle morbid?" he said pleasantly.

She stooped for her golf ball, retaining a hold on his arm. He picked up his ball, too, put away her clubs and his, and they started back together in silence, evidently with no desire to make it eighteen holes.

"It's a confounded shame," he muttered, "just as you were becoming so rested and so delightfully well, to have anything—any unpleasant flash of memory cut in to upset you—"

"I brought it on myself. I should not have risked stirring up the sinister minds that were asleep."

"Hang it all!—and I asked you to amuse me."

"It was not wise in me," she said under her breath. "It is easy to disturb the unknown currents which enmesh the globe. I ought not to have shown you Yian. I ought not to have shown you Yulun. It was my fault for doing that. I was a little lonely, and I wanted to see Yulun."

They came down the river back to the canoe, threw in their golf bags, and embarked on the glassy stream.

Over the calm flood, stained deep with crimson, the canoe glided in the sanguine evening light. But Tressa sang no more and her head was bent sideways as though listening—always listening—to something inaudible to Cleves—something very, very far away which she seemed to hear through the still drip of the paddles.

They were not yet in sight of their landing when she spoke to him, partly turning:

"I think some of your men have arrived."

"Where?" he asked, astonished.

"At the house."

"Why do you think so?"

"I think so."

They paddled a little faster. In a few minutes their dock came into view.

"It's funny," he said, "that you should think some of our men have arrived from the North. I don't see anybody on the dock."

"It's Mr. Recklow," she said in a low voice. "He is seated on our veranda."

As it was impossible to see the house, let alone the veranda, Cleves made no reply. He beached the canoe; Tressa stepped out; he followed, carrying the golf bags.

A mousy light lingered in the shrubbery; bats were flying against a salmon-tinted sky as they took the path homeward.

With an impulse quite involuntary, Cleves encircled his young wife's shoulders with his left arm.

"Girl-comrade," he said lightly, "I'd kill any man who even looked as though he'd harm you."

He smiled, but she had not missed the ugly undertone in his words.

They walked slowly, his arm around her shoulders. Suddenly he felt her start. They halted.

"What was it?" he whispered.

"I thought there was something white in the woods."

"Where, dear?" he asked coolly.

"Over there beyond the lawn."

What she called the "lawn" was only a vast sheet of pink and white phlox, now all misty with the whirring wings of sphinx-moths and Noctuidæ.

The oak grove beyond was dusky. Cleves could see nothing among the trees.

After a moment they went forward. His arm had fallen away from her shoulders.

There were no lights except in the kitchen when they came in sight of the house. At first nobody was visible on the screened veranda under the orange trees. But when he opened the swing door for her a shadowy figure arose from a chair.

It was John Recklow. He came forward, bent his strong white head, and kissed Tressa's hand.

"Is all well with you, Mrs. Cleves?"

"Yes. I am glad you came."

Cleves clasped the elder man's firm hand.

"I'm glad too, Recklow. You'll stop with us, of course."

"Do you really want me?"

"Of course," said Cleves.

"All right. I've a coon and a surrey behind your house."

So Cleves went around in the dusk and sent the outfit back to the hotel, and he himself carried in Recklow's suitcase.

Then Tressa went away to give instructions, and the two men were left together on the dusky veranda.

"Well?" said Recklow quietly.

Cleves went to him and rested both hands on his shoulders:

"I'm playing absolutely square. She's a perfectly fine girl and she'll have her chance some day, God willing."

"Her chance?" repeated Recklow.

"To marry whatever man she will some day care for."

"I see," said Recklow drily.

There was a silence, then:

"She's simply a splendid specimen of womanhood," said Cleves earnestly. "And intensely interesting to me. Why, Recklow, I haven't known a dull moment—though I fear she has known many—"

"Why?"

"Why? Well, being married to a—a sort of temporary figurehead—shut up here all day alone with a man of no particular interest to her—"

"Don't you interest her?"

"Well, how could I? She didn't choose me because she liked me particularly."

"Didn't she?" asked Recklow, still more drily. "Well, that does make it a trifle dull for you both."

"Not for me," said the younger man naïvely. "She is one of the most interesting women I ever met. And good heavens!—what psychic knowledge that child possesses! She did a thing to-day—merely to amuse me—" He checked himself and looked at Recklow out of sombre eyes.

"What did she do?" inquired the older man.

"I think I'll let her tell you—if she wishes.... And that reminds me. Why did you come down here, Recklow?"

"I want to show you something, Cleves. May we step into the house?"

They went into a little lamplit living-room. Recklow handed a newspaper clipping to Cleves; the latter read it, standing:

## "HAD DEADLIEST GAS READY FOR GERMANS
### *"'Lewisite' Might Have Killed Millions*

"WASHINGTON, APRIL 24.—Guarded night and day and far out of human reach on a pedestal at the Interior Department Exposition here is a tiny vial. It contains a specimen of the deadliest poison ever known, 'Lewisite,' the product of an American scientist.

"Germany escaped this poison by signing the armistice before all the resources of the United States were turned upon her.

"Ten airplanes carrying 'Lewisite' would have wiped out, it is said, every vestige of life—animal and vegetable—in Berlin. A single day's output would snuff out the millions of lives on Manhattan Island. A drop poured in the palm of the hand would penetrate to the blood, reach the heart and kill the victim in agony.

"What was coming to Germany may be imagined by the fact that when the armistice was signed 'Lewisite' was being manufactured at the rate of ten tons a day. Three thousand tons of this most terrible instrument ever conceived for killing would have been ready for business on the American front in France on November 1.

"'Lewisite' is another of the big secrets of the war just leaking out. It was developed in the Bureau of Mines by Professor W. Lee Lewis, of Northwestern University, Evanston, Ill., who took a commission as a captain in the army.

"The poison was manufactured in a specially built plant near Cleveland, called the 'Mouse Trap,' because every workman who entered the stockade went under an agreement not to leave the eleven-acre space until the war was won. The object of this, of course, was to protect the secret.

"Work on the plant was started eighteen days after the Bureau of Mines had completed its experiments.

"Experts are certain that no one will want to steal the sample. Everybody at the Exposition, which shows what Secretary Lane's department is doing, keeps as far away from it as possible."

When Cleves had finished reading, he raised his eyes in silence.

"That vial was stolen a week ago," said Recklow gravely, "by a young man who killed one guard and fatally wounded the other."

"Was there any ante-mortem statement?"

"Yes. I've followed the man. I lost all trace of him at Palm Beach, but I picked it up again at Ormond. *And now I'm here*, Cleves."

"You don't mean you've traced him here!" exclaimed Cleves under his breath.

"He's here on the St. Johns River, somewhere. He came up in a motor-boat, but left it east of Orchard Cove. Benton knows this country. He's covering the motor-boat. And I—came here to see how you are getting on."

"And to warn us," added Cleves quietly.

"Well—yes. He's got that stuff. It's deadlier than the newspaper suspects. And I guess—I guess, Cleves, he's one of those damned Yezidee witch-doctors—or sorcerers, as they call them;—one of that sect of Assassins sent over here to work havoc on feeble minds and do murder on the side."

"Why do you think so?"

"Because the dirty beast lugs his shroud around with him—a bed-sheet stolen from the New Willard in Washington.

"We were so close to him in Jacksonville that we got it, and his luggage. But we didn't get him, the rat! God knows how he knew we were waiting for him in his room. He never came back to get his luggage.

"But he stole a bed-sheet from his hotel in St. Augustine, and that is how we picked him up again. Then, at Palm Beach, we lost the beggar, but somehow or other I felt it in my bones that he was after you—you and your wife. So I sent Benton to Ormond and I went to Palatka. Benton picked up his trail. It led toward you—toward the St. Johns. And the reptile has been here forty-eight hours, trying to nose you out, I suppose—"

Tressa came into the room. Both men looked at her.

Cleves said in a guarded voice:

"To-day, on the golf links at Orchard Cove, there was a young man in white flannels—very polite and courteous to us—but—Tressa thought she saw him slinking through the woods as though following and watching us."

"My man, probably," said Recklow. He turned quietly to Tressa and sketched for her the substance of what he had just told Cleves.

"The man in white flannels on the golf links," said Cleves, "was well built and rather handsome, and not more than twenty-five. I thought he was a Jew."

"I thought so too," said Tressa, calmly, "until I saw him in the woods. And then—and then—suddenly it came to me that his smile was the smile of a treacherous Shaman sorcerer.

"...And the idea haunts me—the memory of those smooth-faced, smiling men in white—men who smile only when they slay—when they slay body and soul under the iris skies of Yian!—O God, merciful, long suffering," she whispered, staring into the East, "deliver our souls from Satan who was stoned, and our bodies from the snare of the Yezidee!"

CHAPTER IX
# THE WEST WIND

The night grew sweet with the scent of orange bloom, and all the per-fumed darkness was vibrant with the feathery whirr of hawk-moths' wings.

Tressa had taken her moon-lute to the hammock, but her fingers rested motionless on the strings.

Cleves and Recklow, shoulder to shoulder, paced the moonlit path along the hedges of oleander and hibiscus which divided garden from jungle.

And they moved cautiously on the white-shell road, not too near the shadow line. For in the cypress swamp the bloated grey death was awake and watching under the moon; and in the scrub palmetto the diamond-dotted death moved lithely.

And somewhere within the dark evil of the jungle a man in white might be watching.

So Recklow's pistol swung lightly in his right hand and Cleves' weapon lay in his side-pocket, and they strolled leisurely around the drive and up and down the white-shell walks, passing Tressa at regular intervals, where she sat in her hammock with the moon-lute across her knees.

Once Cleves paused to place two pink hibiscus blossoms in her hair above her ears; and the girl smiled gravely at him in the light.

Again, pausing beside her hammock on one of their tours of the garden, Recklow said in a low voice: "If the beast would only show himself, Mrs. Cleves, we'd not miss him. Have you caught a glimpse of anything white in the woods?"

"Only the night mist rising from the branch and a white ibis stealing through it."

Cleves came nearer: "Do you think the Yezidee is in the woods watching us, Tressa?"

"Yes, he is there," she said calmly.

"You *know* it?"

"Yes."

Recklow stared at the woods. "We can't go in to hunt for him," he said. "That fellow would get us with his Lewisite gas before we could discover and destroy him."

"Suppose he waits for a west wind and squirts his gas in this direction?" whispered Cleves.

"There is no wind," said Tressa tranquilly. "He has been waiting for it, I think. The Yezidee is very patient. And he is a Shaman sorcerer."

"My God!" breathed Recklow. "What sort of hellish things has the Old World been dumping into America for the last fifty years? An ordinary anarchist is bad enough, but this new breed of devil—these Yezidees—this sect of Assassins—"

"Hush!" whispered Tressa.

All three listened to the great cat-owl howling from the jungle. But Tressa had heard another sound—the vague stir of leaves in the live-oaks. Was it a passing breeze? Was a night wind rising? She listened. But heard no brittle clatter from the palm-fronds.

"Victor," she said.

"Yes, Tressa."

"If a wind comes, we must hunt him. That will be necessary."

"Either we hunt him and get him, or he kills us here with his gas," said Recklow quietly.

"If the night wind comes," said Tressa, "we must hunt the darkness for the Yezidee." She spoke coolly.

"If he'd only show himself," muttered Recklow, staring into the darkness.

The girl picked up her lute, caught Cleves' worried eyes fixed on her, suddenly comprehended that his anxiety was on her account, and blushed brightly in the moonlight. And he saw her teeth catch at her underlip; saw her look up again at him, confused.

"If I dared leave you," he said, "I'd go into the hammock and start that reptile. This won't do—this standing pat while he comes to some deadly decision in the woods there."

"What else is there to do?" growled Recklow.

"Watch," said the girl. "Out-watch the Yezidee. If there is no night-wind he may tire of waiting. Then you must shoot fast—very, very fast and straight. But if the night-wind comes, then we must hunt him in darkness."

Recklow, pistol in hand, stood straight and sturdy in the moonlight, gazing fixedly at the forest. Cleves sat down at his wife's feet.

She touched her moon-lute tranquilly and sang in her childish voice:

> "Ring, ring, Buddha bells,
> Gilded gods are listening.
> Swing, swing, lily bells,
> In my garden glistening.
> Now I hear the Shaman drum;
> Now the scarlet horsemen come;
> Ding-dong!
> Ding-dong!
> Through the chanting of the throng

*Thunders now the temple gong.*
*Boom-boom!*
*Ding-dong!*

*"Let the gold gods listen!*
*In my garden; what care I*
*Where my lily bells hang mute!*
*Snowy-sweet they glisten*
*Where I'm singing to my lute.*
*In my garden; what care I*
*Who is dead and who shall die?*
*Let the gold gods save or slay*
*Scented lilies bloom in May.*
*Boom, boom, temple gong!*
*Ding-dong!*
*Ding-dong!"*

"What are you singing?" whispered Cleves.

"'The Bells of Yian.'"

"Is it old?"

"Of the 13th century. There were few Buddhist bells in Yian then. It is Lamaism that has destroyed the Mongols and that has permitted the creed of the Assassins to spread—the devil worship of Erlik."

He looked at her, not understanding. And she, pale, slim prophetess, in the moonlight, gazed at him out of lost eyes—eyes which saw, perhaps, the bloody age of men when mankind took the devil by the throat and all Mount Alamout went up in smoking ruin; and the Eight Towers were dark as death and as silent before the blast of the silver clarions of Ghenghis Khan.

"Something is stirring in the forest," whispered Tressa, her fingers on her lips.

"Damnation," muttered Recklow, "it's the wind!"

They listened. Far in the forest they heard the clatter of palm-fronds. They waited. The ominous warning grew faint, then rose again,—a long, low rattle of palm-fronds which became a steady monotone.

"We hunt," said Recklow bluntly. "Come on!"

But the girl sprang from the hammock and caught her husband's arm and drew Recklow back from the hibiscus hedge.

"Use me," she said. "You could never find the Yezidee. Let me do the hunting; and then shoot very, very fast."

"We've got to take her," said Recklow. "We dare not leave her."

"I can't let her lead the way into those black woods," muttered Cleves.

"The wind is blowing in my face," insisted Recklow. "We'd better hurry."
Tressa laid one hand on her husband's arm.

"I can find the Yezidee, I think. You never could find him before he finds
you! Victor, let me use my own *knowledge!* Let me find the way. Please let
me lead! Please, Victor. Because, if you don't, I'm afraid we'll all die here
in the garden where we stand."

Cleves cast a haggard glance at Recklow, then looked at his wife.

"All right," he said.

The girl opened the hedge gate. Both men followed with pistols lifted.

The moon silvered the forest. There was no mist, but a night-wind blew
mournfully through palm and cypress, carrying with it the strange, dis-
turbing pungency of the jungle—wild, unfamiliar perfumes,—the acrid
aroma of swamp and rotting mould.

"What about snakes?" muttered Recklow, knee deep in wild phlox.

But there was a deadlier snake to find and destroy, somewhere in the
blotched shadows of the forest.

The first sentinel trees were very near, now; and Tressa was running
across a ghostly tangle, where once had been an orange grove, and where
aged and dying citrus stumps rose stark amid the riot of encroaching jungle.

"She's circling to get the wind at our backs," breathed Recklow, running
forward beside Cleves. "That's our only chance to kill the dirty rat—catch
him with the wind at our backs!"

Once, traversing a dry hammock where streaks of moonlight alter-
nated with velvet-black shadow a rattlesnake sprang his goblin alarm.

They could not locate the reptile. They shrank together and moved warily, chilled with fear.

Once, too, clear in the moonlight, the Grey Death reared up from
bloated folds and stood swaying rhythmically in a horrible shadow dance
before them. And Cleves threw one arm around his wife and crept past,
giving death a wide berth there in the checkered moonlight.

Now, under foot, the dry hammock lay everywhere and the night wind
blew on their backs.

Then Tressa turned and halted the two men with a gesture. And went
to her husband where he stood in the palm forest, and laid her hands on
his shoulders, looking him very wistfully in the eyes.

Under her searching gaze he seemed oddly to comprehend her appeal.

"You are going to use—to use your *knowledge*," he said mechanically. "You
are going to find the man in white."

"Yes."

"You are going to find him in a way we don't understand," he continued, dully.

"Yes.... You will not hold me in—in horror—will you?"

Recklow came up, making no sound on the spongy palm litter underfoot.

"Can you find this devil?" he whispered.

"I—think so."

"Does your super-instinct—finer sense—knowledge—whatever it is—give you any inkling as to his whereabouts, Mrs. Cleves?"

"I think he is here in this hammock. Only—" she turned again, with swift impulse, to her husband, "—only if you—if *you* do not hold me in—in horror—because of what I do—"

There was a silence; then:

"What are you about to do?" he asked hoarsely.

"Slay this man."

"We'll do that," said Cleves with a shudder. "Only show him to us and we'll shoot the dirty reptile to slivers—"

"Suppose we hit the jar of gas," said Recklow.

After a silence, Tressa said:

"I have got to give him back to Satan. There is no other way. I understood that from the first. He can not die by your pistols, though you shoot very fast and straight. No!"

After another silence, Recklow said:

"You had better find him before the wind changes. We hunt down wind or—we die here together."

She looked at her husband.

"Show him to us in your own way," he said, "and deal with him as he must be dealt with."

A gleam passed across her pale face and she tried to smile at her husband.

Then, turning down the hammock to the east, she walked noiselessly forward over the fibrous litter, the men on either side of her, their pistols poised.

They had halted on the edge of an open glade, ringed with young pines in fullest plumage.

Tressa was standing very straight and still in a strange, supple, agonised attitude, her left forearm across her eyes, her right hand clenched, her slender body slightly twisted to the left.

The men gazed pallidly at her with tense, set faces, knowing that the girl was in terrible mental conflict against another mind—a powerful, sinister mind which was seeking to grasp her thoughts and control them.

Minute after minute sped: the girl never moved, locked in her psychic duel with this other brutal mind,—beating back its terrible thought-waves which were attacking her, fighting for mental supremacy, struggling in silence with an unseen adversary whose mental dominance meant death.

Suddenly her cry rang out sharply in the moonlight, and then, all at once, a man in white stood there in the lustre of the moon—a young, graceful man dressed in white flannels and carrying on his right arm what seemed to be a long white cloak.

Instantly the girl was transformed from a living statue into a lithe, supple, lightly moving thing that passed swiftly to the west of the glade, keeping the young man in white facing the wind, which was blowing and tossing the plumy young pines.

"So it is *you*, young man, with whom I have been wrestling here under the moon of the only God!" she said in a strange little voice, all vibrant and metallic with menacing laughter.

"It is I, Keuke Mongol," replied the young man in white, tranquilly; yet his words came as though he were tired and out of breath, and the hand he raised to touch his small black moustache trembled as if from physical exhaustion.

"Yarghouz!" she exclaimed. "Why did I not know you there on the golf links, Assassin of the Seventh Tower? And why do you come here with your shroud over your arm and hidden under it, in your right hand, a flask full of death?"

He said, smiling:

"I come because you are to die, Heavenly-Azure Eyes. I bring you your shroud." And he moved warily westward around the open circle of young pines.

Instantly the girl flung her right arm straight upward.

"Yarghouz!"

"I hear thee, Heavenly Azure."

"Another step to the west and I shatter thy flask of gas."

"With what?" he demanded; but stood discreetly motionless.

"With what I grasp in an empty palm. Thou knowest, Yarghouz."

"I have heard," he said with smiling uncertainty, "but to hear of force that can be hurled out of an empty palm is one thing, and to see it and feel it is another. I think you lie, Heavenly Azure."

"So thought Gutchlug. And died of a yellow snake."

The young man seemed to reflect. Then he looked up at her in his frank, smiling way.

"Wilt thou listen, Heavenly Eyes?"

"I hear thee, Yarghouz."

"Listen then, Keuke Mongol. Take life from us as we offer it. Life is sweet. Erlik, like a spider, waits in darkness for lost souls that flutter to his net."

"You think my soul was lost there in the temple, Yarghouz?"

"Unutterably lost, little temple girl of Yian. Therefore, live. Take life as a gift!"

"Whose gift?"

"Sanang's."

"It is written," she said gravely, "that we belong to God and we return to him. Now then, Yezidee, do your duty as I do mine! Kai!"

At the sound of the formula always uttered by the sect of Assassins when about to do murder, the young man started and shrank back. The west wind blew fresh in his startled eyes.

"Sorceress," he said less firmly, "you leave your Yiort to come all alone into this forest and seek me. Why then have you come, if not to submit!—if not to take the gift of life—if not to turn away from your seducers who are hunting me, and who have corrupted you?"

"Yarghouz, I come to slay you," she said quietly.

Suddenly the man snarled at her, flung the shroud at her feet, and crept deliberately to the left.

"Be careful!" she cried sharply; "look what you're about! Stand still, son of a dog! May your mother bewail your death!"

Yarghouz edged toward the west, clasping in his right hand the flask of gas.

"Sorceress," he laughed, "a witch of Thibet prophesied with a drum that the three purities, the nine perfections, and the nine times nine felicities shall be lodged in him who slays the treacherous temple girl, Keuke Mongol! There is more magic in this bottle which I grasp than in thy mind and body. Heavenly Eyes! I pray God to be merciful to this soul I send to Erlik!"

All the time he was advancing, edging cautiously around the circle of little plumy pines; and already the wind struck his left cheek.

"Yarghouz Khan!" cried the girl in her clear voice. "Take up your shroud and repeat the fatha!"

"Backward!" laughed the young man, "—as do you, Keuke Mongol!"

"Heretic!" she retorted. "Do you also refuse to name the ten Imaums in your prayers? Dog! Toad! Spittle of Erlik! May all your cattle die and all your horses take the glanders and all your dogs the mange!"

"Silence, sorceress!" he shouted, pale with fear and fury. "Witch! Mud worm! May Erlik seize you! May your skin be covered with putrefying sores! May all the demons torment you! May God remember you in hell!"

"Yarghouz! Stand still!"

"Is your word then the Rampart of Gog and Magog, you young witch of Yian, that a Khan of the Seventh Tower need fear you!" he sneered, stealing stealthily westward through the feathery pines.

"I give thee thy last chance, Yarghouz Khan," she said in an excited voice that trembled. "Recite thy prayer naming the ten, because with their holy names upon thy lips thou mayest escape damnation. For I am here to slay thee, Yarghouz! Take up thy shroud and pray!"

The young man felt the west wind at the back of his left ear. Then he began to laugh.

"Heavenly Eyes," he said, "thy end is come—together with the two police who hide in the pines yonder behind thee! Behold the bottle magic of Yarghouz Khan!"

And he lifted the glass flask in the moonlight as though he were about to smash it at her feet.

Then a terrible thing occurred. The entire flask glowed red hot in his grasp; and the man screamed and strove convulsively to fling the bottle; but it stuck to his hand, melted into the smoking flesh.

Then he screamed again—or tried to—but his entire lower jaw came off and he stood there with the awful orifice gaping in the moonlight—stood, reeled a moment—and then—and *then*—his whole face slid off, leaving nothing but a bony mask out of which burst shriek after shriek—

Keuke Mongol had fainted dead away. Cleves took her into his arms.

Recklow, trembling and deathly white, went over to the thing that lay among the young pines and forced himself to bend over it.

The glass flask still stuck to one charred hand, but it was no longer hot. And Recklow rolled the unspeakable thing into the white shroud and pushed it into the swamp.

An evil ooze took it, slowly sucked it under and engulfed it. A few stinking bubbles broke.

Recklow went back to the little glade among the pines.

A young girl lay sobbing convulsively in her husband's arms, asking God's pardon and his for the justice she had done upon an enemy of all mankind.

CHAPTER X
# AT THE RITZ

When Victor Cleves telegraphed from St. Augustine to Washington that he and his wife were on their way North, and that they desired to see John Recklow as soon as they arrived, John Recklow remarked that he knew of no place as private as a public one. And he came on to New York and established himself at the Ritz, rather regally.

To dine with him that evening were two volunteer agents of the United States Secret Service, *ZB-303*, otherwise James Benton, a fashionable architect; and *XYL-371*, Alexander Selden, sometime junior partner in the house of Milwin, Selden & Co.

A single lamp was burning in the white-and-rose rococo room. Under its veiled glow these three men sat conversing in guarded voices over coffee and cigars, awaiting the advent of *53-6-26*, otherwise Victor Cleves, recently Professor of Ornithology at Cambridge; and his young wife, Tressa, known officially as *V-69*.

"Did the trip South do Mrs. Cleves any good?" inquired Benton.

"Some," said Recklow. "When Selden and I saw her she was getting better."

"I suppose that affair of Yarghouz upset her pretty thoroughly."

"Yes." Recklow tossed his cigar into the fireplace and produced a pipe. "Victor Cleves upsets her more," he remarked.

"Why?" asked Benton, astonished.

"She's beginning to fall in love with him and doesn't know what's the matter with her," replied the elder man drily. "Selden noticed it, too."

Benton looked immensely surprised. "I supposed," he said, "that she and Cleves considered the marriage to be merely a temporary necessity. I didn't imagine that they cared for each other."

"I don't suppose they did at first," said Selden. "But I think she's interested in Victor. And I don't see how he can help falling in love with her, because she's a very beautiful thing to gaze on, and a most engaging one to talk to."

"She's about the prettiest girl I ever saw," admitted Benton, "and about the cleverest. All the same—"

"All the same—*what?*"

"Well, Mrs. Cleves has her drawbacks, you know—as a real wife, I mean."

Recklow said: "There is a fixed idea in Cleves's head that Tressa Norne married him as a last resort, which is true. But he'll never believe she's changed her ideas in regard to him unless she herself enlightens him. And the girl is too shy to do that. Besides, she believes the same thing of him. There's a mess for you!"

Recklow filled his pipe carefully.

"In addition," he went on, "Mrs. Cleves has another and very terrible fixed idea in her charming head, and that is that she really did lose her soul among those damned Yezidees. She believes that Cleves, though kind to her, considers her merely as something uncanny—something to endure until this Yezidee campaign is ended and she is safe from assassination."

Benton said: "After all, and in spite of all her loveliness, I myself should not feel entirely comfortable with such a girl for a real wife."

"Why?" demanded Recklow.

"Well—good heavens, John!—those uncanny things she does—her rather terrifying psychic knowledge and ability—make a man more or less uneasy." He laughed without mirth.

"For example," he added, "I never was nervous in any physical crisis; but since I've met Tressa Norne—to be frank—I'm not any too comfortable in my mind when I remember Gutchlug and Sanang and Albert Feke and that dirty reptile Yarghouz—and when I recollect *how that girl dealt with them!* Good God, John, I'm not a coward, I hope, but that sort of thing worries me!"

Recklow lighted his pipe. He said: "In the Government's campaign against these eight foreigners who have begun a psychic campaign against the unsuspicious people of this decent Republic, with the purpose of surprising, overpowering and enslaving the minds of mankind by a misuse of psychic power, we agents of the Secret Service are slowly gaining the upper hand.

"In this battle of minds we are gaining a victory. But we are winning solely and alone through the psychic ability and the loyalty and courage of a young girl who, through tragedy of circumstances, spent the years of her girlhood in the infamous Yezidee temple at Yian, and who learned from the devil-worshipers themselves not only this so-called magic of the Mongol sorcerers, but also how to meet its psychic menace and defeat it."

He looked at Benton, shrugged:

"If you and if Cleves really feel the slightest repugnance toward the strange psychic ability of this brave and generous girl, I for one do not share it."

Benton reddened: "It isn't exactly repugnance—" But Recklow interrupted sharply:

"Do you realise, Benton, what she's already accomplished for us in our secret battle against Bolshevism?—against the very powers of hell itself, led by these Mongol sorcerers?

"Of the Eight Assassins—or Sheiks-el-Djebel—who came to the United States to wield the dreadful weapon of psychic power against the minds of our people, and to pervert them and destroy all civilisation,—of the Eight Chief Assassins of the Eight Towers, this girl already has discovered and identified four,—Sanang, Gutchlug, Albert Feke, and Yarghouz; and she has destroyed the last three."

He sat calmly enjoying his pipe for a few moments' silence, then:

"Five of this sect of Assassins remain—five sly, murderous, psychic adepts who call themselves sorcerers. Except for Prince Sanang, I do not know who these other four men may be. I haven't a notion. Nor have you. Nor do I believe that with all the resources of the United States Secret Service we ever should be able to discover these four Sheiks-el-Djebel except for the astounding spiritual courage and psychic experience of the young wife of Victor Cleves."

After a moment Selden nodded. "That is quite true," he said simply. "We are utterly helpless against unknown psychic forces. And I, for one, feel no repugnance toward what Mrs. Cleves has done for all mankind and in the name of God."

"She's a brave girl," muttered Benton, "but it's terrible to possess such knowledge and horrible to use it."

Recklow said: "The horror of it nearly killed the girl herself. Have you any idea how she must suffer by being forced to employ such terrific knowledge? by being driven to use it to combat this menace of hell? Can you imagine what this charming, sensitive, tragic young creature must feel when, with powers natural to her but unfamiliar to us, she destroys with her own mind and will-power demons in human shape who are about to destroy her?

"Talk of nerve! Talk of abnegation! Talk of perfect loyalty and courage! There is more than these in Tressa Cleves. There is that dauntless bravery which faces worse than physical death. Because the child still believes that her soul is damned for whatever happened to her in the Yezidee temple; and that when these Yezidees succeed in killing her body, Erlik will surely seize the soul that leaves it."

There was a knocking at the door. Benton got up and opened it. Victor Cleves came in with his young wife.

Tressa Cleves seemed to have grown since she had been away. Taller, a trifle paler, yet without even the subtlest hint of that charming maturity which the young and happily married woman invariably wears, her virginal allure now verged vaguely on the delicate edges of austerity.

Cleves, sunburnt and vigorous, looked older, somehow—far less boyish—and he seemed more silent than when, nearly seven months before, he had been assigned to the case of Tressa Norne.

Recklow, Selden and Benton greeted them warmly; to each in turn Tressa gave her narrow, sun-tanned hand. Recklow led her to a seat. A servant came with iced fruit juice and little cakes and cigarettes.

Conversation, aimless and general, fulfilling formalities, gradually ceased.

A full June moon stared through the open windows—searching for the traditional bride, perhaps—and its light silvered a pale and lovely figure that might possibly have passed for the pretty ghost of a bride, but not for any girl who had married because she was loved.

Recklow broke the momentary silence, bluntly:

"Have you anything to report, Cleves?"

The young fellow hesitated:

"My wife has, I believe."

The others turned to her. She seemed, for a moment, to shrink back in her chair, and, as her eyes involuntarily sought her husband, there was in them a vague and troubled appeal.

Cleves said in a sombre voice: "I need scarcely remind you how deeply distasteful this entire and accursed business is to my wife. But she is going to see it through, whatever the cost. And we four men understand something of what it has cost her—is costing her—in violence to her every instinct."

"We honour her the more," said Recklow quietly.

"We couldn't honour her too much," said Cleves.

A slight colour came into Tressa's face; she bent her head, but Recklow saw her eyes steal sideways toward her husband.

Still bowed a little in her chair, she seemed to reflect for a while concerning what she had to say; then, looking up at John Recklow:

"I saw Sanang."

"Good heavens! Where?" he demanded.

"I—don't—know."

Cleves, flushing with embarrassment, explained: "She saw him clairvoyantly. She was lying in the hammock. You remember I had a trained nurse for her after—what happened in Orchid Lodge."

Tressa looked miserably at Recklow,—dumbly, for a moment. Then her lips unclosed.

"I saw Prince Sanang," she repeated. "He was near the sea. There were rocks—cottages on cliffs—and very brilliant flowers in tiny, pocket-like gardens.

"Sanang was walking on the cliffs with another man. There were forests, inland."

"Do you know who the other man was?" asked Recklow gently.

"Yes. He was one of the Eight. I recognised him. When I was a girl he came once to the Temple of Yian, all alone, and spread his shroud on the pink marble steps. And we temple girls mocked him and threw stemless roses on the shroud, telling him they were human heads with which to grease his toug."

She became excited and sat up straighter in her chair, and her strange little laughter rippled like a rill among pebbles.

"I threw a big rose without a stem upon the shroud," she exclaimed, "and I cried out, 'Niaz!' which means, 'Courage,' and I mocked him, saying, 'Djamouk Khagan,' when he was only a Khan, of course; and I laughed and rubbed one finger against the other, crying out, 'Toug is glachakho!' which means, 'The toug is anointed.' And which was very impudent of me, because Djamouk was a Sheik-el-Djebel and Khan of the Fifth Tower, and entitled to a toug and to eight men and a Toughtchi. And it is a grave offence to mock at the anointing of a toug."

She paused, breathless, her splendid azure eyes sparkling with the memory of that girlish mischief. Then their brilliancy faded; she bit her lip and stole an uncertain glance at her husband.

And after a pause she explained in a very subdued voice that the "Iagla michi," or action of "greasing the toug," or standard, was done when a severed human head taken in battle was cast at the foot of the lance shaft stuck upright in the ground.

"You see," she said sadly, "we temple girls, being already damned, cared little what we said, even to such a terrible man as Djamouk Khan. And even had the ghost of old Tchinguiz Khagan himself come to the temple and looked at us out of his tawny eyes, I think we might have done something saucy."

Tressa's pretty face was spiritless, now; she leaned back in her armchair and they heard an unconscious sigh escape her.

"Ai-ya! Ai-ya!" she murmured to herself, "what crazy things we did on the rose-marble steps, Yulun and I, so long—so long ago."

Cleves got up and went over to stand beside his wife's chair.

"What happened is this," he said heavily. "During my wife's convalescence after that Yarghouz affair, she found herself, at a certain moment, clairvoyant. And she thought she saw—she *did* see—Sanang, and an Asiatic she recognised as being one of the chiefs of the Assassins sect, whose name is Djamouk.

"But, except that it was somewhere near the sea—some summer colony probably on the Atlantic coast—she does not know where this pair of jailbirds roost. And this is what we have come here to report."

Benton, politely appalled, tried not to look incredulous. But it was evident that Selden and Recklow had no doubts.

"Of course," said Recklow calmly, "the thing to do is for you and your wife to try to find this place she saw."

"Make a tour of all such ocean-side resorts until Mrs. Cleves recognises the place she saw," added Selden. And to Recklow he added: "I believe there are several perfectly genuine cases on record where clairvoyants have aided the police."

"Several authentic cases," said Recklow quietly. But Benton's face was a study.

Tressa looked up at her husband. He dropped his hand reassuringly on her shoulder and nodded with a slight smile.

"There—there was something else," she said with considerable hesitation—"something not quite in line of duty—perhaps—"

"It seems to concern Benton," added Cleves, smiling.

"What is it?" inquired Selden, smiling also as Benton's features froze to a mask.

"Let me tell you, first," interrupted Cleves, "that my wife's psychic ability and skill can make me visualise and actually see scenes and people which, God knows, I never before laid eyes upon, but which she has both seen and known.

"And one morning, in Florida, I asked her to do something strange—something of that sort to amuse me—and we were sitting on the steps of our cottage—you know, the old club-house at Orchid!—and the first I knew I saw, in the mist on the St. Johns, a Chinese bridge humped up over that very commonplace stream, and thousands of people passing over it,—and a city beyond—the town of Yian, Tressa tells me,—and I heard the Buddhist bells and the big temple gong and the noises in streets and on the water—"

He was becoming considerably excited at the memory, and his lean face reddened and he gesticulated as he spoke:

"It was astounding, Recklow! There was that bridge, and all those people moving over it; and the city beyond, and the boats and shipping, and the vast murmur of multitudes.... And then, there on the bridge crossing toward Yian, I saw a young girl, who turned and looked back at my wife and laughed."

"And I told him it was Yulun," said Tressa, simply.

"A playfellow of my wife's in Yian," explained Cleves. "But if she were really Chinese she didn't look like what are my own notions of a Chinese girl."

"Yulun came from Black China," said Mrs. Cleves. "I taught her English. I loved her dearly. I was her most intimate friend in Yian."

There ensued a silence, broken presently by Benton; and:

"Where do I appear in this?" he asked stiffly.

Tressa's smile was odd; she looked at Selden and said:

"When I was convalescent I was lonely.... I made the effort one evening. And I found Yulun. And again she was on a bridge. But she was dressed as I am. And the bridge was one of those great, horrible steel monsters that sprawl across the East River. And I was astonished, and I said, 'Yulun, darling, are you really here in America and in New York, or has a demon tangled the threads of thought to mock my mind in illness?'

"Then Yulun looked very sorrowfully at me and wrote in Arabic characters, in the air, the name of our enemy who once came to the Lake of Ghosts for love of her—Yaddin-ed-Din, Tougtchi to Djamouk the Fox.... And who went his way again amid our scornful laughter.... He is a demon. And he was tangling my thread of thought!"

Tressa became exceedingly animated once more. She rose and came swiftly to where Benton was standing.

"And what do you think!" she said eagerly. "I said to her, 'Yulun Yulun! Will you *make the effort* and come to me if I *make the effort?* Will you come to me, beloved?' And Yulun made 'Yes,' with her lips."

After a silence: "But—where do I come in?" inquired Benton, stiffly fearful of such matters.

"You *came* in."

"I don't understand."

"You came in the door while Yulun and I were talking."

"When?"

"When you came to see me after I was better, and you and Mr. Selden were going North with Mr. Recklow. Don't you remember; I was lying in the hammock in the moonlight, and Victor told you I was asleep?"

"Yes, of course—"

"I was not asleep. I had *made the effort* and I was with Yulun.... I did not know you were standing beside my hammock in the moonlight until Yulun told me.... And *that* is what I am to tell you; Yulun saw you.... And Yulun has written it in Chinese, in Eighur characters and in Arabic,—tracing them with her forefinger in the air—that Yulun, loveliest in Yian, flame-slender and very white, has seen her heart, like a pink pearl afire, burning between your august hands."

"My hands!" exclaimed Benton, very red. There fell an odd silence. Nobody laughed. Tressa came nearer to Benton, wistful, uncertain, shy.

"Would you care to see Yulun?" she asked.

"Well—no," he said, startled. "I—I shall not deny that such things worry me a lot, Mrs. Cleves. I'm a—an Episcopalian."

The tension released, Selden was the first to laugh. "There's no use blinking the truth," he said; "we're up against something absolutely new. Of course, it isn't magic. It can, of course, be explained by natural laws about which we happen to know nothing at present."

Recklow nodded. "What do we know about the human mind? It has been proven that no thought can originate within that mass of convoluted physical matter called the brain. It has been proven that *something outside* the brain originates thought and uses the brain as a vehicle to incubate it. What do we know about thought?"

Selden, much interested, sat cogitating and looking at Mrs. Cleves. But Benton, still flushed and evidently nervous, sat staring out of the window at the full moon, and twisting an unlighted cigarette to shreds.

"Why didn't you tell Benton when the thing occurred down there at Orchid Lodge, the night we called to say good-bye?" asked Selden, curiously.

Tressa gave him a distressed smile: "I was afraid he wouldn't believe me. And I was afraid that you and Mr. Recklow, even if you believed it, might not like—like me any the better for—for being clairvoyant."

Recklow came over, bent his handsome grey head, and kissed her hand.

"I never liked any woman better, nor respected any woman as deeply," he said. And, lifting his head, he saw tears sparkling in her eyes.

"My dear," he said in a low voice, and his firm hand closed over the slim fingers he had kissed.

Benton got up from his chair, went to the window, turned shortly and came over to Tressa.

"You're braver than I ever could learn to be," he said shortly. "I ask your pardon if I seem sceptical. I'm more worried than incredulous. There's something born in me—part of me—that shrinks from anything that upsets my orthodox belief in the future life. But—if you wish me to see this—this girl—Yulun—it's quite all right."

She said softly, and with gentle wonder: "I know of nothing that could upset your belief, Mr. Benton. There is only one God. And if Mahomet be His prophet, or if he be Lord Buddha, or if your Lord Christ be vice-regent to the Most High, I do not know. All I know is that God is God, and that He prevailed over Satan who was stoned. And that in Paradise is eternal life, and in hell demons hide where dwells Erlik, Prince of Darkness."

Benton, silent and secretly aghast at her theology, said nothing. Recklow pleasantly but seriously denied that Satan and his demons were actual and concrete creatures.

Again Cleves's hand fell lightly on his wife's shoulder, in a careless gesture of reassurance. And, to Benton, "No soul is ever lost," he said, calmly. "I don't exactly know how that agrees with your orthodoxy, Benton. But it is surely so."

"I don't know myself," said Benton. "I hope it's so." He looked at Tressa a moment and then blurted out: "Anyway, if ever there was a soul in God's keeping and guarded by His angels, it's your wife's!"

"That also is true," said Cleves quietly.

"By the way," remarked Recklow carelessly, "I've arranged to have you stop at the Ritz while you're in town, Mrs. Cleves. You and your band are to occupy the apartment adjoining this. Where is your luggage, Victor?"

"In our apartment."

"That won't do," said Recklow decisively. "Telephone for it."

Cleves went to the telephone, but Recklow took the instrument out of his hand and called the number. The voice of one of his own agents answered.

Cleves was standing alone by the open window when Recklow hung up the telephone. Tressa, on the sofa, had been whispering with Benton. Selden, looking over the evening paper by the rose-shaded lamp, glanced up as Recklow went over to Cleves.

"Victor," he said, "your man has been murdered. His throat was cut; his head was severed completely. Your luggage has been ransacked and so has your apartment. Three of my men are in possession, and the local police seem to comprehend the necessity of keeping the matter out of the newspapers. What was in your baggage?"

"Nothing," said Cleves, ghastly pale.

"All right. We'll have your effects packed up again and brought over here. Are you going to tell your wife?"

Cleves, still deathly pale, cast a swift glance toward her. She sat on the sofa in animated conversation with Benton. She laughed once, and Benton smiled at what she was saying.

"Is there any need to tell her, Recklow?"

"Not for a while, anyway."

"All right. I suppose the Yezidees are responsible for this horrible business."

"Certainly. Your poor servant's head lay at the foot of a curtain-pole which had been placed upright between two chairs. On the pole were tied three tufts of hair from the dead man's head. The pole had been rubbed with blood."

"That's Mongol custom," muttered Cleves. "They made a toug and 'greased' it!—the murderous devils!"

"They did more. They left at the foot of your bed and at the foot of your wife's bed two white sheets. And a knife lay in the centre of each sheet. That, of course, is the symbol of the Sect of Assassins."

Cleves nodded. His body, as he leaned there on the window sill in the moonlight, trembled. But his face had grown dark with rage.

"If I could—could only get my hands on one of them," he whispered hoarsely.

"Be careful. Don't wear a face like that. Your wife is looking at us," murmured Recklow.

With an effort Cleves raised his head and smiled across the room at his wife.

"Our luggage will be sent over shortly," he said. "If you're tired, we'll say good-night."

So she rose and the three men came to make their adieux and pay their compliments and devoirs. Then, with a smile that seemed almost happy, she went into her own apartment on her husband's arm.

Cleves and his wife had connecting bedrooms and a sitting-room between. Here they paused for a moment before the always formal ceremony of leave-taking at night. There were roses on the centre table. Tressa dropped one hand on the table and bent over the flowers.

"They seem so friendly," she said under her breath.

He thought she meant that she found even in flowers a refuge from the solitude of a loveless marriage.

He said quietly: "I think you will find the world very friendly, if you wish." But she shook her head, looking at the roses.

Finally he said good-night and she extended her hand, and he took it formally.

Then their hands fell away. Tressa turned and went toward her bedroom. At the door she stopped, turned slowly.

"What shall I do about Yulun?" she asked.

"What is there to do? Yulun is in China."

"Yes, her body is."

"Do you mean that the rest of her—whatever it is—could come here?"

"Why, of course."

"So that Benton could see her?"

"Yes."

"Could he see her just as she is? Her face and figure—clothes and everything?"

"Yes."

"Would she seem real or like a ghost—spirit—whatever you choose to call such things?"

Tressa smiled. "She'd be exactly as real as you or I, Victor. She'd seem like anybody else."

"That's astonishing," he muttered. "Could Benton hear her speak?"

"Certainly."

"Talk to her?"

Tressa laughed: "Of course. If Yulun should *make the effort* she could leave her body as easily as she undresses herself. It is no more difficult to divest one's self of one's body than it is to put off one garment and put on another.... And, somehow, I think Yulun will do it to-night."

"Come *here?*"

"It would be like her." Tressa laughed. "Isn't it odd that she should have become so enamoured of Mr. Benton—just seeing him there in the moonlight that night at Orchid Lodge?"

For a moment the smile curved her lips, then the shadow fell again across her eyes, veiling them in that strange and lovely way which Cleves knew so well; and he looked into her impenetrable eyes in troubled silence.

"Victor," she said in a low voice, "were you afraid to tell me that your man had been murdered?"

After a moment: "You always know everything," he said unsteadily. "When did you learn it?"

"Just before Mr. Recklow told you."

"How did you learn it, Tressa?"

"I looked into our apartment."

"When?"

"While you were telephoning."

"You mean you looked into our rooms from *here?*"

"Yes, clairvoyantly."

"What did you see?"

"The Iaglamichi!" she said with a shudder. "Kai! The Toug of Djamouk is anointed at last!"

"Is that the beast of a Mongol who did this murder?"

"Djamouk and Prince Sanang planned it," she said, trembling a little. "But that butchery was Yaddin's work, I think. Kai! The work of Yaddin-ed-Din, Tougtchi to Djamouk the Fox!"

They stood confronting each other, the length of the sitting-room between them. And after the silence had lasted a full minute Cleves reddened and said: "I am going to sleep on the couch at the foot of your bed, Tressa."

His young wife reddened too.

He said: "This affair has thoroughly scared me. I can't let you sleep out of my sight."

"I am quite safe. And you would have an uncomfortable night," she murmured.

"Do you mind if I sleep on the couch, Tressa?"

"No."

"Will you call me when you are ready?"

"Yes."

She went into her bedroom and closed the door. When he was ready he slipped a pistol into the pocket of his dressing-gown, belted it over his pyjamas, and walked into the sitting-room. His wife called him presently, and he went in. Her night-lamp was burning and she extended her hand to extinguish it.

"Could you sleep if it burns?" he asked bluntly.

"Yes."

"Then let it burn. This business has got on my nerves," he muttered.

They looked at each other in an expressionless way. Both really understood how useless was this symbol of protection—this man the girl called husband;—how utterly useless his physical strength, and the pistol sagging in the pocket of his dressing-gown. Both understood that the only real protection to be looked for must come from her—from the gifted and guardian mind of this young girl who lay there looking at him from the pillows.

"Good-night," he said, flushing; "I'll do my best. But only one of God's envoys, like you, knows how to do battle with things that come out of hell."

After a moment's silence she said in a colourless voice: "I wish you'd lie down on the bed."

"Had you rather I did?"

"Yes."

So he went slowly to the bed, placed his pistol under the pillow, drew his dressing-gown around him, and lay down.

After he had lain unstirring for half an hour: "Try to sleep, Tressa," he said, without turning his head.

"Can't you seem to sleep, Victor?" she asked. And he heard her turn her head.

"No."

"Shall I help you?"

"Do you mean use hypnosis—the power of suggestion—on me?"

"No. I can help you to sleep very gently. I can make you very drowsy.... You are drowsy now.... You are very close to the edge of sleep.... Sleep, dear.... Sleep, easily, naturally, confidently as a tired boy.... You are sleeping... deeply... sweetly... my dear... my dear, dear husband."

CHAPTER XI
# YULUN THE BELOVED

Cleves opened his eyes. He was lying on his left side. In the pink glow of the night-lamp he saw his wife in her night-dress, seated sideways on the farther edge of the bed, talking to a young girl.

The strange girl wore what appeared to be a chamber-robe of frail gold tissue that clung to her body and glittered as she moved. He had never before seen such a dress; but he had seen the girl; he recognised her instantly as the girl he had seen turn to look back at Tressa as she crossed the phantom bridge over that misty Florida river. And Cleves comprehended that he was looking at Yulun.

But this charming young thing was no ghost, no astral projection. This girl was warm, living, breathing flesh. The delicate scent of her strange garments and of her hair, her very breath, was in the air of the room. Her half-hushed but laughing voice was deliciously human; her delicate little hands, caressing Tressa's, were too eagerly real to doubt.

Both talked at the same time, their animated voices mingling in the breathless delight of the reunion. Their exclamations, enchanting laughter, bubbling chatter, filled his ears. But not one word of what they were saying to each other could he understand.

Suddenly Tressa looked over her shoulder and met his astonished eyes.

"Tokhta!" she exclaimed. "Yulun! My lord is awake!"

Yulun swung around swiftly on the edge of the bed and looked laughingly at Cleves. But when her red lips unclosed she spoke to Tressa: and, "Darling," she said in English, "I think your dear lord remembers that he saw me on the Bridge of Dreams. And heard the bells of Yian across the mist."

Tressa said, laughing at her husband: "This is Yulun, flame-slender, very white, loveliest in Yian. On the rose-marble steps of the Yezidee Temple she flung a stemless rose upon Djamouk's shroud, where he had spread it like a patch of snow in the sun.

"And at the Lake of the Ghosts, where there is freedom to love, for those who desire love, came Yaddin, Tougtchi to Djamouk the Fox, in search of love—and Yulun, flame-slim, and flower-white.... Tell my dear lord, Yulun!"

Yulun laughed at Cleves out of her dark eyes that slanted charmingly at the corners.

"Kai!" she cried softly, clapping her palms. "I took his roses and tore them with my hands till their petals rained on him and their golden hearts were a powdery cloud floating across the water.

"I said: 'Even the damned do not mate with demons, my Tougtchi! So go to the devil, my Banneret, and may Erlik seize you!'"

Cleves, his ears ringing with the sweet confusion of their girlish laughter, rose from his pillow, supporting himself on one arm.

"You are Yulun. You are alive and real—" He looked at Tressa: "She is real, isn't she?" And, to Yulun: "Where do you come from?"

The girl replied seriously: "I come from Yian." She turned to Tressa with a dazzling smile: "Thou knowest, my heart's gold, how it was I came. Tell thy dear lord in thine own way, so that it shall be simple for his understanding.... And now—because my visit is ending—I think thy dear lord should sleep. Bid him sleep, my heart's gold!"

At that calm suggestion Cleves sat upright on the bed,—or attempted to. But sank back gently on his pillow and met there a dark, delicious rush of drowsiness.

He made an effort—or tried to: the smooth, sweet tide of sleep swept over him to the eyelids, leaving him still and breathing evenly on his pillow.

The two girls leaned over and looked down at him.

"Thy dear lord," murmured Yulun. "Does he love thee, rosebud of Yian?"

"No," said Tressa, under her breath.

"Does he know thou art damned, heart of gold?"

"He says no soul is ever really harmed," whispered Tressa.

"Kai! Has he never heard of the Slayer of Souls?" exclaimed Yulun incredulously.

"My lord maintains that neither the Assassin of Khorassan nor the Sheiks-el-Djebel of the Eight Towers, nor their dark prince Erlik, can have power over God to slay the human soul."

"Tokhta, Rose of Yian! Our souls were slain there in the Yezidee temple."

Tressa looked down at Cleves:

"My dear lord says no," she said under her breath.

"And—Sanang?"

Tressa paled: "His mind and mine did battle. I tore my heart from his grasp. I have laid it, bleeding, at my dear lord's feet. Let God judge between us, Yulun."

"There was a day," whispered Yulun, "when Prince Sanang went to the Lake of the Ghosts."

Tressa, very pallid, looked down at her sleeping husband. She said:

"Prince Sanang came to the Lake of the Ghosts. The snow of the cherry-trees covered the young world.

"The water was clear as sunlight; and the lake was afire with scarlet carp.... Yulun—beloved—the nightingale sang all night long—all night long.... Then I saw Sanang shining, all gold, in the moonlight.... May God remember him in hell!"

"May God remember him."

"Sanang Noïane. May he be accursed in the Namaz Ga!"

"May he be tormented in Jehaunum!—Sanang, Slayer of Souls."

Tressa leaned forward on the bed, stretched herself out, and laid her face gently across her husband's feet, touching them with her lips.

Then she straightened herself and sat up, supported by one hand, and looking silently down at the sleeping man.

"No soul shall die," she said. "Niaz!"

"Is it written?" asked Yulun, surprised.

"My lord has said it."

"Allahou Ekber," murmured Yulun; "thy lord is only a man."

Tressa said: "Neither the Tekbir nor the fatha, nor the warning of Khidr, nor the Yacaz of the Khagan, nor even the prayers of the Ten Imaums are of any value to me unless my dear lord confirms the truth of them with his own lips."

"And Erlik? Is he nothing, then?"

"Erlik!" repeated Tressa insolently. "Who is Erlik but the servant of Satan who was stoned?"

Her beautiful, angry lips were suddenly distorted; her blue eyes blazed. Then she spat, her mouth still tremulous with hatred. She said in a voice shaking with rage:

"Yulun, beloved! Listen attentively. I have slain two of the Slayers of the Eight Towers. With God's help I shall slay them all—all!—Djamouk, Yaddin, Arrak Sou-Sou—all!—every one!—Tiyang Khan, Togrul,—all shall I slay, even to the last one among them!"

"*Sanang, also?*"

"I leave him to God. It is a fearful thing to fall into the hands of the living God!"

Yulun calmly paraphrased the cant phrase of the Assassins: "For it is written that we belong to God and we return to Him. Heart of gold, I shall execute my duty!"

Then Yulun slipped from the edge of the bed to the floor, and stood there looking oddly at Tressa, her eyes rain-bright as though choking back tears—or laughter.

"Heart of a rose," she said in a suppressed voice, "my time is nearly ended.... So... I go to the chamber of this strange young man who holds my soul like a pearl afire between his hands.... I think it is written that I shall love him."

Tressa rose also and placed her lips close to Yulun's ear: "His name, beloved, is Benton. His room is on this floor. Shall we *make the effort* together?"

"Yes," said Yulun. "Lay your body down upon the bed beside your lord who sleeps so deeply.... And now stretch out.... And fold both hands.... And now put off thy body like a silken garment.... So! And leave it there beside thy lord, asleep."

They stood together for a moment, shining like dewy shapes of tall flowers, whispering and laughing together in the soft glow of the night lamp.

Cleves slept on, unstirring. There was the white and sleeping figure of his wife lying on the bed beside him.

But Tressa and Yulun were already melting away between the wall and the confused rosy radiance of the lamp.

Benton, in night attire and chamber-robe belted in, fresh from his bath and still drying his curly hair on a rough towel, wandered back into his bedroom.

When his short, bright hair was dry, he lighted a cigarette, took the automatic from his dresser, examined the clip, and shoved it under his pillow.

Then he picked up the little leather-bound Testament, seated himself, and opened it. And read tranquilly while his cigarette burned.

When he was ready he turned out the ceiling light, leaving only the night lamp lighted. Then he knelt beside his bed,—a custom surviving the nursery period,—and rested his forehead against his folded hands.

Then, as he prayed, something snapped the thread of prayer as though somebody had spoken aloud in the still room; and, like one who has been suddenly interrupted, he opened his eyes and looked around and upward.

The silent shock of her presence passed presently. He got up from his knees, looking at her all the while.

"You are Yulun," he said very calmly.

The girl flushed brightly and rested one hand on the foot of the bed.

"Do you remember in the moonlight where you walked along the hedge of white hibiscus and oleander—that night you said good-bye to Tressa in the South?"

"Yes."

"Twice," she said, laughing, "you stopped to peer at the blossoms in the moonlight."

"I thought I saw a face among them."

"You were not sure whether it was flowers or a girl's face looking at you from the blossoming hedge of white hibiscus," said Yulun.

"I know now," he said in an odd, still voice, unlike his own.

"Yes, it was I," she murmured. And of a sudden the girl dropped to her knees without a sound and laid her head on the velvet carpet at his feet.

So swiftly, noiselessly was it done that he had not comprehended—had not moved—when she sat upright, resting on her knees, and grasped the collar of her tunic with both gemmed hands.

"Have pity on me, lord of my lost soul!" she cried softly.

Benton stooped in a dazed way to lift the girl; but found himself knee deep in a snowy drift of white hibiscus blossoms—touched nothing but silken petals—waded in them as he stepped forward. And saw her standing before him still grasping the collar of her golden tunic.

A great white drift of bloom lay almost waist deep between them; the fragrance of oleander, too, was heavy in the room.

"There are years of life before the flaming gates of Jehaunum open. And I am very young," said Yulun wistfully.

Somebody else laughed in the room. Turning his head, he saw Tressa standing by the empty fireplace.

"What you see and hear need not disturb you," she said, looking at Benton out of brilliant eyes. "There is no god but God; and His prophet has been called by many names." And to Yulun: "Have I not told you that nothing can harm our souls?"

Yulun's expression altered and she turned to Benton: "Say it to me!" she pleaded.

As in a dream he heard his own words: "Nothing can ever really harm the soul."

Yulun's hands fell from her tunic collar. Very slowly she lifted her head, looking at him out of lovely, proud young eyes.

She said, evenly, her still gaze on him: "I am Yulun of the Temple. My heart is like a blazing pearl which you hold between your hands. May the four Blessed Companions witness the truth of what I say."

Then a delicate veil of colour wrapped her white skin from throat to temple; she looked at Benton with sudden and exquisite distress, frightened and ashamed at his silence.

In the intense stillness Benton moved toward her. Into his outstretched hands her two hands fell; but, bending above them, his lips touched only two white hibiscus flowers that lay fresh and dewy in his palms.

Bewildered, he straightened up; and saw the girl standing by the mantel beside Tressa, who had caught her by the left hand.

"Tokhta! Look out!" she said distinctly.

Suddenly he saw two men in the room, close to him—their broad faces, slanting eyes, and sparse beards thrust almost against his shoulder.

"Djamouk! Yaddin-ed-Din!" cried Tressa in a terrible voice. But quick as a flash Yulun tore a white sheet from the bed, flung it on the floor, and, whipping a tiny, jewelled knife from her sleeve, threw it glittering upon the sheet at the feet of the two men.

"One shroud for two souls!" she said breathlessly. "—and a knife like that to sever them from their bodies!"

The two men sprang backward as the sheet touched their feet, and now they stood there as though confounded.

"Djamouk, Kahn of the Fifth Tower!" cried Tressa in a clear voice, "you have put off your body like a threadbare cloak, and your form that stands there is only your mind! And it is only the evil will of Yaddin in the shape of his body that confronts us in this room of a man you have doomed!"

Yulun, intent as a young leopardess on her prey, moved soundlessly toward Yaddin.

"Tougtchi!" she said coldly, "you did murder this day, my Banneret, and the Toug of Djamouk has been greased. Now look out for yourself!"

"Don't stir!" came Tressa's warning voice, as Benton snatched his pistol from the pillow. "Don't fire! Those men have no real substance! For God's sake don't fire! I tell you they have no bodies!"

Suddenly something—some force—flung Benton on the bed. The two men did not seem to touch him at all, but he lay there struggling, crushed, held by something that was strangling him.

Through his swimming eyes he saw Yaddin trying to drive a long nail into his skull with a hammer,—felt the piercing agony of the first crashing blow,—struggled upright, drenched in blood, his ears ringing with the screaming of Yaddin.

Then, there in the little rococo bedroom of the Ritz-Carlton, began a strange and horrible struggle—the more dreadful because the struggle was not physical and the combatants never touched each other—scarcely moved at all.

Yaddin, still screaming, confronted Yulun. The girl's eyes were ablaze, her lips parted with the violence of her breathing. And Yaddin writhed and screamed under the terrible concentration of her gaze, his inferior but ferocious mind locked with her mind in deadly battle.

The girl said slowly, showing a glimmer of white teeth: "Your will to do evil to my young lord is breaking, Yaddin-ed-Din... I am breaking it. The nail and hammer were but symbols. It was your brain that brooded murder—that willed he should die as though shattered by lightning when that blood-vessel burst in his brain!"

"Sorceress!" shrieked Yaddin, "what are you doing to my heart, where my body lies asleep in a berth on the Montreal Express!"

"Your heart is weak, Yaddin. Soon the valves shall fail. A negro porter shall discover you dead in your berth, my Banneret!"

The man's swarthy face became livid with the terrific mental battle.

"Let me go back to my body!" he panted. "What are you doing to me that I can not go back? I will go back! I wish it!—I—"

"Let us go back and rejoin our bodies!" cried Djamouk in an agonised voice. "There are teeth in my throat, deep in my throat, biting and tear-ing out the cords."

"Cancer," said Tressa calmly. "Your body shall die of it while your soul stumbles on through darkness."

"My Tougtchi!" shouted Djamouk, "I hear my soul bidding my body farewell! I must go before my mind expires in the terrible gaze of this young sorceress!"

He turned, drifted like something misty to the solid wall.

"My soul be ransom for yours!" cried Yulun to Tressa. "Bar that man's path to life!"

Tressa flung out her right hand and, with her forefinger, drew a barrier through space, bar above bar.

And Benton, half swooning on his bed, saw a cage of terrible and living light penning in Djamouk, who beat upon the incandescent bars and grasped them and clawed his way about, squealing like a tortured rat in a red-hot cage.

Through the deafening tumult Yulun's voice cut like a sword:

"Their bodies are dying, Heart of a Rose!... Listen! I hear their souls bidding their minds farewell!"

And, after a dreadful silence: "The train speeding north carries two dead men! God is God. Niaz!"

The bars of living fire faded. Two cinder-like and shapeless shadows floated and eddied like whitened ashes stirred by a wind on the hearth; then drifted through the lamp-light, fading, dissolving, lost gradually in thin air.

Tressa, leaning back against the mantel, covered her face with both hands.

Yulun crept to the bed where Benton lay, breathing evenly in deepest sleep.

With the sheer sleeve of her tunic she wiped the blood from his face. And, at her touch, the wound in the temple closed and the short, bright hair dried and curled over a forehead as clean and fresh as a boy's.

Then Yulun laid her lips against his, rested so a moment.

"Seek me, dear lord," she whispered. "Or send me a sign and I shall come."

And, after a pause, she said, her lips scarcely stirring: "Love me. My heart is a flaming pearl burning between your hands."

Then she lifted her head.

But Tressa had rejoined her body, where it lay asleep beside her deeply sleeping husband.

So Yulun stood a moment, her eyes remote. Then, after a while, the little rococo bedroom in the Ritz-Carlton was empty save for a young man asleep on the bed, holding in his clenched hand a white hibiscus blossom.

CHAPTER XII
# HIS EXCELLENCY

His Excellency President Tintinto, Chief Executive of one of the newer and cruder republics, visiting New York incognito with his Secretaries of War and of the Navy, had sent for John Recklow. And now the reception was in full operation.

Recklow was explaining. "In the beginning," he said, "the Bolsheviks' aim was to destroy everything and everybody except themselves, and then to re-organise for their own benefit what was left of a wrecked world. That was their programme—"

"Quite a programme," interrupted the Secretary of War, with something that almost resembled a giggle. But his prominent eyes continued to stare at Recklow untouched by the mirth which stretched his large, silly mouth.

The face of the Secretary of the Navy resembled the countenance of a benevolent manatee. The visage of the President was a study in tinted chalks.

Recklow said: "To combat that sort of Bolshevism was a business that we of the United States Secret Service understood—or supposed we understood.

"Then, suddenly, out of unknown Mongolia and into the civilised world stepped eight men."

"Yezidees," said the President mechanically. "Your Government has sent me a very full report."

"Yezidees of the Sect of the Assassins," continued Recklow; "—the most ancient sect in the world surviving from ancient times—the Sorcerers of Asia. And, as it was in ancient times, so it is now: the Yezidees are devil worshipers; their god is Satan; *his* prophet is Erlik, Prince of Darkness; *his* regent on earth is the old man of Mount Alamout; and to this ancient and sinister title a Yezidee sorcerer called Prince Sanang, or Sanang Noïane, has succeeded.

"His murderous deputies were the Eight Khans of the Eight Towers. Four of these assassins are dead—Gutchlug, Yarghouz, Djamouk the Fox, and Yaddin-ed-Din. One is in prison charged with murder,—Albert Feke.

"Four of the sorcerers remain alive: Tiyang Khan, Togrul, Arrak, Sou-Sou, called The Squirrel, and the Old Man of the Mountain himself, Saï-Sanang, Prince of the Yezidees."

Recklow paused; the pop-eyes of the War Secretary were upon him; the benevolent manatee gazed mildly at him; the countenance of the President seemed more like a Rocky Mountain goat than ever—chiselled out of a block of tinted chalk.

Recklow said: "To the menace of Bolshevism, which endangers this Republic and yours, has been added a more terrible threat—the threat of powerful and evil minds made formidable by psychic knowledge.

"For these Yezidee Sorcerers are determined to conquer, seize, and subdue the minds of mankind. They are here for that frightful purpose. Powerfully, terrifically equipped to surprise and capture the unarmed minds of our people, enslave their very thoughts and use them to their own purposes, these Sorcerers of the Yezidees assumed control of the Bolsheviki, who were merely envious and ferocious bandits, but whose crippled minds are now utterly enslaved by these Assassins from Asia.

"And this is what the United States Secret Service has to combat. And its weapons are not warrants, not pistols. For in this awful battle between decency and evil, it is mind against mind in an occult death grapple. And our only weapon against these minds made powerful by psychic knowledge and made terrible by an esoteric ability akin to what is called black magic,—our only weapon is the mind of a young girl."

"I understand," said the President, "that she became an adept in occult practices while imprisoned in the Yezidee Temple of Erlik at Yian."

Recklow looked into the President's face, which had grown very pale. "Yes, sir," he said. "God alone knows what this child learned in the Yezidee Temple. All I know is that with this knowledge she has met the Yezidees in a battle of minds, has halted them, confounded them, fought them with their own occult knowledge, and has slain four of them."

The intense silence was broken by the frivolous titter of the Secretary of War:

"Of course I don't believe any of this supernatural stuff," he said with the split grin which did not modify his protruding stare. "This girl is merely a clever detective, that is the gist of the matter. And I don't believe anything else."

"Perhaps, sir, you will believe this, then," said John Recklow quietly. "I cut it from the *Times* this morning." And he handed the clipping to the Secretary of War.

NEW PLOT IN EAST

Moslem and Hindu Conspirators
Have Formed Secret
Organisation

Have World Revolution in View

Think to Rouse Asia, America, and Africa
to Outbreaks by Their
Propaganda.

---

July 1.—A significant event has recently taken place. Under the name of the Oriental League has recently been established a central organisation uniting all the various secret societies of Moslem and Hindu nationalists. The aim of the new association is to prepare for joint revolutionary action in Asia, America, and Africa.

The effects of this vast conspiracy may already be traced in recent events in Egypt, India, and Afghanistan. For the first time, through the creation of this league, the racial and religious differences which have divided Eastern conspirators have been overcome. The Ottoman League, founded by Mahmud Muktar Pasha, Munir Pasha, and Ahmed Rechid Bey, has adhered to the new organisation. So have the extreme Egyptian nationalists and the Hindu revolutionary group, "Pro India," emissaries of which were recently sentenced for bringing bombs into Switzerland during the war at the instigation of the German General Staff.

At a "Constituent Assembly" of the league, which took place in Yian, there were present, besides Young Turks, Egyptians and Hindus, delegates representing Persia, Afghanistan, Algeria, Morocco, and Mongolia.

The league is of Mongolian origin. Its leading spirit is a certain Prince Sanang, of whom little is known.

Associated with this mischievous and rather mysterious Mongolian personage are three better known criminals, now fugitives from justice—Talaat, Enver, and Djemal. It is to Enver Pasha's talent for intrigue that the union between Moslems and Hindus, the most striking and dangerous feature of the movement, is chiefly due.

Considerable funds are at the disposal of the league. These are partly supplied from Germany. Besides enjoying the support of the Germans, the league is also in close touch with Lenine, who very soon after his advent to power organised an Oriental Department in Moscow.

The alliance between the league and the Russian Bolsheviki was brought about by the notorious German Socialist agent, "Parvus," who is now in Switzerland. Many weeks ago he conferred with the Soviet rulers in Moscow, whence he went to Afghanistan, hoping to re-organise the new Amir's army and establish lines of communication for propaganda in India.

Evidence exists that the recent insurrection in Egypt, the sudden attack of the Afghans, and the rising in India, remarkable for co-operation between Moslems and Hindus, were connected with the activities of the league.

The Secretary looked up after he finished the reading.

"I don't see anything about Black Magic in this?" he remarked flippantly.

Recklow's features became very grave.

"I think," he said, "that everybody—myself included—and, with all respect, even yourself, sir,—and your honourable colleague,—and perhaps even his Excellency your President,—should be on perpetual guard over their minds, and the thoughts that range there, lest, surreptitiously, stealthily, some taint of Yezidee infection lodge there and take root—and spread—perhaps—throughout your new Republic."

The Secretary of War grinned. "They say I'm something of a socialist already," he chuckled. "Do you think your magic Yezidees are responsible?"

The President, troubled and pallid, gazed steadily at Recklow.

"Mine is a single-track mind," he remarked as though to himself.

Recklow said nothing. It is one kind of mind, after all. However, single-track roads are now obsolete.

"A single-track mind," repeated the President. "And—I should not like anything to happen to the switch. It would mean ditching—or a rusty siding at best.... Please do all that is possible to get those four Yezidees, Mr. Recklow."

Recklow said calmly: "Our only hope is in this young girl, Tressa Norne, who is now Mrs. Cleves."

"My conscience!" piped the Secretary of the Navy. "What would happen to us if these Yezidees should murder her?"

"God knows," replied John Recklow, unsmiling.

"Why not put her aboard our new dreadnought?" suggested the Secretary, "and keep her cruising until you United States Secret Service fellows get the rest of these infernal Yezidees and clap 'em into jail?"

"We can do nothing without her," said Recklow sombrely.

There was a painful silence. The President joined his finger tips and stared palely into space.

"May I not say," he suggested, "that I think it a vital necessity that these Yezidees be caught and destroyed before they do any damage to the minds of myself and my cabinet?"

"God grant it, sir," said Recklow grimly.

"Mine," murmured the President, "is a single-track mind. I should be very much annoyed if anybody tampered with the rails—very much annoyed indeed, Mr. Recklow."

"They mustn't murder that girl," said the Secretary of the Navy. "Do you need any Marines, Mr. Recklow? Why not ask your Government for a few?"

Recklow rose: "Mr. President," he said, "I shall not deny that my Government is very deeply disturbed by this situation. In the beginning, these eight Assassins, and Sanang, came here for the purpose of attacking, overpowering, and enslaving the minds of the people of the United States and of the South American Republics.

"But now, after four of their infamous colleagues have been destroyed, the ferocious survivors, thoroughly alarmed, have turned their every energy to-ward accomplishing the death of Mrs. Cleves! Why, sir, scarcely a day passes but that some attempt upon her life is made by these Yezidees.

"Scarcely a day passes that this young girl is not suddenly summoned to defend her mind as well as her body against the occult attacks of these Mongol Sorcerers. Yes, sir, Sorcerers!" repeated Recklow, his calm voice deep with controlled passion, "—whatever your honourable Secretary of War may think about it!"

His cold, grey eyes measured the President as he stood there.

"Mr. President, I am at my wits' end to protect her from assassination! Her husband is always with her—Victor Cleves, sir, of our Secret Service. But wherever he takes her these devils follow and send their emissaries to watch her, to follow, to attempt her mental destruction or her physical death.

"There is no end to their stealthy cunning, to their devilish devices, to their hellish ingenuity!

"And all we can do is to guard her person from the approach of strangers, and stand ready, physically, to aid her.

"She is our only barrier—*your* only defence—between civilisation and horrors worse than Bolshevism.

"I believe, Mr. President, that civilisation in North and South America—in your own Republic as well as in ours—depends, literally, upon the safety of Tressa Cleves. For, if the Yezidees kill her, then I do not see what is to save civilisation from utter disintegration and total destruction."

There was a silence. Recklow was not certain that the President had been listening.

His Excellency sat with finger tips joined, gazing pallidly into space; and Recklow heard him murmuring under his breath and all to himself, as though to fix the deathless thought forever in his brain:

"May I not say that mine is a single-track mind? May I not say it? May

I not,—may I not,—not, not, not—"

## CHAPTER XIII
# SA-N'SA

June sunshine poured through the window of his bedroom in the Ritz; and Cleves had just finished dressing when he heard his wife's voice in the adjoining sitting-room.

He had not supposed that Tressa was awake. He hastened to tie his tie and pull on a smoking jacket, listening all the while to his wife's modulated but gay young voice.

Then he opened the sitting-room door and went in. And found his wife entirely alone.

She looked up at him, her lips still parted as though checked in what she had been saying, the smile still visible in her blue eyes.

"Who on earth are you talking to?" he asked, his bewildered glance sweeping the sunny room again.

She did not reply; her smile faded as a spot of sunlight wanes, veiled by a cloud—yet a glimmer of it remained in her gaze as he came over to her.

"I thought they'd brought our breakfast," he said, "—hearing your voice.... Did you sleep well?"

"Yes, Victor."

He seated himself, and his perplexed scrutiny included her frail morning robe of China silk, her lovely bare arms, and her splendid hair twisted up and pegged down with a jade dagger. Around her bare throat and shoulders, too, was a magnificent necklace of imperial jade which he had never before seen; and on one slim, white finger a superb jade ring.

"By Jove!" he said, "you're very exotic this morning, Tressa. I never before saw that negligee effect."

The girl laughed, glanced at her ring, lifted a frail silken fold and examined the amazing embroidery.

"I wore it at the Lake of the Ghosts," she said.

The name of that place always chilled him. He had begun to hate it, perhaps because of all that he did not know about it—about his wife's strange girlhood—about Yian and the devil's Temple there—and about Sanang.

He said coldly but politely that the robe was unusual and the jade very wonderful.

The alteration in his voice and expression did not escape her. It meant merely masculine jealousy, but Tressa never dreamed he cared in that way.

Breakfast was brought, served; and presently these two young people were busy with their melons, coffee, and toast in the sunny room high above the softened racket of traffic echoing through avenue and street below.

"Recklow telephoned me this morning," he remarked.

She looked up, her face serious.

"Recklow says that Yezidee mischief is taking visible shape. The Socialist Party is going to be split into bits and a new party, impudently and publicly announcing itself as the Communist Party of America, is being organised. Did you ever hear of anything as shameless—as outrageous—in this Republic?"

She said very quietly: "Sanang has taken prisoner the minds of these wretched people. He and his remaining Yezidees are giving battle to the unarmed minds of our American people."

"Gutchlug is dead," said Cleves, "—and Yarghouz and Djamouk, and Yaddin."

"But Tiyang Khan is alive, and Togrul, and that cunning demon Arrak Sou-Sou, called The Squirrel," she said. She bent her head, considering the jade ring on her finger. "—And Prince Sanang," she added in a low voice.

"Why didn't you let me shoot him when I had the chance?" said Cleves harshly.

So abrupt was his question, so rough his sudden manner, that the girl looked up in dismayed surprise. Then a deep colour stained her face.

"Once," she said, "Prince Sanang held my heart prisoner—as Erlik held my soul.... I told you that."

"Is that the reason you gave the fellow a chance?"

"Yes."

"Oh.... And possibly you gave Sanang a chance because he still holds your—affections!"

She said, crimson with the pain of the accusation:

"I tore my heart out of his keeping.... I told you that.... And, believing—trying to believe what you say to me, I have tried to tear my soul out of the claws of Erlik.... Why are you angry?"

"I don't know.... I'm not angry.... The whole horrible situation is breaking my nerve, I guess.... With whom were you talking before I came in?"

After a silence the girl's smile glimmered. "I'm afraid you won't like it if I tell you."

"Why not?"

"You—such things perplex and worry you.... I am afraid you won't like me any the better if I tell you who it was I had been talking with."

His intent gaze never left her. "I want you to tell me," he repeated.

"I—I was talking with Sa-n'sa," she faltered.

"With whom?"

"With Sa-n'sa.... We called her Sansa."

"Who the dickens is Sansa?"

"We were three comrades at the Temple," she said timidly, "—Yulun, Sansa, and myself. We loved each other. We always went to the Lake of the Ghosts together—for protection—"

"Go on!"

"Sansa was a girl of the Aroulads, born at Buldak—as was Temujin. The night she was born three moon-rainbows made circles around her Yaïlak. The Baroulass horsemen saw this and prayed loudly in their saddles. Then they galloped to Yian and came crawling on their bellies to Sanang Noïane with the news of the miracle. And Sanang came with a thousand riders in leather armour. And, 'What is this child's name?' he shouted, riding into the Yaïlak with his black banners flapping around him like devil's wings.

"A poor Manggoud came out of the tent of skins, carrying the new born infant, and touched his head to Sanang's stirrup. 'This babe is called Tchagane,' he said, trembling all over. 'No!' cries Sanang, 'she is called Sansa. Give her to me and may Erlik seize you!'

"And he took the baby on his saddle in front of him and struck his spurs deep; and so came Sansa to Yian under a roaring rustle of black silk banners.... It is so written in the Book of Iron.... Alla-hou Ekber."

Cleves had leaned his elbow on the table, his forehead rested in his palm.

Perhaps he was striving in a bewildered way to reconcile such occult and amazing things with the year 1920—with the commonplace and noisy city of New York—with this pretty, modern, sunlit sitting-room in the Ritz-Carlton on Madison Avenue—with this girl in her morning negligee opposite, her coffee and melon fragrant at her elbow, her wonderful blue eyes resting on him.

"Sansa," he repeated slowly, as though striving to grasp even a single word from the confusion of names and phrases that were sounding still in his ears like the vibration of distant and unfamiliar seas.

"Is this the girl you were talking with just now? In—in *this* room?" he added, striving to understand.

"Yes."

"She wasn't here, of course."

"Her body was not."

"Oh!"

Tressa said in her sweet, humorous way: "You must try to accustom yourself to such things, Victor. You know that Yulun talks to me.... I wanted to talk to Sansa. The longing awakened me. So—*I made the effort.*"

"And she came—I mean the part of her which is not her body."

"Yes, she came. We talked very happily while I was bathing and dressing. Then we came in here. She is such a darling!"

"Where is she?"

"In Yian, feeding her silk-worms and making a garden. You see, Sansa is quite wealthy now, because when the Japanese came she filled a bullock cart with great lumps of spongy gold from the Temple and filled another cart with Yu-stone, and took the Hezar of Baroulass horsemen on guard at the Lake of the Ghosts. And with this Keutch, riding a Soubz horse, and dressed like an Urieng lancer, my pretty little comrade Tchagane, who is called Sansa, marched north preceded by two kettle-drums and a toug with two tails—"

Tressa's clear laughter checked her; she clapped her hands, breathless with mirth at the picture she evoked.

"Kai!" she laughed; "what adorable impudence has Sansa! Neither Tchortcha nor Khiounnou dared ask her who were her seven ancestors! No! And when her caravan came to the lovely Yliang river, my darling Sansa rode out and grasped the lance from her Tougtchi and drove the point deep into the fertile soil, crying in a clear voice: 'A place for Tchagane and her people! Make room for the toug!'

"Then her Manggoud, who carried the spare steel tip for her lance, got out of his saddle and, gathering a handful of mulberry leaves, rubbed the shaft of the lance till it was all pale green.

"'Toug iaglachakho!' cries my adorable Sansa! 'Build me here my Urdu!*—my Mocalla!** And upon it pitch my tent of skins!'"

Again Tressa's laughter checked her, and she strove to control it with the jade ring pressed to her lips.

"Oh, Victor," she added in a stifled voice, looking at him out of eyes full of mischief, "you don't realise how funny it was—Sansa and her toug and her Urdu—Oh, Allah!—the bones of Tchinguiz must have rattled in his tomb!"

Her infectious laughter evoked a responsive but perplexed smile from Cleves; but it was the smile of a bewildered man who has comprehended very little of an involved jest; and he looked around at the modern room as though to find his bearings.

Suddenly Tressa leaned forward swiftly and laid one hand on his.

"You don't think all this is very funny. You don't like it," she said in soft concern.

"It isn't that, Tressa. But this is New York City in the year 1920. And I can't—I absolutely can not get into touch—hook up, mentally, with such

---

*Urdu=An imperial encampment.
**Mocalla=A platform used as a Moslem pulpit.

things—with the unreal Oriental life that is so familiar to you."

She nodded sympathetically: "I know. You feel like a Mergued Pagan from Lake Baïkal when all the lamps are lighted in the Mosque;—like a camel driver with his jade and gold when he enters Yarkand at sunrise."

"Probably I feel like that," said Cleves, laughing outright. "I take your word, dear, anyway."

But he took more; he picked up her soft hand where it still rested on his, pressed it, and instantly reddened because he had done it. And Tressa's bright flush responded so quickly that neither of them understood, and both misunderstood.

The girl rose with heightened colour, not knowing why she stood up or what she meant to do. And Cleves, misinterpreting her emotion as a silent rebuke to the invasion of that convention tacitly accepted between them, stood up, too, and began to speak carelessly of commonplace things.

She made the effort to reply, scarcely knowing what she was saying, so violently had his caress disturbed her heart,—and she was still speaking when their telephone rang.

Cleves went; listened, then, still listening, summoned Tressa to his side with a gesture.

"It's Selden," he said in a low voice. "He says he has the Yezidee Arrak Sou-Sou under observation, and that he needs you desperately. Will you help us?"

"I'll go, of course," she replied, turning quite pale.

Cleves nodded, still listening. After a while: "All right. We'll be there. Good-bye," he said sharply; and hung up.

Then he turned and looked at his wife.

"I wish to God," he muttered, "that this business were ended. I—I can't bear to have you go."

"I am not afraid.... Where is it?"

"I never heard of the place before. We're to meet Selden at 'Fool's Acre.'"

"Where is it, Victor?"

"I don't know. Selden says there are no roads,—not even a spotted trail. It's a wilderness left practically blank by the Geological Survey. Only the contours are marked, and Selden tells me that the altitudes are erroneous and the unnamed lakes and water courses are all wrong. He says it is his absolute conviction that the Geological Survey never penetrated this wilderness at all, but merely skirted it and guessed at what lay inside, because the map he has from Washington is utterly misleading, and the entire region is left blank except for a few vague blue lines and spots indicating water, and a few heights marked '1800.'"

He turned and began to pace the sitting-room, frowning, perplexed, undecided.

"Selden tells me," he said, "that the Yezidee, Arrak Sou-Sou, is in there and very busy doing something or other. He says that he can do nothing without you, and will explain why when we meet him."

"Yes, Victor."

Cleves turned on his heel and came over to where his wife stood beside the sunny window.

"I hate to ask you to go. I know that was the understanding. But this incessant danger—your constant peril—"

"That does not count when I think of my country's peril," she said in a quiet voice. "When are we to start? And what shall I pack in my trunk?"

"Dear child," he said with a brusque laugh, "it's a wilderness and we carry what we need on our backs. Selden meets us at a place called Glenwild, on the edge of this wilderness, and we follow him in on our two legs."

He glanced across at the mantel clock.

"If you'll dress," he said nervously, "we'll go to some shop that outfits sportsmen for the North. Because, if we can, we ought to leave on the one o'clock train."

She smiled; came up to him. "Don't worry about me," she said. "Because I also am nervous and tired; and I mean to make an end of every Yezidee remaining in America."

"Sanang, too?"

They both flushed deeply.

She said in a steady voice: "Between God and Erlik there is a black gulf where a million million stars hang, lighting a million million other worlds.

"Prince Sanang's star glimmers there. It is a sun, called Yramid. And it lights the planet, Yu-tsung. Let him reign there between God and Erlik."

"You will slay this man?"

"God forbid!" she said, shuddering. "But I shall send him to his own star. Let my soul be ransom for his! And may Allah judge between us—between this man and me."

Then, in the still, sunny room, the girl turned to face the East. And her husband saw her lips move as though speaking, but heard no sound.

"What on earth are you saying there, all to yourself?" he demanded at last.

She turned her head and looked at him across her left shoulder.

"I asked Sansa to help me.... And she says she will."

Cleves nodded in a dazed way. Then he opened a window and leaned there in the sunshine, looking down into Madison Avenue. And the roar of traffic seemed to soothe his nerves.

But "Good heavens!" he thought; "do such things really go on in New York in 1920! Is the entire world becoming a little crazy? Am I really in my right mind when I believe that the girl I married is talking, without wireless, to another girl in China!"

He leaned there heavily, gazing down into the street with sombre eyes.

"What a ghastly thing these Yezidees are trying to do to the world—these Assassins of men's minds!" he thought, turning away toward the door of his bedroom.

As he crossed the threshold he stumbled, and looking down saw that he had tripped over a white sheet lying there. For a moment he thought it was a sheet from his own bed, and he started to pick it up. Then he saw the naked blade of a knife at his feet.

With an uncontrollable shudder he stepped out of the shroud and stood staring at the knife as though it were a snake. It had a curved blade and a bone hilt coarsely inlaid with Arabic characters in brass.

The shroud was a threadbare affair—perhaps a bed-sheet from some cheap lodging house. But its significance was so repulsive that he hesitated to touch it.

However, he was ashamed to have it discovered in his room. He picked up the brutal-looking knife and kicked the shroud out into the corridor, where they could guess if they liked how such a rag got into the Ritz-Carlton.

Then he searched his bedroom, and, of course, discovered nobody hiding. But chills crawled on his spine while he was about it, and he shivered still as he stood in the centre of the room examining the knife and testing edge and point.

Then, close to his ear, a low voice whispered: "Be careful, my lord; the Yezidee knife is poisoned. But it is written that a poisoned heart is more dangerous still."

He had turned like a flash; and he saw, between him and the sitting-room door, a very young girl with slightly slanting eyes, and rose and ivory features as perfect as though moulded out of tinted bisque.

She wore a loose blue linen robe, belted in, short at the elbows and skirt, showing two creamy-skinned arms and two bare feet in straw sandals. In one hand she had a spray of purple mulberries, and she looked coolly at Cleves and ate a berry or two.

"Give me the knife," she said calmly.

He handed it to her; she wiped it with a mulberry leaf and slipped it through her girdle.

"I am Sansa," she said with a friendly glance at him, busy with her fruit.

Cleves strove to speak naturally, but his voice trembled.

"Is it you—I mean your real self—your own body?"

"It's my real self. Yes. But my body is asleep in my mulberry grove."

"In—in China?"

"Yes," she said calmly, detaching another mulberry and eating it. A few fresh leaves fell on the centre table.

Sansa chose another berry. "You know," she said, "that I came to Tressa this morning,—to my little Heart of Fire I came when she called me. And I was quite sleepy, too. But I heard her, though there was a night wind in the mulberry trees, and the river made a silvery roaring noise in the dark.... And now I must go. But I shall come again very soon."

She smiled shyly and held out her lovely little hand. "—As Tressa tells me is your custom in America," she said, "I offer you a good-bye."

He took her hand and found it a warm, smooth thing of life and pulse.

"Why," he stammered in his astonishment, "you *are* real! You are not a ghost!"

"Yes, I am real," she answered, surprised, "but I'm not in my body,—if you mean that." Then she laughed and withdrew her hand, and, going, made him a friendly gesture.

"Cherish, my lord, my darling Heart of Fire. Serpents twist and twine. So do rose vines. May their petals make your path of velvet and sweet scented. May everything that is round be a pomegranate for you two to share; may everything that sways be lilies bordering a path wide enough for two. In the name of the Most Merciful God, may the only cry you hear be the first sweet wail of your firstborn. And when the tenth shall be born, may you and Heart of Fire bewail your fate because both of you desire more children!"

She was laughing when she disappeared. Cleves thought she was still there, so radiant the sunshine, so sweet the scent in the room.

But the golden shadow by the door was empty of her. If she had slipped through the doorway he had not noticed her departure. Yet she was no longer there. And, when he understood, he turned back into the empty room, quivering all over. Suddenly a terrible need of Tressa assailed him— an imperative necessity to speak to her—hear her voice.

"Tressa!" he called, and rested his hand on the centre table, feeling weak and shaken to the knees. Then he looked down and saw the mulberry leaves lying scattered there, tender and green and still dewy with the dew of China.

"Oh, my God!" he whispered, "such things *are!* It isn't my mind that has gone wrong. There *are* such things!"

The conviction swept him like a tide till his senses swam. As though peering through a mist of gold he saw his wife enter and come to him;— felt her arm about him, sustaining him where he swayed slightly with one hand on the table among the mulberry leaves.

"Ah," murmured Tressa, noticing the green leaves, "she oughtn't to have done that. That was thoughtless of her, to show herself to you."

Cleves looked at her in a dazed way. "The body is nothing," he muttered. "The rest only is real. That is the truth, isn't it?"

"Yes."

"I seem to be beginning to believe it.... Sansa said things—I shall try to tell you—some day—dear.... I'm so glad to hear your voice."

"Are you?" she murmured.

"And so glad to feel your touch.... I found a shroud on my threshold. And a knife."

"The Yezidees are becoming mountebanks. Where is the knife?" she asked scornfully.

"Sansa said it was poisoned. She took it. She—she said that a poisoned heart is more dangerous still."

Then Tressa threw up her head and called softly into space: "Sansa! Little Silk-Moth! What are these mischievous things you have told to my lord?"

She stood silent, listening. And, in the answer which he could not hear, there seemed to be something that set his young wife's cheeks aflame.

"Sansa! Little devil!" she cried, exasperated. "May Erlik send his imps to pinch you if you have said to my lord these shameful things. It was impudent! It was mischievous! You cover me with shame and confusion, and I am humbled in the dust of my lord's feet!"

Cleves looked at her, but she could not sustain his gaze.

"Did Sansa say to you what she said to me?" he demanded unsteadily.

"Yes.... I ask your pardon.... And I had already *told* her you did not—did not—were not in—in love—with me.... I ask your pardon."

"Ask more.... Ask your heart whether it would care to hear that I am in love. And with whom. Ask your heart if it could ever care to listen to what my heart could say to it."

"Y-yes—I'll ask—my heart," she faltered.... "I think I had better finish dressing—" She lifted her eyes, gave him a breathless smile as he caught her hand and kissed it.

"It—it would be very wonderful," she stammered, "—if our necessity should be-become our choice."

But that speech seemed to scare her and she fled, leaving her husband standing tense and upright in the middle of the room.

Their train on the New York Central Railroad left the Grand Central Terminal at one in the afternoon.

Cleves had made his arrangements by wire. They travelled lightly, carrying, except for the clothing they wore, only camping equipment for two.

It was raining in the Hudson valley; they rushed through the outlying towns and Po'keepsie in a summer downpour.

At Hudson the rain slackened. A golden mist enveloped Albany, through which the beautiful tower and façades along the river loomed, masking the huge and clumsy Capitol and the spires beyond.

At Schenectady, rifts overhead revealed glimpses of blue. At Amsterdam, where they descended from the train, the flag on the arsenal across the Mohawk flickered brilliantly in the sunny wind.

By telegraphic arrangement, behind the station waited a touring car driven by a trooper of State Constabulary, who, with his comrade, saluted smartly as Cleves and Tressa came up.

There was a brief, low-voiced conversation. Their camping outfit was stowed aboard, Tressa sprang into the tonneau followed by Cleves, and the car started swiftly up the inclined roadway, turned to the right across the railroad bridge, across the trolley tracks, and straight on up the steep hill paved with blocks of granite.

On the level road which traversed the ridge at last they speeded up, whizzed past the great hedged farm where racing horses are bred, rushing through the afternoon sunshine through the old-time Scotch settlements which once were outposts of the old New York frontier.

Nine miles out the macadam road ended. They veered to the left over a dirt road, through two hamlets; then turned to the right.

The landscape became rougher. To their left lay the long, low Maxon hills; behind them the May, field range stretched northward into the open jaws of the Adirondacks.

All around them were woods, now. Once a Gate House appeared ahead; and beyond it they crossed four bridges over a foaming, tumbling creek where Cleves caught glimpses of shadowy forms in amber-tinted pools— big yellow trout that sank unhurriedly out of sight among huge submerged boulders wet with spray.

The State trooper beside the chauffeur turned to Cleves, his purple tie whipping in the wind. "Yonder is Glenwild, sir," he said.

It was a single house on the flank of a heavily forested hill. Deep below to the left the creek leaped two cataracts and went flashing out through a belt of cleared territory ablaze with late sunshine.

The car swung into the farm-yard, past the barn on the right, and continued on up a very rough trail.

"This is the road to the Ireland Vlaie," said the trooper. "It is possible for cars for another mile only."

Splendid spruce, pine, oak, maple, and hemlock fringed the swampy, uneven trail which was no more than a wide, rough vista cut through the forest.

And, as the trooper had said, a little more than a mile farther the trail became a tangle of bushes and swale; the car slowed down and stopped;

and a man rose from where he was seated on a mossy log and came forward, his rifle balanced across the hollow of his left arm.

The man was Alek Selden.

It was long after dark and they were still travelling through pathless woods by the aid of their electric torches.

There was little underbrush; the forest of spruce and hemlock was first growth.

Cleves shined the trees but could discover no blazing, no trodden path.

In explanation, Selden said briefly that he had hunted the territory for years.

"But I don't begin to know it," he added. "There are vast and ugly regions of bog and swale where a sea of alders stretches to the horizon. There are desolate wastes of cat-briers and witch-hopple under leprous tangles of grey birches, where stealthy little brooks darkle deep under matted débris. Only wild things can travel such country.

"Then there are strange, slow-flowing creeks in the perpetual shadows of tamarack woods, where many a man has gone in never to come out."

"Why?" asked Tressa.

"Under the tender carpet of green tresses are shining black bogs set with tussock; and under the bog stretches quicksand,—and death."

"Do you know these places?" asked Cleves.

"No."

Cleves stepped forward to Tressa's side.

"Keep flashing the ground," he said harshly. "I don't want you to step into some hell-hole. I'm sorry I brought you, anyway."

"But I had to come," she said in a low voice. Like the two men, she wore a grey flannel shirt, knickers, and spiral puttees.

They, however, carried rifles as well as packs; and the girl's pack was lighter.

They had halted by a swift, icy rivulet to eat, without building a fire. After that they crossed the Ireland Vlaie and the main creek, where remains of a shanty stood on the bluff above the right bank—the last sign of man.

Beyond lay the uncharted land, skimped and shirked entirely in certain regions by map-makers;—an unknown wilderness on the edges of which Selden had often camped when deer shooting.

It was along this edge he was leading them, now, to a lean-to which he had erected, and from which he had travelled in to Glenwild to use the superintendent's telephone to New York.

There seemed to be no animal life stirring in this forest; their torches illuminated no fiery orbs of dazed wild things surprised at graze in the wilderness; no leaping furry form crossed their flashlights' fan-shaped radiance.

There were no nocturnal birds to be seen or heard, either: no bittern squawked from hidden sloughs; no herons howled; not an owl-note, not a whispering cry of a whippoorwill, not the sudden uncanny twitter of those little birds that become abruptly vocal after dark, interrupted the dense stillness of the forest.

And it was not until his electric torch glimmered repeatedly upon reaches of dusk-hidden bog that Cleves understood how Selden took his bearings—for the night was thick and there were no stars.

"Yes," said Selden tersely, "I'm trying to skirt the bog until I shine a peeled stick."

An hour later the peeled alder-stem glittered in the beam of the torches. In ten minutes something white caught the electric rays.

It was Selden's spare undershirt drying on a bush behind the lean-to.

"Can we have a fire?" asked Cleves, relieving his wife of her pack and striding into the open-faced camp.

"Yes, I'll fix it," replied Selden. "Are you all right, Mrs. Cleves?"

Tressa said: "Delightfully tired, thank you." And smiled faintly at her husband as he let go his own pack, knelt, and spread a blanket for his wife.

He remained there, kneeling, as she seated herself.

"Are you quite fit?" he asked bluntly. Yet, through his brusqueness her ear caught a vague undertone of something else—anxiety perhaps—perhaps tenderness. And her heart stirred deliciously in her breast.

He inflated a pillow for her; the firelight glimmered, brightened, spread glowing across her feet. She lay back with a slight sigh, relaxed.

Then, suddenly, the thrill of her husband's touch flooded her face with colour; but she lay motionless, one arm flung across her eyes, while he unrolled her puttees and unlaced her muddy shoes.

A heavenly warmth from the fire dried her stockinged feet. Later, on the edge of sleep, she opened her eyes and found herself propped upright on her husband's shoulder.

Drowsily, obediently she swallowed spoonfuls of the hot broth which he administered.

"Are you really quite comfortable, dear?" he whispered.

"Wonderfully.... And so very happy.... Thank you—dear."

She lay back, suffering him to bathe her face and hands with warm water.

When the fire was only a heap of dying coals, she turned over on her right side and extended her hand a little way into the darkness. Searching, half asleep, she touched her husband, and her hand relaxed in his nervous clasp. And she fell into the most perfect sleep which she had known in years.

She dreamed that somebody whispered to her, "Darling, darling, wake up. It is morning, beloved."

Suddenly she opened her eyes; and saw her husband set a tray, freshly plaited out of Indian willow, beside her blanket.

"Here's your breakfast, pretty lady," he said, smilingly. "And over there is an exceedingly frigid pool of water. You're to have the camp to yourself for the next hour or two."

"You dear fellow," she murmured, still confused by sleep, and reached out to touch his hand. He caught hers and kissed it, back and palm, and got up hastily as though scared.

"Selden and I will stand sentry," he muttered. "There is no hurry, you know."

She heard him and his comrade walking away over dried leaves; their steps receded; a dry stick cracked distantly; then silence stealthily invaded the place like a cautious living thing, creeping unseen through the golden twilight of the woods.

Seated in her blanket, she drank the coffee; ate a little; then lay down again in the early sun, feeling the warmth of the heap of whitening coals at her feet, also.

For an hour she dozed awake, drowsily opening her eyes now and then to look across the glade at the pool over which a single dragon-fly glittered on guard.

Finally she rose resolutely, grasped a bit of soap, and went down to the edge of the pool.

Tressa was in flannel shirt and knickers when her husband and Selden hailed the camp and presently appeared walking slowly toward the dead fire.

Their grave faces checked her smile of greeting; her husband came up and laid one hand on her arm, looking at her out of thoughtful, preoccupied eyes.

"What is the Tchordagh?" he said in a low voice.

The girl's quiet face went white.

"The—the Tchordagh!" she stammered.

"Yes, dear. What is it?"

"I don't—don't know where you heard that term," she whispered. "The Tchordagh is the—the power of Erlik. It is a term…. In it is comprehended all the evil, all the cunning, all the perverted spiritual intelligence of Evil,— its sinister might,—its menace. It is an Alouäd-Yezidee term, and it is written in brass in Eighur characters on the Eight Towers, and on the Rampart of Gog and Magog;—nowhere else in the world!"

"It is written on a pine tree a few paces from this camp," said Cleves absently.

Selden said: "It has not been there more than an hour or two, Mrs. Cleves. A square of bark was cut out and on the white surface of the wood this word is written in English."

"Can you tell us what it signifies?" asked Cleves, quietly.

Tressa's studied effort at self-control was apparent to both men.

She said: "When that word is written, then it is a death struggle between all the powers of Darkness and those who have read the written letters of that word.... For it is written in The Iron Book that no one but the Assassin of Khorassan—excepting the Eight Sheiks—shall read that written word and live to boast of having read it."

"Let us sit here and talk it over," said Selden soberly.

And when Tressa was seated on a fallen log, and Cleves settled down cross-legged at her feet, Selden spoke again, very soberly:

"On the edges of these woods, to the northwest, lies a sea of briers, close growing, interwoven and matted, strong and murderous as barbed wire.

"Miles out in this almost impenetrable region lies a patch of trees called Fool's Acre.

"At Wells I heard that the only man who had ever managed to reach Fool's Acre was a trapper, and that he was still living.

"I found him at Rainbow Lake—a very old man, who had a fairly clear recollection of Fool's Acre and his exhausting journey there.

"And he told me that man had been there before he had. For there was a roofless stone house there, and the remains of a walled garden. And a skull deep in the wild grasses."

Selden paused and looked down at the recently healed scars on his wrists and hands.

"It was a rotten trip," he said bluntly. "It took me three days to cut a tunnel through that accursed tangle of matted brier and grey birch.... Fool's Acre is a grove of giant trees—first growth pine, oak, and maple. Great outcrops of limestone ledges bound it on the east. A brook runs through the woods.

"There is a house there, *no longer roofless*, and built of slabs of fossil-pitted limestone. The glass in the windows is so old that it is iridescent.

"A seven-foot wall encloses the house, built also of slabs blasted out of the rock outcrop, and all pitted with fossil shells.

"Inside is a garden—not the *remains* of one—a beautiful garden full of unfamiliar flowers. And in this garden I saw the Yezidee on his knees *making living things out of lumps of dead earth!*"

"The Tchordagh!" whispered the girl.

"What was the Yezidee doing?" demanded Cleves nervously.

Involuntarily all three drew nearer each other there in the sunshine.

"It was difficult for me to see," said Selden in his quiet, serious voice. "It was nearly twilight: I lay flat on top of the wall under the curving branches of a huge syringa bush in full bloom. The Yezidees—"

"Were there two!" exclaimed Cleves.

"Two. They were squatting on the old stone path bordering one of the flower-beds." He turned to Tressa: "They both wore white cloths twisted around their heads, and long soft garments of white. Under these their bare, brown legs showed, but they wore things on their naked feet which were shaped like what we call Turkish slippers—only different."

"Black and green," nodded Tressa with the vague horror growing in her face.

"Yes. The soles of their shoes were bright green."

"Green is the colour sacred to Islam," said Tressa. "The priests of Satan defile it by staining with green the soles of their footwear."

After an interval: "Go on," said Cleves nervously.

Selden drew closer, and they bent their heads to listen:

"I don't, even now, know what the Yezidees were actually doing. In the twilight it was hard to see clearly. But I'll tell you what it looked like to me. One of these squatting creatures would scoop out a handful of soil from the flower-bed, and mould it for a few moments between his lean, sinewy fingers, and then he'd open his hands and—and something *alive*—something small like a rat or a toad, or God knows what, would escape from between his palms and run out into the grass—"

Selden's voice failed and he looked at Cleves with sickened eyes.

"I can't—can't make you understand how repulsive to me it was to see a wriggling live thing creep out between their fingers and—and go running or scrambling away—little loathsome things with humpy backs that hopped or scurried through the grass—"

"What on earth *were* these Yezidees doing, Tressa?" asked Cleves almost roughly.

The girl's white face was marred by the imprints of deepening horror.

"It is the Tchor-Dagh," she said mechanically. "They are using every resource of hell to destroy me—testing the gigantic power of Evil—as though it were some vast engine charged with thunderous destruction!—and they were testing it to discover its terrific capacity to annihilate—"

Her voice died in her dry throat; she dropped her bloodless visage into both hands and remained seated so.

Both men looked at her in silence, not daring to interfere. Finally the girl lifted her pallid face from her hands.

"That is what they were doing," she said in a dull voice. "Out of inanimate earth they were making things animate—living creatures—to—to test the hellish power which they are storing—concentrating—for my destruction."

"What is their purpose?" asked Cleves harshly. "What do these Mongol Sorcerers expect to gain by making little live things out of lumps of garden dirt?"

"They are testing their power," whispered the girl.

"Like tuning up a huge machine?" muttered Selden.

"Yes."

"For what purpose?"

"To make larger living creatures out of—of clay."

"They can't—they can't *create!*" exclaimed Cleves. "I don't know how—by what filthy tricks—they make rats out of dirt. But they can't make a—anything—like a—like a man!"

Tressa's body trembled slightly.

"Once," she said, "in the temple, Prince Sanang took dust which was brought in sacks of goat-skin, and fashioned the heap of dirt with his hands, so that it resembled the body of a man lying there on the marble floor under the shrine of Erlik.... And—and then, there in the shadows where only the Dark Star burned—that black lamp which is called the Dark Star—the long heap of dust lying there on the marble pavement began to—to *breathe!*—"

She pressed both hands over her breast as though to control her trembling body: "I saw it; I saw the long shape of dust begin to breathe, to stir, move, and slowly lift itself—"

"A Yezidee trick!" gasped Cleves; but he also was trembling now.

"God!" whispered the girl. "Allah alone knows—the Merciful, the Long Suffering—He knows what it was that we temple girls saw there—that Yulun saw—that Sa-n'sa and I beheld there rising up like a man from the marble floor—and standing erect in the shadowy twilight of the Dark Star...."

Her hands gripped at her breast; her face was deathly.

"Then," she said, "I saw Prince Sanang draw his sabre of Indian steel, and he struck... once only.... And a dead man fell down where the *thing* had stood. And all the marble was flooded with scarlet blood."

"A trick," repeated Cleves, in the ghost of his own voice. But his gaze grew vacant.

Presently Selden spoke in tones that sounded weakly querulous from emotional reaction:

"There is a path—a tunnel under the matted briers. It took me more than a week to cut it out. It is possible to reach Fool's Acre. We can try—with our rifles—if you say so, Mrs. Cleves."

The girl looked up. A little colour came into her cheeks. She shook her head.

"Their bodies may not be there in the garden," she said absently. "What you saw may not have been that part of them—the material which dies by knife or bullet.... And it is necessary that these Yezidees should die."

"Can you do anything?" asked Cleves, hoarsely. She looked at her husband; tried to smile:

"I must try.... I think we had better not lose any time—if Mr. Selden will lead us."

"Now?"

"Yes, we had better go, I think," said the girl.

Her smile still remained stamped on her lips, but her eyes seemed preoccupied as though following the movements of something remote that was passing across the far horizon.

## CHAPTER XIV
# A DEATH TRAIL

The way to Fool's Acre was under a tangled canopy of thorns, under rotting windfalls of grey march, through tunnel after tunnel of fallen debris woven solidly by millions of strands of tough cat-briers which cut the flesh like barbed wire.

There was blood on Tressa, where her flannel shirt had been pierced in a score of places. Cleves and Selden had been painfully slashed.

Silent, thread-like streams flowed darkling under the tangled mass that roofed them. Sometimes they could move upright; more often they were bent double; and there were long stretches where they had to creep forward on hands and knees through sparse wild grasses, soft, rotten soil, or paths of sphagnum which cooled their feverish skin in velvety, icy depths.

At noon they rested and ate, lying prone under the matted roof of their tunnel.

Cleves and Selden had their rifles. Tressa lay like a slender boy, her brier-torn hands empty.

And, as she lay there, her husband made a sponge of a handful of sphagnum moss, and bathed her face and her arms, cleansing the dried blood from the skin, while the girl looked up at him out of grave, inscrutable eyes.

The sun hung low over the wilderness when they came to the woods of Fool's Acre. They crept cautiously out of the briers, among ferns and open spots carpeted with pine needles and dead leaves which were beginning to burn ruddy gold under the level rays of the sun.

Lying flat behind an enormous oak, they remained listening for a while. Selden pointed through the woods, eastward, whispering that the house stood there not far away.

"Don't you think we might risk the chance and use our rifles?" asked Cleves in a low voice.

"No. It is the Tchor-Dagh that confronts us. I wish to talk to Sansa," she murmured.

A moment later Selden touched her arm.

"My God," he breathed, "who is that!"

"It is Sansa," said Tressa calmly, and sat up among the ferns. And the next instant Sansa stepped daintily out of the red sunlight and seated herself among them without a sound.

Nobody spoke. The newcomer glanced at Selden, smiled slightly, blushed, then caught a glimpse of Cleves where he lay in the brake, and a mischievous glimmer came into her slanting eyes.

"Did I not tell my lord truths?" she inquired in a demure whisper. "As surely as the sun is a dragon, and the flaming pearl burns between his claws, so surely burns the soul of Heart of Flame between thy guarding hands. There are as many words as there are demons, my lord, but it is written that *Niaz* is the greatest of all words save only the name of God."

She laughed without any sound, sweetly malicious where she sat among the ferns.

"Heart of Flame," she said to Tressa, "you called me and I *made the effort.*"

"Darling," said Tressa in her thrilling voice, "the Yezidees are making living things out of dust,—as Sanang Noïane made that thing in the Temple.... And slew it before our eyes."

"The Tchor-Dagh," said Sansa calmly.

"The Tchor-Dagh," whispered Tressa.

Sansa's smooth little hands crept up to the collar of her odd, blue tunic; grasped it.

"In the name of God the Merciful," she said without a tremor, "listen to me, Heart of Flame, and may my soul be ransom for yours!"

"I hear you, Sansa."

Sansa said, her fingers still grasping the embroidered collar of her tunic:

"Yonder, behind walls, two Tower Chiefs meddle with the Tchor-Dagh, making living things out of the senseless dust they scrape from the garden."

Selden moistened his dry lips. Sansa said:

"The Yezidees who have come into this wilderness are Arrak Sou-Sou, the Squirrel; and Tiyang Khan.... May God remember them in Hell!"

"May God remember them," said Tressa mechanically.

"And these two Yezidee Sorcerers," continued Sansa coolly, "have advanced thus far in the Tchor-Dagh; for they now roam these woods, digging like demons for the roots of Ginseng; and thou knowest, O Heart of Flame, what that indicates."

"Does Ginseng grow in these woods!" exclaimed Tressa with a new terror in her widening eyes.

"Ginseng grows here, little Rose-Heart, and the roots are as perfect as human bodies. And Tiyang Khan squats in the walled garden moulding the Ginseng roots in his unclean hands, while Sou-Sou the Squirrel scratches among the dead leaves of the woods for roots as perfect as a naked human body.

"All day long the Sou-Sou rummages among the trees; all day long Tiyang pats and rubs and moulds the Ginseng roots in his skinny fingers.

It is the Tchor-Dagh, Heart of Flame. And these Sorcerers must be destroyed."

"Are their bodies here?"

"Arrak is in the body. And thus it shall be accomplished: listen attentively, Rose Heart Afire!—I shall remain here with—" she looked at Selden and flushed a trifle, "—with you, my lord. And when the Squirrel comes a-digging, so shall my lord slay him with a bullet.... And when I hear his soul bidding his body farewell, then I shall make prisoner his soul.... And send it to the Dark Star.... And the rest shall be in the hands of Allah."

She turned to Tressa and caught her hands in both of her own:

"It is written on the Iron Pages," she whispered, "that we belong to Erlik and we return to him. But in the Book of Gold it is written otherwise: 'God preserve us from Satan who was stoned!'... Therefore, in the name of Allah! Now then, Heart of Flame, do your duty!"

A burning flush leaped over Tressa's features.

"Is my soul, then, my own!"

"It belongs to God," said Sansa gravely.

"And—Sanang?"

"God is greatest."

"But—was God there—at the Lake of the Ghosts?"

"God is everywhere. It is so written in the Book of Gold," replied Sansa, pressing her hands tenderly.

"Recite the Fatha, Heart of Flame. Thy lips shall not stiffen; God listens."

Tressa rose in the sunset glory though dazed, and all crimsoned in the last fiery bars of the declining sun.

Cleves also rose.

Sansa laughed noiselessly: "My lord would go whither thou goest, Heart of Fire!" she whispered. "And thy ways shall be his ways!"

Tressa's cheeks flamed and she turned and looked at Cleves.

Then Sansa rose and laid a hand on Tressa's arm and on her husband's:

"Listen attentively. Tiyang Khan must be destroyed. The signal sounds when my lord's rifle-shot makes a loud noise here among these trees."

"Can I prevail against the Tchor-Dagh?" asked Tressa, steadily.

"Is not that event already in God's hands, darling?" said Sansa softly. She smiled and resumed her seat beside Selden, amid the drooping fern fronds.

"Bid thy dear lord leave his rifle here," she added quietly.

Cleves laid down his weapon. Selden pointed eastward in silence.

So they went together into the darkening woods.

In the dusk of heavy foliage overhanging the garden, Tressa lay flat as a lizard on the top of the wall. Beside her lay her husband.

In the garden below them flowers bloomed in scented thickets, bordered by walks of flat stone slabs split from boulders. A little lawn, very green, centred the garden.

And on this lawn, in the clear twilight still tinged with the sombre fires of sundown, squatted a man dressed in a loose white garment.

Save for a twisted breadth of white cloth, his shaven head was bare. His sinewy feet were naked, too, the lean, brown toes buried in the grass.

Tressa's lips touched her husband's ear.

"Tiyang Khan," she breathed. "Watch what he does!"

Shoulder to shoulder they lay there, scarcely daring to breathe. Their eyes were fastened on the Mongol Sorcerer, who, squatted below on his haunches, grave and deliberate as a great grey ape, continued busy with the obscure business which so intently preoccupied him.

In a short semi-circle on the grass in front of him he had placed a dozen wild Ginseng roots. The roots were enormous, astoundingly shaped like the human body, almost repulsive in their weird symmetry.

The Yezidee had taken one of these roots into his hands. Squatting there in the semi-dusk, he began to massage it between his long, muscular fingers, rubbing, moulding, pressing the root with caressing deliberation.

His unhurried manipulation, for a few moments, seemed to produce no result. But presently the Ginseng root became lighter in colour and more supple, yielding to his fingers, growing ivory pale, sinuously limber in a newer and more delicate symmetry.

"Look!" gasped Cleves, grasping his wife's arm. "*What* is that man doing!"

"The Tchor-Dagh!" whispered Tressa. "Do you see what lies twisting there in his hands!"

The Ginseng root had become the tiny naked body of a woman—a little ivory-white creature, struggling to escape between the hands that had created it—dark, powerful, masterly hands, opening leisurely now, and releasing the living being they had fashioned.

The thing scrambled between the fingers of the Sorcerer, leaped into the grass, ran a little way and hid, crouched down, panting, almost hidden by the long grass. The shocked watchers on the wall could still see the creature. Tressa felt Cleves's body trembling beside her. She rested a cool, steady hand on his.

"It is the Tchor-Dagh," she breathed close to his face. "The Mongol Sorcerer is becoming formidable."

"Oh, God!" murmured Cleves, "that thing he made is *alive!* I saw it. I can see it hiding there in the grass. It's frightened—breathing! It's alive!"

His pistol, clutched in his right hand, quivered. His wife laid her hand on it and cautiously shook her head.

"No," she said, "that is of no use."

"But what that Yezidee, is doing is—is blasphemous—"

"Watch him! His mind is stealthily feeling its way among the laws and secrets of the Tchor-Dagh. He has found a thread. He is following it through the maze into hell's own labyrinth! He has created a tiny thing in the image of the Creator. He will try to create a larger being now. Watch him with his Ginseng roots!"

Tiyang, looming ape-like on his haunches in the deepening dusk, moulded and massaged the Ginseng roots, one after another. And one after another, tiny naked creatures wriggled out of his palms between his fingers and scuttled away into the herbage.

Already the dim lawn was alive with them, crawling, scurrying through the grass, creeping in among the flower-beds, little, ghostly-white things that glimmered from shade into shadow like moonbeams.

Tressa's mouth touched her husband's ear:

"It is for the secret of Destruction that the Yezidee seeks. But first he must learn the secret of creation. He is learning.... And he must learn no more than he has already learned."

"That Yezidee is a living man. Shall I fire?"

"No."

"I can kill him with the first shot."

"Hark!" she whispered excitedly, her hand closing convulsively on her husband's arm.

The whip-crack of a rifle-shot still crackled in their ears.

Tiyang had leaped to his feet in the dusk, a Ginseng root, half-alive, hanging from one hand and beginning to squirm.

Suddenly the first moonbeam fell across the wall. And in its lustre Tressa rose to her knees and flung up her right hand.

Then it was as though her palm caught and reflected the moon's ray, and hurled it in one blinding shaft straight into the dark visage of Tiyang Khan.

The Yezidee fell as though he had been pierced by a shaft of steel, and lay sprawling there on the grass in the ghastly glare.

And where his features had been there gaped only a hole into the head.

Then a dreadful thing occurred; for everywhere the grass swarmed with the little naked creatures he had made, running, scrambling, scuttling, darting into the black hole which had been the face of Tiyang Khan.

They poured into the awful orifice, crowding, jostling one another so violently that the head jerked from side to side on the grass, a wabbling, inert, soggy mass in the moonlight.

And presently the body of Tiyang Khan, Warden of the Rampart of Gog and Magog, and Lord of the Seventh Tower, began to burn with white fire—a low, glimmering combustion that seemed to clothe the limbs like an incandescent mist.

On the wall knelt Tressa, the glare from her lifted hand streaming over the burning form below.

Cleves stood tall and shadowy beside his wife, the useless pistol hanging in his grasp.

Then, in the silence of the woods, and very near, they heard Sansa laughing. And Selden's anxious voice:

"Arrak is dead. The Sou-Sou hangs across a rock, head down, like a shot squirrel. Is all well with you?"

"Tiyang is on his way to his star," said Tressa calmly. "Somewhere in the world his body has bid its mind farewell.... And so his body may live for a little, blind, in mental darkness, fed by others, and locked in all day, all night, until the end."

Sansa, at the base of the wall, turned to Selden.

"Shall I bring my body with me, one day, my lord?" she asked demurely.

"Oh, Sansa—" he whispered, but she placed a fragrant hand across his lips and laughed at him in the moonlight.

CHAPTER XV
# IN THE FIRELIGHT

In 1920 the whole spiritual world was trembling under the thundering shock of the Red Surf pounding the frontiers of civilisation from pole to pole.

Up out of the hell-pit of Asia had boiled the molten flood, submerging Russia, dashing in giant waves over Germany and Austria, drenching Italy, France, England with its bloody spindrift.

And now the Red Rain was sprinkling the United States from coast to coast, and the mindless administration, scared out of its stupidity at last, began a frantic attempt to drain the country of the filthy flood and throw up barriers against the threatened deluge.

In every state and city Federal agents made wholesale arrests—too late!

A million minds had already been perverted and dominated by the terrible Sect of the Assassins. A million more were sickening under the awful psychic power of the Yezidee.

Thousands of the disciples of the Yezidee devil-worshipers had already been arrested and held for deportation,—poor, wretched creatures whose minds were no longer their own, but had been stealthily surprised, seized and mastered by Mongol adepts and filled with ferocious hatred against their fellow men.

Yet, of the Eight Yezidee Assassins only two now remained alive in America,—Togrul, and Sanang, the Slayer of Souls.

Yarghouz was dead; Djamouk the Fox, Kahn of the Fifth Tower was dead; Yaddin-ed-Din, Arrak the Sou-Sou, Gutchlug, Tiyang Khan, all were dead. Six Towers had become dark and silent. From them the last evil thought, the last evil shape had sped; the last wicked prayer had been said to Erlik, Khagan of all Darkness.

But his emissary on earth, Prince Sanang, still lived. And at Sanang's heels stole Togrul, Tougtchi to Sanang Noïane, the Slayer of Souls.

In the United States there had been a cessation of the active campaign of violence toward those in authority. Such unhappy dupes of the Yezidees as the I.W.W. and other radicals were, for the time, physically quiescent. Crude terrorism with its more brutal outrages against life and law ceased. But two million sullen eyes, in which all independent human thought had been extinguished, watched unblinking the wholesale arrests by the government—watched panic-stricken officials rushing hither and thither to execute the mandate of a miserable administration—watched and waited in dreadful silence.

In that period of ominous quiet which possessed the land, the little group of Secret Service men that surrounded the young girl who alone stood between a trembling civilisation and the threat of hell's own chaos, became convinced that Sanang was preparing a final and terrible effort to utterly overwhelm the last vestige of civilisation in the United States. What shape that plan would develop they could not guess.

John Recklow sent Benton to Chicago to watch that centre of infection for the appearance there of the Yezidee Togrul.

Selden went to Boston where a half-witted group of parlour-socialists at Cambridge were talking too loudly and loosely to please even the most tolerant at Harvard.

But neither Togrul nor Sanang had, so far, materialised in either city; and John Recklow prowled the purlieus of New York, haunting strange byways and obscure quarters where the dull embers of revolution always smouldered, watching for the Yezidee who was the deep-bedded, vital root of this psychic evil which menaced the minds of all mankind,—Sanang, the Slayer of Souls.

Recklow's lodgings were tucked away in Westover Court—three bedrooms, a parlour and a kitchenette.

Tressa Cleves occupied one bedroom; her husband another; Recklow the third.

And in this tiny apartment, hidden away among a group of old buildings, the very existence of which was unknown to the millions who swarmed the streets of the greatest city in the world,—here in Westover Court, a dozen paces from the roar of Broadway, was now living a young girl upon whose psychic power the only hope of the world now rested.

The afternoon had turned grey and bitter; ragged flakes still fell; a pallid twilight possessed the snowy city, through which lighted trains and taxis moved in the foggy gloom.

By three o'clock in the afternoon all shops were illuminated; the south windows of the Hotel Astor across the street spread a sickly light over the old buildings of Westover Court as John Recklow entered the tiled hallway, took the stairs to the left, and went directly to his apartment.

He unlocked the door and let himself in and stood a moment in the entry shaking the snow from his hat and overcoat.

The sitting-room lamp was unlighted but he could see a fire in the grate, and Tressa Cleves seated near, her eyes fixed on the glowing coals.

He bade her good evening in a low voice; she turned her charming head and nodded, and he drew a chair to the fender and stretched out his wet shoes to the warmth.

"Is Victor still out?" he inquired.

She said that her husband had not yet returned. Her eyes were on the fire, Recklow's rested on her shadowy face.

"Benton got his man in Chicago," he said. "It was not Togrul Kahn."

"Who was it?"

"Only a Swami fakir who'd been preaching sedition to a little group of greasy Bengalese from Seattle.... I've heard from Selden, too."

She nodded listlessly and lifted her eyes.

"Neither Sanang nor Togrul have appeared in Boston," he said. "I think they're here in New York."

The girl said nothing.

After a silence:

"Are you worried about your husband?" he asked abruptly.

"I am always uneasy when he is absent," she said quietly.

"Of course.... But I don't suppose he knows that."

"I suppose not."

Recklow leaned over, took a coal in the tongs and lighted a cigar. Leaning back in his armchair, he said in a musing voice:

"No, I suppose your husband does not realize that you are so deeply concerned over his welfare."

The girl remained silent.

"I suppose," said Recklow softly, "he doesn't dream you are in love with him."

Tressa Cleves did not stir a muscle. After a long silence she said in her even voice:

"Do you think I am in love with my husband, Mr. Recklow?"

"I think you fell in love with him the first evening you met him."

"I did."

Neither of them spoke again for some minutes. Recklow's cigar went wrong; he rose and found another and returned to the fire, but did not light it.

"It's a rotten day, isn't it?" he said with a shiver, and dumped a scuttle of coal on the fire.

They watched the blue flames playing over the grate.

Tressa said: "I could no more help falling in love with him than I could stop my heart beating.... But I did not dream that anybody knew."

"Don't you think he ought to know?"

"Why? He is not in love with me."

"Are you sure, Mrs. Cleves?"

"Yes. He is wonderfully sweet and kind. But he could not fall in love with a girl who has been what I have been."

Recklow smiled. "What have you been, Tressa Norne?"

"You know."

"A temple girl at Yian?"

"And at the Lake of the Ghosts," she said in a low voice.

"What of it?"

"I can not tell you, Mr. Recklow.... Only that I lost my soul in the Yezidee Temple—"

"That is untrue!"

"I wish it were untrue.... My husband tells me that nothing can really harm the soul. I try to believe him.... But Erlik lives. And when my soul at last shall escape my body, it shall not escape the Slayer of Souls."

"That is monstrously untrue—"

"No. I tell you that Prince Sanang slew my soul. And my soul's ghost belongs to Erlik. How can any man fall in love with such a girl?"

"Why do you say that Sanang slew your soul?" asked Recklow, peering at her averted face through the reddening firelight.

She lay still in her chair for a moment, then turned suddenly on him:

"He *did* slay it! He came to the Lake of the Ghosts as my lover; he meant to have done it there; but I would not have him—would not listen, nor suffer his touch!—I mocked at him and his passion. I laughed at his Tchortchas. They were afraid of me!—"

She half rose from her chair, grasped the arms, then seated herself again, her eyes ablaze with the memory of wrongs.

"How dare I show my dear lord that I am in love with him when Sanang's soul caught my soul out of my body one day—surprised my soul while my body lay asleep in the Yezidee Temple!—and bore it in his arms to the very gates of hell!"

"Good God," whispered Recklow, "what do you mean? Such things can't happen."

"Why not? They do happen. I was caught unawares.... It was one golden afternoon, and Yulun and Sansa and I were eating oranges by the fountain in the inner shrine. And I lay down by the pool and *made the effort*— you understand?"

"Yes."

"Very well. My soul left my body asleep and I went out over the tops of the flowers—idly, without aim or intent—as the winds blow in summer.... It was in the Wood of the White Moth that I saw Sanang's soul flash downward like a streak of fire and wrap my soul in flame!... And, in a flash, we were at the gates of hell before I could free myself from his embrace.... Then, by the Temple pool, among the oranges, I cried out asleep; and my terrified body sat up sobbing and trembling in Yulun's arms. But the Slayer of Souls had slain mine in the Wood of the White Moth—slain it as he caught me in his flaming arms.... And now you know why such a woman as I dare not bend to kiss the dust from my dear Lord's feet—Aie-a! Aie-a! I who have lost my girl's soul to him who slew it in the Wood of the White Moth!"

She sat rocking in her chair in the red firelight, her hands framing her lovely face, her eyes staring straight ahead as though they saw opening before them through the sombre shadows of that room all the dread magic of the East where the dancing flame of Sanang's blazing soul lighted their path to hell through the enchanted forest.

Recklow had grown pale, but his voice was steady.

"I see no reason," he said, "why your husband should not love you."

"I tell you my girl's soul belonged to Sanang—was part of his, for an instant."

"It is burned pure of dross."

"It is *burned.*"

Recklow remained silent. Tressa lay deep in her armchair, twisting her white fingers.

"What makes him so late?" she said.... "I sent my soul out twice to look for him, and could not find him."

"Send it again," said Recklow, fearfully.

For ten minutes the girl lay as though asleep, then her eyes unclosed and she said drowsily: "I can not find him."

"Did—did you learn anything while—while you were—away?" asked Recklow cautiously.

"Nothing. There is a thick darkness out there—I mean a darkness gathering over the whole land. It is like a black fog. When the damned pray to Erlik there is a darkness that gathers like a brown mist—"

Her voice ceased; her hands tightened on the arms of her chair.

"*That* is what Sanang is doing!" she said in a breathless voice.

"What?" demanded Recklow.

"*Praying!* That is what he is doing! A million perverted minds which he has seized and obsessed are being concentrated on blasphemous prayers to Erlik! Sanang is directing them. Do you understand the terrible power of a million minds all *willing*, in unison, the destruction of good and the triumph of evil? A million human minds! More! For that is what he is doing. That is the thick darkness that is gathering over the entire Western world. It is the terrific materialisation of evil power from evil minds, all focussed upon the single thought that evil must triumph and good die!"

She sat, gripping the arms of her chair, pale, rigid, terribly alert, dreadfully enlightened, now, concerning the awful and new menace threatening the sanity of mankind.

She said in her steady, emotionless voice: "When the Yezidee Sorcerers desire to overwhelm a nomad people—some yort perhaps that has resisted the Sheiks of the Eight Towers, then the Slayer of Souls rides with his Black Banners to the Namaz-Ga or Place of Prayer.

"Two marble bridges lead to it. There are fourteen hundred mosques there. Then come the Eight, each with his shroud, chanting the prayers for those dead in hell. And there the Yezidees pray blasphemously, all their minds in ferocious unison.... And I have seen a little yort full of Broad Faces with their slanting eyes and sparse beards, sicken and die, and turn black in the sun as though the plague had breathed on them. And I have seen the Long Noses and bushy beards of walled towns wither and perish in the blast and blight from the Namaz-Ga where the Slayer of Souls sat his saddle and prayed to Erlik, and half a million Yezidees prayed in blasphemous unison."

Recklow's head rested on his left hand. The other, unconsciously, had crept toward his pistol—the weapon which had become so useless in this awful struggle between this girl and the loosened forces of hell.

"Is that what you think Sanang is about?" he asked heavily.

"Yes. I know it. He has seized the minds of a million men in America. Every anarchist is to-day concentrating in one evil and supreme mental effort, under Sanang's direction, to will the triumph of evil and the doom of civilisation.... I wish my husband would come home."

"Tressa?"

She turned her pallid face in the firelight: "If Sanang has appointed a Place of Prayer," she said, "he himself will pray on that spot. That will be the Namaz-Ga for the last two Yezidee Sorcerers still alive in the Western World."

"That's what I wished to ask you," said Recklow softly. "Will you try once more, Tressa?"

"Yes. I will send out my soul again to look for the Namaz-Ga."

She lay back in her armchair and closed her eyes.

"Only," she added, as though to herself, "I wish my dear lord were safe in this room beside me.... May God's warriors be his escort. And surely they are well armed, and can prevail over demons. Aie-a! I wish my lord would come home out of the darkness.... Mr. Recklow?"

"Yes, Tressa."

"I thought I heard him on the stairs."

"Not yet."

"Aie-a!" she sighed and closed her eyes again. She lay like one dead. There was no sound in the room save the soft purr of the fire.

Suddenly from the sleeping girl a frightened voice burst: "Yulun! Yulun! Where is that yellow maid of the Baroulass?... What is she doing? That sleek young thing belongs to Togrul Kahn? Yulun! I am afraid of her! Tell Sansa to watch that she does not stir from the Lake of the Ghosts!... Warn that young Baroulass Sorceress that if she stirs I slay her. And know how to do it in spite of Sanang and all the prayers from the Namaz-Ga! Yulun! Sansa! Watch her, follow her, hearts of flame! My soul be ransom for yours! Tokhta!"

The girl's eyes unclosed. Presently she stirred slightly, passed one hand across her forehead, turned her head toward Recklow.

"I could not discover the Namaz-Ga," she said wearily. "I wish my husband would return."

CHAPTER XVI
# THE PLACE OF PRAYER

Her husband called her on the telephone a few minutes later:

"Fifty-three, Six-twenty-six speaking! Who is this?"

"V-sixty-nine," replied his young wife happily. "Are you all right?"

"Yes. Is M. H. 2479 there?"

"He is here."

"Very well. An hour ago I saw Togrul Khan in a limousine and chased him in a taxi. His car got away in the fog but it was possible to make out the number. An empty Cadillac limousine bearing that number is now waiting outside the 44th Street entrance to the Hotel Astor. The doorman will hold it until I finish telephoning. Tell M. H. 2479 to send men to cover this matter—"

"Victor!"

"Be careful! Yes, what is it?"

"I beg you not to stir in this affair until I can join you—"

"Hurry then. It's just across the street from Westover Court—" His voice ceased; she heard another voice, faintly, and an exclamation from her husband; then his hurried voice over the wire: "The doorman just sent word to hurry. The car number is N.Y. *015 F 0379!* I've got to run! Good-b—"

He left the booth at the end of Peacock Alley, ran down the marble steps to the left and out to the snowy sidewalk, passing on his way a young girl swathed to the eyes in chinchilla who was hurrying into the hotel. As he came to where the limousine was standing, he saw that it was still empty although the door stood open and the engine was running. Around the chauffeur stood the gold laced doorman, the gorgeously uniformed carriage porter and a mounted policeman.

"Hey!" said the latter when he saw Cleves,—"what's the matter here? What are you holding up this car for?"

Cleves beckoned him, whispered, then turned to the doorman.

"Why did you send for me? Was the chauffeur trying to pull out?"

"Yes, sir. A lady come hurrying out an' she jumps in, and the shawfur he starts her humming—"

"A lady! Where did she go?"

"It was that young lady in chinchilla fur. The one you just met when you run out. Yessir! Why, as soon as I held up the car and called this here cop, she opens the door and out she jumps and beats it into the hotel again—"

"Hold that car, Officer!" interrupted Cleves. "Keep it standing here and arrest anybody who gets into it! I'll be back again—"

He turned and hurried into the hotel, traversed Peacock Alley scanning every woman he passed, searching for a slim shape swathed in chinchilla. There were no chinchilla wraps in Peacock Alley; none in the dining-room where people already were beginning to gather and the orchestra was now playing; no young girl in chinchilla in the waiting room, or in the north dining-room.

Then, suddenly, far across the crowded lobby, he saw a slender, bare-headed girl in a chinchilla cloak turn hurriedly away from the room-clerk's desk, holding a key in her white gloved hand.

Before he could take two steps in her direction she had disappeared in the crowd.

He made his way through the packed lobby as best he could amid throngs of people dressed for dinner, theatre, or other gaiety awaiting them somewhere out there in the light-smeared winter fog; but when he arrived at the room clerk's desk he looked for a chinchilla wrap in vain.

Then he leaned over the desk and said to the clerk in a low voice: "I am a Federal agent from the Department of Justice. Here are my credentials. Now, who was that young woman in chinchilla furs to whom you gave her door key a moment ago?"

The clerk leaned over his counter and, dropping his voice, answered that the lady in question had arrived only that morning from San Francisco; had registered as Madame Aoula Baroulass; and had been given a suite on the fourth floor numbered from 408 to 414.

"Do you mean to arrest her?" added the clerk in a weird whisper.

"I don't know. Possibly. Have you the master-key?"

The clerk handed it to him without a word; and Cleves hurried to the elevator.

On the fourth floor the matron on duty halted him, but when he murmured an explanation she nodded and laid a finger on her lips.

"Madame has gone to her apartment," she whispered.

"Has she a servant? Or friends with her?"

"No, sir.... I did see her speak to two foreign looking gentlemen in the elevator when she arrived this morning."

Cleves nodded; the matron pointed out the direction in silence, and he went rapidly down the carpeted corridor, until he came to a door numbered 408.

For a second only he hesitated, then swiftly fitted the master-key and opened the door.

The room—a bedroom—was brightly lighted; but there was nobody there. The other rooms—dressing closet, bath-room and parlour, all were brilliantly lighted by ceiling fixtures and wall brackets; but there was not a person to be seen in any of the rooms—nor, save for the illumination, was there any visible sign that anybody inhabited the apartment.

Swiftly he searched the apartment from end to end. There was no baggage to be seen, no garments, no toilet articles, no flowers in the vases, no magazines or books, not one article of feminine apparel or of personal bric-a-brac visible in the entire place.

Nor had the bed even been turned down—nor any preparation for the night's comfort been attempted. And, except for the blazing lights, it was as though the apartment had not been entered by anybody for a month.

All the windows were closed, all shades lowered and curtains drawn. The air, though apparently pure enough, had that vague flatness which one associates with an unused guest-chamber when opened for an airing.

Now, deliberately, Cleves began a more thorough search of the apartment, looking behind curtains, under beds, into clothes presses, behind sofas.

Then he searched the bureau drawers, dressers, desks for any sign or clew of the girl in the chinchillas. There was no dust anywhere,—the hotel management evidently was particular—but there was not even a pin to be found.

Presently he went out into the corridor and looked again at the number on the door. He had made no mistake.

Then he turned and sped down the long corridor to where the matron was standing beside her desk preparing to go off duty as soon as the other matron arrived to relieve her.

To his impatient question she replied positively that she had seen the girl in chinchillas unlock 408 and enter the apartment less than five minutes before he had arrived in pursuit.

"And I saw her lights go on as soon as she went in," added the matron, pointing to the distant illuminated transom.

"Then she went out through into the next apartment," insisted Cleves.

"The fire-tower is on one side of her; the scullery closet on the other," said the matron. "She could not have left that apartment without coming out into the corridor. And if she had come out I should have seen her."

"I tell you she isn't in those rooms!" protested Cleves.

"She must be there, sir. I saw her go in a few seconds before you came up."

At that moment the other matron arrived. There was no use arguing. He left the explanation of the situation to the woman who was going off duty, and, hastening his steps, he returned to apartment 408.

The door, which he had left open, had swung shut. Again he fitted the master-key, entered, paused on the threshold, looked around nervously, his nostrils suddenly filled with a puff of perfume.

And there on the table by the bed he saw a glass bowl filled with a mass of Chinese orchids—great odorous clusters of orange and snow-white bloom that saturated all the room with their freshening scent.

So astounded was he that he stood stock still, one hand still on the door-knob; then in a trice he had closed and locked the door from inside.

*Somebody* was in that apartment. There could be no doubt about it. He dropped his right hand into his overcoat pocket and took hold of his automatic pistol.

For ten minutes he stood so, listening, peering about the room from bed to curtains, and out into the parlour. There was not a sound in the place. Nothing stirred.

Now, grasping his pistol but not drawing it, he began another stealthy tour of the apartment, exploring every nook and cranny. And, at the end, had discovered nothing new.

When at length he realised that, as far as he could discover, there was not a living thing in the place excepting himself, a very faint chill grew along his neck and shoulders, and he caught his breath suddenly, deeply.

He had come back to the bedroom, now. The perfume of the orchids saturated the still air.

And, as he stood staring at them, all of a sudden he saw, where their twisted stalks rested in the transparent bowl of water, something moving—something brilliant as a live ember gliding out from among the mass of submerged stems—a living fish glowing in scarlet hues and winnowing the water with grotesquely trailing fins as delicate as filaments of scarlet lace.

To and fro swam the fish among the maze of orchid stalks. Even its eyes were hot and red as molten rubies; and as its crimson gills swelled and relaxed and swelled, tints of cherry-fire waxed and waned over its fat and glowing body.

And vaguely, now, in the perfume saturated air, Cleves seemed to sense a subtle taint of evil,—something sinister in the intense stillness of the place—in the jewelled fish gliding so silently in and out among the pallid convolutions of the drowned stems.

As he stood staring at the fish, the drugged odour of the orchids heavy in his throat and lungs, something stirred very lightly in the room.

Chills crawling over every limb, he looked around across his shoulder.

There was a figure seated cross-legged in the middle of the bed!

Then, in the perfumed silence, the girl laughed.

For a full minute neither of them moved. No sound had echoed her low laughter save the deadened pulsations of his own heart. But now there grew a faint ripple of water in the bowl where the scarlet fish, suddenly restless, was swimming hither and thither as though pursued by an invisible hand.

With the slight noise of splashing water in his ears, Cleves stood staring at the figure on the bed. Under her chinchilla cloak the girl seemed
to be all a pale golden tint—hair, skin, eyes. The scant shred of an evening
gown she wore, the jewels at her throat and breast, all were yellow and
amber and saffron-gold.

And now, looking him in the eyes, she leisurely disengaged the robe of
silver fur from her naked shoulders and let it fall around her on the bed.
For a second the lithe, willowy golden thing gathered there as gracefully
as a coiled snake filled him with swift loathing. Then, almost instantly, the
beauty of the lissome creature fascinated him.

She leaned forward and set her elbows on her two knees, and rested her
face between her hands—like a gold rose-bud between two ivory petals,
he thought, dismayed by this young thing's beauty, shaken by the dull confusion of his own heart battering his breast like the blows of a rising tide.

"What do you wish?" she inquired in her soft young voice. "Why have
you come secretly into my rooms to search—and clasping in your hand a
loaded pistol deep within your pocket?"

"Why have you hidden yourself until now?" he retorted in a dull and
laboured voice.

"I have been here."

"Where?"

"Here!... Looking at you.... And watching my scarlet fish. His name is Dze-
lim. He is nearly a thousand years old and as wise as a magician. Look upon
him, my lord! See how rapidly he darts around his tiny crystal world!—
like a comet through outer star-dust, running the eternal race with Time....
And—yonder is a chair. Will my lord be seated—at his new servant's feet?"

A strange, physical weariness seemed to weight his limbs and shoulders.
He seated himself near the bed, never taking his heavy gaze from the smiling, golden thing which squatted there watching him so intently.

"Whose limousine was that which you entered and then left so
abruptly?" he asked.

"My own."

"What was the Yezidee Togrul Kahn doing in it?"

"Did you see anybody in my car?" she asked, veiling her eyes a little with
their tawny lashes.

"I saw a man with a thick beard dyed red with henna, and the bony face
and slant eyes of Togrul the Yezidee."

"May my soul be ransom for yours, my lord, but you lie!" she said softly.
Her lips parted in a smile; but her half-veiled eyes were brilliant as two
topazes.

"Is that your answer?"

She lifted one hand and with her forefinger made signs, from right to left and then downward as though writing in Turkish and in Chinese characters.

"It is written," she said in a low voice, "that we belong to God and we return to him. Look out what you are about, my lord!"

He drew his pistol from his overcoat and, holding it, rested his hand on his knee.

"Now," he said hoarsely, "while we await the coming of Togrul Kahn, you shall remain exactly where you are, and you shall tell me exactly who you are in order that I may decide whether to arrest you as an alien enemy inciting my countrymen to murder, or to let you go as a foreigner who is able to prove her honesty and innocence."

The girl laughed:

"Be careful," she said. "My danger lies in your youth and mine—somewhere between your lips and mine lies my only danger from you, my lord."

A dull flush mounted to his temples and burned there.

"I am the golden comrade to Heavenly Azure," she said, still smiling. "I am the Third Immaum in the necklace Keuke wears where Yulun hangs as a rose-pearl, and Sansa as a pearl on fire.

"Look upon me, my lord!"

There was a golden light in his eyes which seemed to stiffen the muscles and confuse his vision. He heard her voice again as though very far away:

"It is written that we shall love, my lord—thou and I—this night—this night. Listen attentively. I am thy slave. My lips shall touch thy feet. Look upon me, my lord!"

There was a dazzling blindness in his eyes and in his brain. He swayed a little still striving to fix her with his failing gaze. His pistol hand slipped sideways from his knee, fell limply, and the weapon dropped to the thick carpet. He could still see the glimmering golden shape of her, still hear her distant voice:

"It is written that we belong to God... Tokhta!..."

Over his knees was settling a snow-white sheet; on it, in his lap, lay a naked knife. There was not a sound in the room save the rushing and splashing of the scarlet fish in its crystal bowl.

Bending nearer, the girl fixed her yellow eyes on the man who looked back at her with dying gaze, sitting upright and knee deep in his shroud.

Then, noiselessly she uncoiled her supple golden body, extending her right arm toward the knife.

"Throw back thy head, my lord, and stretch thy throat to the knife's sweet edge," she whispered caressingly. "No!—do not close your eyes. Look upon me. Look into my eyes. I am Aoula, temple girl of the Baroulass! I am mistress to the Slayer of Souls! I am a golden plaything to Sanang Noïane, Prince of the Yezidees. Look upon me attentively, my lord!"

Her smooth little hand closed on the hilt; the scarlet fish splashed furiously in the bowl, dislodging a blossom or two which fell to the carpet and slowly faded into mist.

Now she grasped the knife, and she slipped from the bed to the floor and stood before the dazed man.

"This is the Namaz-Ga," she said in her silky voice. "Behold, this is the appointed Place of Prayer. Gaze around you, my lord. These are the shadows of mighty men who come here to see you die in the Place of Prayer."

Cleves's head had fallen back, but his eyes were open. The Baroulass girl took his head in both hands and turned it hither and thither. And his glazing eyes seemed to sweep a throng of shadowy white-robed men crowding the room. And he saw the bloodless, symmetrical visage of Sanang among them, and the great red beard of Togrul; and his stiffening lips parted in an uttered cry, and sagged open, flaccid and soundless.

The Baroulass sorceress lifted the shroud from his knees and spread it on the carpet, moving with leisurely grace about her business and softly intoning the Prayers for the Dead.

Then, having made her arrangements, she took her knife into her right hand again and came back to the half-conscious man, and stood close in front of him, bending near and looking curiously into his dimmed eyes.

"Ayah!" she said smilingly. "This is the Place of Prayer. And you shall add your prayer to ours before I use my knife. So! I give you back your power of speech. Pronounce the name of Erlik!"

Very slowly his dry lips moved and his dry tongue trembled. The word they formed was,

"Tressa!"

Instantly the girl's yellow eyes grew incandescent and her lovely mouth became distorted. With her left hand she caught his chin, forced his head back, exposing his throat, and using all her strength drew the knife's edge across it.

But it was only her clenched fingers that swept the taut throat—clenched and empty fingers in which the knife had vanished.

And when the Baroulass girl saw that her clenched hand was empty, felt her own pointed nails cutting into the tender flesh of her own palm, she stared at her blood-stained fingers in sudden terror—stared, spread them, shrieked where she stood, and writhed there trembling and screaming as though gripped in an invisible trap.

But she fell silent when the door of the room opened noiselessly behind her;—and it was as though she dared not turn her head to face the end of all things which had entered the room and was drawing nearer in utter silence.

Suddenly she saw its shadow on the wall; and her voice burst from her lips in a last shuddering scream.

Then the end came slowly, without a sound, and she sank at the knees, gently, to a kneeling posture, then backward, extending her supple golden shape across the shroud; and lay there limp as a dead snake.

Tressa went to the bowl of water and drew from it every blossom. The scarlet fish was now thrashing the water to an iridescent spume; and Tressa plunged in her hands and seized it and flung it out—squirming and wheezing crimson foam—on the shroud beside the golden girl of the Baroulass. Then, very slowly, she drew the shroud over the dying things; stepped back to the chair where her husband lay unconscious; knelt down beside him and took his head on her shoulder, gazing, all the while, at the outline of the dead girl under the snowy shroud.

After a long while Cleves stirred and opened his eyes. Presently he turned his head sideways on her shoulder.

"Tressa," he whispered.

"Hush," she whispered, "all is well now." But she did not move her eyes from the shroud, which now outlined the still shapes of two human figures.

"John Recklow!" she called in a low voice.

Recklow entered noiselessly with drawn pistol. She motioned to him; he bent and lifted the edge of the shroud, cautiously. A bushy red beard protruded.

"Togrul!" he exclaimed.... "But who is this young creature lying dead beside him?"

Then Tressa caught the collar of her tunic in her left hand and flung back her lovely face looking upward out of eyes like sapphires wet with rain:

"In the name of the one and only God," she sobbed—"if there be no resurrection for dead souls, then I have slain this night in vain!

"For what does it profit a girl if her soul be lost to a lover and her body be saved for her husband?"

She rose from her knees, the tears still falling, and went and looked down at the outlined shapes beneath the shroud.

Recklow had gone to the telephone to summon his own men and an ambulance. Now, turning toward Tressa from his chair:

"God knows what we'd do without you, Mrs. Cleves. I believe this accounts for all the Yezidees except Sanang."

"Excepting Prince Sanang," she said drearily. Then she went slowly to where her husband lay in his armchair, and sank down on the floor, and laid her cheek across his feet.

CHAPTER XVII

# THE SLAYER OF SOULS

In that great blizzard which, on the 4th of February, struck the eastern coast of the United States from Georgia to Maine, John Recklow and his men hunted Sanang, the last of the Yezidees.

And Sanang clung like a demon to the country which he had doomed to destruction, imbedding each claw again as it was torn loose, battling for the supremacy of evil with all his dreadful psychic power, striving still to seize, cripple, and slay the bodies and souls of a hundred million Americans.

Again he scattered the uncounted myriads of germs of the Black Plague which he and his Yezidees had brought out of Mongolia a year before; and once more the plague swept over the country, and thousands on thousands died.

But now the National, State and City governments were fighting, with physicians, nurses, and police, this gruesome epidemic which had come into the world from they knew not where. And National, State and City governments, aroused at last, were fighting the more terrible plague of anarchy.

Nation-wide raids were made from the Atlantic to the Pacific, and from the Gulf to the Lakes. Thousands of terrorists of all shades and stripes whose minds had been seized and poisoned by the Yezidees were being arrested. Deportations had begun; government agents were everywhere swarming to clean out the foulness that had struck deeper into the body of the Republic than any one had supposed.

And it seemed, at last, as though the Red Plague, too, was about to be stamped out along with the Black Death called Influenza.

But only a small group of Secret Service men knew that a resurgence of these horrors was inevitable unless Sanang, the Slayer of Souls, was destroyed. And they knew, too, that only one person in America could hope to destroy Sanang, the last of the Yezidees, and that was Tressa Cleves.

Only by the sudden onset of the plague in various cities of the land had Recklow any clew concerning the whereabouts of Sanang.

In Boston, then Washington, then Kansas City, and then New York the epidemic suddenly blazed up. And in these places of death the Secret Service men always found a clew, and there they hunted Sanang, the Yezidee, to kill him without mercy where they might find him.

But they never found Sanang Noïane; only the ghastly marks of his poisoned claws on the body of the sickened nation—only minds diseased by the Red Plague and bodies dying of the Black Death—civil and social centres disorganized, disrupted, depraved, dying.

When the blizzard burst upon New York, struggling in the throes of the plague, and paralysed the metropolis for a week, John Recklow sent out a special alarm, and New York swarmed with Secret Service men searching the snow-buried city for a graceful, slender, dark young man whose eyes slanted a trifle in his amber-tinted face; who dressed fashionably, lived fastidiously, and spoke English perfectly in a delightfully modulated voice.

And to New York, thrice stricken by anarchy, by plague, and now by God, hurried, from all parts of the nation, thousands of secret agents who had been hunting Sanang in distant cities or who had been raiding the traitorous and secret gatherings of his mental dupes.

Agent ZB-303, who was volunteer agent James Benton, came from Boston with his new bride who had just arrived by way of England—a young girl named Yulun who landed swathed in sables, and stretched out both lovely little hands to Benton the instant she caught sight of him on the pier. Whereupon he took the slim figure in furs into his arms, which was interesting because they had never before met in the flesh.

So,—their honeymoon scarce begun, Benton and Yulun came from Boston in answer to Recklow's emergency call.

And all the way across from San Francisco came volunteer agent XLY-371, otherwise Alek Selden, bringing with him a girl named Sansa whom he had gone to the coast to meet, and whom he had immediately married after she had landed from the Japanese steamer *Nan-yang Maru*. Which, also, was remarkable, because, although they recognised each other instantly, and their hands and lips clung as they met, neither had ever before beheld the living body of the other.

The third man who came to New York at Recklow's summons was volunteer agent 53-6-26, otherwise Victor Cleves.

His young wife, suffering from nervous shock after the deaths of Togrul Khan and of the Baroulass girl, Aoula, had been convalescing in a private sanitarium in Westchester.

Until the summons came to her husband from Recklow, she had seen him only for a few moments every day. But the call to duty seemed to have effected a miraculous cure in the slender, blue-eyed girl who had lain all day long, day after day, in her still, sunny room scarcely unclosing her eyes at all save only when her husband was permitted to enter for the few minutes allowed them every day.

The physician had just left, after admitting that Mrs. Cleves seemed to be well enough to travel if she insisted; and she and her maid had already begun to pack when her husband came into her room.

She looked around over her shoulder, then rose from her knees, flung an armful of clothing into the trunk before which she had been kneeling, and came across the room to him. Then she dismissed her maid from the room. And when the girl had gone:

"I am well, Victor," she said in a low voice. "Why are you troubled?"

"I can't bear to have you drawn into this horrible affair once more."

"Who else is there to discover and overcome Sanang?" she asked calmly. He remained silent.

So, for a few moments they stood confronting each other there in the still, sunny chamber—husband and wife who had never even exchanged the first kiss—two young creatures more vitally and intimately bound together than any two on earth—yet utterly separated body and soul from each other—two solitary spirits which had never merged; two bodies virginal and inviolate.

Tressa spoke first: "I must go. That was our bargain."

The word made him wince as though it had been a sudden blow. Then his face flushed red.

"Bargain or no bargain," he said, "I don't want you to go because I'm afraid you can not endure another shock like the last one.... And every time you have thrown your own mind and body between this Nation and destruction you have nearly died of it."

"And if I die?" she said in a low voice.

What answer she awaited—perhaps hoped for—was not the one he made. He said: "If you die in what you believe to be your line of duty, then it will be I who have killed you."

"That would not be true. It is you who have saved me."

"I have not. I have done nothing except to lead you into danger of death since I first met you. If you mean spiritually, that also is untrue. You have saved yourself—if that indeed were necessary. You have redeemed yourself—if it is true you needed redemption—which I never believed—"

"Oh," she sighed swiftly, "Sanang surprised my soul when it was free of my body—followed my soul into the Wood of the White Moth—caught it there all alone—and—slew it!"

His lips and throat had gone dry as he watched the pallid terror grow in her face.

Presently he recovered his voice: "You call that Yezidee the Slayer of Souls," he said, "but I tell you there is no such creature, no such power!

"I suppose I—I know what you mean—having seen what we call souls dissociated from their physical bodies—but that this Yezidee could do you any spiritual damage I do not for one instant believe. The idea is monstrous, I tell you—"

"I—I fought him—soul battling against soul—" she stammered, breathing faster and irregularly. "I struggled with Sanang there in the Wood of the White Moth. I called on God! I called on my two great dogs, Bars and Alaga! I recited the Fatha with all my strength—fighting convulsively whenever his soul seized mine; I cried out the name of Khidr, begging for wisdom! I called on the Ten Imaums, on Ali the Lion, on the Blessed Companions. Then I tore my spirit out of the grasp of his soul—but there was no escape!—no escape," she wailed. "For on every side I saw the cloud-topped rampart of Gog and Magog, and the woods rang with Erlik's laughter—the dissonant mirth of hell—"

She began to shudder and sway a little, then with an effort she controlled herself in a measure.

"There never has been," she began again with lips that quivered in spite of her—"there never has been one moment in our married lives when my soul dared forget the Wood of the White Moth—dared seek yours.... God lives. But so does Erlik. There are angels; but there are as many demons.... My soul is ashamed.... And very lonely... very lonely... but no fit companion—for yours—"

Her hands dropped listlessly beside her and her chin sank.

"So you believe that Yezidee devil caught your soul when it was wandering somewhere out of your body, and destroyed it," he said.

She did not answer, did not even lift her eyes until he had stepped close to her—closer than he had ever come. Then she looked up at him, but closed her eyes as he swept her into his arms and crushed her face and body against his own.

Now her red lips were on his; now her face and heart and limbs and breast melted into his—her breath, her pulse, her strength flowed into his and became part of their single being and single pulse and breath. And she felt their two souls flame and fuse together, and burn together in one heavenly blaze—felt the swift conflagration mount, overwhelm, and sweep her clean of the last lingering taint; felt her soul, unafraid, clasp her husband's spirit in its white embrace—clung to him, uplifted out of hell, rising into the blinding light of Paradise.

Far—far away she heard her own voice in singing whispers—heard her lips pronounce *The Name*—"Ata—Ata! Allahou—"

Her blue eyes unclosed; through a mist, in which she saw her husband's face, grew a vast metallic clamour in her ears.

Her husband kissed her, long, silently; then, retaining her hand, he turned and lifted the receiver from the clamouring telephone.

"Yes! Yes, this is 53-6-26. Yes, V-69 is with me.... When?... To-day?... Very well.... Yes, we'll come at once.... Yes, we can get a train in a few minutes.... All right. Good-bye."

He took his wife into his arms again.

"Dearest of all in the world," he said, "Sanang is cornered in a row of houses near the East River, and Recklow has flung a cordon around the entire block. Good God! I *can't* take you there!"

Then Tressa smiled, drew his head down, looked into his face till the clear blue splendour of her gaze stilled the tumult in his brain.

"I alone know how to deal with Prince Sanang," she said quietly. "And if John Recklow, or you, or Mr. Benton or Mr. Selden should kill him with your pistols, it would be only his body you slay, not the evil thing that would escape you and return to Erlik."

"*Must* you do this thing, Tressa?"

"Yes, I must do it."

"But—if our pistols cannot kill this sorcerer, how are you going to deal with him?"

"I know how."

"Have you the strength?"

"Yes—the bodily and the spiritual. Don't you know that I am already part of you?"

"We shall be nearer still," he murmured.

She flushed but met his gaze.

"Yes.... We shall be but one being.... Utterly.... For already our hearts and souls are one. And we shall become of one mind and one body.

"I am no longer afraid of Sanang Noïane!"

"No longer afraid to slay him?" he asked quietly.

A blue light flashed in her eyes and her face grew still and white and terrible.

"Death to the body? That is nothing, my lord!" she said, in a hard, sweet voice. "It is written that we belong to God and that we return to Him. All living things must die, Heart of the World! It is only the death of souls that matters. And it has arrived at a time in the history of mankind, I think, when the Slayer of Souls shall slay no more."

She looked at him, flushed, withdrew her hand and went slowly across the room to the big bay window where potted flowers were in bloom.

From a window-box she took a pinch of dry soil and dropped it into the bosom of her gown.

Then, facing the East, with lowered arms and palms turned outward:

"There is no god but God," she whispered—"the merciful, the long-suffering, the compassionate, the just.

"For it is written that when the heavens are rolled together like a scroll, every soul shall know what it hath wrought.

"And those souls that are dead in Jehannum shall arise from the dead, and shall have their day in court. Nor shall Erlik stay them till all has been said.

"And on that day the soul of a girl that hath been put to death shall ask for what reason it was slain.

"Thus it has been written."

Then Tressa dropped to her knees, touched the carpet with her forehead, straightened her lithe body and, looking over her shoulder, clapped her hands together sharply.

Her maid opened the door. "Hasten with my lord's luggage!" she cried happily; and, still kneeling, lifted her head to her husband and laughed up into his eyes.

"You should call the porter for we are nearly ready. Shall we go to the station in a sleigh? Oh, wonderful!"

She leaped to her feet, extended her hand and caught his.

"Horses for the lord of the Yiort!" she cried, laughingly. "Kosh! Take me out into this new white world that has been born to-day of the ten purities and the ten thousand felicities! It has been made anew for you and me who also have been born this day!"

He scarcely knew this sparkling, laughing girl with her quick grace and her thousand swift little moods and gaieties.

Porters came to take his luggage from his own room; and then her trunk and bags were ready, and were taken away.

The baggage sleigh drove off. Their own jingling sleigh followed; and Tressa, buried in furs, looked out upon a dazzling, unblemished world, lying silvery white under a sky as azure as her eyes.

"Keuke Mongol—Heavenly Azure," he whispered close to her crimsoned cheek, "do you know how I have loved you—always—always?"

"No, I did not know that," she said.

"Nor I, in the beginning. Yet it happened, also, from the beginning when I first saw you."

"That is a delicious thing to be told. Within me a most heavenly glow is spreading.... Unglove your hand."

She slipped the glove from her own white fingers and felt for his under the furs.

"Aie," she sighed, "you are more beautiful than Ali; more wonderful than the Flaming Pearl. Out of ice and fire a new world has been made for us."

"Heavenly Azure—my darling!"

"Oh-h," she sighed, "your words are sweeter than the breeze in Yian! I shall be a bride to you such as there never has been since the days of the Blessed Companions—may their names be perfumed and sweet-scented!... Shall I truly be one with you, my lord?"

"Mind, soul, and body, one being, you and I, little Heavenly Azure."

"Between your two hands you hold me like a burning rose, my lord."

"Your sweetness and fire penetrate my soul."

"We shall burn together then till the sky-carpet be rolled up. Kosh! We shall be one, and on that day I shall not be afraid."

The sleigh came to a clashing, jingling halt; the train plowed into the depot buried in vast clouds of snowy steam.

But when they had taken the places reserved for them, and the train was moving swifter and more swiftly toward New York, fear suddenly overwhelmed Victor Cleves, and his face grew grey with the menacing tumult of his thoughts.

The girl seemed to comprehend him, too, and her own features became still and serious as she leaned forward in her chair.

"It is in God's hands, Heart of the World," she said in a low voice. "We are one, thou and I,—or nearly so. Nothing can harm my soul."

"No.... But the danger—to your life—"

"I fear no Yezidee."

"The beast will surely try to kill you. And what can I do? You say my pistol is useless."

"Yes.... But I want you near me."

"Do you imagine I'd leave you for a second? Good God," he added in a strangled voice, "isn't there any way I can kill this wild beast? With my naked hands—?"

"You must leave him to me, Victor."

"And you believe you can slay him? *Do* you?"

She remained silent for a long while, bent forward in her armchair, and her hands clasped tightly on her knees.

"My husband," she said at last, "what your astronomers have but just begun to suspect is true, and has long, long been known to the Sheiks-el-Djebel.

"For, near to this world we live in, are other worlds—planets that do not reflect light. And there is a dark world called Yrimid, close to the earth—a planet wrapped in darkness—a black star.... And upon it Erlik dwells.... And it is peopled by demons.... And from it comes sickness and evil—"

She moistened her lips; sat for a while gazing vaguely straight before her.

"From this black planet comes all evil upon earth," she resumed in a hushed voice. "For it is very near to the earth. It is not a hundred miles away. All strange phenomena for which our scientists can not account are due to this invisible planet,—all new and sudden pestilences; all convulsions of nature; the newly noticed radio disturbances; the new, so-called inter-planetary signals—all—all have their hidden causes within that black and demon-haunted planet long known to the Yezidees, and by them called Yrimid, or Erlik's World.

"And—it is to this black planet that I shall send Sanang, Slayer of Souls. I shall tear him from this earth, though he cling to it with every claw; and

I shall fling his soul into darkness—out across the gulf—drive his soul forth—hurl it toward Erlik like a swift rocket charred and falling from the sky into endless night.

"So shall I strive to deal with Prince Sanang, Sorcerer of Mount Alamout, the last of the Assassins, Sheik-el-Djebel, and Slayer of Souls.... May God remember him in hell."

Already their train was rolling into the great terminal.

Recklow was awaiting them. He took Tressa's hands in his and gazed earnestly into her face.

"Have you come to show us how to conclude this murderous business?" he asked grimly.

"I shall try," she said calmly. "Where have you cornered Sanang?"

"Could you and Victor come at once?"

"Yes." She turned and looked at her husband, who had become quite pale.

Recklow saw the look they exchanged. There could be no misunderstanding what had happened to these two. Their tragedy had ended. They were united at last. He understood it instantly,—realised how terrible was this new and tragic situation for them both.

Yet, he knew also that the salvation of civilisation itself now depended upon this girl. She must face Sanang. There was nothing else possible.

"The streets are choked with snow," he said, "but I have a coupé and two strong horses waiting."

He nodded to one of his men standing near. Cleves gave him the hand luggage and checks.

"All right," he said in a low voice to Recklow; and passed one arm through Tressa's.

The coupé was waiting on Forty-second Street, guarded by a policeman. When they had entered and were seated, two mounted policemen rode ahead of the lurching vehicle, picking a way amid the monstrous snowdrifts, and headed for the East River.

"We've got him somewhere in a wretched row of empty houses not far from East River Park. I'm taking you there. I've drawn a cordon of my men around the entire block. He can't get away. But I dared take no chances with this Yezidee sorcerer—dared not let one of my men go in to look for him—go anywhere near him,—until I could lay the situation before you, Mrs. Cleves."

"Yes," she said calmly, "it was the only way, Mr. Recklow. There would have been no use shooting him—no use taking him prisoner. A prisoner, he remains as deadly as ever; dead, his mind still lives and breeds evil. You are quite right; it is for me to deal with Sanang."

Recklow shuddered in spite of himself. "Can you tear his claws from the vitals of the world, and free the sick brains of a million people from the slavery of this monster's mind?"

The girl said seriously:

"Even Satan was stoned. It is so written. And was cast out. And dwells forever and ever in Abaddon. No star lights that Pit. None lights the Black Planet, Yrimid. It is where evil dwells. And there Sanang Noïane belongs."

And now, beyond the dirty edges of the snow-smothered city, under an icy mist they caught sight of the river where ships lay blockaded by frozen floes.

Gulls circled over it; ghostly factory chimneys on the further shore loomed up gigantic, ranged like minarettes.

The coupé, jolting along behind the mounted policemen, struggled up toward the sidewalk and stopped. The two horses stood steaming, knee deep in snow. Recklow sprang out; Tressa gave him one hand and stepped lithely to the sidewalk. Then Cleves got out and came and took hold of his wife's arm again.

"Well," he said harshly to Recklow, "where is this damned Yezidee hidden?"

Recklow pointed in silence, but he and Tressa had already lifted their gaze to the stark, shabby row of abandoned three-story houses where every dirty blind was closed.

"They're to be demolished and model tenements built," he said briefly.

A man muffled in a fur overcoat came up and took Tressa's hand and kissed it.

She smiled palely at Benton, spoke of Yulun, wished him happiness. While she was yet speaking Selden approached and bent over her gloved hand. She spoke to him very sweetly of Sansa, expressing pleasure at the prospect of seeing her again in the body.

"The Seldens and ourselves have adjoining apartments at the Ritz," said Benton. "We have reserved a third suite for you and Victor."

She inclined her lovely head, gravely, then turned to Recklow, saying that she was ready.

"It makes no difference which front door I unlock," he said. "All these tenements are connected by human rat-holes and hidden runways leading from one house to another.... How many men do you want?"

"I want you four men,—nobody else."

Recklow led the way up a snow-covered stoop, drew a key from his pocket, fitted it, and pulled open the door.

A musty chill struck their faces as they entered the darkened and empty hallway. Involuntarily every man drew his pistol.

"I must ask you to do exactly what I tell you to do," she said calmly.

"Certainly," said Recklow, caressing his white moustache and striving to pierce the gloom with his keen eyes.

Then Tressa took her husband's hand. "Come," she said. They mounted the stairway together; and the three others followed with pistols lifted.

There was a vague grey light on the second floor; the broken rear shutters let it in.

As though she seemed to know her way, the girl led them forward, opened a door in the wall, and disclosed a bare, dusty room in the next house.

Through this she stepped; the others crept after her with weapons ready. She opened a second door, turned to the four men.

"Wait here for me. Come only when I call," she whispered.

"For God's sake take me with you," burst out Cleves.

"In God's name stay where you are till you hear me call your name!" she said almost breathlessly.

Then, suddenly she turned, swiftly retracing her steps; and they saw her pass through the first door and disappear into the first house they had entered.

A terrible silence fell among them. The sound of her steps on the bare boards had died away. There was not a sound in the chilly dusk.

Minute after minute dragged by. One by one the men peered fearfully at Cleves. His visage was ghastly and they could see his pistol-hand trembling.

Twice Recklow looked at his wrist watch. The third time he said, unsteadily: "She has been gone three-quarters of an hour."

Then, far away, they heard a heavy tread on the stairs. Nearer and nearer came the footsteps. Every pistol was levelled at the first door as a man's bulky form darkened it.

"It's one of my men," said Recklow in a voice like a low groan. "Where on earth is Mrs. Cleves?"

"I came to tell you," said the agent, "Mrs. Cleves came out of the first house nearly an hour ago. She got into the coupé and told the driver to go to the Ritz."

"What!" gasped Recklow.

"She's gone to the Ritz," repeated the agent. "No one else has come out. And I began to worry—hearing nothing of you, Mr. Recklow. So I stepped in to see—"

"You say that Mrs. Cleves went out of the house we entered, got into the coupé, and told the driver to go to the Ritz?" demanded Cleves, astounded.

"Yes, sir."

"Where is that coupé? Did it return?"

"It had not returned when I came in here."

"Go back and look for it. Look in the other street," said Recklow sharply. The agent hurried away over the creaking boards. The four men gazed at one another.

"The thing to do is to obey her and stay where we are," said Recklow grimly. "Who knows what peril we may cause her if we move from—"

His words froze on his lips as Tressa's voice rang out from the darkness beyond the door they were guarding:

"Victor! I—I need you! Come to me, my husband!"

As Cleves sprang through the door into the darkness beyond, Benton smashed a window sash with all the force of his shoulder, and, reaching out through the shattered glass, tore the rotting blinds from their hinges, letting in a flood of sickly light.

Against the bare wall stood Tressa, both arms extended, her hands flat against the plaster, and each hand transfixed and pinned to the wall by a knife.

A white sheet lay at her feet. On it rested a third knife. And, bending on one knee to pick it up, they caught a glimpse of a slender young man in fashionable afternoon attire, who, as they entered with the crash of the shattered window in their ears, sprang to his nimble feet and stood confronting them, knife in hand.

Instantly every man fired at him and the bullets whipped the plaster to a smoke behind him, but the slender, dark skinned young man stood motionless, looking at them out of brilliant eyes that slanted a trifle.

Again the racket of the fusillade swept him and filled the room with plaster dust.

Cleves, frantic with horror, laid hold of the knives that pinned his wife's hands to the wall, and dragged them out.

But there was no blood, no wound to be seen on her soft palms. She took the murderous looking blades from him, threw one terrible look at Sanang, kicked the shroud across the floor toward him, and flung both knives upon it.

The place was still dim with plaster dust and pistol fumes as she stepped forward through the acrid mist, motioning the four men aside.

"Sanang!" she cried in a clear voice, "may God remember you in hell, for my feet have spurned your shroud, and your knives, which could not scar my palms, shall never pierce my heart! Look out for yourself, Prince Sanang!"

"Tokhta!" he said, calmly. "My soul be ransom for yours!"

"That is a lie! My soul is already ransomed! My mind is the more powerful. It has already halted yours. It is conquering yours. It is seizing your mind and enslaving it. It is mastering your will, Sanang! Your mind bends before mine. You know it! You know it is bending. You feel it is breaking down!"

Sanang's eyes began to glitter but his pale brown face had grown almost white.

"I slew you once—in the Wood of the White Moth," he said huskily. "There is no resurrection from such a death, little Heavenly Azure. Look upon me! My soul and yours are one!"

"You are looking upon my soul," she said.

"A lie! You are in your body!"

The girl laughed. "My body lies asleep in the Ritz upon my husband's bed," she said. "My body is his, my mind belongs to him, my soul is already one with his. Do you not know it, dog of a Yezidee? Look upon me, Sanang Noïane! Look upon my unwounded hands! My shroud lies at your feet. And there lie the knives that could not pierce my heart! I am thrice clean! Listen to my words, Sanang! There is no other god but God!"

The young man's visage grew pasty and loose and horrible; his lips became flaccid like dewlaps; but out of these sagging folds of livid skin his voice burst whistling, screaming, as though wrenched from his very belly:

"May Erlik strangle you! May you rot where you stand! May your face become a writhing mass of maggots and your body a corruption of living worms!

"For what you are doing to me this day may every demon in hell torment you!

"Have a care what you are about!" he screeched. "You are slaying my mind, you sorceress! You have seized my mind and are crushing it! You are putting out its light, you Yezidee witch!—you are quenching the last spark—of reason—in—me—"

"Sanang!"

His knife fell clattering to the floor. But he stood stock still, his hands clutching his head—stood motionless, while scream on scream tore through the loose and gaping lips, blowing them into ghastly, distorted folds.

"Sanang Noïane!" she cried in her clear voice, "the Eight Towers are darkened! The Rampart of Gog and Magog is fallen! On Mount Alamout nothing is living. The minds of mankind are free again!"

She stepped forward, slowly, and stood near him, chanting in a low voice the Prayers for the Dead.

She bent down and unrolled the shroud, laid it on his shoulders and drew it up and across his face, covering his dying eyes, and swathed him so, slowly, from head to foot.

Then she gathered up the three knives, cast them upward into the air. They did not fall again. They disappeared. And all the while, under her breath, the girl was chanting the Prayers for the Dead as she moved silently about her business.

Shrouded to the forehead in its white cerements, the muffled figure of Sanang stood upright, motionless as a swathed and frozen corpse.

Outside, the daylight had become greyer. It had begun to snow again, and a few flakes blew in through the shattered windows and clung to the winding sheet of Sanang.

And now Tressa drew close to the shrouded shape and stood before it, gazing intently upon the outlined features of the last of the Yezidees.

"Sanang," she said very softly, "I hear your soul bidding your body farewell. Tokhta!"

Then, under the strained gaze of the four men gathered there, the shroud fell to the floor in a loose heap of white folds. There was nobody under it; no trace of Sanang. The human shape of the Yezidee had disappeared; but a greyish mist had filled the room, wavering up like smoke from the shroud, and, like smoke, blowing in a long streamer toward the window where the draught drew it out through the falling snow and scattered the last shred of it against the greying sky.

In the room the mist thinned swiftly; the four men could now see one another. But Tressa was no longer in the room. And in place of the white shroud a piece of filthy tattered carpet lay on the floor. And a dead rat, flattened out, dry and dusty, lay upon it.

"For God's sake," whispered Recklow hoarsely, "let us get out of this!"

Cleves, his pistol clutched convulsively, stared at him in terror. But Recklow took him by the arm and drew him away, muttering that Tressa was waiting for him, and might be ill, and that there was nothing further to expect in this ghastly spot.

They went with Cleves to the Ritz. At the desk the clerk said that Mrs. Cleves had the keys and was in her apartment.

The three men entered the corridor with him; watched him try the door; saw him open it; lingered a moment after it had closed; heard the key turn.

At the sound of the door closing the maid came. "Madame is asleep in her room," she whispered.

"When did she come in?"

"More than two hours ago, sir. I have drawn her bath, but when I opened the door a few moments ago, Madame was still asleep."

He nodded; he was trembling when he put off his overcoat and dropped hat and gloves on the carpet.

From the little rose and ivory reception room he could see the closed door of his wife's chamber. And for a while he stood staring at it.

Then, slowly, he crossed this room, opened the door; entered.

In her bedroom the tinted twilight was like ashes of roses. He went to the bed and looked down at her shadowy face; gazed intently; listened; then, in sudden terror, bent and laid his hand on her heart. It was beating as tranquilly as a child's; but as she stirred, turned her head, and unclosed her eyes, under his hand her heart leaped like a wild thing caught unawares and the snowy skin glowed with an exquisite and deepening tint as she lifted her arms and clasped them around her husband's neck, drawing his quivering face against her own.

THE END

# THE MAKER OF MOONS

# OF MOONS

## BY ROBERT W. CHAMBERS

For My Father

"I am myself just as much evil as good, and my nation is —
    And I say there is in fact no evil;
Or if there is, I say it is just as important to you, to
    the land, or to me, as anything else.

Each is not for its own sake;
I say the whole earth, and all the stars in the sky, are
    for Religion's sake.
I say no man has ever yet been half devout enough;
None has ever yet adored or worshipped half enough;
None has begun to think how divine he himself is, and
    how certain the future is."
                                    WALT WHITMAN.

# THE MAKER OF MOONS

"I have heard what the Talkers were talking,—the talk
Of the beginning and the end;
But I do not talk of the beginning or the end."

## I.

Concerning Yue-Laou and the Xin I know nothing more than you shall know. I am miserably anxious to clear the matter up. Perhaps what I write may save the United States Government money and lives, perhaps it may arouse the scientific world to action; at any rate it will put an end to the terrible suspense of two people. Certainty is better than suspense.

If the Government dares to disregard this warning and refuses to send a thoroughly equipped expedition at once, the people of the State may take swift vengeance on the whole region and leave a blackened devastated waste where to-day forest and flowering meadow land border the lake in the Cardinal Woods.

You already know part of the story; the New York papers have been full of alleged details. This much is true: Barris caught the "Shiner," red handed, or rather yellow handed, for his pockets and boots and dirty fists were stuffed with lumps of gold. I say gold, advisedly. You may call it what you please. You also know how Barris was—but unless I begin at the beginning of my own experiences you will be none the wiser after all.

On the third of August of this present year I was standing in Tiffany's, chatting with George Godfrey of the designing department. On the glass counter between us lay a coiled serpent, an exquisite specimen of chiselled gold.

"No," replied Godfrey to my question, "it isn't my work; I wish it was. Why, man, it's a masterpiece!"

"Whose?" I asked.

"Now I should be very glad to know also," said Godfrey. "We bought it from an old jay who says he lives in the country somewhere about the Cardinal Woods. That 's near Starlit Lake, I believe—"

"Lake of the Stars?" I suggested.

"Some call it Starlit Lake,—it's all the same. Well, my rustic Reuben says that he represents the sculptor of this snake for all practical and business purposes. He got his price too. We hope he'll bring us something more. We have sold this already to the Metropolitan Museum."

I was leaning idly on the glass case, watching the keen eyes of the artist in precious metals as he stooped over the gold serpent.

"A masterpiece!" he muttered to himself, fondling the glittering coil; "look at the texture! Whew!" But I was not looking at the serpent. Something was moving,—crawling out of Godfrey's coat pocket,—the pocket nearest to me,—something soft and yellow with crab-like legs all covered with coarse yellow hair.

"What in Heaven's name," said I, "have you got in your pocket? It's crawling out—it's trying to creep up your coat, Godfrey!"

He turned quickly and dragged the creature out with his left hand.

I shrank back as he held the repulsive object dangling before me, and he laughed and placed it on the counter.

"Did you ever see anything like that?" he demanded.

"No," said I truthfully, "and I hope I never shall again. What is it?"

"I don't know. Ask them at the Natural History Museum—they can't tell you. The Smithsonian is all at sea too. It is, I believe, the connecting link between a sea-urchin, a spider, and the devil. It looks venomous but I can't find either fangs or mouth. Is it blind? These things may be eyes but they look as if they were painted. A Japanese sculptor might have produced such an impossible beast, but it is hard to believe that God did. It looks unfinished too. I have a mad idea that this creature is only one of the parts of some larger and more grotesque organism,—it looks so lonely, so hopelessly dependent, so cursedly unfinished. I'm going to use it as a model. If I don't out-Japanese the Japs my name isn't Godfrey."

The creature was moving slowly across the glass case towards me. I drew back.

"Godfrey," I said, "I would execute a man who executed any such work as you propose. What do you want to perpetuate such a reptile for? I can stand the Japanese grotesque but I can't stand that—spider—"

"It's a crab."

"Crab or spider or blind-worm—ugh! What do you want to do it for? It's a nightmare—it's unclean!"

I hated the thing. It was the first living creature that I had ever hated.

For some time I had noticed a damp acrid odour in the air, and Godfrey said it came from the reptile.

"Then kill it and bury it," I said; "and by the way, where did it come from?"

"I don't know that either," laughed Godfrey; "I found it clinging to the box that this gold serpent was brought in. I suppose my old Reuben is responsible."

"If the Cardinal Woods are the lurking places for things like this," said I, "I am sorry that I am going to the Cardinal Woods."

"Are you?" asked Godfrey; "for the shooting?"

"Yes, with Barris and Pierpont. Why don't you kill that creature?"

"Go off on your shooting trip, and let me alone," laughed Godfrey.

I shuddered at the "crab," and bade Godfrey good-bye until December.

That night, Pierpont, Barris, and I sat chatting in the smoking-car of the Quebec Express when the long train pulled out of the Grand Central Depot. Old David had gone forward with the dogs; poor things, they hated to ride in the baggage car, but the Quebec and Northern road provides no sportsman's cars, and David and the three Gordon setters were in for an uncomfortable night.

Except for Pierpont, Barris, and myself, the car was empty. Barris, trim, stout, ruddy, and bronzed, sat drumming on the window ledge, puffing a short fragrant pipe. His gun-case lay beside him on the floor.

"When I have white hair and years of discretion," said Pierpont languidly, "I'll not flirt with pretty serving-maids; will you, Roy?"

"No," said I, looking at Barris.

"You mean the maid with the cap in the Pullman car?" asked Barris.

"Yes," said Pierpont.

I smiled, for I had seen it also.

Barris twisted his crisp grey moustache, and yawned.

"You children had better be toddling off to bed," he said. "That lady's-maid is a member of the Secret Service."

"Oh," said Pierpont, "one of your colleagues?"

"You might present us, you know," I said; "the journey is monotonous."

Barris had drawn a telegram from his pocket, and as he sat turning it over and over between his fingers he smiled. After a moment or two he handed it to Pierpont who read it with slightly raised eyebrows.

"It's rot,—I suppose it's cipher," he said; "I see it's signed by General Drummond—"

"Drummond, Chief of the Government Secret Service," said Barris.

"Something interesting?" I enquired, lighting a cigarette.

"Something so interesting," replied Barris, "that I'm going to look into it myself—"

"And break up our shooting trio—"

"No. Do you want to hear about it? Do you, Billy Pierpont?"

"Yes," replied that immaculate young man. Barris rubbed the amber mouth-piece of his pipe on his handkerchief, cleared the stem with a bit of wire, puffed once or twice, and leaned back in his chair.

"Pierpont," he said, "do you remember that evening at the United States Club when General Miles, General Drummond, and I were examining that gold nugget that Captain Mahan had? You examined it also, I believe."

"I did," said Pierpont.

"Was it gold?" asked Barris, drumming on the window.

"It was," replied Pierpont.

"I saw it too," said I; "of course, it was gold."

"Professor La Grange saw it also," said Barris; "he said it was gold."

"Well?" said Pierpont.

"Well," said Barris, "it was not gold."

After a silence Pierpont asked what tests had been made.

"The usual tests," replied Barris. "The United States Mint is satisfied that it is gold, so is every jeweller who has seen it. But it is not gold,—and yet—it is gold."

Pierpont and I exchanged glances.

"Now," said I, "for Barris's usual coup-de-théâtre: what was the nugget?"

"Practically it was pure gold; but," said Barris, enjoying the situation intensely, "really it was not gold. Pierpont, what is gold?"

"Gold's an element, a metal—"

"Wrong! Billy Pierpont," said Barris coolly.

"Gold was an element when I went to school," said I.

"It has not been an element for two weeks," said Barris; "and, except General Drummond, Professor La Grange, and myself, you two youngsters are the only people, except one, in the world who know it,—or have known it."

"Do you mean to say that gold is a composite metal?" said Pierpont slowly.

"I do. La Grange has made it. He produced a scale of pure gold day before yesterday. That nugget was manufactured gold."

Could Barris be joking? Was this a colossal hoax? I looked at Pierpont. He muttered something about that settling the silver question, and turned his head to Barris, but there was that in Barris's face which forbade jesting, and Pierpont and I sat silently pondering.

"Don't ask me how it's made," said Barris, quietly; "I don't know. But I do know that somewhere in the region of the Cardinal Woods there is a gang of people who do know how gold is made, and who make it. You understand the danger this is to every civilized nation. It's got to be stopped of course. Drummond and I have decided that I am the man to stop it. Wherever and whoever these people are—these gold makers,—they must be caught, every one of them,—caught or shot."

"Or shot," repeated Pierpont, who was owner of the Cross-Cut Gold Mine and found his income too small; "Professor La Grange will of course be prudent;—science need not know things that would upset the world!"

"Little Willy," said Barris laughing, "your income is safe."

"I suppose," said I, "some flaw in the nugget gave Professor La Grange the tip."

"Exactly. He cut the flaw out before sending the nugget to be tested. He worked on the flaw and separated gold into its three elements."

"He is a great man," said Pierpont, "but he will be the greatest man in the world if he can keep his discovery to himself."

"Who?" said Barris.

"Professor La Grange."

"Professor La Grange was shot through the heart two hours ago," replied Barris slowly.

## II.

We had been at the shooting box in the Cardinal Woods five days when a telegram was brought to Barris by a mounted messenger from the nearest telegraph station, Cardinal Springs, a hamlet on the lumber railroad which joins the Quebec and Northern at Three Rivers Junction, thirty miles below.

Pierpont and I were sitting out under the trees, loading some special shells as experiments; Barris stood beside us, bronzed, erect, holding his pipe carefully so that no sparks should drift into our powder box. The beat of hoofs over the grass aroused us, and when the lank messenger drew bridle before the door, Barris stepped forward and took the sealed telegram. When he had torn it open he went into the house and presently reappeared, reading something that he had written.

"This should go at once," he said, looking the messenger full in the face.

"At once, Colonel Barris," replied the shabby countryman.

Pierpont glanced up and I smiled at the messenger who was gathering his bridle and settling himself in his stirrups. Barris handed him the written reply and nodded good-bye: there was a thud of hoofs on the greensward, a jingle of bit and spur across the gravel, and the messenger was gone. Barris's pipe went out and he stepped to windward to relight it.

"It is queer," said I, "that your messenger—a battered native,—should speak like a Harvard man."

"He is a Harvard man," said Barris.

"And the plot thickens," said Pierpont; "are the Cardinal Woods full of your Secret Service men, Barris?"

"No," replied Barris, "but the telegraph stations are. How many ounces of shot are you using, Roy?"

I told him, holding up the adjustable steel measuring cup. He nodded.

After a moment or two he sat down on a camp-stool beside us and picked up a crimper.

"That telegram was from Drummond," he said; "the messenger was one of my men as you two bright little boys divined. Pooh! If he had spoken the Cardinal County dialect you wouldn't have known."

"His make-up was good," said Pierpont.

Barris twirled the crimper and looked at the pile of loaded shells. Then he picked up one and crimped it.

"Let 'em alone," said Pierpont, "you crimp too tight."

"Does his little gun kick when the shells are crimped too tight?" enquired Barris tenderly; "well, he shall crimp his own shells then,—where's his little man?"

"His little man," was a weird English importation, stiff, very carefully scrubbed, tangled in his aspirates, named Howlett. As valet, gilly, gunbearer, and crimper, he aided Pierpont to endure the ennui of existence, by doing for him everything except breathing. Lately, however, Barris's taunts had driven Pierpont to do a few things for himself. To his astonishment he found that cleaning his own gun was not a bore, so he timidly loaded a shell or two, was much pleased with himself, loaded some more, crimped them, and went to breakfast with an appetite. So when Barris asked where "his little man" was, Pierpont did not reply but dug a cupful of shot from the bag and poured it solemnly into the half filled shell.

Old David came out with the dogs and of course there was a pow-wow when "Voyou," my Gordon, wagged his splendid tail across the loading table and sent a dozen unstopped cartridges rolling over the grass, vomiting powder and shot.

"Give the dogs a mile or two," said I; "we will shoot over the Sweet Fern Covert about four o'clock, David."

"Two guns, David," added Barris.

"Are you not going?" asked Pierpont, looking up, as David disappeared with the dogs.

"Bigger game," said Barris shortly. He picked up a mug of ale from the tray which Howlett had just set down beside us and took a long pull. We did the same, silently. Pierpont set his mug on the turf beside him and returned to his loading.

We spoke of the murder of Professor La Grange, of how it had been concealed by the authorities in New York at Drummond's request, of the certainty that it was one of the gang of gold-makers who had done it, and of the possible alertness of the gang.

"Oh, they know that Drummond will be after them sooner or later," said Barris, "but they don't know that the mills of the gods have already begun to grind. Those smart New York papers builded better than they knew when their ferret-eyed reporter poked his red nose into the house on 58th Street and sneaked off with a column on his cuffs about the 'suicide' of Professor La Grange. Billy Pierpont, my revolver is hanging in your room; I'll take yours too—"

"Help yourself," said Pierpont.

"I shall be gone over night," continued Barris; "my poncho and some bread and meat are all I shall take except the 'barkers.'"

"Will they bark to-night?" I asked.

"No, I trust not for several weeks yet. I shall nose about a bit. Roy, did it ever strike you how queer it is that this wonderfully beautiful country should contain no inhabitants?"

"It's like those splendid stretches of pools and rapids which one finds on every trout river and in which one never finds a fish," suggested Pierpont.

"Exactly,—and Heaven alone knows why," said Barris; "I suppose this country is shunned by human beings for the same mysterious reasons."

"The shooting is the better for it," I observed.

"The shooting is good," said Barris, "have you noticed the snipe on the meadow by the lake? Why it's brown with them! That's a wonderful meadow."

"It's a natural one," said Pierpont, "no human being ever cleared that land."

"Then it's supernatural," said Barris; "Pierpont, do you want to come with me?" Pierpont's handsome face flushed as he answered slowly, "It's awfully good of you,—if I may."

"Bosh," said I, piqued because he had asked Pierpont, "what use is little Willy without his man?"

"True," said Barris gravely, "you can't take Howlett you know."

Pierpont muttered something which ended in "d—n."

"Then," said I, "there will be but one gun on the Sweet Fern Covert this afternoon. Very well, I wish you joy of your cold supper and colder bed. Take your night-gown, Willy, and don't sleep on the damp ground."

"Let Pierpont alone," retorted Barris, "you shall go next time, Roy."

"Oh, all right,—you mean when there's shooting going on?"

"And I?" demanded Pierpont, grieved.

"You too, my son; stop quarelling! Will you ask Howlett to pack our kits—lightly mind you,—no bottles,—they clink."

"My flask doesn't," said Pierpont, and went off to get ready for a night's stalking of dangerous men.

"It is strange," said I, "that nobody ever settles in this region. How many people live in Cardinal Springs, Barris?"

"Twenty counting the telegraph operator and not counting the lumbermen; they are always changing and shifting. I have six men among them."

"Where have you no men? In the Four Hundred?"

"I have men there also,—chums of Billy's only he doesn't know it. David tells me that there was a strong flight of woodcock last night. You ought to pick up some this afternoon."

Then we chatted about alder-cover and swamp until Pierpont came out of the house and it was time to part.

"Au revoir," said Barris, buckling on his kit, "come along, Pierpont, and don't walk in the damp grass."

"If you are not back by to-morrow noon," said I, "I will take Howlett and David and hunt you up. You say your course is due north?"

"Due north," replied Barris, consulting his compass.

"There is a trail for two miles and a spotted lead for two more," said Pierpont.

"Which we won't use for various reasons," added Barris pleasantly; "don't worry, Roy, and keep your confounded expedition out of the way; there's no danger."

He knew, of course, what he was talking about and I held my peace.

When the tip end of Pierpont's shooting coat had disappeared in the Long Covert, I found myself standing alone with Howlett. He bore my gaze for a moment and then politely lowered his eyes.

"Howlett," said I, "take these shells and implements to the gun room, and drop nothing. Did Voyou come to any harm in the briers this morning?"

"No 'arm, Mr. Cardenhe, sir," said Howlett.

"Then be careful not to drop anything else," said I, and walked away leaving him decorously puzzled. For he had dropped no cartridges. Poor Howlett!

# III✦

About four o'clock that afternoon I met David and the dogs at the spinney which leads into the Sweet Fern Covert. The three setters, Voyou, Gamin, and Mioche were in fine feather,—David had killed a woodcock and a brace of grouse over them that morning,—and they were thrashing about the spinney at short range when I came up, gun under arm and pipe lighted.

"What's the prospect, David," I asked, trying to keep my feet in the tangle of wagging, whining dogs; "hello, what's amiss with Mioche?"

"A brier in his foot sir; I drew it and stopped the wound but I guess the gravel's got in. If you have no objection, sir, I might take him back with me."

"It's safer," I said; "take Gamin too, I only want one dog this afternoon. What is the situation?"

"Fair, sir; the grouse lie within a quarter of a mile of the oak second-growth. The woodcock are mostly on the alders. I saw any number of snipe on the meadows. There's something else in by the lake,—I can't just tell what, but the wood-duck set up a clatter when I was in the thicket and they come dashing through the wood as if a dozen foxes was snappin' at their tail feathers."

"Probably a fox," I said; "leash those dogs,—they must learn to stand it. I'll be back by dinner time."

"There is one more thing sir," said David, lingering with his gun under his arm.

"Well," said I.

"I saw a man in the woods by the Oak Covert,—at least I think I did."

"A lumberman?"

"I think not sir—at least,—do they have Chinamen among them?"

"Chinese? No. You didn't see a Chinaman in the woods here?"

"I—I think I did sir,—I can't say positively. He was gone when I ran into the covert."

"Did the dogs notice it?"

"I can't say—exactly. They acted queer like. Gamin here lay down and whined—it may have been colic—and Mioche whimpered,—perhaps it was the brier."

"And Voyou?"

"Voyou, he was most remarkable sir, and the hair on his back stood up. I did see a groundhog makin' for a tree near by."

"Then no wonder Voyou bristled. David, your Chinaman was a stump or tussock. Take the dogs now."

"I guess it was sir; good afternoon sir," said David, and walked away with the Gordons leaving me alone with Voyou in the spinney. I looked at the dog and he looked at me.

"Voyou!"

The dog sat down and danced with his fore feet, his beautiful brown eyes sparkling.

"You're a fraud," I said; "which shall it be, the alders or the upland? Upland? Good!—now for the grouse,—heel, my friend, and show your miraculous self-restraint."

Voyou wheeled into my tracks and followed close, nobly refusing to notice the impudent chipmunks and the thousand and one alluring and important smells which an ordinary dog would have lost no time in investigating.

The brown and yellow autumn woods were crisp with drifting heaps of leaves and twigs that crackled under foot as we turned from the spinney into the forest. Every silent little stream, hurrying toward the lake was gay with painted leaves afloat, scarlet maple or yellow oak. Spots of sunlight fell upon the pools, searching the brown depths, illuminating the gravel bottom where shoals of minnows swam to and fro, and to and fro again, busy with the purpose of their little lives. The crickets were chirping in the long brittle grass on the edge of the woods, but we left them far behind in the silence of the deeper forest.

"Now!" said I to Voyou.

The dog sprang to the front, circled once, zigzagged through the ferns around us and, all in a moment, stiffened stock still, rigid as sculptured bronze. I stepped forward, raising my gun, two paces, three paces, ten perhaps, before a great cock-grouse blundered up from the brake and burst through the thicket fringe toward the deeper growth. There was a flash and puff from my gun, a crash of echoes among the low wooded cliffs, and through the faint veil of smoke something dark dropped from mid-air amid a cloud of feathers, brown as the brown leaves under foot.

"Fetch!"

Up from the ground sprang Voyou, and in a moment he came galloping back, neck arched, tail stiff but waving, holding tenderly in his pink mouth a mass of mottled bronzed feathers. Very gravely he laid the bird at my feet and crouched close beside it, his silky ears across his paws, his muzzle on the ground.

I dropped the grouse into my pocket, held for a moment a silent caressing communion with Voyou, then swung my gun under my arm and motioned the dog on.

It must have been five o'clock when I walked into a little opening in the woods and sat down to breathe. Voyou came and sat down in front of me.

"Well?" I enquired.

Voyou gravely presented one paw which I took.

"We will never get back in time for dinner," said I, "so we might as well take it easy. It's all your fault, you know. Is there a brier in your foot?—let's see,—there! it's out my friend and you are free to nose about and lick it. If you loll your tongue out you'll get it all over twigs and moss. Can't you lie down and try to pant less? No, there is no use in sniffing and looking at that fern patch, for we are going to smoke a little, doze a little, and go home by moonlight. Think what a big dinner we will have! Think of Howlett's despair when we are not in time! Think of all the stories you will have to tell to Gamin and Mioche! Think what a good dog you have been! There—you are tired old chap; take forty winks with me."

Voyou was a little tired. He stretched out on the leaves at my feet but whether or not he really slept I could not be certain, until his hind legs twitched and I knew he was dreaming of mighty deeds.

Now I may have taken forty winks, but the sun seemed to be no lower when I sat up and unclosed my lids. Voyou raised his head, saw in my eyes that I was not going yet, thumped his tail half a dozen times on the dried leaves, and settled back with a sigh.

I looked lazily around, and for the first time noticed what a wonderfully beautiful spot I had chosen for a nap. It was an oval glade in the heart of the forest, level and carpeted with green grass. The trees that surrounded it were gigantic; they formed one towering circular wall of verdure, blotting out all except the turquoise blue of the sky-oval above. And now I noticed that in the centre of the greensward lay a pool of water, crystal clear, glimmering like a mirror in the meadow grass, beside a block of granite. It scarcely seemed possible that the symmetry of tree and lawn and lucent pool could have been one of nature's accidents. I had never before seen this glade nor had I ever heard it spoken of by either Pierpont or Barris. It was a marvel, this diamond clear basin, regular and graceful as a Roman fountain, set in the gem of turf. And these great trees,—they also belonged, not in America but in some legend-haunted forest of France, where moss-grown marbles stand neglected in dim glades, and the twilight of the forest shelters fairies and slender shapes from shadow-land.

I lay and watched the sunlight showering the tangled thicket where masses of crimson Cardinal-flowers glowed, or where one long dusty sunbeam tipped the edge of the floating leaves in the pool, turning them to palest gilt. There were birds too, passing through the dim avenues of trees like jets of flame,—the gorgeous Cardinal-Bird in his deep stained crimson robe,—the bird that gave to the woods, to the village fifteen miles away, to the whole county, the name of Cardinal.

I rolled over on my back and looked up at the sky. How pale,—paler than a robin's egg,—it was. I seemed to be lying at the bottom of a well, walled with verdure, high towering on every side. And, as I lay, all about me the air became sweet scented. Sweeter and sweeter and more penetrating grew the perfume, and I wondered what stray breeze, blowing over acres of lilies could have brought it. But there was no breeze; the air was still. A gilded fly alighted on my hand,—a honey-fly. It was as troubled as I by the scented silence.

Then, behind me, my dog growled.

I sat quite still at first, hardly breathing, but my eyes were fixed on a shape that moved along the edge of the pool among the meadow grasses. The dog had ceased growling and was now staring, alert and trembling.

At last I rose and walked rapidly down to the pool, my dog following close to heel.

The figure, a woman's, turned slowly toward us.

# IV.

She was standing still when I approached the pool. The forest around us was so silent that when I spoke the sound of my own voice startled me.

"No," she said,—and her voice was smooth as flowing water, "I have not lost my way. Will he come to me, your beautiful dog?"

Before I could speak, Voyou crept to her and laid his silky head against her knees.

"But surely," said I, "you did not come here alone."

"Alone? I did come alone."

"But the nearest settlement is Cardinal, probably nineteen miles from where we are standing."

"I do not know Cardinal," she said.

"Ste. Croix in Canada is forty miles at least,—how did you come into the Cardinal Woods?" I asked amazed.

"Into the woods?" she repeated a little impatiently.

"Yes."

She did not answer at first but stood caressing Voyou with gentle phrase and gesture.

"Your beautiful dog I am fond of, but I am not fond of being questioned," she said quietly. "My name is Ysonde and I came to the fountain here to see your dog."

I was properly quenched. After a moment or two I did say that in another hour it would be growing dusky, but she neither replied nor looked at me.

"This," I ventured, "is a beautiful pool,—you call it a fountain,—a delicious fountain: I have never before seen it. It is hard to imagine that nature did all this."

"Is it?" she said.

"Don't you think so?" I asked.

"I haven't thought; I wish when you go you would leave me your dog."

"My—my dog?"

"If you don't mind," she said sweetly, and looked at me for the first time in the face.

For an instant our glances met, then she grew grave, and I saw that her eyes were fixed on my forehead. Suddenly she rose and drew nearer, looking intently at my forehead. There was a faint mark there, a tiny crescent, just over my eyebrow. It was a birthmark.

"Is that a scar?" she demanded, drawing nearer.

"That crescent shaped mark? No."

"No? Are you sure?" she insisted.

"Perfectly," I replied, astonished.

"A—a birthmark?"

"Yes,—may I ask why?"

As she drew away from me, I saw that the color had fled from her cheeks. For a second she clasped both hands over her eyes as if to shut out my face, then slowly dropping her hands, she sat down on a long square block of stone which half encircled the basin, and on which to my amazement I saw carving. Voyou went to her again and laid his head in her lap.

"What is your name?" she asked at length.

"Roy Cardenhe."

"Mine is Ysonde. I carved these dragon-flies on the stone, these fishes and shells and butterflies you see."

"You! They are wonderfully delicate,—but those are not American dragon-flies—"

"No—they are more beautiful. See, I have my hammer and chisel with me."

She drew from a queer pouch at her side a small hammer and chisel and held them toward me.

"You are very talented," I said, "where did you study?"

"I? I never studied,—I knew how. I saw things and cut them out of stone. Do you like them? Some time I will show you other things that I have done. If I had a great lump of bronze I could make your dog, beautiful as he is."

Her hammer fell into the fountain and I leaned over and plunged my arm into the water to find it.

"It is there, shining on the sand," she said, leaning over the pool with me.

"Where," said I, looking at our reflected faces in the water. For it was only in the water that I had dared, as yet, to look her long in the face.

The pool mirrored the exquisite oval of her head, the heavy hair, the eyes. I heard the silken rustle of her girdle, I caught the flash of a white arm, and the hammer was drawn up dripping with spray.

The troubled surface of the pool grew calm and again I saw her eyes reflected.

"Listen," she said in a low voice, "do you think you will come again to my fountain?"

"I will come," I said. My voice was dull; the noise of water filled my ears.

Then a swift shadow sped across the pool; I rubbed my eyes. Where her reflected face had bent beside mine there was nothing mirrored but the rosy evening sky with one pale star glimmering. I drew myself up and

turned. She was gone. I saw the faint star twinkling above me in the afterglow, I saw the tall trees motionless in the still evening air, I saw my dog
slumbering at my feet.

The sweet scent in the air had faded, leaving in my nostrils the heavy
odor of fern and forest mould. A blind fear seized me, and I caught up my
gun and sprang into the darkening woods. The dog followed me, crashing through the undergrowth at my side. Duller and duller grew the light,
but I strode on, the sweat pouring from my face and hair, my mind a chaos.
How I reached the spinney I can hardly tell. As I turned up the path I
caught a glimpse of a human face peering at me from the darkening
thicket,—a horrible human face, yellow and drawn with high-boned
cheeks and narrow eyes.

Involuntarily I halted; the dog at my heels snarled. Then I sprang
straight at it, floundering blindly through the thicket, but the night had
fallen swiftly and I found myself panting and struggling in a maze of
twisted shrubbery and twining vines, unable to see the very undergrowth that ensnared me.

It was a pale face, and a scratched one that I carried to a late dinner that
night. Howlett served me, dumb reproach in his eyes, for the soup had been
standing and the grouse was juiceless.

David brought the dogs in after they had had their supper, and I drew
my chair before the blaze and set my ale on a table beside me. The dogs
curled up at my feet, blinking gravely at the sparks that snapped and flew
in eddying showers from the heavy birch logs.

"David," said I, "did you say you saw a Chinaman today?"

"I did sir."

"What do you think about it now?"

"I may have been mistaken sir—"

"But you think not. What sort of whiskey did you put in my flask today?"

"The usual sir."

"Is there much gone?"

"About three swallows sir, as usual."

"You don't suppose there could have been any mistake about that
whiskey,—no medicine could have gotten into it for instance."

David smiled and said, "No sir."

"Well," said I, "I have had an extraordinary dream."

When I said "dream," I felt comforted and reassured. I had scarcely dared
to say it before, even to myself.

"An extraordinary dream," I repeated; "I fell asleep in the woods about
five o'clock, in that pretty glade where the fountain—I mean the pool is.
You know the place?"

"I do not sir."

I described it minutely, twice, but David shook his head.

"Carved stone did you say sir? I never chanced on it. You don't mean the New Spring—"

"No, no! This glade is way beyond that. Is it possible that any people inhabit the forest between here and the Canada line?"

"Nobody short of Ste. Croix; at least I have no knowledge of any."

"Of course," said I, "when I thought I saw a Chinaman, it was imagination. Of course I had been more impressed than I was aware of by your adventure. Of course you saw no Chinaman, David."

"Probably not sir," replied David dubiously.

I sent him off to bed, saying I should keep the dogs with me all night; and when he was gone, I took a good long draught of ale, "just to shame the devil," as Pierpont said, and lighted a cigar. Then I thought of Barris and Pierpont, and their cold bed, for I knew they would not dare build a fire, and, in spite of the hot chimney corner and the crackling blaze, I shivered in sympathy.

"I'll tell Barris and Pierpont the whole story and take them to see the carved stone and the fountain," I thought to myself; "what a marvellous dream it was—Ysonde,—if it was a dream."

Then I went to the mirror and examined the faint white mark above my eyebrow.

## V.

About eight o'clock next morning, as I sat listlessly eyeing my coffee cup which Howlett was filling, Gamin and Mioche set up a howl, and in a moment more I heard Barris's step on the porch.

"Hello, Roy," said Pierpont, stamping into the dining room, "I want my breakfast by jingo! Where's Howlett,—none of your *café au lait* for me,— I want a chop and some eggs. Look at that dog, he'll wag the hinge off his tail in a moment—"

"Pierpont," said I, "this loquacity is astonishing but welcome. Where's Barris? You are soaked from neck to ankle."

Pierpont sat down and tore off his stiff muddy leggings.

"Barris is telephoning to Cardinal Springs,—I believe he wants some of his men,—down! Gamin, you idiot! Howlett, three eggs poached and more toast,—what was I saying? Oh, about Barris; he's struck something or other which he hopes will locate these gold-making fellows. I had a jolly time,— he'll tell you about it."

"Billy! Billy!" I said in pleased amazement, "you are learning to talk! Dear me! You load your own shells and you carry your own gun and you fire it yourself—hello! here's Barris all over mud. You fellows really ought to change your rig—whew! what a frightful odor!"

"It's probably this," said Barris tossing something onto the hearth where it shuddered for a moment and then began to writhe; "I found it in the woods by the lake. Do you know what it can be, Roy?"

To my disgust I saw it was another of those spidery wormy crablike creatures that Godfrey had in Tiffany's.

"I thought I recognized that acrid odor," I said; "for the love of the Saints take it away from the breakfast table, Barris!"

"But what is it?" he persisted, unslinging his field-glass and revolver.

"I'll tell you what I know after breakfast," I replied firmly, "Howlett, get a broom and sweep that thing into the road.—what are you laughing at, Pierpont?"

Howlett swept the repulsive creature out and Barris and Pierpont went to change their dew-soaked clothes for dryer raiment. David came to take the dogs for an airing and in a few minutes Barris reappeared and sat down in his place at the head of the table.

"Well," said I, "is there a story to tell?"

"Yes, not much. They are near the lake on the other side of the woods,— I mean these gold-makers. I shall collar one of them this evening. I haven't located the main gang with any certainty,—shove the toast rack this way will you, Roy,—no, I am not at all certain, but I've nailed one anyway. Pierpont was a great help, really,—and, what do you think, Roy? He wants to join the Secret Service!"

"Little Willy!"

"Exactly. Oh I'll dissuade him. What sort of a reptile was that I brought in? Did Howlett sweep it away?"

"He can sweep it back again for all I care," I said indifferently, "I've finished my breakfast."

"No," said Barris, hastily swallowing his coffee, "it's of no importance; you can tell me about the beast—"

"Serve you right if I had it brought in on toast," I returned.

Pierpont came in radiant, fresh from the bath.

"Go on with your story, Roy," he said; and I told them about Godfrey and his reptile pet.

"Now what in the name of common sense can Godfrey find interesting in that creature?" I ended, tossing my cigarette into the fireplace.

"It's Japanese, don't you think?" said Pierpont.

"No," said Barris, "it is not artistically grotesque, it's vulgar and horrible,—it looks cheap and unfinished—"

"Unfinished,—exactly," said I, "like an American humorist—"

"Yes," said Pierpont, "cheap. What about that gold serpent?"

"Oh, the Metropolitan Museum bought it; you must see it, it's marvellous."

Barris and Pierpont had lighted their cigarettes and, after a moment, we all rose and strolled out to the lawn, where chairs and hammocks were placed under the maple trees.

David passed, gun under arm, dogs heeling.

"Three guns on the meadows at four this afternoon," said Pierpont.

"Roy," said Barris as David bowed and started on, "what did you do yesterday?"

This was the question that I had been expecting. All night long I had dreamed of Ysonde and the glade in the woods, where, at the bottom of the crystal fountain, I saw the reflection of her eyes. All the morning while bathing and dressing I had been persuading myself that the dream was not worth recounting and that a search for the glade and the imaginary stone carving would be ridiculous. But now, as Barris asked the question, I suddenly decided to tell him the whole story.

"See here, you fellows," I said abruptly, "I am going to tell you something queer. You can laugh as much as you please too, but first I want to ask Barris a question or two. You have been in China, Barris?"

"Yes," said Barris, looking straight into my eyes.

"Would a Chinaman be likely to turn lumberman?"

"Have you seen a Chinaman?" he asked in a quiet voice.

"I don't know; David and I both imagined we did."

Barris and Pierpont exchanged glances.

"Have you seen one also?" I demanded, turning to include Pierpont.

"No," said Barris slowly; "but I know that there is, or has been, a Chinaman in these woods."

"The devil!" said I.

"Yes," said Barris gravely; "the devil, if you like,—a devil,—a member of the Kuen-Yuin."

I drew my chair close to the hammock where Pierpont lay at full length, holding out to me a ball of pure gold.

"Well?" said I, examining the engraving on its surface, which represented a mass of twisted creatures,—dragons, I supposed.

"Well," repeated Barris, extending his hand to take the golden ball, "this globe of gold engraved with reptiles and Chinese hieroglyphics is the symbol of the Kuen-Yuin."

"Where did you get it?" I asked, feeling that something startling was impending.

"Pierpont found it by the lake at sunrise this morning. It is the symbol of the Kuen-Yuin," he repeated, "the terrible Kuen-Yuin, the sorcerers of China, and the most murderously diabolical sect on earth."

We puffed our cigarettes in silence until Barris rose, and began to pace backward and forward among the trees, twisting his grey moustache.

"The Kuen-Yuin are sorcerers," he said, pausing before the hammock where Pierpont lay watching him; "I mean exactly what I say,—sorcerers. I've seen them,—I've seen them at their devilish business, and I repeat to you solemnly, that as there are angels above, there is a race of devils on earth, and they are sorcerers. Bah!" he cried, "talk to me of Indian magic and Yogis and all that clap-trap! Why, Roy, I tell you that the Kuen-Yuin have absolute control of a hundred millions of people, mind and body, body and soul. Do you know what goes on in the interior of China? Does Europe know,—could any human being conceive of the condition of that gigantic hell-pit? You read the papers, you hear diplomatic twaddle about Li Hung Chang and the Emperor, you see accounts of battles on sea and land, and you know that Japan has raised a toy tempest along the jagged edge of the great unknown. But you never before heard of the Kuen-Yuin; no, nor has any European except a stray missionary or two, and yet I tell you that when the fires from this pit of hell have eaten through the continent to the coast, the explosion will inundate half a world,—and God help the other half."

Pierpont's cigarette went out; he lighted another, and looked hard at Barris.

"But," resumed Barris quietly, "'sufficient unto the day,' you know,—I didn't intend to say as much as I did,—it would do no good,—even you and Pierpont will forget it,—it seems so impossible and so far away,—like the burning out of the sun. What I want to discuss is the possibility or probability of a Chinaman,—a member of the Kuen-Yuin, being here, at this moment, in the forest."

"If he is," said Pierpont, "possibly the gold-makers owe their discovery to him."

"I do not doubt it for a second," said Barris earnestly.

I took the little golden globe in my hand, and examined the characters engraved upon it.

"Barris," said Pierpont, "I can't believe in sorcery while I am wearing one of Sanford's shooting suits in the pocket of which rests an uncut volume of the 'Duchess.'"

"Neither can I," I said, "for I read the *Evening Post*, and I know Mr. Godkin would not allow it. Hello! What's the matter with this gold ball?"

"What is the matter?" said Barris grimly.

"Why—why—it's changing color—purple, no, crimson—no, it's green I mean—good Heavens! these dragons are twisting under my fingers—"

"Impossible!" muttered Pierpont, leaning over me; "those are not dragons—"

"No!" I cried excitedly; "they are pictures of that reptile that Barris brought back—see—see how they crawl and turn—"

"Drop it!" commanded Barris; and I threw the ball on the turf. In an instant we had all knelt down on the grass beside it, but the globe was again golden, grotesquely wrought with dragons and strange signs.

Pierpont, a little red in the face, picked it up, and handed it to Barris. He placed it on a chair, and sat down beside me.

"Whew!" said I, wiping the perspiration from my face, "how did you play us that trick, Barris?"

"Trick?" said Barris contemptuously.

I looked at Pierpont, and my heart sank. If this was not a trick, what was it? Pierpont returned my glance and colored, but all he said was, "It's devilish queer," and Barris answered, "Yes, devilish." Then Barris asked me again to tell my story, and I did, beginning from the time I met David in the spinney to the moment when I sprang into the darkening thicket where that yellow mask had grinned like a phantom skull.

"Shall we try to find the fountain?" I asked after a pause.

"Yes,—and—er—the lady," suggested Pierpont vaguely.

"Don't be an ass," I said a little impatiently, "you need not come, you know."

"Oh, I'll come," said Pierpont, "unless you think I am indiscreet—"

"Shut up, Pierpont," said Barris, "this thing is serious; I never heard of such a glade or such a fountain, but it's true that nobody knows this forest thoroughly. It's worth while trying for; Roy, can you find your way back to it?"

"Easily," I answered; "when shall we go?"

"It will knock our snipe shooting on the head," said Pierpont, "but then when one has the opportunity of finding a live dream-lady—"

I rose, deeply offended, but Pierpont was not very penitent and his laughter was irresistible.

"The lady's yours by right of discovery," he said, "I'll promise not to infringe on your dreams,—I'll dream about other ladies—"

"Come, come," said I, "I'll have Howlett put you to bed in a minute. Barris, if you are ready,—we can get back to dinner—"

Barris had risen and was gazing at me earnestly.

"What's the matter?" I asked nervously, for I saw that his eyes were fixed on my forehead, and I thought of Ysonde and the white crescent scar.

"Is that a birthmark?" said Barris.

"Yes—why, Barris?"

"Nothing,—an interesting coincidence—"

"What!—for Heaven's sake!"

"The scar,—or rather the birthmark. It is the print of the dragon's claw,—the crescent symbol of Yue-Laou—"

"And who the devil is Yue-Laou?" I said crossly.

"Yue-Laou,—the Moon Maker, Dzil-Nbu of the Kuen-Yuin;—it's Chinese Mythology, but it is believed that Yue-Laou has returned to rule the Kuen-Yuin—"

"The conversation," interrupted Pierpont, "smacks of peacocks' feathers and yellow-jackets. The chicken-pox has left its card on Roy, and Barris is guying us. Come on, you fellows, and make your call on the dream-lady. Barris, I hear galloping; here come your men."

Two mud splashed riders clattered up to the porch and dismounted at a motion from Barris. I noticed that both of them carried repeating rifles and heavy Colt's revolvers.

They followed Barris, deferentially, into the dining-room, and presently we heard the tinkle of plates and bottles and the low hum of Barris's musical voice.

Half an hour later they came out again, saluted Pierpont and me, and galloped away in the direction of the Canadian frontier. Ten minutes passed, and, as Barris did not appear, we rose and went into the house, to find him. He was sitting silently before the table, watching the small golden globe, now glowing with scarlet and orange fire, brilliant as a live coal. Howlett, mouth ajar, and eyes starting from the sockets, stood petrified behind him.

"Are you coming," asked Pierpont, a little startled. Barris did not answer. The globe slowly turned to pale gold again,—but the face that Barris raised to ours was white as a sheet. Then he stood up, and smiled with an effort which was painful to us all.

"Give me a pencil and a bit of paper," he said. Howlett brought it. Barris went to the window and wrote rapidly. He folded the paper, placed it in the top drawer of his desk, locked the drawer, handed me the key, and motioned us to precede him.

When again we stood under the maples, he turned to me with an impenetrable expression. "You will know when to use the key," he said: "Come, Pierpont, we must try to find Roy's fountain."

# VI.

At two o'clock that afternoon, at Barris's suggestion, we gave up the search for the fountain in the glade and cut across the forest to the spinney where David and Howlett were waiting with our guns and the three dogs.

Pierpont guyed me unmercifully about the "dream-lady" as he called her, and, but for the significant coincidence of Ysonde's and Barris's questions concerning the white scar on my forehead, I should long ago have been perfectly persuaded that I had dreamed the whole thing. As it was, I had no explanation to offer. We had not been able to find the glade although fifty times I came to landmarks which convinced me that we were just about to enter it. Barris was quiet, scarcely uttering a word to either of us during the entire search. I had never before seen him depressed in spirits. However, when we came in sight of the spinney where a cold bit of grouse and a bottle of Burgundy awaited each, Barris seemed to recover his habitual good humor.

"Here's to the dream-lady!" said Pierpont, raising his glass and standing up.

I did not like it. Even if she was only a dream, it irritated me to hear Pierpont's mocking voice. Perhaps Barris understood,—I don't know, but he bade Pierpont drink his wine without further noise, and that young man obeyed with a childlike confidence which almost made Barris smile.

"What about the snipe, David," I asked; "the meadows should be in good condition."

"There is not a snipe on the meadows, sir," said David solemnly.

"Impossible," exclaimed Barris, "they can't have left."

"They have, sir," said David in a sepulchral voice which I hardly recognized.

We all three looked at the old man curiously, waiting for his explanation of this disappointing but sensational report.

David looked at Howlett and Howlett examined the sky.

"I was going," began the old man, with his eyes fastened on Howlett, "I was going along by the spinney with the dogs when I heard a noise in the covert and I seen Howlett come walkin' very fast toward me. In fact," continued David, "I may say he was runnin'. Was you runnin', Howlett?"

Howlett said "Yes," with a decorous cough.

"I beg pardon," said David, "but I'd rather Howlett told the rest. He saw things which I did not."

"Go on, Howlett," commanded Pierpont, much interested.

Howlett coughed again behind his large red hand.

"What David says is true sir," he began; "I h'observed the dogs at a distance 'ow they was a workin' sir, and David stood a lightin' of 's pipe be'ind the spotted beech when I see a 'ead pop up in the covert 'oldin a stick like 'e was h'aimin' at the dogs sir—"

"A head holding a stick?" said Pierpont severely.

"The 'ead 'ad 'nds, sir," explained Howlett, "'ands that 'eld a painted stick,—like that, sir. 'Owlett, thinks I to meself, this 'ere's queer, so I jumps in an' runs, but the beggar 'e seen me an' w'en I comes alongside of David, 'e was gone. "Ello 'Owlett,' sez David, 'what the 'ell'—I beg pardon, sir,— "ow did you come 'ere,' sez 'e very loud. 'Run!' sez I, 'the Chinaman is harryin' the dawgs!' 'For Gawd's sake wot Chinaman?' sez David, h'aimin' 'is gun at every bush. Then I thinks I see 'im an' we run an' run, the dawgs a boundin' close to heel sir, but we don't see no Chinaman."

"I'll tell the rest," said David, as Howlett coughed and stepped in a modest corner behind the dogs.

"Go on," said Barris in a strange voice.

"Well sir, when Howlett and I stopped chasin', we was on the cliff overlooking the south meadow. I noticed that there was hundreds of birds there, mostly yellow-legs and plover, and Howlett seen them too. Then before I could say a word to Howlett, something out in the lake gave a splash—a splash as if the whole cliff had fallen into the water. I was that scared that I jumped straight into the bush and Howlett he sat down quick, and all those snipe wheeled up—there was hundreds,—all a squeelin' with fright, and the wood-duck came bowlin' over the meadows as if the old Nick was behind."

David paused and glanced meditatively at the dogs.

"Go on," said Barris in the same strained voice.

"Nothing more sir. The snipe did not come back."

"But that splash in the lake?"

"I don't know what it was sir."

"A salmon? A salmon couldn't have frightened the duck and the snipe that way?"

"No—oh no, sir. If fifty salmon had jumped they couldn't have made that splash. Couldn't they, Howlett?"

"No 'ow," said Howlett.

"Roy," said Barris at length, "what David tells us settles the snipe shooting for to-day. I am going to take Pierpont up to the house. Howlett and David will follow with the dogs,—I have something to say to them. If you care to come, come along; if not, go and shoot a brace of grouse for dinner and be back by eight if you want to see what Pierpont and I discovered last night."

David whistled Gamin and Mioche to heel and followed Howlett and his hamper toward the house. I called Voyou to my side, picked up my gun and turned to Barris.

"I will be back by eight," I said; "you are expecting to catch one of the gold-makers are you not?"

"Yes," said Barris listlessly.

Pierpont began to speak about the Chinaman but Barris motioned him to follow, and, nodding to me, took the path that Howlett and David had followed toward the house. When they disappeared I tucked my gun under my arm and turned sharply into the forest, Voyou trotting close to my heels.

In spite of myself the continued apparition of the Chinaman made me nervous. If he troubled me again I had fully decided to get the drop on him and find out what he was doing in the Cardinal Woods. If he could give no satisfactory account of himself I would march him in to Barris as a gold-making suspect,—I would march him in anyway, I thought, and rid the forest of his ugly face. I wondered what it was that David had heard in the lake. It must have been a big fish, a salmon, I thought; probably David's and Howlett's nerves were overwrought after their Celestial chase.

A whine from the dog broke the thread of my meditation and I raised my head. Then I stopped short in my tracks.

*The lost glade lay straight before me.*

Already the dog had bounded into it, across the velvet turf to the carved stone where a slim figure sat. I saw my dog lay his silky head lovingly against her silken kirtle; I saw her face bend above him, and I caught my breath and slowly entered the sun-lit glade.

Half timidly she held out one white hand.

"Now that you have come," she said, "I can show you more of my work. I told you that I could do other things besides these dragon-flies and moths carved here in stone. Why do you stare at me so? Are you ill?"

"Ysonde," I stammered.

"Yes," she said, with a faint color under her eyes.

"I—I never expected to see you again," I blurted out, "—you—I—I—thought I had dreamed—"

"Dreamed, of me? Perhaps you did, is that strange?"

"Strange? N—no—but—where did you go when—when we were leaning over the fountain together? I saw your face,—your face reflected beside mine and then—then suddenly I saw the blue sky and only a star twinkling."

"It was because you fell asleep," she said, "was it not?"

"I—asleep?"

"You slept—I thought you were very tired and I went back—"

"Back?—where?"

"Back to my home where I carve my beautiful images; see, here is one I brought to show you to-day."

I took the sculptured creature that she held toward me, a massive golden lizard with frail claw-spread wings of gold so thin that the sunlight burned through and fell on the ground in flaming gilded patches.

"Good Heavens!" I exclaimed, "this is astounding! Where did you learn to do such work? Ysonde, such a thing is beyond price!"

"Oh, I hope so," she said earnestly, "I can't bear to sell my work, but my step-father takes it and sends it away. This is the second thing I have done and yesterday he said I must give it to him. I suppose he is poor."

"I don't see how he can be poor if he gives you gold to model in," I said, astonished.

"Gold!" she exclaimed, "gold! He has a room full of gold! He makes it."

I sat down on the turf at her feet completely unnerved.

"Why do you look at me so?" she asked, a little troubled.

"Where does your step-father live?" I said at last.

"Here."

"Here!"

"In the woods near the lake. You could never find our house."

"A house!"

"Of course. Did you think I lived in a tree? How silly. I live with my step-father in a beautiful house,—a small house, but very beautiful. He makes his gold there but the men who carry it away never come to the house, for they don't know where it is and if they did they could not get in. My step-father carries the gold in lumps to a canvas satchel. When the satchel is full he takes it out into the woods where the men live and I don't know what they do with it. I wish he could sell the gold and become rich for then I could go back to Yian where all the gardens are sweet and the river flows under the thousand bridges."

"Where is this city?" I asked faintly.

"Yian? I don't know. It is sweet with perfume and the sound of silver bells all day long. Yesterday I carried a blossom of dried lotus buds from Yian, in my breast, and all the woods were fragrant. Did you smell it?"

"Yes."

"I wondered, last night, whether you did. How beautiful your dog is; I love him. Yesterday I thought most about your dog but last night—"

"Last night," I repeated below my breath.

"I thought of you. Why do you wear the dragon-claw?"

I raised my hand impulsively to my forehead, covering the scar.

"What do you know of the dragon-claw?" I muttered.

"It is the symbol of Yue-Laou, and Yue-Laou rules the Kuen-Yuin, my step-father says. My step-father tells me everything that I know. We lived in Yian until I was sixteen years old. I am eighteen now; that is two years we have lived in the forest. Look!—see those scarlet birds! What are they? There are birds of the same color in Yian."

"Where is Yian, Ysonde?" I asked with deadly calmness.

"Yian? I don't know."

"But you have lived there?"

"Yes, a very long time."

"Is it across the ocean, Ysonde?"

"It is across seven oceans and the great river which is longer than from the earth to the moon."

"Who told you that?"

"Who? My step-father; he tells me everything."

"Will you tell me his name, Ysonde?"

"I don't know it, he is my step-father, that is all."

"And what is your name?"

"You know it, Ysonde."

"Yes, but what other name."

"That is all, Ysonde. Have you two names? Why do you look at me so impatiently?"

"Does your step-father make gold? Have you seen him make it?"

"Oh yes. He made it also in Yian and I loved to watch the sparks at night whirling like golden bees. Yian is lovely,—if it is all like our garden and the gardens around. I can see the thousand bridges from my garden and the white mountain beyond—"

"And the people—tell me of the people, Ysonde!" I urged gently.

"The people of Yian? I could see them in swarms like ants—oh! many, many millions crossing and recrossing the thousand bridges."

"But how did they look? Did they dress as I do?"

"I don't know. They were very far away, moving specks on the thousand bridges. For sixteen years I saw them every day from my garden but I never went out of my garden into the streets of Yian, for my step-father forbade me."

"You never saw a living creature near by in Yian?" I asked in despair.

"My birds, oh such tall, wise-looking birds, all over grey and rose color."

She leaned over the gleaming water and drew her polished hand across the surface.

"Why do you ask me these questions," she murmured; "are you displeased?"

"Tell me about your step-father," I insisted. "Does he look as I do? Does he dress, does he speak as I do? Is he American?"

"American? I don't know. He does not dress as you do and he does not look as you do. He is old, very, very old. He speaks sometimes as you do, sometimes as they do in Yian. I speak also in both manners."

"Then speak as they do in Yian," I urged impatiently, "speak as—why, Ysonde! why are you crying? Have I hurt you?—I did not intend,—I did not dream of your caring! There Ysonde, forgive me,—see, I beg you on my knees here at your feet."

I stopped, my eyes fastened on a small golden ball which hung from her waist by a golden chain. I saw it trembling against her thigh, I saw it change color, now crimson, now purple, now flaming scarlet. It was the symbol of the KuenYuin.

She bent over me and laid her fingers gently on my arm.

"Why do you ask me such things?" she said, while the tears glistened on her lashes. "It hurts me here,—" she pressed her hand to her breast,—"it pains.—I don't know why. Ah, now your eyes are hard and cold again; you are looking at the golden globe which hangs from my waist. Do you wish to know also what that is?"

"Yes," I muttered, my eyes fixed on the infernal color flames which subsided as I spoke, leaving the ball a pale gilt again.

"It is the symbol of the Kuen-Yuin," she said in a trembling voice; "why do you ask?"

"Is it yours?"

"Y—yes."

"Where did you get it?" I cried harshly.

"My—my step fa—"

Then she pushed me away from her with all the strength of her slender wrists and covered her face.

If I slipped my arm about her and drew her to me,—if I kissed away the tears that fell slowly between her fingers,—if I told her how I loved her—how it cut me to the heart to see her unhappy,—after all that is my own business. When she smiled through her tears, the pure love and sweetness in her eyes lifted my soul higher than the high moon vaguely glimmering through the sun-lit blue above. My happiness was so sudden, so fierce and overwhelming that I only knelt there, her fingers clasped in mine, my eyes raised to the blue vault and the glimmering moon. Then something in the long grass beside me moved close to my knees and a damp acrid odor filled my nostrils.

"Ysonde!" I cried, but the touch of her hand was already gone and my two clenched fists were cold and damp with dew.

"Ysonde!" I called again, my tongue stiff with fright;—but I called as one awaking from a dream—a horrid dream, for my nostrils quivered with the damp acrid odor and I felt the crab-reptile clinging to my knee. Why had the night fallen so swiftly,—and where was I—where?—stiff, chilled, torn, and bleeding, lying flung like a corpse over my own threshold with Voyou licking my face and Barris stooping above me in the light of a lamp that flared and smoked in the night breeze like a torch. Faugh! the choking stench of the lamp aroused me and I cried out:

"Ysonde!"

"What the devil's the matter with him?" muttered Pierpont, lifting me in his arms like a child, "has he been stabbed, Barris?"

# VII.

In a few minutes I was able to stand and walk stiffly into my bedroom where Howlett had a hot bath ready and a hotter tumbler of Scotch. Pierpont sponged the blood from my throat where it had coagulated. The cut was slight, almost invisible, a mere puncture from a thorn. A shampoo cleared my mind, and a cold plunge and alcohol friction did the rest.

"Now," said Pierpont, "swallow your hot Scotch and lie down. Do you want a broiled woodcock? Good, I fancy you are coming about."

Barris and Pierpont watched me as I sat on the edge of the bed, solemnly chewing on the woodcock's wishbone and sipping my Bordeaux, very much at my ease.

Pierpont sighed his relief.

"So," he said pleasantly, "it was a mere case of ten dollars or ten days. I thought you had been stabbed—"

"I was not intoxicated," I replied, serenely picking up a bit of celery.

"Only jagged?" enquired Pierpont, full of sympathy.

"Nonsense," said Barris, "let him alone. Want some more celery, Roy?— it will make you sleep."

"I don't want to sleep," I answered; "when are you and Pierpont going to catch your Gold-maker?"

Barris looked at his watch and closed it with a snap.

"In an hour; you don't propose to go with us?"

"But I do,—toss me a cup of coffee, Pierpont, will you,—that's just what I propose to do. Howlett, bring the new box of Panatella's,—the mild imported;—and leave the decanter. Now Barris, I'll be dressing, and you and Pierpont keep still and listen to what I have to say. Is that door shut tight?"

Barris locked it and sat down.

"Thanks," said I. "Barris, where is the city of Yian?"

An expression akin to terror flashed into Barris's eyes and I saw him stop breathing for a moment.

"There is no such city," he said at length, "have I been talking in my sleep?"

"It is a city," I continued, calmly, "where the river winds under the thousand bridges, where the gardens are sweet scented and the air is filled with the music of silver bells—"

"Stop!" gasped Barris, and rose trembling from his chair. He had grown ten years older.

"Roy," interposed Pierpont coolly, "what the deuce are you harrying Barris for?"

I looked at Barris and he looked at me. After a second or two he sat down again.

"Go on, Roy," he said.

"I must," I answered, "for now I am certain that I have not dreamed."

I told them everything; but, even as I told it, the whole thing seemed so vague, so unreal, that at times I stopped with the hot blood tingling in my ears, for it seemed impossible that sensible men, in the year of our Lord 1896 could seriously discuss such matters.

I feared Pierpont, but he did not even smile. As for Barris, he sat with his handsome head sunk on his breast, his unlighted pipe clasped tight in both hands.

When I had finished, Pierpont turned slowly and looked at Barris. Twice he moved his lips as if about to ask something and then remained mute.

"Yian is a city," said Barris, speaking dreamily; "was that what you wished to know, Pierpont?"

He nodded silently.

"Yian is a city," repeated Barris, "where the great river winds under the thousand bridges,—where the gardens are sweet scented, and the air is filled with the music of silver bells."

My lips formed the question, "Where is this city?"

"It lies," said Barris, almost querulously, "across the seven oceans and the river which is longer than from the earth to the moon."

"What do you mean?" said Pierpont.

"Ah," said Barris, rousing himself with an effort and raising his sunken eyes, "I am using the allegories of another land; let it pass. Have I not told you of the Kuen-Yuin? Yian is the centre of the Kuen-Yuin. It lies hidden in that gigantic shadow called China, vague and vast as the midnight Heavens,—a continent unknown, impenetrable."

"Impenetrable," repeated Pierpont below his breath.

"I have seen it," said Barris dreamily. "I have seen the dead plains of Black Cathay and I have crossed the mountains of Death, whose summits are above the atmosphere. I have seen the shadow of Xangi cast across Abaddon. Better to die a million miles from Yezd and Ater Quedah than to have seen the white water-lotus close in the shadow of Xangi! I have slept among the ruins of Xaindu where the winds never cease and the Wulwulleh is wailed by the dead."

"And Yian," I urged gently.

There was an unearthly look on his face as he turned slowly toward me.

"Yian,—I have lived there—and loved there: When the breath of my body shall cease, when the dragon's claw shall fade from my arm,"—he tore up his sleeve, and we saw a white crescent shining above his elbow,—"when the light of my eyes has faded forever, then, even then I shall not forget the city of Yian. Why, it is my home,—mine! The river and the thousand bridges, the white peak beyond, the sweet-scented gardens, the lilies, the pleasant noise of the summer wind laden with bee music and the music of bells,—all these are mine. Do you think because the Kuen-Yuin feared the dragon's claw on my arm that my work with them is ended? Do you think that because Yue-Laou could give, that I acknowledge his right to take away? Is he Xangi in whose shadow the white water-lotus dares not raise its head? No! No!" he cried violently, "it was not from Yue-Laou, the sorcerer, the Maker of Moons, that my happiness came! It was real, it was not a shadow to vanish like a tinted bubble! Can a sorcerer create and give a man the woman he loves? Is Yue-Laou as great as Xangi then? Xangi is God. In His own time, in His infinite goodness and mercy He will bring me again to the woman I love. And I know she waits for me at God's feet."

In the strained silence that followed I could hear my heart's double beat and I saw Pierpont's face, blanched and pitiful. Barris shook himself and raised his head. The change in his ruddy face frightened me.

"Heed!" he said, with a terrible glance at me; "the print of the dragon's claw is on your forehead and Yue-Laou knows it. If you must love, then love like a man, for you will suffer like a soul in hell, in the end. What is her name again?"

"Ysonde," I answered simply.

# VIII.

At nine o'clock that night we caught one of the gold-makers. I do not know how Barris had laid his trap; all I saw of the affair can be told in a minute or two.

We were posted on the Cardinal road about a mile below the house, Pierpont and I with drawn revolvers on one side, under a butternut tree, Barris on the other, a Winchester across his knees.

I had just asked Pierpont the hour, and he was feeling for his watch when far up the road we heard the sound of a galloping horse, nearer, nearer, clattering, thundering past. Then Barris's rifle spat flame and the dark mass, horse and rider, crashed into the dust. Pierpont had the half stunned horseman by the collar in a second,—the horse was stone dead,—and, as we lighted a pine knot to examine the fellow, Barris's two riders galloped up and drew bridle beside us.

"Hm!" said Barris with a scowl, "it's the 'Shiner,' or I'm a moonshiner."

We crowded curiously around to see the "Shiner." He was red-headed, fat and filthy, and his little red eyes burned in his head like the eyes of an angry pig.

Barris went through his pockets methodically while Pierpont held him and I held the torch. The Shiner was a gold mine; pockets, shirt, bootlegs, hat, even his dirty fists, clutched tight and bleeding, were bursting with lumps of soft yellow gold. Barris dropped this "moonshine gold," as we had come to call it, into the pockets of his shooting-coat, and withdrew to question the prisoner. He came back again in a few minutes and motioned his mounted men to take the Shiner in charge. We watched them, rifle on thigh, walking their horses slowly away into the darkness, the Shiner, tightly bound, shuffling sullenly between them.

"Who is the Shiner?" asked Pierpont, slipping the revolver into his pocket again.

"A moonshiner, counterfeiter, forger, and highwayman," said Barris, "and probably a murderer. Drummond will be glad to see him, and I think it likely he will be persuaded to confess to him what he refuses to confess to me."

"Wouldn't he talk?" I asked.

"Not a syllable. Pierpont, there is nothing more for you to do."

"For me to do? Are you not coming back with us, Barris?"

"No," said Barris.

We walked along the dark road in silence for a while, I wondering what Barris intended to do, but he said nothing more until we reached our own verandah. Here he held out his hand, first to Pierpont, then to me, saying good-bye as though he were going on a long journey.

"How soon will you be back?" I called out to him as he turned away toward the gate. He came across the lawn again and again took our hands with a quiet affection that I had never imagined him capable of.

"I am going," he said, "to put an end to his gold-making to-night. I know that you fellows have never suspected what I was about on my little solitary evening strolls after dinner. I will tell you. Already I have unobtrusively killed four of these gold-makers,—my men put them under ground just below the new wash-out at the four mile stone. There are three left alive,—the Shiner whom we have, another criminal named 'Yellow,' or 'Yaller' in the vernacular, and the third—"

"The third," repeated Pierpont, excitedly.

"The third I have never yet seen. But I know who and what he is,—I know; and if he is of human flesh and blood, his blood will flow to-night."

As he spoke a slight noise across the turf attracted my attention. A mounted man was advancing silently in the starlight over the spongy meadowland. When he came nearer Barris struck a match, and we saw that he bore a corpse across his saddle bow.

"Yaller, Colonel Barris," said the man, touching his slouched hat in salute.

This grim introduction to the corpse made me shudder, and, after a moment's examination of the stiff wide-eyed dead man, I drew back.

"Identified," said Barris, "take him to the four mile post and carry his effects to Washington,—under seal, mind, Johnstone."

Away cantered the rider with his ghastly burden, and Barris took our hands once more for the last time. Then he went away, gaily, with a jest on his lips, and Pierpont and I turned back into the house.

For an hour we sat moodily smoking in the hall before the fire, saying little until Pierpont burst out with: "I wish Barris had taken one of us with him to-night!"

The same thought had been running in my mind, but I said: "Barris knows what he's about." This observation neither comforted us nor opened the lane to further conversation, and after a few minutes Pierpont said good night and called for Howlett and hot water. When he had been warmly tucked away by Howlett, I turned out all but one lamp, sent the dogs away with David and dismissed Howlett for the night.

I was not inclined to retire for I knew I could not sleep. There was a book lying open on the table beside the fire and I opened it and read a page or two, but my mind was fixed on other things.

The window shades were raised and I looked out at the star-set firmament. There was no moon that night but the sky was dusted all over with sparkling stars and a pale radiance, brighter even than moonlight, fell over meadow and wood. Far away in the forest I heard the voice of the wind, a soft warm wind that whispered a name, Ysonde.

"Listen," sighed the voice of the wind, and "listen" echoed the swaying trees with every little leaf a-quiver. I listened.

Where the long grasses trembled with the cricket's cadence I heard her name, Ysonde; I heard it in the rustling woodbine where grey moths hovered; I heard it in the drip, drip, drip of the dew from the porch. The silent meadow brook whispered her name, the rippling woodland streams repeated it, Ysonde, Ysonde, until all earth and sky were filled with the soft trill, Ysonde, Ysonde, Ysonde.

A night-thrush sang in a thicket by the porch and I stole to the verandah to listen. After a while it began again, a little further on. I ventured out into the road. Again I heard it far away in the forest and I followed it, for I knew it was the singing of Ysonde.

When I came to the path that leaves the main road and enters the Sweet Fern Covert below the spinney, I hesitated; but the beauty of the night lured me on and the night-thrushes called me from every thicket. In the starry radiance, shrubs, grasses, field flowers, stood out distinctly, for there was no moon to cast shadows. Meadow and brook, grove and stream, were illuminated by the pale glow. Like great lamps lighted the planets hung from the high domed sky and through their mysterious rays the fixed stars, calm, serene, stared from the heavens like eyes.

I waded on waist deep through fields of dewy golden-rod, through late clover and wild-oat wastes, through crimson fruited sweetbrier, blueberry, and wild plum, until the low whisper of the Wier Brook warned me that the path had ended.

But I would not stop, for the night air was heavy with the perfume of water-lilies and far away, across the low wooded cliffs and the wet meadowland beyond, there was a distant gleam of silver, and I heard the murmur of sleepy waterfowl. I would go to the lake. The way was clear except for the dense young growth and the snares of the moose-bush.

The night-thrushes had ceased but I did not want for the company of living creatures. Slender, quick darting forms crossed my path at intervals, sleek mink, that fled like shadows at my step, wiry weasels and fat muskrats, hurrying onward to some tryst or killing.

I never had seen so many little woodland creatures on the move at night. I began to wonder where they all were going so fast, why they all hurried on in the same direction. Now I passed a hare hopping through the brushwood, now a rabbit scurrying by, flag hoisted. As I entered the beech second-growth two foxes glided by me; a little further on a doe crashed out of the underbrush, and close behind her stole a lynx, eyes shining like coals.

He neither paid attention to the doe nor to me, but loped away toward the north.

The lynx was in flight.

"From what?" I asked myself, wondering. There was no forest fire, no cyclone, no flood.

If Barris had passed that way could he have stirred up this sudden exodus? Impossible; even a regiment in the forest could scarcely have put to rout these frightened creatures.

"What on earth," thought I, turning to watch the headlong flight of a fisher-cat, "what on earth has started the beasts out at this time of night."

I looked up into the sky. The placid glow of the fixed stars comforted me and I stepped on through the narrow spruce belt that leads down to the borders of the Lake of the Stars.

Wild cranberry and moose-bush entwined my feet, dewy branches spattered me with moisture, and the thick spruce needles scraped my face as I threaded my way over mossy logs and deep spongy tussocks down to the level gravel of the lake shore.

Although there was no wind the little waves were hurrying in from the lake and I heard them splashing among the pebbles. In the pale star glow thousands of water-lilies lifted their half-closed chalices toward the sky.

I threw myself full length upon the shore, and, chin on hand, looked out across the lake. Splash, splash, came the waves along the shore, higher, nearer, until a film of water, thin and glittering as a knife blade, crept up to my elbows. I could not understand it; the lake was rising, but there had been no rain. All along the shore the water was running up; I heard the waves among the sedge grass; the weeds at my side were awash in the ripples. The lilies rocked on the tiny waves, every wet pad rising on the swells, sinking, rising again until the whole lake was glimmering with undulating blossoms. How sweet and deep was the fragrance from the lilies. And now the water was ebbing, slowly, and the waves receded, shrinking from the shore rim until the white pebbles appeared again, shining like froth on a brimming glass.

No animal swimming out in the darkness along the shore, no heavy salmon surging, could have set the whole shore aflood as though the wash from a great boat were rolling in. Could it have been the overflow, through the Weir Brook, of some cloud-burst far back in the forest? This was the only way I could account for it, and yet when I had crossed the Wier Brook I had not noticed that it was swollen.

And as I lay there thinking, a faint breeze sprang up and I saw the surface of the lake whiten with lifted lily pads.

All around me the alders were sighing; I heard the forest behind me stir; the crossed branches rubbing softly, bark against bark. Something—it may have been an owl—sailed out of the night, dipped, soared, and was again engulfed, and far across the water I heard its faint cry, Ysonde.

Then first, for my heart was full, I cast myself down upon my face, calling on her name. My eyes were wet when I raised my head,—for the spray from the shore was drifting in again,—and my heart beat heavily; "No more, no more." But my heart lied, for even as I raised my face to the calm stars, I saw her standing still, close beside me; and very gently I spoke her name, Ysonde. She held out both hands.

"I was lonely," she said, "and I went to the glade, but the forest is full of frightened creatures and they frightened me. Has anything happened in the woods? The deer are running toward the heights."

Her hand still lay in mine as we moved along the shore, and the lapping of the water on rock and shallow was no lower than our voices.

"Why did you leave me without a word, there at the fountain in the glade?" she said.

"I leave you!—"

"Indeed you did, running swiftly with your dog, plunging through thickets and brush,—oh —you frightened me."

"Did I leave you so?"

"Yes—after—"

"After?"

"You had kissed me—"

Then we leaned down together and looked into the black water set with stars, just as we had bent together over the fountain in the glade.

"Do you remember?" I asked.

"Yes. See, the water is inlaid with silver stars,—everywhere white lilies floating and the stars below, deep, deep down."

"What is the flower you hold in your hand?"

"White water-lotus."

"Tell me about Yue-Laou, Dzil Nbu of the Kuen-Yuin," I whispered, lifting her head so I could see her eyes.

"Would it please you to hear?"

"Yes, Ysonde."

"All that I know is yours, now, as I am yours, all that I am. Bend closer. Is it of Yue-Laou you would know? Yue-Laou is Dzil-Nbu of the Kuen-Yuin. He lived in the Moon. He is old—very, very old, and once, before he came to rule the Kuen-Yuin, he was the old man who unites with a silken cord all predestined couples, after which nothing can prevent their union. But all that is changed since he came to rule the Kuen-Yuin. Now he has perverted the Xin,—the good genii of China,—and has fashioned from their warped bodies a monster which he calls the Xin. This monster is horrible, for it not only lives in its own body, but it has thousands of loathsome satellites,—living creatures without mouths, blind, that move when the Xin moves, like a mandarin and his escort. They are part of the Xin although they are not attached. Yet if one of these satellites is injured the Xin writhes with agony. It is fearful—this huge living bulk and these creatures spread out like severed fingers that wriggle around a hideous hand."

"Who told you this?"

"My step-father."

"Do you believe it?"

"Yes. I have seen one of the Xin's creatures."

"Where, Ysonde?"

"Here in these woods."

"Then you believe there is a Xin here?"

"There must be,—perhaps in the lake—"

"Oh, Xins inhabit lakes?"

"Yes, and the seven seas. I am not afraid here."

"Why?"

"Because I wear the symbol of the Kuen-Yuin."

"Then I am not safe," I smiled.

"Yes you are, for I hold you in my arms. Shall I tell you more about the Xin? When the Xin is about to do to death a man, the Yeth-hounds gallop through the night—"

"What are the Yeth-hounds, Ysonde?"

"The Yeth-hounds are dogs without heads. They are the spirits of murdered children, which pass through the woods at night, making a wailing noise."

"Do you believe this?"

"Yes, for I have worn the yellow lotus—"

"The yellow lotus—"

"Yellow is the symbol of faith—"

"Where?"

"In Yian," she said faintly.

After a while I said, "Ysonde, you know there is a God?"

"God and Xangi are one."

"Have you ever heard of Christ?"

"No," she answered softly.

The wind began again among the tree tops. I felt her hands closing in mine.

"Ysonde," I asked again, "do you believe in sorcerers?"

"Yes, the Kuen-Yuin are sorcerers; Yue-Laou is a sorcerer."

"Have you seen sorcery?"

"Yes, the reptile satellite of the Xin—"

"Anything else ?"

"My charm,—the golden ball, the symbol of the Kuen-Yuin. Have you seen it change,—have you seen the reptiles writhe—?"

"Yes," said I shortly, and then remained silent, for a sudden shiver of apprehension had seized me. Barris also had spoken gravely, ominously of the sorcerers, the Kuen-Yuin, and I had seen with my own eyes the graven reptiles turning and twisting on the glowing globe.

"Still," said I aloud, "God lives and sorcery is but a name."

"Ah," murmured Ysonde, drawing closer to me, "they say, in Yian, the Kuen-Yuin live; God is but a name."

"They lie," I whispered fiercely.

"Be careful," she pleaded, "they may hear you. Remember that you have the mark of the dragon's claw on your brow."

"What of it?" I asked, thinking also of the white mark on Barris's arm.

"Ah don't you know that those who are marked with the dragon's claw are followed by Yue-Laou, for good or for evil,—and the evil means death if you offend him?"

"Do you believe that!" I asked impatiently.

"I know it," she sighed.

"Who told you all this? Your step-father? What in Heaven's name is he then,—a Chinaman!"

"I don't know; he is not like you."

"Have—have you told him anything about me?"

"He knows about you—no, I have told him nothing,—ah, what is this—see—it is a cord, a cord of silk about your neck—and about mine!"

"Where did that come from?" I asked astonished.

"It must be—it must be Yue-Laou who binds me to you,—it is as my step-father said—he said Yue-Laou would bind us—"

"Nonsense," I said almost roughly, and seized the silken cord, but to my amazement it melted in my hand like smoke.

"What is all this damnable jugglery!" I whispered angrily, but my anger vanished as the words were spoken, and a convulsive shudder shook me to the feet. Standing on the shore of the lake, a stone's throw away, was a figure, twisted and bent,—a little old man, blowing sparks from a live coal which he held in his naked hand. The coal glowed with increasing radiance, lighting up the skull-like face above it, and threw a red glow over the sands at his feet. But the face!—the ghastly Chinese face on which the light flickered,—and the snaky slitted eyes, sparkling as the coal glowed hotter. Coal! It was not a coal but a golden globe staining the night with crimson flames,—it was the symbol of the Kuen-Yuin.

"See! See!" gasped Ysonde, trembling violently, "see the moon rising from between his fingers! Oh I thought it was my step-father and it is Yue-Laou the Maker of Moons—no! no! it is my step-father—ah God! they are the same!"

Frozen with terror I stumbled to my knees, groping for my revolver which bulged in my coat pocket; but something held me—something which bound me like a web in a thousand strong silky meshes. I struggled and turned but the web grew tighter; it was over us—all around us, drawing, pressing us into each other's arms until we lay side by side, bound hand and body and foot, palpitating, panting like a pair of netted pigeons.

And the creature on the shore below! What was my horror to see a moon, huge, silvery, rise like a bubble from between his fingers, mount higher, higher into the still air and hang aloft in the midnight sky, while another moon rose from his fingers, and another and yet another until the vast span of Heaven was set with moons and the earth sparkled like a diamond in the white glare.

A great wind began to blow from the east and it bore to our ears a long mournful howl,—a cry so unearthly that for a moment our hearts stopped.

"The Yeth-hounds!" sobbed Ysonde, "do you hear—they are passing through the forest! The Xin is near!"

Then all around us in the dry sedge grasses came a rustle as if some small animals were creeping, and a damp acrid odor filled the air. I knew the smell, I saw the spidery crab-like creatures swarm out around me and drag their soft yellow hairy bodies across the shrinking grasses. They passed, hundreds of them, poisoning the air, tumbling, writhing, crawling with their blind mouthless heads raised. Birds, half asleep and confused by the darkness fluttered away before them in helpless fright, rabbits sprang from their forms, weasels glided away like flying shadows. What remained of the forest creatures rose and fled from the loathsome invasion; I heard the squeak of a terrified hare, the snort of stampeding deer, and the lumbering gallop of a bear; and all the time I was choking, half suffocated by the poisoned air.

Then, as I struggled to free myself from the silken snare about me, I cast a glance of deadly fear at the sorcerer below, and at the same moment I saw him turn in his tracks.

"Halt!" cried a voice from the bushes.

"Barris!" I shouted, half leaping up in my agony.

I saw the sorcerer spring forward, I heard the bang! bang! bang! of a revolver, and, as the sorcerer fell on the water's edge, I saw Barris jump out into the white glare and fire again, once, twice, three times, into the writhing figure at his feet.

Then an awful thing occurred. Up out of the black lake reared a shadow, a nameless shapeless mass, headless, sightless, gigantic, gaping from end to end.

A great wave struck Barris and he fell, another washed him up on the pebbles, another whirled him back into the water and then,—and then the thing fell over him,—and I fainted.

□  □  □

This, then, is all that I know concerning Yue-Laou and the Xin. I do not fear the ridicule of scientists or of the press for I have told the truth. Barris is gone and the thing that killed him is alive to-day in the Lake of the Stars while the spider-like satellites roam through the Cardinal Woods. The game has fled, the forests around the lake are empty of any living creatures save the reptiles that creep when the Xin moves in the depths of the lake.

General Drummond knows what he has lost in Barris, and we, Pierpont and I, know what we have lost also. His will we found in the drawer, the key of which he had handed me. It was wrapped in a bit of paper on which was written:

"Yue-Laou the sorcerer is here in the Cardinal Woods. I must kill him or he will kill me. He made and gave to me the woman I loved,—he made her,—I saw him,—he made her out of a white water-lotus bud. When our child was born, he came again before me and demanded from me the woman I loved. Then, when I refused, he went away, and that night my wife and child vanished from my side, and I found upon her pillow a white lotus bud. Roy, the woman of your dream, Ysonde, may be my child. God help you if you love her for Yue-Laou will give,— and take away, as though he were Xangi, which is God. I will kill Yue-Laou before I leave this forest,—or he will kill me.
                                        FRANKLYN BARRIS."

Now the world knows what Barris thought of the Kuen-Yuin and of Yue-Laou. I see that the newspapers are just becoming excited over the glimpses that Li-Hung-Chang has afforded them of Black Cathay and the demons of the Kuen Yuin. The Kuen-Yuin are on the move.

Pierpont and I have dismantled the shooting-box in the Cardinal Woods. We hold ourselves ready at a moment's notice to join and lead the first Government party to drag the Lake of the Stars and cleanse the forest of the crab reptiles. But it will be necessary that a large force assembles, and a well-armed force, for we never have found the body of Yue-Laou, and, living or dead, I fear him. Is he living?

Pierpont, who found Ysonde and myself lying unconscious on the lake shore, the morning after, saw no trace of corpse or blood on the sands. He may have fallen into the lake, but I fear and Ysonde fears that he is alive. We never were able to find either her dwelling place or the glade and the fountain again. The only thing that remains to her of her former life is the gold serpent in the Metropolitan Museum and her golden globe, the symbol of the Kuen-Yuin; but the latter no longer changes color.

"There was never any more inception than there is now,
Nor any more youth or age than there is now;
And will never be any more perfection than there is now,
Nor any more heaven or hell than there is now."

WALT WHITMAN.

# THE SILENT LAND

"And the woman fled into the wilderness, where
she hath a place prepared of God."

## I.

Ferris and I had had a dispute, a bitter one, and, as usual, Ferris had
pushed his cap over his eyes until the hair on the back of his head stuck
out.

"You can't do it," he said, shoving both hands up to the wrists in his canvas fishing-coat.

"I'll prove it," said I. "What a stubborn mule you are, Ferris!"

"Stubborn nothing," he retorted, "you and your theories must have
your little airing, I suppose, but I don't intend to assist."

"I'm right sometimes," I said.

"Sometimes you're wrong, too," said Ferris. Then he walked off toward
the cliffs, whistling, uncompromising, untidy.

"There's a hole in your leggings!" I called after him, but he did not deign
to answer me.

"Obstinate ass," I thought, for we were very fond of each other, "if he
wastes his time with the Silver Doctor he'll rue it." Then I looked at
Solomon and lighted a cigarette.

Solomon was a bird, an enervating bird of the Ibis species, wrinkled and
wizened, like the mummies of his native land, which was Egypt. The bird
was mine, a sarcastic tribute from Ferris, and the bird and the sarcasm both
bore directly on the only disputes which ever arose between Ferris and myself. The cause of these disputes was a trout-fly, an innocent toy of scarlet
and tinsel, known to anglers as the "Red Ibis." I swore by it, Ferris swore
at it. In the long winter nights when the streams gurgled under the frozen
forests and the lake was a sheet of soggy snow, Ferris and I loafed before
the fire pulling tangled masses of leaders and flies about and dragging the
silken lines over the rugs to hear the reels click. Every fly known to the
brethren of the angle was discussed—every fly except the Red Ibis. We
both honestly tried to avoid this bone of contention. We talked of Duns
and Hackles; and Spinners and Gnats, but in spite of every precaution the
Red Ibis would occasionally rise like a fiery spectre between us, and then

we disputed vehemently.

"No angler with a rag of self-respect would use the Ibis," said Ferris, with that obstinate shrug which added gall to the insult, and I—well, the crowning insult came when Ferris sent to Cairo and imported a live Egyptian Ibis for me.

"Pull out his tail feathers when you're short of Red Ibis," gasped Ferris, weak with laughter, as I stood silently inspecting the bird in my studio.

"I'll send him to Central Park," said I, swallowing my wrath; but I thought better of it, and Solomon, the wizened, became an important member of my household.

The bird was a mystery. I never cared to encounter his filmy eyes. Centuries seemed to roll away when he unclosed them, visions of tombs and obelisks filled my mind—glimpses of desert sunsets and the warm waters of lazy rivers. His black shrivelled head, bare as a skull, lay like a withered gourd among the garish flame-coloured feathers on his breast.

"Solly," said I, when Ferris disappeared below the cliff, "do you want a frog?"

The bird unclosed one eye. I went to a pail of water in which I kept minnows, and Solomon followed me, solemnly hopping.

"Help yourself, Solly," said I, uncovering the pail.

I called him Solly because I wished to put myself at ease with this relic of Egyptian Royalty. The splendour of Pharo's court had not dimmed this hoary prophet's eye, which was piercing when the sleepy film left it—piercing enough to make me feel thousands of years young, and very bourgeois. In vain I addressed him as Solly, in vain I gave him chocolate creams,—he was the aristocrat, the venerable high-priest of an Empire dead—and I was his man-servant, his ass, and his ox.

Solomon dabbed once or twice at a sportive minnow, pecked pensively at the handle of the pail, swallowed a pebble or two, and then, ruffling his scarlet feathers, sidled aimlessly back into the sedge by the frog-pond. I watched him for awhile, brooding dreamily among the rushes, but he paid no further attention either to me or to the small green frogs that squatted on the lily-pads or floated half submerged, watching him with enormous eyes.

A noisy blue-jay flitted through the orchard and alighted on a crab-apple tree solely to insult Solomon. He of course was unsuccessful, and his language became so utterly unfit for publication that I moved away, shocked and annoyed.

The sun was very hot. It glittered with a blinding light across the rippling pond, where dragon-flies darted and sailed and chased each other over the water, or flitted among the clouds of dancing midges, searching for prey.

A sweet smell came to me from orchard and sedge; there was an odour of scented rushes in the air, and the lingering summer wind bore puffs of perfume from clover-fields and meadows fragrant with flowering mint. I looked again toward the cliffs. Ferris was not in sight.

"Obstinate mule," I thought, and, picking up my rod and fly-book, I sauntered toward the forest.

"Ferris," said I to myself, "is after that big trout by the Red Rock Rapids, but he'll never raise him with a Silver Doctor, and he'll come home in a devil of a temper."

I sat down in a clump of sweet fern and joined my rod. When I had run the silk through the guides and had fastened the nine-foot leader, I opened my fly-book and sought for a Red Ibis fly. There was not one in the book.

"I must send to New York to-morrow," I thought, turning the aluminum leaves impatiently; "fancy my being out of Red Ibis!" I selected a yellow Oak fly for the dropper and a nameless Gnat for the hand-fly, and, drawing the leader down to the reel, started on again, carrying my rod with the tip behind me.

The forest was dim and moist and silent. Where the sunshine fell among the ferns a few flies buzzed in the gilded warmth; but except for this and a strange grey bird which flitted before me silently as I walked, there was no sign of life, nothing stirring, not a rustle among the leaves, not a movement, not a bird-note.

Over moss and dead leaves aglisten in the pale forest light I passed,—over crumbling logs, damp and lichen-covered, half submerged in little pools; and the musty fragrance of the forest mould set me dreaming of dryads, and fauns, and lost altars, whose marbles, stained with tender green, glimmer in ancient forests.

This belt of woods was always silent; I often wondered why. There were no birds—none except this strange grey creature which kept flitting ahead of me, uttering no note. It was the first bird I had ever seen in the western forest belt—the first bird except Solomon, who occasionally accompanied me on my trips to the long pool in the river which borders the wooded belt on the west.

It was an unknown bird to me,—I could catch fleeting glimpses of it,—and its long slender wings and dark eyes brought no recollections to my mind.

To the north, south, and east the woods were full of thrushes and woodpeckers; full of game, too—grouse, deer, foxes, and an occasional mink and otter, but the shy wood creatures left the western forest belt alone, and even the trout seemed to shun the dark pools where the river swept the edges of the wood until it curved out again by Lynx Peak. I say the trout shunned it, but there was one, a monstrous fish, wily and subtile, that lived in the long amber pool below. Early in the season Ferris had raised him with a Silver Doctor, and Ferris's madness on the Silver Doctor dated from that moment. His mania for this fly lead him to use it in season and out, and no amount of persuasion or of ridicule moved him.

"Because," said I, "you had a Silver Doctor snapped off by a big fish, do you imagine it's the only fly in the world?"

"It's good enough for me," he said.

There were two things which Ferris used to say that maddened me. One was, "The Silver Doctor's good enough for me"; the other was, "New York's good enough for me."

We never discussed the latter question after Ferris had alluded to me as a "Latin Quarter Nondescript," but the battle still raged over the merits of the Silver Doctor and the Red Ibis.

When I came to the wooded slope which overhung the river I buttoned my shooting coat and began a cautious descent, trailing my rod carefully. I headed for the foot of the pool, for one of my theories, which ruffled Ferris, was that certain pools should be fished up stream. This was one of those pools, according to my theory; and when I had reached the rocks and had waded into the rushing water, I faced up stream and cast straight out into the rapids which curled among the boulders at the foot of the pool.

At the second cast I hooked a snag and waded out to disengage it. Fumbling about under the foaming water I found my fly imbedded in something which refused to give way. I tugged cautiously and gently; it was useless. Then I rolled up my sleeve and plunged my arm into the water up to the shoulder. This time it did give way; I drew out my arm and held up something glistening and dripping, in which my hook was firmly imbedded. It was a shoe, small, pointed, high-heeled, and buckled with a silver buckle.

"This," said I, "is most extraordinary," and I sat down on a flat rock, holding the shoe close to my eyes.

"Besnard—Paris," I read stamped on the lining over the heel. And the buckle was of sterling silver. I sat for a moment, thinking.

Our cottage, Ferris's and mine, was the only house in the whole region that I knew of, except the old house in the glade by the White Moss Spring. That was unoccupied and had been for years—a crumbling, abandoned farm, tottering among the young growth of an advancing forest. But as I sat thinking I remembered early in the season having seen smoke above the trees once when we were in the neighbourhood of the White Moss Spring, and I recollected that Ferris had spoken of poachers. We had been too lazy to investigate, too lazy even to remember it until, as I sat there holding the small shoe, the incident came back to me, and I wondered whether anybody had taken up an abode in the abandoned farm.

I didn't like it. The forests and streams belonged to Ferris and me, and although up to the present moment it had not been necessary to employ many keepers, I began to fear that our woods were being invaded and that we should soon be obliged to find protection.

I looked at the shoe, turning it over carefully in my hands. It was new—had scarcely been worn at all.

"Pooh," I thought, "the owner of this could scarcely do much damage among the game, but of course there may be bigger shoes in company with this, and those bigger shoes had better look out!"

My first impulse was to throw the shoe into the underbrush. I started to do this, and then carefully laid it down on a sun-warmed rock.

"Let it dry," I muttered; "it's evidence for Ferris." But as it happened, Ferris was not destined to see the shoe.

## II.

I fished the pool twice, once up and once down, and heaven knows I fished it conscientiously; but no trout rose to the flies, although I changed the cast half a dozen times and even violated my feelings by tying a Silver Doctor. It was true I glanced up and down the river to see whether Ferris was in sight before I did so.

"The wily old devil won't come up," said I to myself, meaning the trout; "I'll give him a rest for a while." And I sat down on the rock where the pointed shoe was drying in the sun, laying my rod beside me.

"What's the use of speculating about this shoe," I thought, and straightway began to speculate.

The strange grey bird with the slender wings and dark eyes slipped through the undergrowth along the opposite side of the pool, but it uttered no call, and I caught only fleeting glimpses of it at intervals. Once, for a moment, it flitted quite near, and a sudden sense of having seen it before came over me, but after a little thinking I found myself associating it with a rare bird I had once noticed in Northern France, and of course it was impossible that this could be a French bird.

"It was an association of ideas," said I to myself, looking at the mark in the slim shoe. "Besnard—Paris." And I began speculating upon the owner of the shoe.

"Young? Probably. Slender? Probably. Pretty? The deuce take the shoe," I muttered, picking up my rod. Presently I laid it down again, softly.

"Now, perhaps," said I to myself, "this little shoe has tapped the gravel of the Luxembourg, patted the asphalt of the Boulevard des Italiens, brushed the lawns of the Bois—ah me! ah me!—the devil take the shoe!"

The sun beat down upon the rock; the little shoe in my hand was nearly dry.

"No," said I to myself, "I'll not show it to Ferris. And I'll not shove it into my pocket—no—for if Ferris finds it he'll rag me to death. I'll throw it away." I stood up.

"I'll just throw it away," I repeated aloud to encourage myself, for I didn't want to throw it away.

"One, two, three," said I, with an attempt at carelessness which changed to astonishment as I raised my eyes to the bank above whither I had intended to hurl the shoe.

For an instant I stood rigid, my right hand clutching the shoe, arrested in mid air. Then I placed the shoe very carefully upon the rock beside me and took off my shooting-cap.

"I beg your pardon," said I, "I did not see you."

I stood silent, politely holding my shooting-cap against my stomach. But I was confused, for she had answered me in French, pure Parisian French, and my ideas were considerably unbalanced.

I am afraid I stared a little. I tried not to. She was slender and very young. Her dark eyes, half shadowed under black lashes, made me think of the strange, dark-eyed bird that had followed me. She sat on the crooked trunk of a tree overhanging the bank, her feet negligently crossed, her hands in the pockets of a leather shooting-jacket. I'm afraid to say how short her skirts were,—but of course this is the age of bicycles and shooting-kilts.

"Madame," I said, trying to keep my eyes from one small stockinged foot, "I have found a shoe—"

"My shoe, Monsieur," she said, serenely.

"Permit me, madame," said I—

"Mademoiselle—" said she—

"Permit me,—a thousand pardons, Mademoiselle,—to return to you your shoe."

"It was very stupid of me to lose it," said she.

"It is nearly dry," said I; "will Mademoiselle pardon the uncommitted stupidity of which I was nearly guilty."

"You were going to throw it away," said she.

"I almost perpetrated that unpardonable crime—"

"Give it to me," she said, with a gracious gesture.

Now when she smiled I smiled too, and picking up the shoe waded across the pool to the bank under her.

"May I come up?" I asked.

"Pardi, Monsieur, how else am I to get my shoe?"

I clambered up, hanging to limbs and branches. It was a miracle I did not break my neck.

"Why do you not take the path?" she asked. "Do you not know you might fall—and all for a shoe?"

"But such a shoe—"

"True, the buckle is silver—"

"Which I claim the privilege of buckling," said I, dragging myself up beside her.

She deliberately held out her slim stockinged foot, and I slipped the shoe on it.

The silver buckle was not easily buckled. There were difficulties—for the tongue had become bent and needed straightening.

"You might take the shoe off again to arrange the buckle," she said.

"I can straighten it without that," said I.

When at last the buckle was clasped we had been talking so long that I had told her my name, my residence, my profession, and more or less about Ferris. I don't know why I told her all this. She seemed to be interested. Then I asked her if she lived at the "Brambles."

"The Brambles?" she repeated, looking at her shoes.

"The deserted Farm by the White Moss Spring—"

"Yes—not alone; I have a housekeeper."

"Aged?"

"Very—and fierce. But I shall do as I please."

"Did you buy the house?"

"No. It was empty, and I walked in. Next day they sent my twelve trunks from Lynne Centre. The furniture was good."

"And you have been there for two months?"

"Yes. I have a horse and dog cart too. Rose drives to Lynne Centre twice a week for the marketing. I think I shall keep a cow—I generally do what I please. I choose to amuse myself with you just now."

"This," said I, "is a very strange history; did you know that Mr. Ferris and myself—existed?"

"It is not a strange history,—no, I once saw your house as I passed through the forest belt, but there was nobody there on the lawn except an ordinary person with little side whiskers."

"Howlett!" I exclaimed.

"Comment?" she asked.

"A servant, an Englishman."

"Probably," said she, looking dreamily at me.

Then I told her all about Ferris and myself; how we came every spring to the Clover Cottage with Howlett, a cook, and three dogs as retinue, how we fished in summer and shot in the autumn, how twice a year men came all the way from Lynne Center to house our hay and repair damages, how the game-keepers lurked at the mouth of the valley, miles to the south, to prevent poachers from entering, but we concluded it was not necessary for keepers to patrol the woods inside the valley.

"Now," I said, "the poachers are in our very midst—here established—and such dangerous poachers, too! What shall we do with them, Mademoiselle?"

"You mean me," she said, with wide open eyes.

"No," said I, "I do not mean you—you are very welcome in our valley."

"But I am sure you do mean me," she said, smiling.

Then we talked of other things, of Paris and France; of trout, and flies, and Ferris, of Normandy, and the beauty of the world; but it was nearly five o'clock before we spoke of love.

"I have never loved," she said, looking at me calmly.

"Oh, how unnecessary!" I thought, for I had believed her clever.

"But," she continued, gravely, "I think it is time that I did."

"I think so too," said I.

"I should like to fall in love," said she; "I have nothing else to do."

"I also am very idle," I said.

"Then," said she, "the opportunity only is lacking."

I think I muttered something about poachers—I was not perfectly cool.

"Now," said she, "I know you mean me!"

"Ah," said I, "I mean a keener poacher than you or I, a free rover more to be dreaded than an army of riflemen."

"Then you don't mean me," she said.

I shook my head.

"Do you know," said she, "I should very much like to be the heroine of a romance."

"I will aid you to be one!" I said, hastily. We had known each other nearly three hours.

"Let us," said she, "pretend that this is the forest of Versailles in the time of Louis Quinze."

"Let us indeed!" I cried, enthusiastically.

"And you are a Count—"

"And you a Marquise—"

"Named Diane; it is my real name."

"Diane."

"And you—"

"My real name is Louis—"

"It will do; you may kiss my hand."

I wondered just where she was going to draw the line. Then, the devil prompting, I entered recklessly into this most extraordinary adventure.

And what an adventure! Words, thoughts even failed me as I looked at her. This wood-land maid with the wonderful eyes! There was no mistaking the challenge in her eyes, the half-innocent smile, the utter disregard for every human conventionality.

"How," thought I—"how can such a woman wear a childlike face!" I had known coquettes,—many,—but the depth of this strange girl's recklessness I feared to sound—I dreaded almost to understand.

"She is too deep," said I to myself—"too deep for me," and I looked her questioningly in the eyes.

I don't know why or how,—I never shall know probably, but a sudden conviction seized me that she was as innocent as she looked. Imagine a man coming to such a conclusion! I felt inclined to laugh, and yet I was as firmly convinced as though I had known her all my life.

"You may kiss my hand," she said, and held it out to me.

I did. I wished I hadn't a moment later, for I tumbled head over heels in love with her and fairly gasped at the idea.

"Lovers in the Court of Louis Quinze resembled us, I think," she said, after a long silence.

"We will try to make the resemblance perfect," said I, taking both her hands in mine.

She bent her head a little,—there was just a shadow of resistance,—then I kissed her on the lips.

There are moments in a man's life when he does not know whether he is a-foot or a-horseback. I remember that I sat down on the bank and carefully uprooted several ferns. When I had regained control of my voice,— the little maid was very silent,— I asked her to tell me of herself, if it might please her to do so.

"I was born," said the little maid, resting her small head on one hand, "in Rouen. Do you know Rouen?"

"Yes."

"Papa was an officer, and he killed his general when I was seven years old. It was something about Mama; I never saw her again. Then we went to Canada very quickly; Papa died there. I had been in a convent school; I ran away, and went to New York. I am nineteen, and very reckless."

"Yes, Diane."

"I have a great deal of money in bank notes. It was Papa's. I have never counted it—it is in a big trunk. I understand English, but do not care to speak it. I do not care what becomes of me; I wish it were over—this life. You are the first man who ever kissed me. Do you believe me?"

"Yes, Diane."

"I wonder you do. Let us go down to the river where the sunlight falls. The descent is easy—"

"Diane—you must not go—"

"With you— will you give me your hand?"

"Come."

"Did you see that shy grey bird?" said the little maid, hesitating on the slope, her hand in in mine.

I could not see it, for we had already begun the descent.

## III◆

"Where the mischief have you been all day?" demanded Ferris that evening as we sat on the veranda after dinner.

"Well," said I lighting a pipe, "when you had your fit of sulks I went off for a brace of trout."

"Did you see anything worth seeing?"

"I saw no trout," said I.

"Unfortunate, eh?"

"Oh not very," I said, looking at Solomon.

"Not very?"

"Look at that ridiculous bird, Ferris."

"Swallowed a frog the wrong way," said Ferris, watching the solemn contortions of Solomon; "he looks like a little Jew in a crimson overcoat with a stomach ache. What fly did you use, Louis?"

"Everything; couldn't raise a fin."

"Oh, you've been trying that old devil down by the west woods! I should think you'd let him alone; it's useless," yawned Ferris.

"I'm going to try for him every day till I get him," said I, trying not to lie more than necessary. "Of course you'll not infringe?"

"Infringe! Not much! You can have the whole west woods to your own sweet self; but you're an idiot!"

"Not at all," said I, thankfully; and in a burst of confidence I confessed that I had used a Silver Doctor.

There was a momentary gleam of triumph in Ferris's eyes, but he was very decent about it and asked me most politely for the loan of a Red Ibis. Oh men of the busy world, learn courtesy from the angler! There are other things you need not learn from anglers.

"My dear fellow," said I, more touched than I had been for a long time, "I haven't a Red Ibis left. I shall write Conroy to-night before I retire. If you really do want an Ibis I will catch Solomon and pluck a plume from his tail feathers."

"I don't want it enough to inconvenience you or hurt Solomon's feelings," said Ferris, laughing.

After a long interval of silent smoking Ferris rose and yawned at the moon.

"Do you know what a Spirit-bird is, Ferris?" I asked, rapping my pipe on the arm of my chair.

"Spirit-bird—the French one—the Oiseau Saint-Esprit? Yes, I've seen one—in the Vosges."

"Grey—with slim wings and big dark eyes?"

"That's the bird," said Ferris; "why?"

"Well, I thought I saw one to-day. Of course that's impossible."

"Of course," said Ferris, yawning again. "I'm going to turn in; good-night, old chap."

"Good-night," said I, tapping nervously on the veranda with my pipe.

Howlett came out a few moments later with my wading-shoes which he had been oiling.

"Well," said I, "are the hob-nails all right?"

"Seving 'ob-nails is h'out, sir," replied Howlett, holding up the shoes for my inspection.

"Put them in as soon as they're dry. Did you oil the bamboo? Good. Is my lamp lighted? Put it out—and you need not sit up, Howlett; I'm going for a stroll."

"Thank you sir," said Howlett,—"and Solomon, sir?"

Now it was one of my delights to see Howlett house Solomon. The wily Ibis loved to snoop about in the moonlight, and he was always ready for Howlett when that dignified servant came to round him up.

I looked at Solomon, who stood gloomily brooding among the water-lilies.

"He ought to be in bed," said I.

Howlett descended the veranda steps with arms extended, but Solomon sidled out into the pond. Howlett pleaded earnestly. He flattered and cajoled, but Solomon was obdurate.

"Nothink I say do move 'im, sir!" said Howlett, stiffly; "he is vicious to-night, sir."

"Then take the boat," I said.

Howlett in a boat chasing a sulky Ibis was one of those rare spectacles that few are permitted to witness. Once a week Solomon turned "vicious" and then, at Ferris's and my suggestion, Howlett took to the boat. A terrestrial Howlett was solemnly ludicrous, but an aquatic Howlett was impossible. Of course Ferris and I never laughed—that is, aloud, but we usually felt rather weak after it was over.

In the course of half an hour Solomon, mad, wet, and rumpled was cornered by Howlett and clasped to his stiff shirt front, muddy, bedraggled, and kicking.

"Are you not mortified, you bad bird?" said I, as Howlett passed toward the kitchen where Kitty the cook was airing his straw-thatched house.

"A vicious bird, sir, good-night, sir," murmured Howlett.

"Good-night, Howlett; breakfast at seven tomorrow," said I, and sauntered out into the moonlit valley.

I had been walking almost half an hour when it occurred to me that I should be in bed.

"What the deuce am I sprinting about the valley at this hour for?" I thought, looking around.

Over the shadowy meadows the night mist hung, silvered by the moonlight, and I heard the meadow-brook rippling through the sedge. Slender birches glimmered among the alders, and all the little poplar leaves were quivering, but I felt no breath of air.

Where the dark forest fringed the meadow I saw the moonbeams sparkling on lonely pools, but the depths of the woodland were black and impenetrable, and the forest itself was vague as the mist that shrouded it.

For a long time I stood, looking at the stars and the mist, and little by little I came to understand why I was there alone.

I knew I should go on, I wished to, but I lingered in the moonlight staring at earth and sky until something moved in the thicket beside me, and I followed it, knowing it was the Spirit-bird.

When I entered the forest I could scarcely see my hand, but I felt a trodden path beneath my feet, and I heard before me the whisper of soft wings, and presently I heard the river, rushing through rocks of the western forest, and when I came to the wooded bank the moonlight fell all around me.

There was a narrow strip in the forest, overgrown with silver birch and poplar and lighted by the moon, but I searched it in vain, up and down, up and down, always with the whisper of soft wings in my ears.

At last I called, "Diane," and before I called again, her hands lay close in mine.

□ □ □

"I came," said the little maid, "because you were coming."

"Who told you I was coming?"

"Told me? No one told me. Rose is asleep. Why did you come?"

"Why did you, Diane?"

"I? Because you came. How did you find my bower?"

"Your bower, Diane?"

"It is yours I know; I call it mine; I call it the Silent Land."

"It is very silent," I said.

"It is always silent—no birds, not even the noise of the water. Do you think it is sad? There are times when sounds,—the song of living creatures and the countless movements of things that live, trouble me. Then I come here. There are flowers."

"The air is very sweet, too sweet. What is the perfume? The trees are heavy with fragrance. Ah!—are you tired, Diane?"

"No—it is the odour of blossoms; I sleep here sometimes."

"Your hair is loose—how long it is! Is it the perfume from your hair—is it your breath—"

"The blossoms are very sweet; the moon has gone."

"There is a star,—how soft your breath is."

"I do not see the star, where, Louis?"

"It is there;—clouds are veiling it;—there is a mist over all—"

"It is my hair—over your eyes."

# IV.

"Howlett," said I, one warm afternoon, "Solomon is unendurable: he follows me everywhere, and I wish you to see that he minds his own business."

"A hobstinate bird, sir," said Howett, "and vicious when crossed,—which I scorn 'is h'anger,—beg pardon sir,—for 'e's took to biting wen 'is vittles disagrees."

"Has he bitten you?"

"Twice, sir,—which 'appily my h'eyes is huninjured, though h'aimed at by 'is beak."

"This is intolerable," said I; "you must punish him, Howlett."

"'Ow, sir?"

"Tie him up when he bites. Have those flies come from Conroy's?"

"Nothink 'as came, sir."

"Where is Mr. Ferris?"

"Mr. Ferris is a whipping of the h'Amber Pool sir, with three sea-trout to the good and a brace of square tails. Solomon followed 'im, sir, and is h'observing the sport."

"Then I can get away without that red feathered Paul Pry tiptoeing after me," I thought, and sent Howlett for my rod-case.

"Tell Mr. Ferris, when he returns, that I may not be back until dinner," I said, when Howlett brought the case.

I selected a four-ounce split bamboo, pocketed my fly-book and a tin box of floating flies for dry fishing, picked up a landing-net, and walked away toward the western woodland, whistling. I had not fished for three weeks, although every day I went away into the western woods with rod and creel. Ferris laughed at my infatuation for the long pool where the great fish lay and jeered at me when I returned evening after evening with no trout, although the river, except the western stretch, was full of trout. He had never come to the pool,—I should have seen him from the Silent Land if he had,—but Solomon sneaked after me on several occasions. Once I caught him craning his neck and peering into the bower,—our bower—and as I did not care to have him pilot Ferris thither, I hustled him off.

The woods were fragrant and warm, stained by the afternoon sun; the quiet murmur of the brook came to me from leafy thickets as I walked, and I heard the river rushing in the distance and the summer wind among the pines. White clouds shimmered in the blue above, sailing, sailing God knows where, but they passed across the azure, one by one, drifting to the south, and I watched them with the vague longing that comes to men who watch white sails at sea.

I had turned my steps toward the long pool, for I had decided to fish that afternoon, wishing to redeem my words to Ferris—at least in part; but as I stepped across the trail I heard the sound of wings, and a shadow glided in front of me toward the forest. It was always so from the first, and now, as always, I turned away, following unquestioningly the Spirit-bird. The noise of the river ceased as I entered the Silent Land. For an instant the grey bird hovered high in the sunshine, then left me alone.

I threw myself full length upon the blossoming bank and waited, chin on hand. And as I waited, she came noiselessly across the moss, so quietly, so silently that I saw her only when her fingers touched mine.

"It has been a long time," we said; and; "Did you sleep?" and; "When did you awake?" Then we asked each other a thousand little questions which are asked when lovers meet, and we answered as lovers answer. We spoke of the Spirit-bird as we always did, wondering, and she told me how that morning it had tapped upon her window as the day broke.

"Rose did not hear it," she said, "but I was already awake and thinking."

"I awoke at sunrise too," I said; "for a moment I thought it was a swallow in the chimney that fluttered so—"

"The Spirit-bird flies swiftly when Love is dreaming,—that is a very old proverb of Normandy. What shall we do, Louis—there is so much to do and so little time in life!—I brought my lute—ah! you are laughing!"

"The lute is such an old-fashioned toy; I didn't know you played. Will you sing too, Diane? Something very old, older than the lute."

"I learned a song this morning because I thought you would care for it. That is why I dared to bring my lute into the Silent Land. The song is called, 'Tristesse.'"

Then the little maid sat up among the blossoms and touched the soft strings, singing:

"J'ai perdu ma force et ma vie,
Et mes amis et ma gaité;
J'ai perdu jusqu' à la fierté
Qui faisait croire à mou génie.

Quand j'ai connu la Vérité
J'ai cru que c'était une amie;
Quand je l'ai comprise et sentie,
J'en etais déjà dégoûté.

Et pourtant elle est éternelle
Et ceux qui se sont passés d'elle
Ici-bas ont tout ignoré.

Dieu parle, il faut qu'on lui réponde;
Le seul bien qui me reste au monde
Est d'avoir quelquefois pleuré."

"That is all," said the little maid.

"Sing, Diane," I said, but I scarcely heard my own voice.

She laughed and bent above me with a graceful gesture. "Not that," she said, "for you at least are not sad. There is a chansonnette,—shall I sing again?—then be very still, here at my feet. Do you not think my lute is sweet?

"Je voudrais pour moi qu'il fut toujours fête
Et tourner la tête
Aux plus orgueilleux;
tre en même temps de glace et de flamme,
La haine dans l'âme,
L'amour dans les yeux."

"You, Diane?" I whispered; but she smiled, and the mystery of love veiled her dark eyes; and she sang:

"Je ne voudrais pas à la contredanse,
Sans quelque prudence
Livrer mon bras nu
Puis, au cotillion, laisser ma main blanche

Trainer sur la manche
Du premier venu."

"Si mon fin corset, si souple et si juste,
        D'un bras trop robuste
        Se sentait serré,
J'aurais, je l'avoue, une peur mortelle
        Qu'un bout de dentelle
        N'en fut déchiré."

She looked at me with soft, unfathomable eyes and touched the lute.
When I moved she started from her reverie with a gay little nod to me:

"Quand on est coquette, it faut être sage,
        L'oiseau de passage
        Qui vole à plein coeur
Ne dort pas en l'air comme une hirondelle,
        Et peut, d'un coup d'aile
        Briser une fleur!"

"Sing," I said in a changed voice.

"I have sung," she said, and laid her lute in my hands. But I knew nothing of minstrelsy and lay silent, idly touching the strings.

She had fashioned for her fair head a wreath of sweet-fern twined with
clustered buds, white as snow and faintly perfumed.

"So I am crowned," she said, "a princess in the Silent Land. Where I step,
all things green shall flourish; where I turn my eyes, blossoms shall open
in the summer wind;—am I not queen?"

"Will you not sing again, Diane?"

"No, it pleases me to hear a legend now. You may begin, Louis."

"Which—the Were-wolf or the Man in Purple Tatters or the—"

"No, no—something new."

"The Seventh Seal?"

"Begin it."

"And when he opened the Seventh Seal there was silence in Heaven—"

"Dear Saints, have we not silence enough in the Silent Land? Tell me
about battles."

"'And the sound of their wings was as the sound of chariots of many
horses running to battle.' I could tell you about battles, Diane."

"Tell me,—don't move your arm,—tell me of battles, Louis."

"There was once a King in Carcosa," I began. But the little maid was already asleep.

I thought I heard a step in the undergrowth and listened.
The forest was silent.

When we awoke it was night. Down from the dark heavens a great star fell, burning like a lamp. Above the low-hanging branches, sombre, drooping, heavy with fragrance, a misty darkness lay like a vast veil spread.

In the stillness I heard her quiet breathing, but we did not speak.

Silence is a Prophet, unveiling mysteries.

Then, through the forest, we heard the sound of wings, and as we moved, stepping together into the shadows, the moon rose above Lynx Peak, gigantic, golden, splendid.

So we passed out of the forest into the star-lit night.

The skies were leaden, the watery clouds hung low over the valley, and a wet wind blew from the west, ruffling the long pool where Diane stood. Kilted and capped in tweeds, creel swinging with every movement of the rod which swayed and bent with her bending wrist, she moved from ripple to shallow, wading noiselessly while the silken line whistled and the gay flies chased each other across the wind-lashed pool.

We spoke in a low voice, glancing at each other when the light cast struck the water.

"Under the alders Diane—" I said; "have you changed the Grey Dun for the Royal?"

"No, what is your new cast?"

"Emerald and Orange Miller—I shall tie an Alder-fly in place of the Miller. Do you think the water warrants a cast of three?"

"It is rough; I don't know,—Louis, was that an offer?"

"I think it was the spray from the rapids. Shall we move up a little? Do you feel the chill of the water?"

"I am cold to my knees," said the little maid, "the river is rising I think—ah, what was that?"

"Nothing,—you touched a floating leaf in the swirl."

"Splash!" A great fish flopped over in the pool, a trout, lazy, unwieldy, monstrous.

"Oh! he missed it!" cried Diane, turning a little white.

"Cast again," I whispered, tossing my rod onto the sandy beach and un-slinging my landing-net.

Trembling a little with excitement she cast across the swirl, once, twice, twenty times, but the monster was invisible. Somewhere in the dusky depths of that amber well the fierce fish lay watching the lightly dropping flies, unmoved. Then we changed the cast; I emptied my fly-book, but nothing stirred except the hurrying water, curling, gurgling, tumbling through the rocks. Finally I broke the silence.

"Diane, it was the spinner that he rose to. He's after something redder. Have you a Scarlet Ibis?"

"No—have you?"

I almost groaned, for Conroy's flies had not arrived, and I hadn't an Ibis in the world.

After a while she reeled in her silken line, and we waded to the sandy beach and sat down.

"Oh, the pity of it," sighed Diane; "never have I seen such a trout before. I suppose it is useless, Louis."

I sat moodily poking holes in the sand with the butt of my landing-net.

We spoke of other things for a time, sinking our voices below the roar of the river. Presently a sunbeam stole through the vapour above, light-ing the depths of the dark pool. And all at once we saw the trout, hang-ing just above the pebbly bottom; we saw the scarlet fins move, the great square tail waving gently in the current, the mottled spotted back, the round staring eyes. The swelling of the gills was scarcely perceptible, the broad mouth hardly moved.

For a long time we sat silent, fascinated; then something stirred behind us on the beach and we slowly turned. It was Solomon.

"Ciel!" faltered Diane, "what is that?"

"My bird—an Egyptian Ibis," I whispered, laughing silently; "he has fol-lowed me, after all."

Solomon ruffled his scarlet plumes, blinked at me, scratched his head with his broad foot, pecked at a bit of mica, and took two solemn steps nearer.

"Diane," said I, suddenly, "I'll get a red fly for you; don't move—the bird will come close to us."

But Solomon was in no hurry. Inch by inch he sidled nearer, dallying with bits of moss and shining pebbles, often pausing to reflect, but grad-ually approaching, for his curiosity concerning Diane was great.

"He looks as if he had stepped off an obelisk," murmured Diane; "I have seen hieroglyphics that resembled him. Oh, what a prehistoric head—so old, so old!"

"His name is Solomon," I whispered. "Solomon in all his glory was not arrayed like one of these. I'm going to have a small bit of Solomon's glory—sh—h! ah! I've got him!"

It was over in a second, and I do not believe it was painful. There was a flurry of sand, a furious flapping of flame-coloured wings, a squawk! a smothered laugh—nothing more.

Mortified, furious, Solomon marched off, shaking the river sand from wing and foot, and Diane and I, with tears of laughter in our eyes, wound the scarlet feather about a spare hook, tied it close with a thread from my coat, and whipped it firmly to the shank. I looped the improvised fly to Diane's leader, and she shook the line free. The reel sang a sweet tune as she drew the silk through the guides, and presently she motioned me to follow her out into the rippling shallows, and I went, swinging my landing-net to my shoulder. She cast once. The fly struck the swirl and sank a little, but she drew it to the surface and the current swept it under the alders. For a moment it sank again; then the ripples parted, and a broad crimson-flecked side rolled just below the surface of the water. At the same moment the light rod curved, deeply quivering, the reel screamed like the wind in the chimney, and the straining line cut through the water, moving up the pool with lightning speed.

"Strike!" I cried, and she struck heavily, but the reel sang out like a whistling buoy, and the fish tumbled into the churning water under the falls at the head of the pool.

"Now," said Diane, with a strange quiet in her voice, "I suppose he is gone, Louis." But the vicious tug and long, fierce strain contradicted her, and I stepped back a pace or two to let her fight the battle to the bitter end.

The struggle was splendid. Once I believe she became a little frightened,—the rod was staggering under the furious fish,—and she spoke in a queer, small voice: "Are you there, Louis?"

"I am here, Diane."

"Close behind?"

"Close behind."

She said nothing more until the great fish lay floating within reach of my net.

"Now!" she gasped.

It was done in a second; and, as I bore the deep-laden net to the beach, I caught a fleeting glimpse of a figure among the trees on the bank above. Diane was kneeling breathlessly on a rock beside me; she did not see the figure. I did, for an instant. It was Ferris.

# VII.

Dinner was over. Ferris and I lingered silently over the Burgundy, and Howlett hovered in the corner with a decanter of port until Ferris shook his head.

It had been a silent dinner. Ferris tried to be cordial, and failed. Then he tried to be indifferent, with better success. We exchanged a word or two concerning a new keeper who was to be stationed at the notch in the north, and I spoke to Howlett about cleaning the lamps.

Neither of us mentioned rods or trout, although Howlett had served us a delicious sea-trout that evening which had fallen to Ferris's rod, over which we ordinarily should have exulted.

Ferris of course knew that I had seen him among the trees on the bank above the long pool. It was my place to speak; we both understood that, but I did not. What was there to say? Suppose I should go back to the beginning and tell him—not all, but all that I was bound in honour to tell him. What would he think if I spoke of the Spirit-bird, of the Silent Land, of my long deception? An explanation was due him—I felt that with a vague sense of anger and humiliation. For weeks I had abandoned him; I never thought about his being lonely, but I knew now that he had felt it deeply. Oh, it was the underhand part of the business that sickened me, the daily deceit, the double dealing. Ferris was no infant. A word would have been enough. I had never by sign or speech spoken that word which would at least have set me right with him, and which I could have spoken honourably. And moreover, if I had spoken that word,—no, not a word even, a look would have been enough,—Ferris would never have entered the western forest belt.

We sat dawdling over our wine in the glow of the long candles while the fire crackled in the chimney place; for the evening was chilly, and Solomon brooded sullenly before the blaze. Howlett, noiseless and pompous, glided from side-board to table, decorously avoiding the evil jabs from Solomon's curved bill, until Ferris woke up and told him he might retire, which he did with a modest "good-night, sir," and a haughty glance at Solomon. A half hour of strained silence followed. I leaned on the table, my head on my hands, watching the candle light reflected on the fragile wine glasses. Myriads of little flames glistened on the crystal bowls, deep stained with the red wine's glow. The fire snapped and sparkled on the hearth, and Solomon slept, his wizened head buried in the depths of his flaming plumage.

And as we sat there, there came a faint tapping at the curtained window. Ferris did not hear it I did, for it was the Spirit-bird.

"I must go," said I, rising suddenly.

"Where?" said Ferris.

I looked at him stupidly for a moment, then sank back into my chair.

Solomon stirred in his slumber and I heard the wind rising in the chimney.

Ferris leaned across the table and touched my sleeve.

I looked at him silently.

"I must speak," he said; "are you ready?"

I did not reply.

"Sadness and silence have no place here, between you and me. Shall I tell you a story I once read?"

"I am half asleep," I muttered.

"This is the story," he said, unheeding my words. "There was once a King in Carcosa—"

My hand fell heavily upon the table.

"—And there was given unto him a mouth speaking great things and blasphemies—"

"For God's sake, Ferris—"

"Yes," he said, "for God's sake."

We sat staring at each other across the table, and if my face was as white as his I do not know, but my hand trembled among the glasses till they tinkled.

"I was born in France," he said at last. "You did not know it, for I never told you. What do you know about me after all? Nothing. What have years of friendship taught you about my past? Nothing. Now learn. My father was shot dead by an inferior officer in Rouen. The assassin escaped to Canada where—I found him. He died by his own hand—from choice. I did not know he had a child."

The dull fear at my heart must have looked from my eyes. Ferris nodded.

"Yes, you know the rest," he said; "the shame and disgrace of the suicide drove the child away—anywhere to escape it—anywhere—here, into the wilderness the woman fled where she hath a place prepared of God."

The Spirit-bird was tapping on the window, I heard the noise of wings beating against the pane.

"I must go," I said, and my voice sounded within me as from a great distance.

"Vengeance is God's," said Ferris, quietly: "I am guilty."

"I must go," I repeated, steadying myself with my hand on the table.

The noise of wings filled my ears. I knew the summons.

"Do you not hear?" I cried.

"The wind," said Ferris.

Then the door slowly opened from without, the long candles flared in the wind, and the ashes stirred and drifted among the embers on the hearth. And out of the night came a slender figure, with dark eyes wide, and timid hands outstretched—outstretched until they fell into my own and lay there.

"I came from the Silent Land," she said; "the bird led me; see, it has entered with me, Louis."

"It is my wife who has entered," I said quietly to Ferris, and the little maid clung close to me, holding out one slim hand to Ferris.

There was an interval of silence.

"Father Gregory will breakfast with us tomorrow," said Ferris to me.

"A Priest?"

"Open the window," smiled Ferris; "there is a small grey bird here."

So I opened the window and it flew away.

"Good-night," whispered the little maid, and kissed her hand to the open window.

"Diane!"

She came to me quietly. Ferris had vanished; Solomon peered dreamily at us with filmy eyes.

"The Spirit-bird has gone," she said.

Then, with her arms about my neck, I raised her head, touching her white brow with my lips.

"Lorsque la coquette Espérance
Nous pousse le coude en passant,
Puis a tire-d'aile s'élance,
Et se retourne en souriaut;

"Où va l'homme! Où son coeur l'appelle!
L'hirondelle suit le zephyr,
Et moins légère est l'hirondelle
Que l'homme qui suit son désir."

# THE BLACK WATER

Oh! could you view the melodie
        Of ev'ry grace,
And musick of her face,
        You'd drop a teare,
Seeing more harmonie
        In her bright eye,
Then now you heare."
                                LOVELACE.

## I♦

Ysonde swung her racquet. Her laughter was very sweet. A robin on the tip of a balsam-tree cocked his head to listen; a shy snow-bird peered at her through the meadow grass.

"What are you laughing at?" I asked, uneasily. I spoke sharply—I had not intended to. The porcupine on the porch lifted his head, his rising quills grating on the piazza; a drab-coloured cow, knee deep in the sedge, stared at me in stupid disapproval.

"I beg your pardon, Ysonde," I said, sulkily, for I felt the rebuke of the cow. Then Ysonde laughed again; the robin chirped in sympathy, and the snow-bird crept to the edge of the tennis-court.

"Deuce," I said, picking up a ball, "are you ready?"

She stepped back, making me a mocking reverence. Her eyes were bluer than the flowering flax behind her.

I had intended to send her a swift service, and I should have done so had I not noticed her eyes.

"Deuce," I repeated, pausing to recover the composure necessary for good tennis. She made a gesture with her racquet. The service was a miserable failure. I drove the second ball into the net, and then, placing the butt of my racquet on the turf, sat down on the rim.

"Vantage out," said I, gritting my teeth; "what were you laughing at, Ysonde?"

"Vantage out," she repeated; "I am not laughing."

"You were," I said; "you are now."

She went to the boxwood hedge, picked out one ball and sent it back; then she drove the other over the net and retired to her corner swinging her racquet. I did not move.

"You are spoiling your racquet," she said.

I was sitting on it. I knew better.

"And your temper," she said, sweetly.

"Vantage out," I repeated, and raised my tennis-bat for a smashing service. The ball whisted close to the net, and the white dust flew from her court, but her racquet caught it fair and square and I heard the ring of the strings as the ball shot along my left alley and dropped exactly on the service line. How I got it I don't know, but the next moment a puff of dust rose in her vantage court, there was a rustle of skirts, a twinkle of small tennis shoes, and the ball rocketed, higher, higher, into the misty sunshine.

"Oh," gasped Ysonde, and bit her lip.

The ball began to come down. I had time to laugh before it struck,—to laugh quietly and twirl my short mustache.

"I shall place that ball," said I, "where you will not find it easily;" and I did, deliberately.

For a second Ysonde was disappointed, I could see that, but I imagined there was the slightest tremour of relief in her voice when she said:

"Brute force is useless, Bobby; listen to the voice of the Prophetess."

"I hear," I said, "the echo of your voice in the throat of every bird."

"Which is very pretty but unfair," said Ysonde, looking at the snow-birds beside her. "It is unfair," she repeated.

"Yes," said I, "it is unfair; are you ready?"

"Let us finish the game this afternoon," she suggested; "look at these snow-birds, Bobby; if I raise my racquet it will frighten them."

"And you imagine," said I, "that these snow-birds are going to interrupt the game—this game?"

"What a pity to frighten them; see—look how close they come to me? Do you think the little things are tamed by hunger?"

"Some creatures are not tamed by anything," I said.

"Are you hungry?" she asked, innocently. I was glad that I suppressed my anger.

"Ysonde," I said, "you know what this game means to me—to us."

"I know nothing about it," she said, hastily, retreating to her corner; "play—it's deuce you know."

"I know," I replied, and sent a merciless ball shooting across her deuce court.

"Vantage in," I observed, trying not to smile. A swift glance from her wide eyes, a perceptible tremble of the long lashes—that was all; but I knew what I knew, for I have hunted wild creatures.

The porcupine on the piazza rose, sniffed, blinked in the sunlight, and lumbered down the steps, every quill erect.

"Billy! Go back this minute!" said Ysonde.

The quills on Billy's back flattened.

"Billy!" I repeated, "go and climb a tree."

"If you speak to him he will bristle again," said Ysonde, walking over to the porcupine.

"Billy, my child, climb this pretty balsam tree for the gentleman; come—you are interrupting the game, and the gentleman is impatient."

"The gentleman is very impatient, Billy," I said.

I saw Ysonde colour—a soft faint tint, nothing more; I saw Billy receive a gentle impulse—oh, very gentle indeed, from the point of her slender tennis shoes. So the porcupine was hustled up the balsam-tree, where he lay like an old mat, untidy, mortified, nursing his wrath, while two blue-birds tittered among the branches above him.

Ysonde came back and stood in the game court.

"It is vantage, I believe," she said, indifferently.

"Out," said I, with significance. Ysonde looked at me.

"Out," I repeated.

"Play," she said, desperately.

"No," I replied, sitting down upon the edge of my racquet again—I knew better—"let us clearly understand the consequences first."

She swung her racquet and looked me full in the eyes.

"What consequences?" she said.

"The consequences incident upon my winning this set."

"What consequences?" she insisted, defiantly.

"The forfeit," said I.

"When you win the set we will discuss that," she said. "Do you imagine you will win?"

She was a better player than I; she could give me thirty on each game.

"Yes," I said, and I believe the misery in my voice would have moved a tigress to pity.

Now perhaps it was because there is nothing of the tigress about Ysonde, perhaps because I showed my fear of her—I don't know which—but I saw her scarlet lips press one upon the other, and I saw her eyes darken like violet velvet at night.

"Play," she said; "I am ready."

The first ball struck the net; the racquet turned in my nerveless hand, and she smiled.

"Play!" I cried, and the second ball bit the lime dust at her feet. I saw the flash of her racquet, I saw a streak of gray lightning, and I lifted my racquet, but something struck me in the face,—the tennis-balls were heavy and wet,—and I staggered about blindly, faint with pain.

"Oh, Bobby!" cried Ysonde, and stood quite still.

"I'm a duffer," I muttered, trying to open my eye, but the pain sickened me. I placed my hand over it and looked out upon the world with one eye. The drab-coloured cow was watching me; she was chewing her cud; the porcupine had one sardonic eye fixed upon me; the robin, balanced on the tip of the balsam, mocked me. It was plain that the creatures were all on her side. The wild snow-birds scarcely moved as Ysonde hastened across the court to my side. I heard the blue-birds tittering over head, but I did not care; I had heard the tones of Ysonde's voice, and I was glad that I had been banged in the eye. It was true she had only said, "Oh, Bobby!"

"Is it very painful?" she asked, standing close beside me.

"Yes," I replied, seriously.

"Let me look," she said, laying one hand on the sleeve of my cricket shirt.

"Billy will rejoice at this," said I, removing my handkerchief so she could see the eyes. The pain was becoming intense. With my uninjured eye I could see how white her hand was.

She stood still a moment; my arm grew warm beneath her hand.

"It will cheer Billy," I suggested; "did I tell you that he bit me yesterday and I whacked him? No? Well, he did, and I did."

"How can you!" she murmured; "how can you speak of that ridiculous Billy when you may have—have to be blind?"

"Nonsense," I said, with a shiver.

She crossed the turf to the spring and brought her handkerchief back soaking and cold as ice. I felt her palm on my cheek as she adjusted it. It was smooth, like an apricot.

"Hold it there," I said, bribing my conscience; "it is very pleasant." She thought I meant the wet handkerchief.

"If—if I have ruined your sight…" she began.

Now it was on the tip of my tongue to add—"and yet you are going to ruin my life by beating me at tennis," but my conscience revolted.

"Do you think it is serious?" she asked, in a voice so low that I bent my head involuntarily. She mistook the gesture for one of silent acquiescence. A tear—a large warm one—fell on my wrist; I thought it was a drop of water from the handkerchief at first. Then I opened my uninjured eye and saw her mistake.

"You misunderstood," I said, wearily. "I don't believe what the oculist told me; the eye will be all right."

"But he warned you that a sudden blow would—"

"Might—"

"Oh—did he say might?"

"Yes—but it won't. I'm all right—don't take away your hand; are you tired?"

"No, no," she said, "shall I get some fresh water?"

"Not yet—don't go. The game was at deuce, wasn't it?"

Ysonde was silent.

"Was it deuce? Does that point count against me?" I insisted.

"How can you think of the game now?" said Ysonde, in a queer voice—like the note of a very young bird.

I sat down on the turf, and the handkerchief fell from my eye. Ysonde hastened to the spring and returned carrying the heavy stone jar full of water. It must have strained her delicate wrist —she said it did not; and, kneeling beside me, she placed the cold bit of cambric over my eye.

"Thank you," I said; "will you sit beside me on the turf?" Both of my eyes were aching and closed, but I heard her skirts rustle and felt the momentary pressure of her palm on my cheek.

"Are you seated?" I asked.

"Yes, Bobby."

"Then tell me whether I lost that point."

"How can I tell," she answered; "I would willingly concede it if it were not—"

"For the forfeit," I added; "then you think I did lose the point?"

"Does your eye pain very much?" she asked.

"Yes," said I, truthfully. Perhaps it was ungenerous, but I dared not reject such an ally as truth. I opened one eye and looked at Ysonde. She was examining a buttercup.

"All buttercups look as though they had been carefully varnished," said she, touching one with the tip of her middle finger.

"Did I win the set?" I began again.

"Oh—no—not the set!" she protested.

"Then I lost that point?"

"Oh! why will you dwell upon tennis at such a moment!"

"Because," said I, "it means so much to me." I suppose there was something in my voice that frightened her.

"Forgive me," I said, bitterly ashamed, for I had broken our compact, not directly, but in substance. "Forgive me, Ysonde," I said, looking at the porcupine with my left eye.

"Ridiculous Billy," for that was his name, stared at me with the insolence born of safety, and his white whiskers twitched in derision.

"You old devil," I thought, remembering the scar on my ankle.

"Where did he bite you?" asked Ysonde unconsciously reading my thoughts. It was a trick of hers.

"In the ankle,—it was nothing. I would rather have him bite the other ankle than get any more of his quills into me!" I replied. "See how the snow-birds have followed you. They are there among the wild strawberries."

She turned her head.

"Hush!" she whispered, raising one palm. It was pinker than the unripe berries. There was an ache in my heart as well as in my eyes, so I said something silly; "There was an old man who said, Hush! I perceive a young bird in this bush—"

"When they said, Is it small? he replied, Not at all! It is four times as big as the bush!" repeated Ysonde, solemnly. We both laughed, but I read a gratitude in her eyes which annoyed me.

"We digress," I said, "speaking of the game—"

"Oh, but we were not speaking of the game!" she said, half-alarmed, half-smiling; "there! I thought you were going to be sensible, Bobby."

"I am. I only wish to know whether I lost that game."

"You know the rules," she said.

"Yes—I know the rules."

"If it were not for the forfeit, I should not insist," she continued, returning to her buttercup. "It seems unfair to take the point;—does the eye pain, Bobby?"

"Not so much," I replied, sticking to the truth to the bitter end. My ally was becoming a nuisance.

"Let me see it," she said, gently removing the handkerchief. The eye must have looked bad, for her face changed.

"Oh, you poor fellow," she said, and I fairly revelled in the delight of my own misery.

"Then I lost that point," said I, stifling conscience.

She replaced the handkerchief. Her hand had become suddenly steady.

"No," she said, "you did not lose the point,—I concede it."

I wondered whether my ears were tricking me. "Then—if I won the point—I won the set," I said.

"Yes."

"And the forfeit—"

"The forfeit was that I should kiss you," said Ysonde, gravely.

"That was not all—"

"No,—you are to be allowed to tell me that you love me," continued Ysonde in calm, even tones.

"Then," said I, flushing uncomfortably, "when will you pay the forfeit?"

"Now, if you wish it. Shall I kiss you?" She leaned on the turf, one hand hidden by the buttercups. She had dropped the handkerchief, and I picked it up and held it to my eye with my left hand. Then, with my right hand, I took her right hand, listlessly drooping beside her, and I looked her full in the eyes.

"When we made the wager," I said, "we were boy and girl. That was almost twenty-four hours ago. You need not kiss me, Ysonde."

"A kiss means more at our age," she said.

"We were very silly," said I.

"It should mean love," she said, faintly.

"Indeed it should," I said.

Ysonde sat straight up among the field flowers.

"I do not love," she said.

"I know it," I replied gaily, and I let the bandage drop from my eye. "The pain is all gone," I said, closing my left eye to see whether my vision was impaired.

I was totally blind in my right eye.

For an instant the shock staggered me. I don't know how long I sat, mouth open, staring at the sun with one sound, one sightless eye. Ysonde, her chin on her hands, lay with her face turned toward the White Lady, a towering peak in the east.

"Come," I said, rising, "your aunt will be impatient; dinner has been served this half hour." She sprang to her feet,—she had been in a reverie,—and gave me a long look winch I could not define.

"And your eye doesn't pain?" she asked, after a moment.

"No," I said, for the pain had disappeared with the sight; "I am all right except a headache."

"And you can see perfectly well?"

"Perfectly."

It was at this point that truth and I parted; for what was a lost eye that it should cause her a moment's regret?

## II.

It was about this time that the oculist came to Holderness and visited me at the Rosebud Inn. I was in a dark room; Ysonde thought it better, believing darkness a cure for headache. When the oculist walked in—his name was Keen,—he said, "What the devil are you doing here?"

"I am blind in one eye—will it be noticeable?" I asked.

"Banged in the eye?" he enquired, opening the shutters.

"Banged in the eye," I repeated, as he bent over me.

His examination lasted scarcely ten seconds. After a moment he rose and closed the shutters, and I stood up in the darkness.

"Will it disfigure me?" I asked again.

"No,—an oculist could tell the difference perhaps. You may go out in three weeks."

"Blind?"

"Nonsense," growled Keen, "you have another eye yet."

"But I am an artist," I said in a low voice, "is there hope?"

I heard Keen sit down in the room, and his rocking-chair squeaked through five minutes of the bitterest darkness I ever knew. I could stand it no longer, so I rose and felt my way towards the rocking-chair,—I wanted to touch him—I was terrified. Well, it only lasted a few moments—most men pass through crises—I was glad he did not attempt to pity me.

"It was Miss—" he began.

"Hush!" I whispered. "Who told you, Keen?"

"She did," he replied. "Of course, she need never know you are—"

"Blind," I said,—"No, she need not know it."

I heard him feeling for the door.

"Turn your back," he said.

I did so.

"Three weeks?" I enquired over my shoulder.

"Yes—don't smoke."

"What the devil shall I do?" I said, savagely.

"Think on your sins, old chap,"—we had studied together in the Latin Quarter—"think of Pepita—"

"I won't," I cried. Keen hummed in a mischievous voice,

> "Quand le sommeil sur to famille
> Autour de toi s'est repondu,
> O Pépita, charmante fille,
> Mon amour, à quoi penses-tu?"

"Keen," I said, "I'll break your head, if I am one-eyed."

"I'm a married man," he replied, "and I refuse your offer; that's better, I like to hear the old ring in your voice, Bobby—keep a stiff upper lip. Surgery and painting are not the only things we learned in the Quarter."

I heard the door close behind him, then turned and groped my way toward the bed.

□ □ □

How I ever lived through those three weeks! Well, I did, and every fresh pipe of Bird's-eye tasted sweeter for my disobedience.

"Write him," I dictated through the closed door to Ysonde,—"write him that I am smoking six pipes a day as he directed." After all, if I was going to be blind in one eye, I did not care whether tobacco hastened the blow, and I was glad to poke a little fun at Keen.

Ysonde could not imagine why the doctor had recommended smoking—

she had heard that it weakened the sight, but she wrote as I directed, merely expressing her distrust in Keen, which amused me, for he is now one of the most famous oculists in the world.

"Yes," said I, through the key-hole, "Keen is young, and has much to learn, but I dare not disobey orders. How is your aunt?"

"My aunt is well, thank you, Bobby; did you like the sherbet she made?"

"Yes—that's six times you have asked me." I was wearying of lying. The sherbet reposed among the soapsuds of my toilet jar.

Ysonde's aunt, a tall aristocratic beauty, whose perfectly arched eye-brows betrayed the complacent vacancy of her mind, had actually prepared, with her own fair hands, a sherbet for me. I cannot bear sweets of any kind.

"Aunt Lynda will make another to-morrow," cooed Ysonde through the key-hole.

"Thank her for me," said I faintly; "Ysonde, I am coming out to-night."

"It is not yet three weeks!" cried Ysonde.

"It will be three weeks to-morrow at 1 p.m. My eyes won't suffer at night. I should like to smell the woods a little. Will you walk with me this evening?"

"If Aunt Lynda will allow me," said Ysonde. After a moment she added: "I will ask her now"; and I heard her rise from her chair outside my door.

When she came back, I was lying face downwards on my bed, miserable, dreading the hour when I should first face my own reflection in a mirror. I heard her step on the stairs, and I jumped up and groped my way toward the door.

"Bobby," she called softly.

"Ysonde," I answered, with my mouth close to the key-hole. She started— I heard her—for she did not know I was so near. I bent my head to listen.

"Aunt Lynda says you are foolish to go out before to-morrow—"

"The evening won't hurt me."

"But suppose—only suppose your disobedience should cost you the sight of your eye?"

"It won't," said I.

"Think how I should feel?"

"It won't," I repeated. The perspiration suddenly dampened my forehead, and I wiped it away.

"Can't you wait?" she pleaded.

"No. Have you your aunt's permission to walk with me this evening?"

"Yes," she said. "Shall I read to you a little while?"

For an hour I listened to her voice, and if it was Lovelace or Herrick or Isaac Walton, I do not know upon my soul, but I do know that my dark room was filled with the delicious murmur; and I heard the trees moving in the evening wind and the twitter of sleepy birds from the hedge. It might have been the perfume from the roses under my window—perhaps it was the fragrance of her hair—she bent so close to my door outside— but a sweet smell tinctured the darkness about me, stealing into my senses; and I rose and opened my blinds a little way.

It was night. I heard the rocky river rushing through the alders and the pines swaying on the ridge. The ray from the moon which silvered the windows caused my eyes no pain.

I listened. Through the low music of her voice crept the song of a night-thrush. A breeze stirred the roses under my window; the music of voice and thrush was stilled. Then, in the silence, some wild creature cried out from the mountain side.

"me damnée!" I muttered; for my soul was heavy with the dread of the coming morning.

"What are you murmuring in there by yourself?" whispered Ysonde, through the door.

"Nothing—was it a lynx on Noon Peak?"

"I heard nothing," she said.

"Nor I," said I, opening the door.

The light from the lamp dazzled but did not hurt me. She laid down the book and came swiftly toward me.

"Now," said I, "we will walk under the stars—with your aunt's permission."

I heard her sigh as she took my arm; "Bobby, I am so glad your eye is well. What could you have done if you had lost the sight of an eye?"

# III.

The morning was magnificent. A gentleman with symmetrical whiskers named Blylock and I were standing on the verandah of the Rosebud Inn. Blylock's mind was neutral. His lineage was long, his voice modulated, his every action acutely impersonal. The subdued polish of Harvard was reflected from his shoes to his collar. When he smoked he smoked judiciously, joylessly.

"And you lost the fish?" said I.

"Yes," said Blylock, with colourless enthusiasm.

"In the West Branch?"

"Near the Forks," said Blylock. "Do you know the pool?"

I regretted that I did not. He had once asked me whether I knew the Stryngbenes of Beacon Street, and I had replied with the same regret. Now he learned that I was culpably ignorant of the pool at the West Branch

Forks.

Blylock looked at the mountains. The White Lady was capped with mist, but except for that there was not a cloud in the sky. The Gilded Dome towered, clear cut as a cameo, against the pure azure of the northern horizon; Lynx Peak, jagged and cold, shot up above the pines of Crested Hawk, whose sweeping base was washed by the icy river.

"Do you think he might weigh five pounds?" I asked.

"Possibly," replied Blylock; "I regret exceedingly that I lost him."

"But, thank God, Plymouth Rock still stands!" was what I felt he expected me to say. I did not; I merely asked him if he had ever experienced emotion. "Why, of course," he answered seriously, but when I begged him to tell me when, he suspected a joke and smiled. If I had a son who smiled like that I would send him to Tony Pastor's. Oh, that smile!—gentle, vacant, blank as the verses of a Brook Farm Bard, bleaker than Bunker Hill.

"For sweet charity's sake," said I, "tell me why you do it, Blylock."

"Do what?" he asked.

"Oh," said I wearily, "nothing—lose a five-pound trout, for instance."

"I had on a brown hackle," said Blylock; "it was defective."

"It bust," said I, brutally, "did you curse?"

"No," replied Blylock. Ysonde came out and we took off our shooting-caps.

"Put them on again directly," said Ysonde, nestling deep into the collar of her jacket; "is it too cold for the trout to rise, Mr. Blylock?"

Blylock looked at the sky and then at his finger tips. There was a seal ring on one of his fingers which I was tired of seeing.

I listened to his even voice, I noticed his graceful carriage—I even noticed the momentary flush on his cold cheeks. Oh, how tired I was of looking at him; it wearied me as it wearies me to read advertisements in the cars of the elevated railroad. But I liked him.

"Blylock," said I, "get a gait on you, and we'll whip the stream to the Intervale before dinner."

"The water will be cold," said Ysonde. "You ought to have waders."

Now Ysonde knew that I had no waders. I loathed them. Blylock always wore waders.

"Thank you," said Blylock, "I will not neglect to wear them."

I looked at Ysonde and met her eyes.

"Oh," said I, spoiling everything with intentional obstinacy, "Mr. Blylock never forgets his waders." For a moment the colour touched her cheek, but she treated me much better than I deserved.

"Bobby," said Ysonde, "remember that you have been ill, and if you wade the river in knickerbockers you will be obliged to eat sherbet again."

So she knew the mystery of the soapsuds.

"I have no waders, Ysonde," I said humbly, "do you think I had better not go?"

"You know best," she said indifferently; and I got my deserts to the placid satisfaction of Blylock.

Ysonde walked away to join her aunt and I loafed about, sniffing the breeze, sulky, undecided, until Blylock appeared with rod and creel.

"Going?" enquired Blylock.

"No, I shall paint," I said, after a moment's silence.

He joined Ysonde and her aunt, and I saw them all walking toward the trail that crosses the river by the White Cascade. Blylock had undertaken to teach Ysonde to cast. I was surprised when she accepted, for I myself had taught her to cast. However I never asked any explanation and she never offered any—to my secret annoyance.

It was just two weeks that I had been out of the dark room. I was totally blind in my right eye, but nobody except Keen and myself knew it. I was becoming used to it—I was only too thankful that the eye, to all appearances, was as perfect as the other eye. But I dreaded to begin painting again. I feared that everything might be colourless and lop-sided, that I should be a ruined man as far as my profession was concerned. I had put off the beginning of work from sheer cowardice. Nobody but an artist can appreciate my mental suffering;—nobody but an artist knows that two eyes are little enough to see with. Had the accident destroyed the balance of my sight? Would my drawing be exaggerated, unstable, badly constructed, out of proportion? Would my colour be weak or brutally crude? I decided to find out without further delay, so when Ysonde and her aunt and Blylock had disappeared, I went to my room, gathered up my well-worn sketching kit, screwed two canvases into the holder, and marched manfully out the door into the sunlit forest.

Ridiculous Billy followed me. This capricious porcupine had taken a violent fancy to me, from the moment I emerged from the dark room. Of course I preferred his friendship to his enmity—I still bore a red scar on my ankle—but what soothed me most was his undisguised hatred of Blylock. Billy bit him whenever he could, and the blood of Bunker Hill appealed to Heaven from the piazza of the Rosebud Inn!

Blylock took it very decently—the porcupine was Ysonde's property—but although he himself suffered in silence, and Ysonde darned his golf-stockings as partial reparation, I always fancied that his blood was importuning Heaven, and, remembering George III, I trembled for Ridiculous Billy.

Sometimes I was sorry for Blylock, sometimes I was not, especially when Ysonde darned his golf-stockings. Blylock was Lynda Sutherland's cousin, but I demonstrated to Ysonde that this did not concern her. Sometimes I wished that Blylock would go back to Beacon Street, and yet I had grown fond of him in a way.

The porcupine followed me into the forest, poking his rat-like muzzle into every soft rotten stump, twitching his white whiskers. A red squirrel followed him from tree to tree, chattering and squealing with rage, but Billy lumbered along, stolid, blasé, entirely wrapped up in his own business. What that business was I dared not enquire, for Billy's malicious eyes boded evil for interlopers, and I respected his privacy.

Walking along the fragrant brown trail, barred with sunlight, I recalled that cold gray morning in camp when Sutherland—Lynda's late lamented—waking from the troubled dreams incident on an overdose of hot whiskey and water, called to me, to take "that thing away!" "That thing" was Billy. From his nest among the pine-clad ridges, he had smelled our pork, and being a freeborn American, he had descended to appropriate it. In the gray of the morning, through the smouldering camp-fire smoke, I saw Billy in the act of removing the pork from the crotches of a spruce tree.

"What is it? Take it away for God's sake!" bellowed Sutherland, associating Billy with other grotesque phantoms incident on overdoses.

"It's a porcupine," said I.

"Pink?" faltered Sutherland.

"Go to sleep, you brute," I muttered, not addressing the porcupine. I took a poncho, a thick one, and ran the porcupine down. Then I enveloped him in the blanket, and got a rope about his neck, tied him to a tree and examined my wounds. One of our guides helped me pull the spines from my person, and that night the other guide led Ridiculous Billy into the settlement which consists of the Rosebud Inn and three barns.

The taking of Billy preceded Sutherland's death by twenty-four hours; he was mauled by a panther whose cubs he was investigating. His wife, Lynda, who had secured a few month's reprieve from his presence, and who first heard of his death at Fortress Monroe, came north with Ysonde. Sutherland was buried in New York, and two weeks later Lynda and Ysonde came to the Rosebud Inn. All this happened three years ago, and during those three years, Billy, gorgeous with a silver collar, had never forgiven me for removing him from his native wilds. His attitude toward the household was unmistakable. Lynda he avoided, Ysonde he followed with every mark of approbation, Blylock he loathed, and now, he had taken this sudden shine to me.

Billy and I followed the trail, solemnly, deliberately. The trail was a blind one, now plain, brown and gold with trampled wet leaves, now invisible, a labyrinth of twisted moose-bush and hemlock, badly blazed. But we knew our business, Billy and I, for presently we crossed a swift brook, darkling among mossy hollows, and turning to the right, entered a moist glade all splashed with dewy sunlight.

"Here," said I, unstrapping my camp-stool, "is a woodland Mecca"; and I drove my white umbrella deep into the bank, where the brook widened in sunny shallows.

Billy eyed me a moment, rolled a pine-cone over with his nose, and mounted a tree. I liked to watch him mount trees. He did not climb, he neither scrambled nor scratched, he simply flowed up the trunk.

"Pleasant dreams," said I, as he curled up in the first moss-covered crotch; and I began to set my palette.

In the fragrant sun-soaked glade the long grass, already crisp as hay, was vibrating with the hum of insects. Shy forest butterflies waved their soft wings over the Linnea, long-legged gnats with spotted wings danced across the fern patches, and I saw a great sleepy moth hanging from a chestnut twig among the green branches overhead. His powdery wings, soft as felt, glistened like gilded dust.

"An Imperial Moth," said I to myself, for I was glad to recognize a friend. Then a wood-thrush ruffled his feathers under the spreading ferns, and I saw a baby rabbit sit up and wriggle its nose at me.

"Lucky for you I'm not a fox," said I, picking up a pointed sable brush; and I drew the outline of the chestnut tree, omitting the porcupine in the branches.

When I had indicated a bit of the forest beyond the glade, using a pointed brush dipped in Garance Rose foncée, I touched in a mousey shadow or two, scrubbed deep warm tones among my trees, using my rag when I pleased, and then, digging up a brushful of sunny greens and yellows, slapped it boldly on the foreground. Over this I drew a wavering sky reflection, indicated a sparkle among the dewy greens, scrubbed more sunlight into the shallow depths of the brook, and leaned back with a nervous sigh. What had God taken from me when he took the light from my eye? I pondered in silence while round me the brown-winged forest flies buzzed and hummed and droned an endless symphony. To me, with my single trembling eye, my painted foreground seemed aglow with sunlight, and the depths of the quiet forest, wrapped in hazy mystery, appeared true and just, slumbering there upon my canvas.

The brook prattled to me of dreams and splendid hopes, the pines whispered of fame, the ferns rustled and nodded consolation. I raised my head. High in the circle of quivering blue above, a gray hawk hung, turning, turning, turning in silence.

A light step sounded among the fallen leaves. Slowly I turned, my sight dazzled by the sky, but before my eye had found its focus I heard her low laughter and felt her touch on my arm.

"You were asleep," she said, "you must not deny it, do you hear me?"

"I was not asleep," I answered, rising from my camp-stool.

"Then you are blind,—why I have been standing there for two minutes."

"Two minutes? then I believe that I must be blind," said I, turning so that I could see her better. She stood on my right.

"I expected to be challenged," said she; "I did not hear your qui vive."

Then she sat down on my camp-stool and gazed at my canvas with amazement.

I watched her in silence, proud of my work, happy that she should recognize it, for she knew good work every time. After a while I began to chafe at her silence, and I bent my head to see her face. I shall never forget the pained surprise in her eyes nor the quiver of her voice as she said:

"Bobby, this is childish, what on earth do you mean by such work?"

The blow had fallen. At first I was stunned. Then terror seized me, and I grasped a low swinging branch to steady myself, for I felt as though I were falling.

"Bobby," she cried, "you are white—are you ill?"

"No," said I, "that sketch was only a joke,—to tease you."

"It is a very stupid joke," she said coldly; "I cannot understand how an artist could bring himself to do such a thing."

"It was a poor joke," said I, red as fire, "pardon me, Ysonde, I don't know what possessed me to paint like that."

She picked up my paint rag and swept it across the face of my canvas; then turning to me:

"Now you are forgiven; come and talk to me, Bobby."

The sun climbed to the zenith and still we sat there, she with her round white chin on her wrist, I at her feet.

Billy, who had descended from his perch in the chestnut tree as soon as he heard Ysonde's voice, rambled about us, snuffling and snooping into every tuft of fern, one evil eye fixed on us, one on the red squirrel who chattered and twitched his brush, and rushed up and down a big oak tree in a delirium of temper.

"No," replied Ysonde to my question, "Mr. Blylock did not fish; he talked to Lynda most of the time. I came here because I had an intuition that you were going to paint."

"But," said I, "how did you know I was coming here? I never before painted in this glade."

"I don't know how I knew it," said Ysonde, slowly.

"Witchcraft?" I asked.

"Possibly," she said, with an almost imperceptible frown.

"I have noticed already," I said, "that you have a mysterious faculty for reading my thoughts and divining my intentions. Are you aware of it?"

"No," she said shortly.

"But you have," I persisted.

"You flatter yourself, Bobby. I am not thinking of you every minute."

"Suppose," said I, after a moment's silence, "that you loved me—"

"I shall not suppose so," she answered haughtily.

"Let us suppose, then," said I, "that I love you—"

"Really, Bobby, you are more than tiresome."

I thought for a while in silence. The wood-thrush, who had come quite close to Ysonde—all wild creatures loved her—began to sing. The baby rabbit sat up to listen and wriggle its nose, and the speckled gnats danced giddily.

"Suppose," said I, with something in my voice that silenced her, "suppose that you loved me, and that I had lost my eye. Would you still love me?"

"Yes," said Ysonde, with an effort.

"And suppose," I continued, "I had been born with an eye blind; could you have loved such a man?"

"I do not think I could," she answered truthfully.

"Probably not," I repeated, biting the stem of a wild strawberry. After a moment I looked up into the sky. The hawk was not there; but I was not looking for the hawk.

"Come," said I, rising, "dinner must be ready and your aunt should not be kept waiting."

I gathered up my sketching kit, tenderly perhaps, for I should never use it again, and whistled Billy to heel,—which he did when he chose.

Perhaps it was something in my face—I don't know—but Ysonde suddenly came up to me and took both my hands.

"Are you going to be sensible, Bobby?" she asked. Her face was very serious.

"Yes, Ysonde," I said.

But she did not seem satisfied—there came a faint glow on her face—it may have been a sunbeam—and she dropped my hands and whistled to Billy.

"Come!" she cried, with a tinge of anger in her voice that I had never before heard,—"heel, Billy!"

But as Billy lingered, sniffing and rooting among the ferns, she picked up a twig and struck Billy on the nose. The blow was gentle—it would not have hurt a mosquito—but I was astounded, for it was the first time I had ever seen her lift her hand in anger to any living creature. Perplexed and wondering I followed her through the forest, my locked colour-box creaking on my shoulder.

# IV.

"To him that hath shall be given, and from him that hath not, shall be taken away even that which he hath," said I, knocking my pipe against the verandah railing.

"Scripture," said Blylock, approvingly.

"For this is the law and the prophets," I continued, grateful that the Bible had received Boston's approval.

"Scripture," repeated Blylock, with the smile of a publisher mentioning the work of a very young author.

"Exactly," I replied, "also the Koran; I forget whether Tupper mentions it."

"Probably," said Blylock seriously.

"Probably," I repeated, inserting a straw in the stem of my pipe. Ysonde frowned at me. "Blylock," I continued, smiling at nothing, "have you read Emerson?"

"Heavens!" murmured Blylock under his breath.

I had aroused him. I made it a point to stir him up once every day, satisfied to allow him to relapse into his normal Beacon Street trance afterward.

"Your scriptural quotation," said Ysonde, with a dangerous light in her eyes, "would indicate that you have suffered a loss."

"From him that hath not, shall be taken away even that which he hath," I repeated; "yes, having nothing, I have lost all I have, which," I continued, "is of course nothing. But I am encroaching on Brook Farm,—and the Koran—"

"And on the patience of your friends," said Ysonde; "don't try to be epigrammatic, Bobby." There was a glass of water standing on a table to my right. I did not see it, my right eye being sightless, and I knocked it over. I was confused and startled at this—it brought back to me my misfortune so cruelly that I apologized more than was necessary, and received a puzzled stare from Ysonde. I noted it and chafed helplessly. Lynda Sutherland came out on the porch, and I rose and brought her a chair.

"The moonlight reminds me of Venice," said Lynda, turning her lovely face to the moon.

We all agreed with her, although we knew it was nonsense, for we all had lived in Venice. If she had said it reminded her of peach ice-cream, we would have agreed. She was too beautiful for one to analyze what she said—she was too beautiful to analyze it herself. I remembered with a shock that the late lamented had once referred to his wife's being "d—nd ornamental," and I was glad the panther had clawed his besotted soul from his body. But Sutherland had never said a truer thing in his life; drunkard that he was, he always spoke the truth.

"Lynda," cooed Ysonde, "do you think that we might camp for a few days with Bobby and Mr. Blylock? They are going to the Black Water to-morrow and Mr. Blylock asked us."

"We take two guides," added Blylock, vaguely.

"We will only stay three days," said I.

"We will have a trout supper," suggested Blylock.

"And flap-jacks for breakfast," said I.

"I should so like to go," pleaded Ysonde. Blylock examined the moon, and I saw Lynda look at him.

"Is there any danger?" she asked.

I was discreetly silent; the question was not addressed to me.

"I think not," said Blylock turning around, "I carry a rifle."

"Three cheers for Bunker Hill," I said, "there is nothing to shoot—"

"Except—panthers," observed Blylock dryly.

At this tactless remark I expected to hear Lynda refuse to go. She did not, although she looked at Blylock a little reproachfully. He, serenely unconscious, examined his seal ring in silence. Possibly Lynda did not believe that panthers ranged so near the Inn, perhaps she was not ungrateful to the last one that had patted her late lamented into a better land.

"There are," said I, truthfully, "a few panthers ranging between the Gilded Dome and Crested Hawk. Sometimes they get as far as Noon Peak and the White Lady, sometimes even as far as Lynx Peak, but I never heard of anything bigger than a lynx being seen near the Black Water."

"I have been in these forests every summer and autumn for twenty years," said Blylock, "and I never saw either panther or lynx; have you?" he ended, turning toward me. Then, recollecting that I had witnessed the mauling of the late lamented, he turned rosy, and I was pleased to see that he was capable of experiencing two whole emotions in one evening.

I did not answer—it was not necessary, of course. I could show him the panther skin in my studio some day when I wanted to take a rise out of him. It measured nine feet from tip to tip—it might have measured more had the panther had time to nourish himself with Sutherland.

Now Ysonde must have read what was passing in my mind, for she looked shocked and nestled closer to Lynda.

"What is a lynx," demanded Lynda, shivering.

"There are two species found here," replied Blylock, glad to change the subject, "one the big grey Canada lynx, the other the short-tailed American lynx—"

"Otherwise Bob-cat, Lucivee, and wild-cat," I interposed; "they make a horrid noise in the woods and are harmless."

"If you let them alone," added Blylock, conscientious to the end.

"Which we will," said Ysonde, gaily, "we are going, are we not, Lynda?"

"No," said Lynda, firmly.

But the next morning when the first sunbeams scattered the mist which clung to copse and meadow, and sent it rolling up the flanks of the Gilded Dome, Lynda said, "Yes," and possibly her pretty mountain costume tipped the balance in Ysonde's favour, for Lynda looked like a fin-de-siècle Diana in that frock and she knew it, bless her fair face!

The guides, Jimmy Ellis and Buck Hanson, were tightening straps and rolling blankets on the lawn outside.

"Buck," said I, "how many pounds do you take in?"

"Fifty, sir," drawled Buck, wiping the sweat from his face with the back of his hand.

"And you, Jimmy?" I asked.

"Abaout forty, sir," replied Ellis, seriously.

"I cal'late," added Buck, "the ladies will want extry blankets."

"They will," I replied, "the wind is hauling around to the northwest." Then I took a step nearer and dropped my voice.

"Any panthers seen lately, Jimmy?"

"I hain't seed none," replied Ellis.

"What was it killed the white heifer two weeks ago?"

"Waal," replied Jimmy reflecting a little, "I cal'late t'war a cat."

"It maught be a b'ar," said Buck, "I seed one daown to Drake's clearin' last week come Sabbath."

"Sho!" drawled Ellis, returning to his blankets.

"I understand," said I, "that Ezra Field found a thirty-pound trap missing last week."

"Whar?" asked Hanson.

"Back of the gum-camp on Swift River," I replied.

Ellis looked cynical and Hanson laughed, the silent confiding laughter of the honest.

"Ezry was scairt haf to deth by a Bob-cat, onct, into Swift River Forks," said Ellis; "he sees things whar there hain't nawthin'."

"Do you think," said I, after a long pull at my pipe, "that panthers ever attack? I mean, when you let their cubs alone."

"Hain't never seed no panther," replied Buck. "You saw Mr. Sutherland when he was brought in three years ago."

"Yes sir—you and Cy Holman toted him in."

"Well, you saw the panther we brought in also, didn't you?"

"Yes sir,—but that was a daid panther," replied Buck, prosaically.

I laughed and walked toward the piazza.

"All I want to know is whether you fellows have heard that these creatures are bothering honest people who mind their business," I said over my shoulder; and both the big guides laughed, and answered "No fear o' that sir!"

Half an hour later we were on the trail to the Black Water.

The morning was perfect, the air keen as September breezes on the moors, and the mottled sunlight spotted our broad trail which twisted and curved through the tangled underbrush along the bank of a mountain stream.

Blylock and Ysonde were well ahead, the latter swinging a light steelshod mountain stick; next came Lynda, beautiful and serene, approving the beauty of the forest in pleased little platitudes. I followed close behind, silent, spellbound by the splendour of the forest, charmed by the soft notes of the nesting thrushes and the softer babble of Lynda and the brook.

Broad dewy leaves slapped our faces, filmy floating spiders' meshes crossed our chins and cheeks and tickled Ysonde's pretty nose.

"You may walk ahead," she said to Blylock, "and break the spiders' webs for me."

"With pleasure," said Blylock, seriously, and I saw him take the lead, his single eyeglass gleaming in the sunshine.

"It is written," said I, flippantly, "that the first shall be last, and the last shall be first;—I believe that I should take the lead."

"Please do," said Ysonde, coolly, "it is your proper place."

Now Ysonde had never before said anything to me quite as sharp as that, although doubtless I had often invited it.

"Do you want me to go?" I asked inanely.

"If you care to clear the path, I would not object," said Ysonde.

"For you and Lynda," said I, feeling that I was speaking regardless of either sound or sense.

"—And for Mr. Blylock," added Ysonde, quietly.

"With pleasure," said I, vaguely wishing my tongue might stop wagging before I said something hopelessly foolish, "I shall clear the way for you—and Mr. Blylock."

I had said it; even Lynda raised her lovely eyes to me in disapproval. As for Ysonde, her face wore that pained expression that I dreaded to see—I had never seen it before but once—in the glade—and I felt that my proper place was among the wits of a country store. A boor in the kitchen of the Rosebud Inn would have had more instinctive tact—unless he was jealous!—that is the word!—I was jealous—vulgarly jealous of Blylock. Perhaps Ysonde read the shame in my face, perhaps she had divined my thoughts as she did when she chose, but she saw I was miserable, disgusted with myself, and she raised me to her own level with a smile so sweet and chivalrous that I felt there was manhood left in me yet.

"Bobby," she said, "you promised to show me how to blaze a trail. Have you forgotten?"

I dropped out of the path to the right, she to the left; Lynda passed us to join Blylock who was waiting, the two big guides tramped by, their boots creaking on the trodden leaves. I drew the light hatchet from my belt, removed the leather blade-cover, and started on.

"This is all it is," I said, and struck a light shaving from the bark of a hemlock, cutting it at the base with the next stroke so that the bit of bark fell, leaving a white scar on the tree trunk.

"Always on both sides," said I, repeating the stroke on the other side of the tree. "Will you try it, Ysonde?"

She took the hatchet in her small gloved hand, and the chips flew along the trail until I begged her to spare the forest.

"But the trees don't die!" she exclaimed. "Oh, Bobby, you're joking; am I overdoing it?"

"A little," said I, "a blind man could follow this forest boulevard."

"You are blind," she said, calmly.

"Blind?" I cried with a start.

"—To your own interests, Bobby. Aunt Lynda likes you, but she doesn't like to hear you speak flippantly. If you destroy her trust in you, she will not let us walk together when we please." We moved on in silence for a while, until Ysonde, tired of blazing, handed me the hatchet.

"Yes," said I, "I am blind—I cannot lead you—on any trail."

"Nor I you," she said simply.

I did not reply, for who but I should know that through the fragrant forest, bathed in sun and dew, the blind led on the blind.

"You have formed a habit," said Ysonde, "of muttering to yourself. Are you afraid to have me know your thoughts?"

"Yes," said I, turning, "I am afraid."

She did not answer, but I saw her colour deepen, and I feared that I had spoken bitterly.

"I was thinking that I had forgotten my flask," I continued gaily.

"Mr. Blylock has your flask—you were not thinking of that," said Ysonde.

"Well," said I, "then tell me of what I was thinking; you know you can read my thoughts—when you take the trouble," I added prudently.

"Bobby," said Ysonde, "I would take more trouble for your sake than you dream of."

I stopped short in the trail and faced her, but she passed me impatiently. I saw her bite her lips as she always did when annoyed.

The chestnut, oak, and dappled beech-woods were giving place to pines and hemlocks as we wheeled from the Gilded Dome trail into the narrower trail that leads over the long divide to the Black Water. Along the rushing stream alder and hazel waved, silver birches gleamed deep-set in tangled depths, and poplars rose along the water's edge, quivering as the breezes freshened, every glistening leaf a-tremble.

Under foot, brown pine-needles spread a polished matting over the forest mould, for we had entered the pine belt and the long trail had just begun.

The breeze in the pines! it will always make me think of Ysonde. Wild wind-swept harmonies swelling from the windy ridge, the whisper and sigh and rush of water, the grey ledges, the deep sweep of precipices where lonely rivers glimmer, lost in the sea of trees,—these I remember as I think of Ysonde, these and more too,—the dome of green, the fragments of sky between mixed branches, the silence, broken by a single birdnote.

□  □  □

The trail crossed a sunny glade, mossy and moist, bordered by black birch thickets and carpeted with winter-green. Ysonde leaned upon her steel-shod staff and looked at her own reflection in the placid spring pool, shining among the ferns.

"I am very much tanned," she said.

"Are you thirsty," I asked.

"There is a little freckle beside my nose," observed Ysonde.

"It is becoming," I said truthfully.

"Yes, I am thirsty," said Ysonde, "—what do you know about freckles?"

I handed her a cup of water; she drank a little, looked over the rim of the cup reflectively, drank a little more, sighed, smiled, and poured what was left of the water upon the moss.

"A libation to the gods," she explained.

"To which?" I asked.

"Ah," she said; "I had not thought of that. Well, then, to—to—"

I looked at her and she tossed the cup to me saying, "I shall not tell you. I am getting into the habit of telling you everything."

"But—but the gentleman's name?" I urged.

"No, no! Goodness! may I not have a secret, all my own?"

"Very well," said I, "you pour out libations to a gentleman god and I shall even up matters. Here's to the lady!"

"Minerva, of course. You are so wise," suggested Ysonde.

"It's neither to Minerva nor to the owl," said I, "it's to the Lady Aphrodite."

"Pooh!" said Ysonde, "you are not clever; Hermes might—"

"Might what?"

"Be careful, Bobby, your sleeve is getting wet—"

"Might what?"

"Now how should I know," exclaimed Ysonde, "mercy, I'm not a little Greek maiden!"

I strapped the cup to my belt, tightened the buckle of my rod-case, lighted my pipe, and sat down on a log.

"Well, Master Bobby," said Ysonde in that bantering voice which she used when perfectly happy.

"Well, Mistress Ysonde," said I.

"Are you going to lose the others?"

I pointed to the foot of the long slope, where, among the tree trunks, something blue fluttered.

"It's Lynda's veil," said Ysonde, "and there is Mr. Blylock, also; they are sitting down."

"True," said I, "let us rest also. We have been hours on the trail. Here is a dry spot on this log."

Ysonde sat down. Now whenever Ysonde seated herself there was something in the pose of her figure that made me think of courts and kings and coronations. The little ceremony of seating herself ended, I resumed my seat also, feeling it a privilege accorded only to the very great. I told her this and she pretended to agree with me.

"You must be something at court," she said, "you cannot be an earl, for earls are blond and slender; you cannot be a count, for counts are dark and dapper; nor a duke, for dukes are big and always red in the face; you might be a baron—no, they are fierce and merciless—"

"So am I."

"No you're not. You can't be a marquis either, for they are plausible and treacherous—"

"Then I'll be a Master of 'Ounds," I insisted, "let the title go by the board."

She agreed, and I was installed Master of Stag-hounds to her petite Majesty—this position permitting me to sit occasionally in her presence.

"I am thirsty again," said Ysonde.

I brought her a cup of ice-cold water into which I dropped a dozen wild strawberries. She touched a berry with the tip of her pink tongue, which was bad manners, and I told her so.

"What do you know about Queen's etiquette?" she said disdainfully, and, finding the berries ripe, she ate three and smiled at me.

A thrush came fearlessly to her very feet and drank from the spring; a mottled wood-toad made futile efforts to clamber up the log into her lap, and two red lizards peeped at her from a cleft in the boulder beside us.

"It's queer," said I, watching the scrambling toad, "how you seem to fascinate all wild creatures. Shall I poke the toad away?"

"No, I am not afraid; I am very glad they all come to me."

"You were possibly a dryad once," I hazarded.

"Possibly. And you?"

"Probably the oak tree that sheltered you."

"Sheltered me?"

There is something in the note of a very young bird that I have noticed in Ysonde's voice, but now, as she laughed—oh, such soft, sweet laughter,—it seemed to me as though the bird had grown, and its note trembled with purer, truer melody.

"Sheltered me! I imagine it!" she said, with a wonderful sweetness in her eyes. "Hark! Mr. Blylock is calling!"

She rose with capricious grace as I answered Blylock in a view-halloo which awoke the echoes among the cliffs above us.

When we came up to them Lynda linked her arm in Ysonde's, and Blylock and I pushed ahead after the plodding guides.

Blylock and I discussed trout-flies and casts and philosophy with an occasional question to the guides, and as we moved I could hear the light laughter of Lynda and the clear voice of Ysonde singing old songs that were made in France when hawk's-bells tinkled in castle courts and tasselled palfreys pawed the drawbridge.

It was noon when we entered the Scaur Valley, and luncheon was grateful; but before the leading guide entered the spotted trail which swings to the west above the third spur of Crested Hawk, the sun had dropped into the notch between Mount Eternity and the White Lady, and the alpen-glow crimsoned every peak as we threw down our packs and looked out across the Black Water. "Here," said I, "our journey ends; Princess Ysonde,"—I took her gloved hand,—"be seated, for below you lies the Black Water—yours by right of conquest."

"I cal'late 't 'l be right cold to-night, Ma' am," said Buck Hanson.

"Yes," said Ysonde listlessly.

## V.

Night fell over the Black Water before the shelter was raised, but the great camp-fire lighted up the cleared space among the trees, and I saw Ellis staggering in under loads of freshly-stripped bark for our roof. Buck Hanson finished thatching the exposed ends with hemlock and spruce. The partition, a broad sheet of heavy bark, separated the lean-to into two sections, one for Lynda and Ysonde, the other for Blylock, myself, and the guides.

I had roamed about the underbrush, lopping off balsam twigs for our bedding which Blylock brought in and spread over the pine-needle floor.

When Ellis finished roofing the hut with his thick rolls of bark I sent him to the spring below with the camp kettle, and picking up an axe, called to Buck to follow.

"I should very much like," said Blylock solemnly, "to chop a tree into sections adequate for the camp fire."

"Take the axe and my blessing," said I, "I hate to chop."

"It's very good of you," said Blylock, following Buck into the forest where our firelight glimmered red on rugged trunks towering into the blackness above.

Ysonde came creeping out of her compartment, her eyes and cheeks brilliant in the fire's glare.

"Lynda is lying down," she said, "isn't supper nearly ready? How delicious our bed of balsam smells; what are you doing with your trout rod?"

I knotted the nine-foot leader to the line, slipped on an orange miller for a dropper, tied a big coachman three feet above it, and picked up my landing-net.

"What is home without a dinner?" I asked, "and what is dinner without a trout? Come down to that rock which hangs over the Black Water, and you shall see your future dinner leaping in the moonlight."

"Bobby the poet," said Ysonde, steadying herself by my arm in the dark descent to the lake. "Poet Bobby, there is no moon on the Black Water."

"Look," said I, pointing to a pale light in the sky above the White Lady, "the moon will come up over that peak in ten minutes; give me your hand, it's very dark."

Clinging closely to my arm, she moved through the undergrowth until we felt the firm flat rock under our feet. The rock ran straight out into the water at right angles from the shore like a pier.

"Be careful—oh, be careful," she urged, "you almost walked off into the water there where the shadows lie so black."

"Then hold me," said I diplomatically, and I felt her warm hands close tightly on my left arm. The moon peeped over the shoulder of the White Lady as I made my first cast into the darkness ahead, and I saw my leader strike the water, now placidly rocking like a lake of molten silver.

"Oh-h!" cried Ysonde, softly, "oh, the wondrous beauty of it all."

In the silence I heard the thwack of an axe from the woods above and Blylock's voice quite plainly. The water lapped the edges of the rock below us, catching thin gleams from the shining sheet beyond, and my silk line whistled and whimpered like a keen wind lashing the sea.

Then a wonderful thing occurred. Out of the depths of the burnished water a slim shape shot, showering the black night with spray. Splash! A million little wavelets hurried away into the darkness, crowding, sparkling, dancing in widening circles, while the harsh whirr of the reel rang in my ears, and the silk line melted away like a thread of smoke. The rod staggered in my hand.

"Ysonde, there are two on now!" I whispered.

"Give me the rod!" she said, excitedly. I handed it to her, and for a moment she felt the splendid strain. Then the fish gave a deep surge to the west, and she gasped and pushed the rod into my hands.

"Living wild things struggling for life," she sighed. "Oh, hurry, Bobby,— it pains me so!" and she pressed both hands to her breast.

For a second the joy of the battle left me. I had an impulse to fling the rod into the Black Water; but I am a hunter by instinct.

Deeper and deeper surged the fish, and the rod swayed and bent until the tip brushed my knuckles.

"Oh, kill the creatures," murmured Ysonde, "it is all so fierce and cruel,— I never thought you were like that!"

"I am," I muttered, checking a savage sweep toward the north,—"quick, Ysonde—pass me my net."

She did so, and I crawled down to the water's edge, shortening my line at every step. It was soon over; I washed my hands in the black water, and flung the fish back into the landing-net.

"Now," said I, tossing rod and net over my shoulder, "we will go to dinner; lean on my shoulder;—how brutal you must think me, Ysonde."

"Yes," said Ysonde.

She passed me—perhaps it was the moonlight that whitened her cheeks—and I saw her enter the circle of red firelight as Lynda came forward to meet her.

"Hello, Ellis!" I called.

"Hallo, sir!" came back from the spring among the rocks below, and Jimmy Ellis appeared, carrying a chunk of pork.

"Two," I said, turning the trout out of the landing-net.

"Good fish, sir," drawled Ellis, "mor'n 'nuff for dinner, I suspicion."

"Split them," said I, "broil both as only you can broil them. Spring all right?"

"Sweet an' full. Dinner is ready above."

Blylock came down with a blazing pine knot to inspect the fish, and I heard him rigging his rod ten minutes later as I walked into camp and sat down, glowing from a dip in the tin bucket below.

Lynda and Ysonde were nibbling away at broiled trout, hot toast, and potted pheasant.

"Dear me," said Lynda, "I really must not eat like this, I have had three cups of bouillon to begin with. Ysonde says you are the cleverest angler in the world."

"That, of course," said Ysonde, "may be an exaggeration, for I have seen very few anglers."

"Oh, you're not exaggerating one bit," I assured her. "Is there any toast over there?"

Lynda deigned to serve me with hot bouillon and Ysonde tossed a slice of toast to me, scandalizing her aunt.

"You little savage," said Lynda, reproachfully.

"Any trout left?" I asked. "Where is Mr. Blylock?"

"Here's the trout," smiled Ysonde, serving me a bit of the crisp pink fish. "Mr. Blylock said 'ha!' several times when he saw your two trout and went down to the rock flourishing his rod very recklessly."

"Mr. Blylock never flourishes anything," observed Lynda.

"No, he waved it as Merlin might have waved—"

"Why, Ysonde!" said Lynda, warmly.

I was discreet enough to finish my toast in silence; I was very happy.

"Now, Sir Fisherman," said Ysonde, "a cup of this white wine with your trout? What! a whole bottle? Oh, Lynda, look at him!"

"I see him," said Lynda, sleepily, "I wonder what time it is."

Buck and Jimmy, having finished their dinner, which included a trout between them and a gallon or so of coffee, piled half a dozen logs on the fire, backed them with half a tree trunk, said goodnight very politely, and ambled away with the dishes and a pail of boiling water. Ten minutes later Blylock came in with three fair-sized fish, which Lynda admired and I encored, and then Lynda and Ysonde rose with deep reverences, and mockingly prayed to be allowed to retire.

Buck and Jimmy were already sound asleep.

"If they snore," said I, "there will be murder done on Black Water shore."

Blylock lighted a cigar and I my pipe.

"I never sleep well in camp the first night," said I.

"No?" asked Blylock, politely.

"No, you old jay," said I, for I was becoming very fond of Blylock. That broke the back of Beacon Street for the moment, and Blylock blossomed out as a story-teller without equal. I laughed till it hurt me, softly, of course, and still Blylock, imperturbable, bland, told story after story, until I marvelled, between my spasms of laughter, at the make-up of this Bostonian. At last he went to bed, mildly suggesting that I follow his example, which I did after I finished my pipe, although I knew I should sleep but little.

About ten o'clock Buck Hanson snored. I leaned over Blylock, already fast asleep, and poked the wretched Buck until he stopped. Ten minutes later

Ellis began a solo which I have never since heard equalled.

"Great heavens!" I muttered, and jabbed him viciously with my rod-butt, but Jimmy Ellis didn't wake, and before I knew it, Buck Hanson, taking a mean advantage, chimed in with a snort that would have done credit to a rogue elephant. This was not all. I dread to record it, but I am trying to tell the truth in this story—I pray the lady to pardon me if I suggest that from the other side of the bark partition came a sound,—delicate, discreet, but continuous, in short, a gentle—no! no! I can never bring myself to write it down. I am no brute, Madam—and, after all, only men snore.

A black fly got into my neck and bothered me; later a midge followed the example of his erring colleague. To slay them both was my intention, and in doing so I awoke Blylock, who sleepily protested. This was exasperating, and I told him so, but he was asleep again before I finished. Why on earth I should never be able to sleep more than an hour or so on my first night in camp,—I who have camped in the forest for years,—I never can understand.

I endured the concerted snores of the whole camp as long as I could, then I crawled to the fire outside, hauled two fresh logs into the blaze, swathed myself in my blankets, lighted a fresh pipe, and sat down with my feet to the heat and my back against a sapling.

Outside the wavering ring of firelight the blackness was so profound, so hopelessly impenetrable that I wondered whether a storm was rolling up behind the Scaur. Trees, brush, rocks, and ledges—the whole huge forest, root and branch, seemed woven together into curtains of utter darkness which wavered, advanced, and receded with the ever dying, ever leaping flames. There was no storm, for I saw stars on the strip of darkness above—little pale stars, timidly glimmering in the depths of a vast vault. The moon had long ago passed behind the Scaur—that sullen mass of menacing ledges, blackening the fathomless stretch of the Black Water. There were noises in the forest, stealthy steps and timid scratchings—now faint, as if across the rocking lake, now nearer, now so sudden and sharp that I involuntarily leaned forward, striving to pierce the outer circle of gloom beyond the fire ring. Once something brushed and rustled among the leaves behind me, and I saw a grey snake glide into the warm glow by my feet.

"Get out," I whispered, with a gesture of annoyance.

The serpent slowly raised its head, flashed a forked tongue at me, swayed a moment, then noiselessly moved on into the night.

"Salut! O mon Roi!" said a low voice behind me, and Ysonde crept out of her fragrant bed of balsam, and curled up in her blanket at my feet.

"Oh, dear," she sighed, "I am so sleepy, but I can't sleep. Why is it, Bobby?—I haven't closed my eyes once."

"Then," said I, under my breath, "it was not you who—"

"Sh-h! Lynda might hear you."

"Not probable, judging from symptoms."

"You're impertinent, Bobby—hark! do you hear? What was it?"

"Anything from a toad to a porcupine; the forest is always full of sounds. Are you warm, Ysonde?"

"Yes,—and so sleepy that—ah! what was that?"

"Anything from a wood-mouse to a weasel."

"I don't believe it."

"A fawn, perhaps—I heard deer among the pitcher-plants at the head of the Black Water a few minutes ago."

"Gentle things," murmured Ysonde, "I wish they would come close to me; I love them—I love everything."

"And everything on earth and sea loves you, Ysonde."

Her lids were drooping, and she smiled, half asleep.

"Bobby," she murmured, "I believe I could sleep here by you—you make me sleepy."

Her head drooped and rested on my blanket. After a moment—it may have been an hour—I whispered, bending above her: "Do you sleep, Ysonde?" and again, "do you sleep?"

The stars flickered and died in the heavens, the flames sank lower, lower, and the great black night crept into the camp, smothering the fading fire with pale shadows, vague and strange, moving, swaying, until my eyes closed and I slept.

Was it a second—was it an hour? I sat bolt upright staring at the dying embers before me. A bit of charred log fell in with a soft crash sending a jet of sparks into the air, where they faded and went out. Went out? There were two—two big green sparks that had not faded with the others, and I, half asleep, watched them, vaguely curious. Ah! they are moving now— no, they are still again, close together.

The hair stirred on my head, my heart ceased, thumped once, stopped— it seemed hours,—and leaped into my throat, almost stifling me with its throbbing. I was not dreaming, for I felt the sweat trickling in my eyebrows, and the roots of my hair were cold and damp.

Ysonde moved in her slumber, frowned and raised her hand.

A low snarl came from the shadows. Slowly the power of thinking returned to me, but my eye never left those two green sparks, now blazing like lamps there in the darkness.

When would the thing spring? Would I have time to fling Ysonde behind me? Would it spring if I called to Blylock? Blylock had a rifle. Would it spring if I moved, or if Ysonde moved again? Gently, scarcely stirring, I tried to free my knees, and the creature snarled twice.

"It's against all precedent in these woods," I thought, "for any of the cat tribe to dare attack a camp." A sudden anger took possession of me, a fury of impatience, and quick as the thought, I sprang among the embers and hurled a glowing branch straight into the creature's eyes. What happened after that I can scarcely tell; I know a heavy soft mass struck me senseless, but my ears at moments ring yet with that horrid scream which seemed to split and tear the night asunder, wavering, quavering, long after I was hurled on my back, and my eyes seemed stark open in oceans of blood.

# VI.

When I came to my senses it was still dark—or so it seemed to me. After a while I felt a hand shifting the bandage which pressed heavily over both eyes, and in a moment or two somebody raised me by the shoulders, somebody else by the knees, and I heard Blylock cock his rifle, and say: "Give me that torch, Buck, and walk faster."

"Blylock," I gasped, "they're lugging me in as I lugged in Sutherland—mauled by a panther," and I laughed miserably.

"Hello!" said Blylock, in a low voice, "I thought you'd brace up; are you bleeding much?"

"I don't know," I muttered; "what in hell's the matter?"

"Matter!" repeated Blylock, "the forest has gone mad—it's preposterous, but the woods are full of bob-cats, troops of 'em, and the skulking brutes have actually got the nerve to follow us."

"Can't I walk?" I groaned. "Where is Ysonde?"—for I was beginning to remember.

"Walk?—yes, if you want to bleed to death—the ladies are here between me and the guides who are toting you."

"Ysonde," I murmured, "pardon me for my profanity—I am dazed—where are you?"

"Here, Bobby," whispered Ysonde—"close beside you; don't talk, dear, you are very much hurt."

"Are you speaking to me, Ysonde?" I said, doubting my senses.

"To you, Bobby," she whispered close to my ear, "didn't you know that I loved you? Ah, try to live and you will know!"

My strength was ebbing fast, but I think I muttered something that she understood, for the light touch of her hand was on my cheek, and I felt it tremble. Somebody gave me water,—I was choking,—and my burning lips shrank and cracked beneath the cool draught. I could hear Jimmy Ellis muttering to Buck Hanson, and Hanson's replies.

"Look out, Buck, here's a rut,—Mr. Blylock, can you dip your pine knot this side?—so fashion,—steady, Buck."

"Steady, it is,—hold up his legs,—Mr. Blylock, throw a stun by that windfall,—there's a lucivee sneakin' araound in behind—"

Crack! spoke Blylock's rifle, and then I heard Buck's nasal drawl: "A stun is jest's good, Mr. Blylock, they're scairt haf to deth—I suspicion it's the pork they're after!"

"Throw that pork into the woods, Jimmy," said Blylock, "we'll be in before long. Good heavens! how dark it is—lay him down and throw that pork away—there may be a panther among them."

"There be," drawled Buck, "I seen him."

"You did? Why didn't you say so! I can't waste cartridges on those infernal lynxes."

"I sez to you, Mr. Blylock, sez I, throw stuns, it's jest as good," replied Buck, placidly; and I was lifted again, fore and aft.

"It's incredible," grumbled Blylock; "what's got into all these moth-eaten lynxes and mangy panthers; I've been twenty years in these woods, and I never before saw even a tom-cat."

"I ain't seed nothing like this,—there's three 'r four bob-cats raound us now, and I ha'n't never seed but one so close before,—Jimmy was there that night. I jest disremember if it was abaout gummin' time—"

Crack! went Blylock's rifle, and I heard a whine from the thickets on the left.

"Thet's the panther—let him hev it again," said Ellis.

Again the rifle cracked.

"The darned cuss!" drawled Buck; "shoot again, Mr. Blylock!"

"No need," said Ellis—"listen! There he goes lopin' off. Hear him snarl!"

"Hit, I guess," said Buck, and we moved on.

Once I heard Buck complain that a particularly bold lynx kept trotting along the trail behind, "smellin' and sniffin' almighty close to my shins," he asserted, and there certainly was an awful yell when Blylock wheeled in his tracks and fired. I heard Ellis laughing, and Buck said, "haow them lucivees du screech!"

"Worse'n a screech-owl," added Ellis.

That is the last thing I remembered until I woke in my bed in the Rosebud Inn.

The bandage was still on my eyes,—I felt too weak to raise a finger,—and the rest of my body seemed stiff and hard as wood. I heard somebody rocking in a rocking-chair and I spoke.

"I am here," said Ysonde,—but her voice seemed choked and unsteady.

"What time is it?" I asked, incoherently.

"Half past eleven," said Ysonde.

"I am hungry," said I, and that was my last effort until they brought me a bowl of beef broth with an egg in it, and I had managed to swallow it all.

I heard the door close, and for a moment I thought I was alone, but presently the rocking-chair creaked, and I called again: "Ysonde."

"I am here."

"What is the matter with me?"

"You have been ill."

"How long?"

"Two days, Bobby. You will get well—the claws poisoned you. Try to sleep now."

"What claws?"

"The—the panther's—don't you remember?"

"No—yes, a little. Where are the lynxes? Where is Blylock?"

Ysonde laughed softly.

"Mr. Blylock has gone to Boston on important business. I will tell you all about it when you can get up. He's to be married."

"And Lynda?"

"Lynda is downstairs. Shall I call her?"

"No."

The next day I drank more broth, and two days later I sat up,— it took me half an hour and some groans to do so.

"I think," said I, listening to the rocking-chair, "that it is high time I saw something. Lift my bandage, please, Ysonde."

"Only one side," she said, and lowered the cloth that concealed my right eye—the sightless one.

There was a silence, a wretched moment of suspense, and then Ysonde cried: "What—what is it—can't you see—can't you see me!—Oh, Bobby!"

When I spoke I hardly knew what I said, but it was something about Keen's assuring me that nobody but an oculist could tell that I was blind in my right eye. I remember I felt very angry at Keen, and demanded to know how Ysonde could see that my right eye was sightless. I am glad I was spared the agony of her face—I would willingly have been spared the agony of her voice as she cried, "Did I do that?"

I tried to move, but her arms were about me,—I tried to explain, but her warm mouth closed my lips; I only thought that it was very pleasant to be blind.

The eyes of an oculist and the eyes of love see everything. Who says that love is blind? Her tears fell on my cheeks; when she asked pardon, I answered by asking pardon, and she—but, after all, that is our own affair.

"And my left eye," said I, "is that gone, too?"

"Almost well," said Ysonde, "it was a sympathetic shock, or something;

I was afraid the claws had struck it, but Dr. Keen—"

"Keen!"

"Yes—he's gone to Holderness now. Don't you remember his being here with Dr. Conroy, the surgeon?"

"No," said I, "I was too badly mauled. I have been clawed by a panther, then?"

"A little," said Ysonde, with gentle sarcasm.

After a moment I inquired about the present health of the panther, and was assured that he was probably flourishing his tail in excellent spirits somewhere among the Scaur crags.

"Then Blylock didn't hit him?"

"He hit something, for I heard it scream—Oh, my darling, what a horrible night!—and you dying, as I believed, and the tangled brush, and the flare of the torch, and the firing"—

□　□　□

"Are you thirsty?—your lips are burning," said Ysonde.

□　□　□

I have a joke on Keen—James Keen, the great oculist, the wise, the infallible,—and I trust he will swallow his medicine like a little man when he reads this. It happened in this way.

I was sitting under the trees by the Tennis Court with Ysonde, watching the snow-birds fluttering in the meadow grass, and listening to the robin who, boldly balanced on the tip of his spruce tree, was doing his best. The blue-birds were teaching their young to navigate the air, twittering and tittering at the efforts of their youngsters, a truly frivolous family. The drab-coloured cow had also done her best, and the result was a miniature copy of herself, also an expert cud-chewer.

Billy—Ridiculous Billy, the white-whiskered and malicious, was spread in the low forks of an apple tree, a splendid representation of a disreputable door-mat.

Lynda sat at the bay-window in the Rosebud Inn, embroidering something in white and gold. She also succeeded in doing her best in her own line, which was to look more beautiful every day. I saw Blylock's shadow behind her.

"When are they to be married, Ysonde?" I asked for the fiftieth time.

"On the twenty-seventh,—oh, Bobby, it's shocking to keep forgetting—and we're to be best man and bride's maid, too!"

The sun dazzled my left eye, and I closed it for a second. Then a miraculous thing happened, an everlasting joke on Keen, for, although I had closed my sound eye, and, by rights, should have been blind as a bat, I was nothing of the kind.

"My right eye—Ysonde—I can see!—Do you understand? I can see!" I stammered.

Oh, it was glorious—glorious as the joyous wonder in Ysonde's eyes!—it was a miracle. I don't care what Keen says about it having happened before, or about it happening once in ten thousand cases, and I don't care a brass farthing for his subsequent observations concerning the optic nerve, and partial paralysis, and retinas, and things,—it was and must remain one of God's miracles, and that is enough for Ysonde and for me.

"We will go to the glade and repaint my picture which you erased," said I.

She understood and forgave me, for I hardly knew what I was saying.

"Come," she said—her eyes were wonderfully sweet, and bluer than the flowering flax around us.

So, with her hand in mine, we walked up the scented path to the Rosebud Inn, Billy lumbering along behind us, twitching his hoary whiskers.

"Et pis, doucett'ment on s'endort,
On fait sa carne, on fait sa sorgue,
On ronfle, et, comme un tuyau d'orgue,
L'tuyau s'met à ronfler pus fort…."
                ARISTIDE BRUANT.

# A PLEASANT EVENING

## I.

As I stepped upon the platform of a Broadway cable-car at Forty-second Street, somebody said; "Hello, Hilton, Jamison's looking for you."

"Hello, Curtis," I replied, "what does Jamison want?"

"He wants to know what you've been doing all the week," said Curtis, hanging desperately to the railing as the car lurched forward; "he says you seem to think that the *Manhattan Illustrated Weekly* was created for the sole purpose of providing salary and vacations for you."

"The shifty old tom-cat!" I said, indignantly, "he knows well enough where I've been. Vacation! Does he think the State Camp in June is a snap?"

"Oh," said Curtis, "you've been to Peekskill?"

"I should say so," I replied, my wrath rising as I thought of my assignment.

"Hot?" inquired Curtis, dreamily.

"One hundred and three in the shade," I answered. "Jamison wanted three full pages and three half pages, all for process work, and a lot of line drawings into the bargain. I could have faked them—I wish I had. I was fool enough to hustle and break my neck to get some honest drawings, and that's the thanks I get!"

"Did you have a camera?"

"No. I will next time—I'll waste no more conscientious work on Jamison," I said sulkily.

"It doesn't pay," said Curtis. "When I have military work assigned me, I don't do the dashing sketch-artist act, you bet; I go to my studio, light my pipe, pull out a lot of old *Illustrated London News*, select several suitable battle scenes by Caton Woodville—and use 'em too."

The car shot around the neck-breaking curve at Fourteenth Street.

"Yes," continued Curtis, as the car stopped in front of the Morton House for a moment, then plunged forward again amid a furious clanging of gongs, "it doesn't pay to do decent work for the fat-headed men who run the *Manhattan Illustrated*. They don't appreciate it."

"I think the public does," I said, "but I'm sure Jamison doesn't. It would serve him right if I did what most of you fellows do—take a lot of Caton

Woodville's and Thulstrup's drawings, change the uniforms, 'chic' a figure or two, and turn in a drawing labelled 'from life.' I'm sick of this sort
of thing anyway. Almost every day this week I've been chasing myself over
that tropical camp, or galloping in the wake of those batteries. I've got a
full page of the 'camp by moonlight,' full pages of 'artillery drill' and 'light
battery in action,' and a dozen smaller drawings that cost me more groans
and perspiration than Jamison ever knew in all his lymphatic life!"

"Jamison's got wheels," said Curtis,—"more wheels than there are bicycles in Harlem. He wants you to do a full page by Saturday."

"A what?" I exclaimed, aghast.

"Yes he does—he was going to send Jim Crawford, but Jim expects to go
to California for the winter fair, and you've got to do it."

"What is it?" I demanded savagely.

"The animals in Central Park," chuckled Curtis.

I was furious. The animals! Indeed! I'd show Jamison that I was entitled
to some consideration! This was Thursday; that gave me a day and a half
to finish a full-page drawing for the paper, and, after my work at the State
Camp I felt that I was entitled to a little rest. Anyway I objected to the subject. I intended to tell Jamison so—I intended to tell him firmly. However,
many of the things that we often intended to tell Jamison were never told.
He was a peculiar man, fat-faced, thin-lipped, gentle-voiced, mild-man-
nered, and soft in his movements as a pussy-cat. Just why our firmness
should give way when we were actually in his presence, I have never quite
been able to determine. He said very little—so did we, although we often
entered his presence with other intentions.

The truth was that the *Manhattan Illustrated Weekly* was the best paying,
best illustrated paper in America, and we young fellows were not anxious
to be cast adrift. Jamison's knowledge of art was probably as extensive as
the knowledge of any "Art editor" in the city. Of course that was saying
nothing, but the fact merited careful consideration on our part, and we
gave it much consideration.

This time, however, I decided to let Jamison know that drawings are not
produced by the yard, and that I was neither a floor-walker nor a hand-
me-down. I would stand up for my rights; I'd tell old Jamison a few
things to set the wheels under his silk hat spinning, and if he attempted
any of his pussy-cat ways on me, I'd give him a few plain facts that would
curl what hair he had left.

Glowing with a splendid indignation I jumped off the car at the City
Hall, followed by Curtis, and a few minutes later entered the office of the
*Manhattan Illustrated News.*

"Mr. Jamison would like to see you, sir," said one of the compositors as
I passed into the long hallway. I threw my drawings on the table and

passed a handkerchief over my forehead.

"Mr. Jamison would like to see you, sir," said a small freckle-faced boy with a smudge of ink on his nose.

"I know it," I said, and started to remove my gloves.

"Mr. Jamison would like to see you, sir," said a lank messenger who was carrying a bundle of proofs to the floor below.

"The deuce take Jamison," I said to myself. I started toward the dark passage that leads to the abode of Jamison, running over in my mind the neat and sarcastic speech which I had been composing during the last ten minutes.

Jamison looked up and nodded softly as I entered the room. I forgot my speech.

"Mr. Hilton," he said, "we want a full page of the Zoo before it is removed to Bronx Park. Saturday afternoon at three o'clock the drawing must be in the engraver's hands. Did you have a pleasant week in camp?"

"It was hot," I muttered, furious to find that I could not remember my little speech.

"The weather," said Jamison, with soft courtesy, "is oppressive everywhere. Are your drawings in, Mr. Hilton?"

"Yes. It was infernally hot and I worked like a nigger—"

"I suppose you were quite overcome. Is that why you took a two days' trip to the Catskills? I trust the mountain air restored you—but—was it prudent to go to Cranston's for the cotillion Tuesday? Dancing in such uncomfortable weather is really unwise. Good-morning, Mr. Hilton, remember the engraver should have your drawings on Saturday by three."

I walked out, half hypnotized, half enraged. Curtis grinned at me as I passed—I could have boxed his ears.

"Why the mischief should I lose my tongue whenever that old tom-cat purrs!" I asked myself as I entered the elevator and was shot down to the first floor. "I'll not put up with this sort of thing much longer—how in the name of all that's foxy did he know that I went to the mountains? I suppose he thinks I'm lazy because I don't wish to be boiled to death. How did he know about the dance at Cranston's? Old cat!"

The roar and turmoil of machinery and busy men filled my ears as I crossed the avenue and turned into the City Hall Park.

From the staff on the tower the flag drooped in the warm sunshine with scarcely a breeze to lift its crimson bars. Overhead stretched a splendid cloudless sky, deep, deep blue, thrilling, scintillating in the gemmed rays of the sun.

Pigeons wheeled and circled about the roof of the grey Post Office or dropped out of the blue above to flutter around the fountain in the square.

On the steps of the City Hall the unlovely politician lounged, exploring his heavy under jaw with wooden toothpick, twisting his drooping black moustache, or distributing tobacco juice over marble steps and close-clipped grass.

My eyes wandered from these human vermin to the calm scornful face of Nathan Hale, on his pedestal, and then to the grey-coated Park police-man whose occupation was to keep little children from the cool grass.

A young man with thin hands and blue circles under his eyes was slum-bering on a bench by the fountain, and the policeman walked over to him and struck him on the soles of his shoes with a short club.

The young man rose mechanically, stared about, dazed by the sun, shiv-ered, and limped away. I saw him sit down on the steps of the white mar-ble building, and I went over and spoke to him. He neither looked at me, nor did he notice the coin I offered.

"You're sick," I said, "you had better go to the hospital."

"Where?" he asked vacantly—"I've been, but they wouldn't receive me."

He stooped and tied the bit of string that held what remained of his shoe to his foot.

"You are French," I said.

"Yes."

"Have you no friends? Have you been to the French Consul?"

"The Consul!" he replied; "no, I haven't been to the French Consul."

After a moment I said, "You speak like a gentleman."

He rose to his feet and stood very straight, looking at me, for the first time, directly in the eyes.

"Who are you?" I asked abruptly.

"An outcast," he said, without emotion, and limped off thrusting his hands into his ragged pockets.

"Huh!" said the Park policeman who had come up behind me in time to hear my question and the vagabond's answer; "don't you know who that hobo is?—An' you a newspaper man!"

"Who is he, Cusick?" I demanded, watching the thin shabby figure mov-ing across Broadway toward the river.

"On the level you don't know, Mr. Hilton?" repeated Cusick, suspiciously.

"No, I don't; I never before laid eyes on him."

"Why," said the sparrow policeman, "that's 'Soger Charlie';—you re-member—that French officer what sold secrets to the Dutch Emperor."

"And was to have been shot? I remember now, four years ago—and he escaped—you mean to say that is the man?"

"Everybody knows it," sniffed Cusick, "I'd a-thought you newspaper gents would have knowed it first."

"What was his name?" I asked after a moment's thought.

"Soger Charlie—"

"I mean his name at home."

"Oh, some French dago name. No Frenchman will speak to him here; sometimes they curse him and kick him. I guess he's dyin' by inches."

I remembered the case now. Two young French cavalry officers were arrested, charged with selling plans of fortifications and other military secrets to the Germans. On the eve of their conviction, one of them, Heaven only knows how, escaped and turned up in New York. The other was duly shot. The affair had made some noise, because both young men were of good families. It was a painful episode, and I had hastened to forget it. Now that it was recalled to my mind, I remembered the newspaper accounts of the case, but I had forgotten the names of the miserable young men.

"Sold his country," observed Cusick, watching a group of children out of the corner of his eyes—"you can't trust no Frenchman nor dagoes nor Dutchmen either. I guess Yankees are about the only white men."

I looked at the noble face of Nathan Hale and nodded.

"Nothin' sneaky about us, eh, Mr. Hilton?"

I thought of Benedict Arnold and looked at my boots.

Then the policeman said, "Well, so long, Mr. Hilton," and went away to frighten a pasty-faced little girl who had climbed upon the railing and was leaning down to sniff the fragrant grass.

"Cheese it, de cop!" cried her shrill-voiced friends, and the whole bevy of small ragamuffins scuttled away across the square.

With a feeling of depression I turned and walked toward Broadway, where the long yellow cable-cars swept up and down, and the din of gongs and the deafening rumble of heavy trucks echoed from the marble walls of the Court House to the granite mass of the Post Office.

Throngs of hurrying busy people passed up town and down town, slim sober-faced clerks, trim cold-eyed brokers, here and there a red-necked politician linking arms with some favourite heeler, here and there a City Hall lawyer, sallow-faced and saturnine. Sometimes a fireman, in his severe blue uniform, passed through the crowd, sometimes a blue-coated policeman, mopping his clipped hair, holding his helmet in his white-gloved hand. There were women too, pale-faced shop girls with pretty eyes, tall blonde girls who might be typewriters and might not, and many, many older women whose business in that part of the city no human being could venture to guess, but who hurried up town and down town, all occupied with *something* that gave to the whole restless throng a common likeness— the expression of one who hastens toward a hopeless goal.

I knew some of those who passed me. There was little Jocelyn of the *Mail and Express;* there was Hood, who had more money than he wanted and was going to have less than he wanted when he left Wall Street; there was Colonel Tidmouse of the 45th Infantry, N.G.S.N.Y., probably coming from the office of the *Army and Navy Journal*, and there was Dick Harding who wrote the best stories of New York life that have been printed. People said his hat no longer fitted,—especially people who also wrote stories of New York life and whose hats threatened to fit as long as they lived.

I looked at the statue of Nathan Hale, then at the human stream that flowed around his pedestal.

"Quand même," I muttered and walked out into Broadway, signalling to the gripman of an uptown cable-car.

I passed into the Park by the Fifth Avenue and 59th Street gate; I could never bring myself to enter it through the gate that is guarded by the hideous pigmy statue of Thorwaldsen.

The afternoon sun poured into the windows of the New Netherlands Hotel, setting every orange-curtained pane a-glitter, and tipping the wings of the bronze dragons with flame.

Gorgeous masses of flowers blazed in the sunshine from the grey terraces of the Savoy, from the high grilled court of the Vanderbilt palace, and from the balconies of the Plaza opposite.

The white marble façade of the Metropolitan Club was a grateful relief in the universal glare, and I kept my eyes on it until I had crossed the dusty street and entered the shade of the trees.

Before I came to the Zoo I smelled it. Next week it was to be removed to the fresh cool woods and meadows in Bronx Park, far from the stifling air of the city, far from the infernal noise of the Fifth Avenue omnibuses.

A noble stag stared at me from his enclosure among the trees as I passed down the winding asphalt walk. "Never mind, old fellow," said I, "you will be splashing about in the Bronx River next week and cropping maple shoots to your heart's content."

On I went, past herds of staring deer, past great lumbering elk, and moose, and long-faced African antelopes, until I came to the dens of the great carnivora.

The tigers sprawled in the sunshine, blinking and licking their paws; the lions slept in the shade or squatted on their haunches, yawning gravely. A slim panther travelled to and fro behind her barred cage, pausing at times to peer wistfully out into the free sunny world. My heart ached for caged wild things, and I walked on, glancing up now and then to encounter the blank stare of a tiger or the mean shifty eyes of some ill-smelling hyena.

Across the meadow I could see the elephants swaying and swinging their great heads, the sober bison solemnly slobbering over their cuds, the sarcastic countenances of camels, the wicked little zebras, and a lot more animals of the camel and llama tribe, all resembling each other, all equally ridiculous, stupid, deadly uninteresting.

Somewhere behind the old arsenal an eagle was screaming, probably a Yankee eagle; I heard the "tchug! tchug!" of a blowing hippopotamus, the squeal of a falcon, and the snarling yap! of quarrelling wolves.

"A pleasant place for a hot day!" I pondered bitterly, and I thought some things about Jamison that I shall not insert in this volume. But I lighted a cigarette to deaden the aroma from the hyenas, unclasped my sketching block, sharpened my pencil, and fell to work on a family group of hippopotami.

They may have taken me for a photographer, for they all wore smiles as if "welcoming a friend," and my sketch block presented a series of wide open jaws, behind which shapeless bulky bodies vanished in alarming perspective.

The alligators were easy; they looked to me as though they had not moved since the founding of the Zoo, but I had a bad time with the big bison, who persistently turned his tail to me, looking stolidly around his flank to see how I stood it. So I pretended to be absorbed in the antics of two bear cubs, and the dreary old bison fell into the trap, for I made some good sketches of him and laughed in his face as I closed the book.

There was a bench by the abode of the eagles, and I sat down on it to draw the vultures and condors, motionless as mummies among the piled rocks. Gradually I enlarged the sketch, bringing in the gravel plaza, the steps leading up to Fifth Avenue, the sleepy park policeman in front of the arsenal—and a slim, white-browed girl, dressed in shabby black, who stood silently in the shade of the willow trees.

After a while I found that the sketch, instead of being a study of the eagles, was in reality a composition in which the girl in black occupied the principal point of interest. Unwittingly I had subordinated everything else to her, the brooding vultures, the trees and walks, and the half indicated groups of sun-warmed loungers.

She stood very still, her pallid face bent, her thin white hands loosely clasped before her. "Rather dejected reverie," I thought, "probably she's out of work." Then I caught a glimpse of a sparkling diamond ring on the slender third finger of her left hand.

"She'll not starve with such a stone as that about her," I said to myself, looking curiously at her dark eyes and sensitive mouth. They were both beautiful, eyes and mouth—beautiful, but touched with pain.

After a while I rose and walked back to make a sketch or two of the lions and tigers. I avoided the monkeys—I can't stand them, and they never seem funny to me, poor dwarfish, degraded caricatures of all that is ignoble in ourselves.

"I've enough now," I thought; "I'll go home and manufacture a full page that will probably please Jamison." So I strapped the elastic band around my sketching block, replaced pencil and rubber in my waistcoat pocket, and strolled off toward the Mall to smoke a cigarette in the evening glow before going back to my studio to work until midnight, up to the chin in charcoal grey and Chinese white.

Across the long meadow I could see the roofs of the city faintly looming above the trees. A mist of amethyst, ever deepening, hung low on the horizon, and through it, steeple and dome, roof and tower, and the tall chimneys where thin fillets of smoke curled idly, were transformed into pinnacles of beryl and flaming minarets, swimming in filmy haze. Slowly the enchantment deepened; all that was ugly and shabby and mean had fallen away from the distant city, and now it towered into the evening sky, splendid, gilded, magnificent, purified in the fierce furnace of the setting sun.

The red disk was half hidden now; the tracery of trees, feathery willow and budding birch, darkened against the glow; the fiery rays shot far across the meadow, gilding the dead leaves, staining with soft crimson the dark moist tree trunks around me.

Far across the meadow a shepherd passed in the wake of a huddling flock, his dog at his heels, faint moving blots of grey.

A squirrel sat up on the gravel walk in front of me, ran a few feet, and sat up again, so close that I could see the palpitation of his sleek flanks.

Somewhere in the grass a hidden field insect was rehearsing last summer's solos; I heard the tap! tap! tat-tat-t-t-tat! of a woodpecker among the branches overhead and the querulous note of a sleepy robin.

The twilight deepened; out of the city the music of bells floated over wood and meadow; faint mellow whistles sounded from the river craft along the north shore, and the distant thunder of a gun announced the close of a June day.

The end of my cigarette began to glimmer with a redder light; shepherd and flock were blotted out in the dusk, and I only knew they were still moving when the sheep bells tinkled faintly.

Then suddenly that strange uneasiness that all have known—that half-awakened sense of having seen it all before, of having been through it all, came over me, and I raised my head and slowly turned.

A figure was seated at my side. My mind was struggling with the instinct to remember. Something so vague and yet so familiar—something that eluded thought yet challenged it, something—God knows what! troubled me. And now, as I looked, without interest, at the dark figure beside me, an apprehension, totally involuntary, an impatience to *understand*, came upon me, and I sighed and turned restlessly again to the fading west.

I thought I heard my sigh re-echoed—I scarcely heeded; and in a moment I sighed again, dropping my burned-out cigarette on the gravel beneath my feet.

"Did you speak to me?" said some one in a low voice, so close that I swung around rather sharply.

"No," I said after a moment's silence.

It was a woman. I could not see her face clearly, but I saw on her clasped hands, which lay listlessly in her lap, the sparkle of a great diamond. I knew her at once. It did not need a glance at the shabby dress of black, the white face, a pallid spot in the twilight, to tell me that I had her picture in my sketch-book.

"Do—do you mind if I speak to you?" she asked timidly. The hopeless sadness in her voice touched me, and I said: "Why, no, of course not. Can I do anything for you?"

"Yes," she said, brightening a little, "if you—you only would."

"I will if I can," said I, cheerfully; "what is it? Out of ready cash?"

"No, not that," she said, shrinking back.

I begged her pardon, a little surprised, and withdrew my hand from my change pocket.

"It is only—only that I wish you to take these,"—she drew a thin packet from her breast,—"these two letters."

"I?" I asked astonished.

"Yes, if you will."

"But what am I to do with them?" I demanded.

"I can't tell you; I only know that I must give them to you. Will you take them?"

"Oh, yes, I'll take them," I laughed, "am I to read them?" I added to myself, "It's some clever begging trick."

"No," she answered slowly, "you are not to read them; you are to give them to somebody."

"To whom? Anybody?"

"No, not to anybody. You will know whom to give them to when the time comes."

"Then I am to keep them until further instructions?"

"Your own heart will instruct you," she said, in a scarcely audible voice. She held the thin packet toward me, and to humour her I took it. It was wet.

"The letters fell into the sea," she said; "There was a photograph which should have gone with them but the salt water washed it blank. Will you care if I ask you something else?"

"I? Oh, no."

"Then give me the picture that you made of me to-day."

I laughed again, and demanded how she knew I had drawn her.

"Is it like me?" she said.

"I think it is very like you," I answered truthfully.

"Will you not give it to me?"

Now it was on the tip of my tongue to refuse, but I reflected that I had enough sketches for a full page without that one, so I handed it to her, nodded that she was welcome, and stood up. She rose also, the diamond flashing on her finger.

"You are sure that you are not in want?" I asked, with a tinge of good-natured sarcasm.

"Hark!" she whispered; "listen!—do you hear the bells of the convent!"

I looked out into the misty night.

"There are no bells sounding," I said, "and anyway there are no convent bells here. We are in New York, mademoiselle"—I had noticed her French accent—"we are in Protestant Yankee-land, and the bells that ring are much less mellow than the bells of France."

I turned pleasantly to say good-night. She was gone.

## III.

"Have you ever drawn a picture of a corpse?" inquired Jamison next morning as I walked into his private room with a sketch of the proposed full page of the Zoo.

"No, and I don't want to," I replied, sullenly.

"Let me see your Central Park page," said Jamison in his gentle voice, and I displayed it. It was about worthless as an artistic production, but it pleased Jamison, as I knew it would.

"Can you finish it by this afternoon?" he asked, looking up at me with persuasive eyes.

"Oh, I suppose so," I said, wearily; "anything else, Mr. Jamison?"

"The corpse," he replied, "I want a sketch by to-morrow—finished."

"What corpse?" I demanded, controlling my indignation as I met Jamison's soft eyes.

There was a mute duel of glances. Jamison passed his hand across his forehead with a slight lifting of the eyebrows.

"I shall want it as soon as possible," he said in his caressing voice.

What I thought was, "Damned purring pussy-cat!" What I said was, "Where is this corpse?"

"In the Morgue—have you read the morning papers? No? Ah,—as you very rightly observe you are too busy to read the morning papers. Young men must learn industry first, of course, of course. What you are to do is this: the San Francisco police have sent out an alarm regarding the disappearance of a Miss Tufft—the millionaire's daughter, you know. To-day a body was brought to the Morgue here in New York, and it has been identified as the missing young lady,—by a diamond ring. Now I am convinced that it isn't, and I'll show you why, Mr. Hilton."

He picked up a pen and made a sketch of a ring on a margin of that morning's *Tribune*.

"That is the description of her ring as sent on from San Francisco. You notice the diamond is set in the centre of the ring where the two gold serpents' *tails* cross! Now the ring on the finger of the woman in the Morgue is like this," and he rapidly sketched another ring where the diamond rested in the *fangs* of the two gold serpents.

"That is the difference," he said in his pleasant, even voice.

"Rings like that are not uncommon," said I, remembering that I had seen such a ring on the finger of the white-faced girl in the Park the evening before. Then a sudden thought took shape—perhaps that was the girl whose body lay in the Morgue!

"Well," said Jamison, looking up at me, "what are you thinking about?"

"Nothing," I answered, but the whole scene was before my eyes, the vultures brooding among the rocks, the shabby black dress, and the pallid face,—and the ring, glittering on that slim white hand!

"Nothing," I repeated, "when shall I go, Mr. Jamison? Do you want a portrait—or what?"

"Portrait,—careful drawing of the ring, and,—er—a centre piece of the Morgue at night. Might as well give people the horrors while we're about it."

"But," said I, "the policy of this paper—"

"Never mind, Mr. Hilton," purred Jamison, "I am able to direct the policy of this paper."

"I don't doubt you are," I said angrily.

"I am," he repeated, undisturbed and smiling; "you see this Tufft case interests society. I am—er—also interested."

He held out to me a morning paper and pointed to a heading.

I read: "Miss Tufft Dead! Her Fiancée was Mr. Jamison, the well known Editor."

"What!" I cried in horrified amazement. But Jamison had left the room, and I heard him chatting and laughing softly with some visitors in the press-room outside.

I flung down the paper and walked out.

"The cold-blooded toad!" I exclaimed again and again;—"making capital out of his fiancée's disappearance! Well, I—I'm d—nd! I knew he was a bloodless, heartless, grip-penny, but I never thought—I never imagined—" Words failed me.

Scarcely conscious of what I did I drew a *Herald* from my pocket and saw the column entitled: "Miss Tufft Found! Identified by a Ring. Wild Grief of Mr. Jamison, her Fiancée."

That was enough. I went out into the street and sat down in City Hall Park. And, as I sat there, a terrible resolution came to me; I would draw that dead girl's face in such a way that it would chill Jamison's sluggish blood, I would crowd the black shadows of the Morgue with forms and ghastly faces, and every face should bear something in it of Jamison. Oh, I'd rouse him from his cold snaky apathy! I'd confront him with Death in such an awful form, that, passionless, base, inhuman as he was, he'd shrink from it as he would from a dagger thrust. Of course I'd lose my place, but that did not bother me, for I had decided to resign anyway, not having a taste for the society of human reptiles. And, as I sat there in the sunny park, furious, trying to plan a picture whose sombre horror should leave in his mind an ineffaceable scar, I suddenly thought of the pale black-robed girl in Central Park. Could it be her poor slender body that lay among the shadows of the grim Morgue! If ever brooding despair was stamped on any face, I had seen its print on hers when she spoke to me in the Park and gave me the letters. The letters! I had not thought of them since, but now I drew them from my pocket and looked at the addresses.

"Curious," I thought, "the letters are still damp; they smell of salt water too."

I looked at the address again, written in the long fine hand of an educated woman who had been bred in a French convent. Both letters bore the same address, in French:

"CAPTAIN D'YNIOL.
(Kindness of a Stranger.)"

"Captain d'Yniol," I repeated aloud—"confound it, I've heard that name! Now, where the deuce—where in the name of all that's queer—"Somebody who had sat down on the bench beside me placed a heavy hand on my shoulder.

It was the Frenchman, "Soger Charlie."

"You spoke my name," he said in apathetic tones.

"Your name!"

"Captain d'Yniol," he repeated; "it is my name."

I recognized him in spite of the black goggles he was wearing, and, at the same moment, it flashed into my mind that d'Yniol was the name of the traitor who had escaped. Ah, I remembered now!

"I am Captain d'Yniol," he said again, and I saw his fingers closing on my coat sleeve.

It may have been my involuntary movement of recoil,—I don't know,—but the fellow dropped my coat and sat straight up on the bench.

"I am Captain d'Yniol," he said for the third time, "charged with treason and under sentence of death."

"And innocent!" I muttered, before I was even conscious of having spoken. What was it that wrung those involuntary words from my lips, I shall never know, perhaps—but it was I, not he, who trembled, seized with a strange agitation, and it was I, not he, whose hand was stretched forth impulsively, touching his.

Without a tremor he took my hand, pressed it almost imperceptibly, and dropped it. Then I held both letters toward him, and, as he neither looked at them nor at me, I placed them in his hand. Then he started.

"Read them," I said, "they are for you."

"Letters!" he gasped in a voice that sounded like nothing human.

"Yes, they are for you,—I know it now—"

"Letters!—letters directed to *me?*"

"Can you not see?" I cried.

Then he raised one frail hand and drew the goggles from his eyes, and, as I looked, I saw two tiny white specks exactly in the centre of both pupils.

"Blind!" I faltered.

"I have been unable to read for two years," he said.

After a moment he placed the tip of one finger on the letters.

"They are wet," I said; "shall—would you like to have me read them?" For a long time he sat silently in the sunshine, fumbling with his cane, and I watched him without speaking. At last he said, "Read, Monsieur," and I took the letters and broke the seals.

The first letter contained a sheet of paper, damp and discoloured, on which a few lines were written:

"My darling, I knew you were innocent—" Here the writing ended, but, in the blur beneath, I read: "Paris shall know—France shall know, for at last I have the proofs and I am coming to find you, my soldier, and to place them in your own dear brave hands. They know, now, at the War Ministry—they have a copy of the traitor's confession—but they dare not make it public—they dare not withstand the popular astonishment and rage. Therefore I sail on Monday from Cherbourg by

the Green Cross Line, to bring you back to your own again, where you
will stand before all the world, without fear, without reproach.

"ALINE."

"This—this is terrible!" I stammered; "can God live and see such things
done!"

But with his thin hand he gripped my arm again, bidding me read the
other letter; and I shuddered at the menace in his voice.

Then, with his sightless eyes on me, I drew the other letter from the wet,
stained envelope. And before I was aware—before I understood the purport of what I saw, I had read aloud these half effaced lines:

"The *Lorient* is sinking—an iceberg—mid-ocean—good-bye—you are
innocent—I love—"

"The *Lorient!*" I cried; "it was the French steamer that was never heard
from—the *Lorient* of the Green Cross Line! I had forgotten—I—"

The loud crash of a revolver stunned me; my ears rang and ached with
it as I shrank back from a ragged dusty figure that collapsed on the bench
beside me, shuddered a moment, and tumbled to the asphalt at my feet.

The trampling of the eager hard-eyed crowd, the dust and taint of powder in the hot air, the harsh alarm of the ambulance clattering up Mail
Street,—these I remember, as I knelt there, helplessly holding the dead
man's hands in mine.

"Soger Charlie," mused the sparrow policeman, "shot his-self, didn't he,
Mr. Hilton? You seen him, sir,—blowed the top of his head off, didn't he,
Mr. Hilton?"

"Soger Charlie," they repeated, "a French dago what shot his-self;" and
the words echoed in my ears long after the ambulance rattled away, and
the increasing throng dispersed, sullenly, as a couple of policemen cleared
a space around the pool of thick blood on the asphalt.

They wanted me as a witness, and I gave my card to one of the policemen who knew me. The rabble transferred its fascinated stare to me, and
I turned away and pushed a path between frightened shop girls and ill-
smelling loafers, until I lost myself in the human torrent of Broadway.

The torrent took me with it where it flowed—East? West?—I did not
notice nor care, but I passed on through the throng, listless, deadly weary
of attempting to solve God's justice—striving to understand His purpose—
His laws—His judgments which are "true and righteous altogether."

# IV.

"More to be desired are they than gold, yea, than much fine gold. Sweeter also than honey and the honey-comb!"

I turned sharply toward the speaker who shambled at my elbow. His sunken eyes were dull and lustreless, his bloodless face gleamed pallid as a death mask above the blood-red jersey—the emblem of the soldiers of Christ.

I don't know why I stopped, lingering, but, as he passed, I said, "Brother, I also was meditating upon God's wisdom and His testimonies."

The pale fanatic shot a glance at me, hesitated, and fell into my own pace, walking by my side. Under the peak of his Salvation Army cap his eyes shone in the shadow with a strange light.

"Tell me more," I said, sinking my voice below the roar of traffic, the clang! clang! of the cable-cars, and the noise of feet on the worn pavements—"tell me of His testimonies."

"Moreover by them is Thy servant warned and in keeping of them there is great reward. Who can understand His errors? Cleanse Thou me from secret faults. Keep back Thy servant also from presumptuous sins. Let them not have dominion over me. Then shall I be upright and I shall be innocent from the great transgression. Let the words of my mouth and the meditation of my heart be acceptable in Thy sight,—O Lord! My strength and my Redeemer!"

"It is Holy Scripture that you quote," I said; "I also can read that when I choose. But it cannot clear for me the reasons—it cannot make me understand—"

"What?" he asked, and muttered to himself.

"That, for instance," I replied, pointing to a cripple, who had been *born* deaf and dumb and horridly misshapen,—a wretched diseased lump on the sidewalk below St. Paul's Churchyard,—a sore-eyed thing that mouthed and mowed and rattled pennies in a tin cup as though the sound of copper could stem the human pack that passed hot on the scent of gold.

Then the man who shambled beside me turned and looked long and earnestly into my eyes. And after a moment a dull recollection stirred within me—a vague something that seemed like the awakening memory of a past, long, long forgotten, dim, dark, too subtle, too frail, too indefinite—ah! the old feeling that all men have known—the old strange uneasiness, that useless struggle to remember when and where it all occurred before.

And the man's head sank on his crimson jersey, and he muttered, muttered to himself of God and love and compassion, until I saw that the fierce heat of the city had touched his brain, and I went away and left him prating of mysteries that none but such as he dare name.

So I passed on through dust and heat; and the hot breath of men touched my cheek and eager eyes looked into mine. Eyes, eyes,—that met my own and looked through them, beyond—far beyond to where gold glittered amid the mirage of eternal hope. Gold! It was in the air where the soft sunlight gilded the floating moats, it was under foot in the dust that the sun made gilt, it glimmered from every window pane where the long red beams struck golden sparks above the gasping gold-hunting hordes of Wall Street.

High, high, in the deepening sky the tall buildings towered, and the breeze from the bay lifted the sun-dyed flags of commerce until they waved above the turmoil of the hives below—waved courage and hope and strength to those who lusted after gold.

The sun dipped low behind Castle William as I turned listlessly into the Battery, and the long straight shadows of the trees stretched away over greensward and asphalt walk.

Already the electric lights were glimmering among the foliage although the bay shimmered like polished brass and the topsails of the ships glowed with a deeper hue, where the red sun rays fall athwart the rigging.

Old men tottered along the sea-wall, tapping the asphalt with worn canes, old women crept to and fro in the coining twilight,—old women who carried baskets that gaped for charity or bulged with mouldy stuffs,—food, clothing?—I could not tell; I did not care to know.

The heavy thunder from the parapets of Castle William died away over the placid bay, the last red arm of the sun shot up out of the sea, and wavered and faded into the sombre tones of the afterglow. Then came the night, timidly at first, touching sky and water with grey fingers, folding the foliage into soft massed shapes, creeping onward, onward, more swiftly now, until colour and form had gone from all the earth and the world was a world of shadows.

And, as I sat there on the dusky sea-wall, gradually the bitter thoughts faded and I looked out into the calm night with something of that peace that comes to all when day is ended.

The death at my very elbow of the poor blind wretch in the Park had left a shock, but now my nerves relaxed their tension and I began to think about it all,—about the letters and the strange woman who had given them to me. I wondered where she had found them,—whether they really were carried by some vagrant current in to the shore from the wreck of the fated Lorient.

Nothing but these letters had human eyes encountered from the *Lorient*, although we believed that fire or berg had been her portion; for there had been no storms when the *Lorient* steamed away from Cherbourg.

And what of the pale-faced girl in black who had given these letters to me, saying that my own heart would teach me where to place them?

I felt in my pockets for the letters where I had thrust them all crumpled and wet. They were there, and I decided to turn them over to the police. Then I thought of Cusick and the City Hall Park and these set my mind running on Jamison and my own work,—ah! I had forgotten that,—I had forgotten that I had sworn to stir Jamison's cold, sluggish blood! Trading on his fiancée's reported suicide,—or murder! True, he had told me that he was satisfied that the body at the Morgue was not Miss Tufft's because the ring did not correspond with his fiancée's ring. But what sort of a man was that!—to go crawling and nosing about morgues and graves for a full-page illustration which might sell a few extra thousand papers. I had never known he was such a man. It was strange too—for that was not the sort of illustration that the *Weekly* used; it was against all precedent—against the whole policy of the paper. He would lose a hundred subscribers where he would gain one by such work.

"The callous brute!" I muttered to myself, "I'll wake him up—I'll—"

I sat straight up on the bench and looked steadily at a figure which was moving toward me under the spluttering electric light.

It was the woman I had met in the Park.

She came straight up to me, her pale face gleaming like marble in the dark, her slim hands outstretched.

"I have been looking for you all day—all day," she said, in the same low thrilling tones, "I want the letters back; have you them here?"

"Yes," I said, "I have them here,—take them in Heaven's name; they have done enough evil for one day!"

She took the letters from my hand; I saw the ring, made of the double serpents, flashing on her slim finger, and I stepped closer, and looked her in the eyes.

"Who are you?" I asked.

"I? My name is of no importance to you," she answered.

"You are right," I said, "I do not care to know your name. That ring of yours—"

"What of my ring?" she murmured.

"Nothing,—a dead woman lying in the Morgue wears such a ring. Do you know what your letters have done? No? Well I read them to a miserable wretch and he blew his brains out!"

"You read them to a man!"

"I did. He killed himself."

"Who was that man?"

"Captain d'Yniol—"

With something between a sob and a laugh she seized my hand and covered it with kisses, and I, astonished and angry, pulled my hand away from her cold lips and sat down on the bench.

"You needn't thank me," I said sharply; "if I had known that,—but no matter. Perhaps after all the poor devil is better off somewhere in other regions with his sweetheart who was drowned,—yes, I imagine he is. He was blind and ill,—and broken-hearted."

"Blind?" she asked gently.

"Yes. Did you know him?"

"I knew him."

"And his sweetheart, Aline?"

"Aline," she repeated softly,—"she is dead. I come to thank you in her name."

"For what?—for his death?"

"Ah, yes, for that."

"Where did you get those letters?" I asked her, suddenly.

She did not answer, but stood fingering the wet letters.

Before I could speak again she moved away into the shadows of the trees, lightly, silently, and far down the dark walk I saw her diamond flashing.

Grimly brooding, I rose and passed through the Battery to the steps of the Elevated Road. These I climbed, bought my ticket, and stepped out to the damp platform. When a train came I crowded in with the rest, still pondering on my vengeance, feeling and believing that I was to scourge the conscience of the man who speculated on death.

And at last the train stopped at 28th Street, and I hurried out and down the steps and away to the Morgue.

When I entered the Morgue, Skelton, the keeper, was standing before a slab that glistened faintly under the wretched gas jets. He heard my footsteps, and turned around to see who was coming. Then he nodded, saying: "Mr. Hilton, just take a look at this here stiff—I'll be back in a moment—this is the one that all the papers take to be Miss Tufft,—but they're all off, because this stiff has been here now for two weeks."

I drew out my sketching-block and pencils.

"Which is it, Skelton?" I asked, fumbling for my rubber.

"This one, Mr. Hilton, the girl what's smilin'. Picked up off Sandy Hook, too. Looks as if she was asleep, eh?"

"What's she got in her hand—clenched tight? Oh,—a letter. Turn up the gas, Skelton, I want to see her face."

The old man turned the gas jet, and the flame blazed and whistled in the damp, fetid air. Then suddenly my eyes fell on the dead.

Rigid, scarcely breathing, I stared at the ring, made of two twisted ser-pents set with a great diamond,—I saw the wet letters crushed in her slen-der hand,—I looked, and—God help me!—I looked upon the dead face of the girl with whom I had been speaking on the Battery!

"Dead for a month at least," said Skelton, calmly.

Then, as I felt my senses leaving me, I screamed out, and at the same in-stant somebody from behind seized my shoulder and shook me sav-agely—shook me until I opened my eyes again and gasped and coughed.

"Now then, young feller!" said a Park policeman bending over me, "if you go to sleep on a bench, somebody'll lift your watch!"

I turned, rubbing my eyes desperately.

Then it was all a dream—and no shrinking girl had come to me with damp letters,—I had not gone to the office—there was no such person as Miss Tufft,—Jamison was not an unfeeling villain,—no, indeed!—he treated us all much better than we deserved, and he was kind and gener-ous too. And the ghastly suicide! Thank God that also was a myth,—and the Morgue and the Battery at night where that pale-faced girl had—ugh!

I felt for my sketch-block, found it; turned the pages of all the animals that I had sketched, the hippopotami, the buffalo, the tigers—ah! where was that sketch in which I had made the woman in shabby black the prin-cipal figure, with the brooding vultures all around and the crowd in the sunshine—? It was gone.

I hunted everywhere, in every pocket. It was gone.

At last I rose and moved along the narrow asphalt path in the falling twi-light.

And as I turned into the broader walk, I was aware of a group, a po-liceman holding a lantern, some gardeners, and a knot of loungers gath-ered about something,—a dark mass on the ground.

"Found 'em just so," one of the gardeners was saying, "better not touch 'em until the coroner comes."

The policeman shifted his bull's-eye a little; the rays fell on two faces, on two bodies, half supported against a park bench. On the finger of the girl glittered a splendid diamond, set between the fangs of two gold serpents. The man had shot himself; he clasped two wet letters in his hand. The girl's clothing and hair were wringing wet, and her face was the face of a drowned person.

"Well, sir," said the policeman, looking at me; "you seem to know these two people—by your looks—"

"I never saw them before," I gasped, and walked on, trembling in every nerve.

For among the folds of her shabby black dress I had noticed the end of a paper,—my sketch that I had missed!

"Awed and afraid I cross the border-land.
Oh, who am I that I dare enter here
Where the great artists of the world have trod?"

ELLA WHEELER WILCOX.

# THE MAN AT THE NEXT TABLE

"The caricaturist is a freebooter. Public tolerance grants him letters of marque...."

MARMADUKE HUMPHREY.

"Ainsi rien ne se passe, rieu de vraiment immortel et d'éternellemeut doux que dans notre âme."

## I.

It was high noon in the city of Antwerp. From slender steeples floated the mellow music of the Flemish bells, and in the spire of the great cathedral across the square the cracked chimes clashed discords until my ears ached.

When the fiend in the cathedral had jerked the last tuneless clang from the chimes, I removed my fingers from my ears and sat down at one of the iron tables in the court. A waiter with his face shaved blue, brought me a bottle of Rhine wine, a tumbler of cracked ice, and a siphon.

"Does Monsieur desire anything else?" he inquired.

"Yes—the head of the cathedral bell-ringer; bring it with vinegar and potatoes," I said, bitterly. Then I began to ponder on my great-aunt and the Crimson Diamond.

The white walls of the Hotel St. Antoine rose in a rectangle around the sunny court, casting long shadows across the basin of the fountain. The strip of blue overhead was cloudless. Sparrows twittered under the eaves; the yellow awnings fluttered, the flowers swayed in the summer breeze, and the jet of the fountain splashed among the water plants. On the sunny side of the piazza the tables were vacant; on the shady side, I was lazily aware that the tables behind me were occupied, but I was indifferent as to their occupants, partly because I shunned all tourists, partly because I was thinking of my great-aunt.

Most old ladies are eccentric, but there is a limit, and my great-aunt had overstepped it. I had believed her to be wealthy;—she died bankrupt. Still, I knew there was one thing she did possess, and that was the famous "Crimson Diamond." Now, of course, you know who my great-aunt was.

Excepting the Koh-i-noor, and the Regent, this enormous and unique stone was, as everybody knows, the most valuable gem in existence. Any ordinary person would have placed that diamond in a safe-deposit. My great-aunt did nothing of the kind. She kept it in a small velvet bag, which she carried about her neck. She never took it off, but wore it dangling openly on her heavy silk gown.

In this same bag she also carried dried catnip leaves of which she was inordinately fond. Nobody but myself, her only living relative, knew that the Crimson Diamond lay among the sprigs of catnip in the little velvet bag.

"Harold," she would say, "do you think I'm a fool? If I place the Crimson Diamond in any safe-deposit vault in New York, somebody would steal it sooner or later." Then she would nibble a sprig of catnip and peer cunningly at me. I loathed the odour of catnip and she knew it. I also loathed cats. This also she knew and of course surrounded herself with a dozen. Poor old lady! On the 1st day of March, 1896, she was found dead in her bed in her apartments at the Waldorf. The doctor said she died from natural causes. The only other occupant of her sleeping room was a cat. The cat fled when we broke open the door, and I heard that she was received and cherished by some people in a neighboring apartment.

Now, although my great-aunt's death was due to purely natural causes, there was one very startling and disagreeable feature of the case. The velvet bag, containing the Crimson Diamond, had disappeared. Every inch of the apartment was searched, the floors torn up, the walls dismantled, but the Crimson Diamond had vanished. Chief of Police Conlin detailed four of his best men on the case, and as I had nothing better to do, I enrolled myself as a volunteer. I also offered $25,000 reward for the recovery of the gem. All New York was agog.

The case seemed hopeless enough, although there were five of us after the thief. McFarlane was in London, and had been for a month, but Scotland Yard could give him no help, and the last I heard of him he was roaming through Surrey after a man with a white spot in his hair. Harrison had gone to Paris. He kept writing me that clues were plenty and the scent hot, but as Dennet, in Berlin, and Clancy, in Vienna, wrote me the same thing, I began to doubt these gentlemen's ability.

"You say," I answered Harrison, "that the fellow is a Frenchman, and that he is now concealed in Paris; but Dennet writes me by the same mail that the thief is undoubtedly a German, and was seen yesterday in Berlin. To-day I received a letter from Clancy, assuring me that Vienna holds the culprit, and that he is an Austrian from Trieste. Now for Heaven's sake," I ended, "let me alone and stop writing me letters until you have something to write about."

The night clerk of the Waldorf had furnished us with our first clue. On the night of my aunt's death he had seen a tall, grave-faced man, hurriedly leave the hotel. As the man passed the desk, he removed his hat and mopped his forehead, and the night clerk noticed that in the middle of his head there was a patch of hair, as white as snow.

We worked this clue for all it was worth, and, a month later, I received a cable dispatch from Paris, saying that a man, answering to the description of the Waldorf suspect, had offered an enormous crimson diamond for sale to a jeweller in the Palais Royal. Unfortunately the fellow took fright and disappeared before the jeweller could send for the police, and since that time, McFarlane in London, Harrison in Paris, Dennet in Berlin, and Clancy in Vienna, had been chasing men with white patches on their hair until no grey-headed patriarch in Europe was free from suspicion. I myself had sleuthed it through England, France, Holland and Belgium, and now I found myself in Antwerp at the Hotel St. Antoine without a clue that promised anything except another outrage on some respectable white-haired citizen. The case seemed hopeless enough, unless the thief tried again to sell the gem. Here was our only hope, for, unless he cut the stone into smaller ones, he had no more chance of selling it than he would have had if he had stolen the Venus of Milo and peddled her about the rue de Seine. Even were he to cut up the stone, no respectable gem collector or jeweller would buy a crimson diamond without first notifying me; for although a few red stones are known to collectors, the colour of the Crimson Diamond was absolutely unique, and there was little probability of an honest mistake.

Thinking of all these things I sat sipping my Rhine wine in the shadow of the yellow awnings. A large white cat came sauntering by and stopped in front of me to perform her toilet until I wished she would go away. After a while she sat up, licked her whiskers, yawned once or twice, and was about to stroll on, when, catching sight of me, she stopped short and looked me squarely in the face. I returned the attention with a scowl because I wished to discourage any advances towards social intercourse which she might contemplate; but after a while her steady gaze disconcerted me, and I turned to my Rhine wine. A few minutes later I looked up again. The cat was still eyeing me.

"Now what the devil is the matter with the animal," I muttered, "does she recognize in me a relative?"

"Perhaps," observed a man at the next table.

"What do you mean by that?" I demanded.

"What I say," replied the man at the next table. I looked him full in the face. He was old and bald and appeared weak-minded. His age protected his impudence. I turned my back on him. Then my eyes fell on the cat again. She was still gazing earnestly at me.

Disgusted that she should take such pointed public notice of me, I wondered whether other people saw it; I wondered whether there was anything peculiar in my own personal appearance. How hard the creature stared. It was most embarrassing.

"What has got into that cat?" I thought. "It's sheer impudence. It's an intrusion, and I won't stand it!" The cat did not move. I tried to stare her out of countenance. It was useless. There was aggressive inquiry in her yellow eyes. A sensation of uneasiness began to steal over me—a sensation of embarrassment not unmixed with awe. All cats looked alike to me, and yet there was something about this one that bothered me—something that I could not explain to myself, but which began to occupy me.

She looked familiar—this Antwerp cat. An odd sense of having seen her before—of having been well acquainted with her in former years slowly settled in my mind, and, although I could never remember the time when I had not detested cats, I was almost convinced that my relations with this Antwerp tabby had once been intimate if not cordial. I looked more closely at the animal. Then an idea struck me,—an idea which persisted and took definite shape in spite of me. I strove to escape from it, to evade it, to stifle and smother it; an inward struggle ensued which brought the perspiration in beads upon my cheeks,—a struggle short, sharp, decisive. It was useless—useless to try to put it from me,—this idea so wretchedly bizarre, so grotesque and fantastic, so utterly inane,—it was useless to deny that the cat bore a distinct resemblance to my great-aunt!

I gazed at her in horror. What enormous eyes the creature had!

"Blood is thicker than water," said the man at the next table.

"What does he mean by that?" I muttered, angrily swallowing a tumbler of Rhine wine and seltzer. But I did not turn. What was the use?

"Chattering old imbecile," I added to myself, and struck a match, for my cigar was out; but as I raised the match to relight it, I encountered the cat's eyes again. I could not enjoy my cigar with the animal staring at me, but I was justly indignant, and I did not intend to be routed. "The idea! forced to leave for a cat!" I sneered, "we will see who will be the one to go!" I tried to give her a jet of seltzer from the siphon, but the bottle was too nearly empty to carry far. Then I attempted to lure her nearer, calling her in French, German, and English, but she did not stir. I did not know the Flemish for "cat."

"She's got a name, and won't come," I thought. "Now, what under the sun can I call her?"

"Aunty," suggested the man at the next table. I sat perfectly still. Could that man have answered my thoughts?—for I had not spoken aloud. Of course not—it was a coincidence,—but a very disgusting one.

"Aunty," I repeated mechanically, "aunty, aunty—good gracious, how horribly human that cat looks!" Then somehow or other, Shakespeare's words crept into my head and I found myself repeating: "the soul of his grandam might happily inhabit a bird; the soul of his grandam might happily inhabit a bird; the soul of—nonsense!" I growled—"it isn't printed correctly! One might possibly say, speaking in poetical metaphor, that the soul of a bird might happily inhabit one's grandam—" I stopped short, flushing painfully. "What awful rot!" I murmured, and lighted another cigar. The cat was still staring; the cigar went out. I grew more and more nervous. "What rot!" I repeated. "Pythagoras must have been an ass, but I do believe that there are plenty of asses alive to-day who swallow that sort of thing."

"Who knows," sighed the man at the next table, and I sprang to my feet and wheeled about. But I only caught a glimpse of a pair of frayed coattails and a bald head vanishing into the dining-room. I sat down again, thoroughly indignant. A moment later the cat got up and went away.

## II◆

Daylight was fading in the city of Antwerp. Down into the sea sank the sun, tinting the vast horizon with flakes of crimson, and touching with rich deep undertones the tossing waters of the Scheldt. Its glow fell like a rosy mantle over red-tiled roofs and meadows; and through the haze the spires of twenty churches pierced the air like sharp, gilded flames. To the west and south the green plains, over which the Spanish armies tramped so long ago, stretched away until they met the sky; the enchantment of the afterglow had turned old Antwerp into fairyland; and sea and sky and plain were beautiful and vague as the night mists floating in the moats below.

Along the sea-wall from the Rubens Gate, all Antwerp strolled, and chattered, and flirted and sipped their Flemish wines from slender Flemish glasses or gossiped over krugs of foaming beer.

From the Scheldt came the cries of sailors, the creaking of cordage, and the puff! puff! of the ferry-boats. On the bastions of the fortress opposite a bugler was standing. Twice the mellow notes of the bugle came faintly over the water, then a great gun thundered from the ramparts, and the Belgian flag fluttered along the lanyards to the ground.

I leaned listlessly on the sea-wall and looked down at the Scheldt below. A battery of artillery was embarking for the fortress. The tublike transport lay hissing and whistling in the slip, and the stamping of horses, the rumbling of gun and caisson, and the sharp cries of the officers came plainly to the ear.

When the last caisson was aboard and stowed, and the last trooper had sprung jingling to the deck, the transport puffed out into the Scheldt, and I turned away through the throng of promenaders, and found a little table on the terrace, just outside of the pretty café. And as I sat down, I became aware of a girl at the next table—a girl all in white—the most ravishingly and distractingly pretty girl that I had ever seen. In the agitation of the moment I forgot that I was a woman-hater, I forgot my name, my fortune, my aunt, and the Crimson Diamond—all these I forgot in a purely human impulse to see clearly; and to that end I removed my monocle from my left eye. Some moments later I came to myself and feebly replaced it. It was too late; the mischief was done. I was not aware at first of the exact state of my feelings,—for I had never before been in love—but I did know that at her request I would have been proud to stand on my head, or turn a flip-flap into the Scheldt.

I did not stare at her, but I managed to see her most of the time when her eyes were in another direction. I found myself drinking something which a waiter brought presumably upon an order which I did not remember having given. Later I noticed that it was a loathsome drink which the Belgians call "American Grog," but I swallowed it and lighted a cigarette. As the fragrant cloud rose in the air, a voice, which I recognized with a chill, broke into my dream of enchantment. Could he have been there all the while,—there sitting beside that vision in white? His hat was off, and the ocean breezes whispered about his bald head. His frayed coat-tails were folded carefully over his knees, and between the thumb and forefinger of his left hand he balanced a bad cigar. He looked at me in a mildly cheerful way, and said, "I know now."

"Know what?" I asked, thinking it better to humour him, for I was convinced that he was mad.

"I know why cats bite."

This was startling. I hadn't the vaguest idea what to say.

"I know why," he repeated; "can you guess why?" There was a covert tone of triumph in his voice and he smiled encouragement. "Come, try and guess," he urged.

I was uneasy, but I told him with stiff civility that I was unequal to problems.

"Listen, young man," he continued, folding his coat-tails closely about his legs—"try to reason it out; why should cats bite? Don't you know? I do."

He looked at me anxiously.

"You take no interest in this problem?" he demanded.

"Oh, yes."

"Then why do you not ask me why?" he said, looking vaguely disappointed.

"Well," I said in desperation, "why do cats bite?—hang it all!" I thought, "it's like a burnt-cork show, and I'm Mr. Bones and he's Tambo!"

Then he smiled gently. "Young man," he said, "cats bite because they feed on cat-nip. I have reasoned it out."

I stared at him in blank astonishment. Was this benevolent looking old party poking fun at me? Was he paying me up for the morning's snub? Was he a malignant and revengeful old party, or was he merely feeble-minded? Who might he be? What was he doing here in Antwerp—what was he doing now!—for the bald one had turned familiarly to the beautiful girl in white.

"Elsie," he said, "do you feel chilly?" The girl shook her head.

"Not in the least, papa."

"Good Lord!" I thought—"her father!"

"I have been to the Zoo to-day," announced the bald one, turning toward me.

"Ah, indeed," I observed,—"er—I trust you enjoyed it."

"I have been contemplating the apes," he continued, dreamily. "Yes, contemplating the apes."

I said nothing, but tried to look interested.

"Yes, the apes," he murmured, fixing his mild eyes on me. Then he leaned toward me confidentially and whispered; "can you tell me what a monkey thinks?"

"I can not," I replied, sharply.

"Ah," he sighed, sinking back in his chair, and patting the slender hand of the girl beside him, "ah, who can tell what a monkey thinks?" His gentle face lulled my suspicions, and I replied very gravely; "who can tell whether they think at all?"

"True, true! Who can tell whether they think at all; and if they do think, ah! who can tell what they think?"

"But," I began, "if you can't tell whether they think at all, what's the use of trying to conjecture what they *would* think if they *did* think?"

He raised his hand in deprecation. "Ah, it is exactly that which is of such absorbing interest, exactly that! It is the abstruseness of the proposition which stimulates research—which stirs profoundly the brain of the thinking world. The question is of vital and instant importance. Possibly you have already formed an opinion."

I admitted that I had thought but little on the subject.

"I doubt," he continued, swathing his knees in his coat-tails,—"I doubt whether you have given much attention to the subject lately discussed by the Boston Dodo Society of Pythagorean Research."

"I am not sure," I said politely, "that I recall that particular discussion. May I ask what was the question brought up?"

"The Felis Domesticus question."

"Ah, that must indeed be interesting! And—er—what may be the Felis Do— do—"

"Domesticus—not Dodo. Felis Domesticus, the common or garden cat."

"Indeed," I murmured.

"You are not listening," he said.

I only half heard him; I could not turn my eyes from her face.

"Cat!" shouted the bald one, and I almost leaped from my chair. "Are you deaf?" he inquired, sympathetically.

"No—oh no!" I replied, colouring with confusion; "you were—pardon me—you were—er —speaking of the Dodo. Extraordinary bird that—"

"I was not discussing the Dodo," he sighed—"I was speaking of cats."

"Of course," I said.

"The question is," he continued, twisting his frayed coat-tails into a sort of rope—"the question is, how are we to ameliorate the present condition and social status of our domestic cats—"

"Feed 'em," I suggested.

He raised both hands. They were eloquent with patient expostulation. "I mean their spiritual condition," he said.

I nodded, but my eyes reverted to that exquisite face. She sat silent, her eyes fixed on the waning flecks of colour in the western sky.

"Yes," repeated the bald one, "the spiritual welfare of our domestic cats—"

"Toms and Tabbies?" I murmured.

"Exactly," he said, tying a large knot in his coat-tails.

"You will ruin your coat," I observed.

"Papa!" exclaimed the girl, turning in dismay, as that gentleman gave a guilty start, "stop it at once!"

He smiled apologetically and made a feeble attempt to conceal his coat-tails.

"My dear," he said, with gentle deprecation, "I am so absent-minded— I always do it in the heat of argument."

The girl rose, and, bending over her untidy parent, deftly untied the knot in his flapping coat. When he was disentangled, she sat down and said, with a ghost of a smile; "he is so very absent-minded."

"Your father is evidently a great student," I said, pleasantly. How I pitied her, tied to this lunatic!

"Yes, he is a great student," she said, quietly.

"I am," he murmured, "that's what makes me so absent-minded. I often go to bed and forget to sleep." Then looking at me he asked me my name, adding, with a bow, that his name was P. Royal Wyeth, Professor of Pythagorean Research and Abstruse Paradox.

"My first name is Penny—named after Professor Penny of Harvard," he said, "but I seldom use my first name in connection with my second, as the combination suggests a household remedy of penetrating odour."

"My name is Kensett," I said, "Harold Kensett of New York."

"Student?"

"Er—a little—"

"Student of diamonds?"

I smiled. "Oh, I see you know who my great-aunt was," I said.

"I know her," he said.

"Ah,—perhaps you are unaware that my great-aunt is not now living—"

"I know her," he repeated, obstinately. I bowed. What a crank he was!

"What do you study? You don't fiddle away all your time, do you?" he asked.

Now that was just what I did, but I was not pleased to have Miss Wyeth know it. Although my time was chiefly spent in shooting and fishing, I had once, in a fit of energy, succeeded in stuffing and mounting a wood-cock, so I evaded a humiliating confession by saying that I had done a little work in ornithology.

"Good!" cried the Professor, beaming all over. "I knew you were a fellow scientist. Possibly you are a brother member of the Boston Dodo Society of Pythagorean Research. Are you a Dodo?"

I shook my head. "No, I am not a Dodo."

"Only a jay?"

"A—what?" I said, angrily.

"A jay. We call the members of the Junior Ornithological Jay Society of New York, jays, just as we refer to ourselves as Dodos. Are you not even a jay?"

"I am not," I said, watching him suspiciously.

"I must convert you, I see," said the Professor, smiling.

"I'm afraid I do not approve of Pythagorean research," I began, but the beautiful Miss Wyeth turned to me very seriously, and looking me frankly in the eyes, said:

"I trust you will be open to conviction."

"Good Lord!" I thought, "can she be another crank." I looked at her steadily. What a little beauty she was. She also then belonged to the Pythagoreans—a sect I despised. Everybody knows all about the Pythagorean craze, its rise in Boston, its rapid spread, and its subsequent consolidation with Theosophy, Hypnotism, the Salvation Army, the Shakers, the Dunkards, and the Mind Cure Cult, upon a business basis. I had hitherto regarded all Pythagoreans with the same scornful indifference which I accorded to the Faith Curists; being a member of the Catholic Church I was scarcely prepared to take any of them seriously. Least of all

did I approve of the "business basis," and I looked very much askance indeed at the "Scientific and Religious Trust Company," duly incorporated
and generally known as the Pythagorean Trust, which, consolidating
with Mind Curists, Faith Curists, and other flourishing Salvation Syndi-
cates, actually claimed a place among ordinary Trusts, and at the same time
pretended to a control over man's future life. No, I could never listen—I
was ashamed of even entertaining the notion, and I shook my head.

"No, Miss Wyeth, I am afraid I do not care to listen to any reasoning on
this subject."

"Don't you believe in Pythagoras?" demanded the Professor, subduing his
excitement with difficulty, and adding another knot to his coat-tails.

"No," I said, "I do not."

"How do you know you don't?" enquired the Professor.

"Because," I said, firmly, "it is nonsense to say that the soul of a human
being can inhabit a hen!"

"Put it in a more simplified form!" insisted the Professor; "do you believe
that the soul of a hen can inhabit a human being?"

"No, I don't!"

"Did you ever hear of a hen-pecked man?" cried the Professor, his voice
ending in a shout.

I nodded, intensely annoyed.

"Will you listen to reason, then?" he continued, eagerly.

"No," I began, but I caught Miss Wyeth's blue eyes fixed on mine with
an expression so sad, so sweetly appealing, that I faltered.

"Yes, I will listen," I said, faintly.

"Will you become my pupil?" insisted the Professor.

I was shocked to find myself wavering, but my eyes were looking into
hers, and I could not disobey what I read there. The longer I looked the
greater inclination I felt to waver. I saw that I was going to give in, and,
strangest of all, my conscience did not trouble me. I felt it coming—a sort
of mild exhilaration took possession of me. For the first time in my life I
became reckless—I even gloried in my recklessness.

"Yes, yes," I cried, leaning eagerly across the table, "I shall be glad—de-
lighted! Will you take me as your pupil?" My single eye-glass fell from its
position—unheeded. "Take me! Oh, will you take me?" I cried. Instead of
answering, the Professor blinked rapidly at me for a moment. I imagined
his eyes had grown bigger, and were assuming a greenish tinge. The corners of his mouth began to quiver, emitting queer, caressing little noises,
and he rapidly added knot after knot to his twitching coat-tails. Suddenly
he bent forward across the table until his nose almost touched mine. The
pupils of his eyes expanded, the iris assuming a beautiful changing golden-
green tinge, and his coat-tails switched violently. Then he began to mew.

I strove to rouse myself from my paralysis—I tried to shrink back, for I felt the end of his cold nose touch mine. I could not move. The cry of terror died in my straining throat, my hands tightened convulsively; I was incapable of speech or motion. At the same time my brain became wonderfully clear. I began to remember everything that had ever happened to me—everything that I had ever done or said. I even remembered things that I had neither done nor said, I recalled distinctly much that had never happened. How fresh and strong my memory! The past was like a mirror, crystal clear, and there, in glorious tints and hues, the scenes of my childhood grew and glowed and faded, and gave place to newer and more splendid scenes. For a moment the episode of the cat at the Hotel St. Antoine flashed across my mind. When it vanished, a chilly stupor slowly clouded my brain; the scenes, the memories, the brilliant colours, faded, leaving me enveloped in a grey vapour, through which the two great eyes of the Professor twinkled with a murky light. A peculiar longing stirred me,—a strange yearning for something—I knew not what—but, oh! how I longed and yearned for it! Slowly this indefinite, incomprehensible longing became a living pain. Ah, how I suffered!—and how the vapours seemed to crowd around me. Then, as at a great distance, I heard her voice, sweet, imperative:

"Mew!" she said.

For a moment I seemed to see the interior of my own skull, lighted as by a flash of fire; the rolling eye-balls, veined in scarlet, the glistening muscles quivering along the jaw, the humid masses of the convoluted brain,—then awful darkness—a darkness almost tangible—an utter blackness, through which now seemed to creep a thin silver thread, like a river crawling across a world—like a thought gliding to the brain—like a song, a thin, sharp song which some distant voice was singing—which I was singing.

And I knew that I was mewing!

I threw myself back in my chair and mewed with all my heart. Oh, that heavy load which was lifted from my breast! How good, how satisfying it was to mew! And how I did mew!

I gave myself up to it, heart and soul; my whole being thrilled with the passionate outpourings of a spirit freed. My voice trembled in the upper bars of a feline love song, quavered, descended, swelling again into an intimation that I brooked no rival, and ended with a magnificent crescendo.

I finished, somewhat abashed, and glanced askance at the Professor and his daughter, but the one sat nonchalantly disentangling his coattails, and the other was apparently absorbed in the distant landscape. Evidently they did not consider me ridiculous. Flushing painfully, I turned in my chair to see how my gruesome solo had affected the people on the terrace. Nobody even looked at me. This, however, gave me little comfort, for, as I began to realize what I had done, my mortification and rage knew no bounds. I was ready to die of shame. What on earth had induced me to mew? I looked wildly about for escape—I would leap up—rush home to bury my burning face in my pillows, and later in the friendly cabin of a homeward-bound steamer. I would fly—fly at once! Woe to the man who blocked my way! I started to my feet, but at that moment I caught Miss Wyeth's eyes fixed on mine.

"Don't go," she said.

What in Heaven's name lay in those blue eyes! I slowly sank back into my chair.

Then the Professor spoke. "Elsie, I have just received a dispatch."

"Where from, Papa?"

"From India. I'm going at once."

She nodded her head, without turning her eyes from the sea. "Is it important, papa?"

"I should say so. The cashier of the Trust has eloped with an Astral body, and has taken all our funds, including a lot of first mortgages on Nirvana. I suppose he's been dabbling in futures, and was short in his accounts. I shan't be gone long."

"Then good-night, papa," she said, kissing him, "try to be back by eleven." I sat stupidly staring at them.

"Oh, it's only to Bombay—I shan't go to Thibet to-night,—good-night, my dear," said the Professor.

Then a singular thing occurred. The Professor had at last succeeded in disentangling his coat tails, and now, jamming his hat over his ears, and waving his arms with a bat-like motion, he climbed upon the seat of his chair, and ejaculated the word "Presto!" Then I found my voice.

"Stop him!" I cried, in terror.

"Presto! Presto!" shouted the Professor, balancing himself on the edge of his chair and waving his arms majestically, as if preparing for a sudden flight across the Scheldt; and, firmly convinced that he not only meditated it but was perfectly capable of attempting it, I covered my eyes with my hands.

"Are you ill, Mr. Kensett?" said the girl, quietly.

I raised my head indignantly. "Not at all, Miss Wyeth, only I'll bid you good-evening, for this is the 19th century, and I'm a Christian."

"So am I," she said. "So is my father."

"The devil he is," I thought.

Her next words made me jump.

"Please do not be profane, Mr. Kensett." How did she know I was profane? I had not spoken a word! Could it be possible she was able to read my thoughts? This was too much, and I rose and bowed stiffly.

"I have the honour to bid you good-evening," I began, and reluctantly turned to include the Professor, expecting to see that gentleman balancing himself on his chair. The Professor's chair was empty.

"Oh," said the girl, faintly, "my father has gone."

"Gone! Where?"

"To—to India, I believe."

I sank helplessly into my own chair.

"I do not think he will stay very long—he promised to return by eleven," she said, timidly.

I tried to realize the purport of it all. "Gone to India? Gone! How? On a broomstick? Good Heavens!" I murmured, "am I sane?"

"Perfectly," she said, "and I am tired; you may take me back to the hotel."

I scarcely heard her; I was feebly attempting to gather up my numbed wits. Slowly I began to comprehend the situation, to review the startling and humiliating events of the day. At noon, in the court of the Hotel St. Antoine, I had been annoyed by a man and a cat. I had retired to my own room and had slept until dinner. In the evening I met two tourists on the sea-wall promenade. I had been beguiled into conversation—yes, into intimacy with these two tourists! I had had the intention of embracing the faith of Pythagoras! Then I had mewed like a cat with all the strength of my lungs. Then the male tourist vanishes—and leaves me in charge of the female tourist, alone and at night in a strange city! And now the female tourist proposes that I take her home!

With a remnant of self-possession I groped for my eye-glass, seized it, screwed it firmly into my eye, and looked long and earnestly at the girl. As I looked, my eyes softened, my monocle dropped, and I forgot everything in the beauty and purity of the face before me. My heart began to beat against my stiff white waistcoat. Had I dared—yes, dared to think of this wondrous little beauty, as a female tourist? Her pale sweet face, turned toward the sea, seemed to cast a spell upon the night. How loud my heart was beating. The yellow moon floated, half dipping in the sea, flooding land and water with enchanted lights. Wind and wave seemed to feel the spell of her eyes, for the breeze died away, the heaving Scheldt tossed noiselessly, and the dark Dutch luggers swung idly on the tide with every sail adroop.

A sudden hush fell over land and water, the voices on the promenade were stilled; little by little the shadowy throng, the terrace, the sea itself vanished, and I only saw her face, shadowed against the moon.

It seemed as if I had drifted miles above the earth, through all space and eternity, and there was nought between me and high Heaven but that white face. Ah, how I loved her! I knew it—I never doubted it. Could years of passionate adoration touch her heart—her little heart, now beating so

calmly with no thought of love to startle it from its quiet and send it fluttering against the gentle breast? In her lap her clasped hands tightened,—her eyelids drooped as though some pleasant thought was passing. I saw the colour dye her temples, I saw the blue eyes turn,
half-frightened to my own, I saw—and I knew she had read my thoughts.
Then we both rose, side by side, and she was weeping softly, yet for my
life I dared not speak. She turned away, touching her eyes with a bit of lace,
and I sprang to her side and offered her my arm.

"You cannot go back alone," I said.

She did not take my arm.

"Do you hate me, Miss Wyeth?"

"I am very tired," she said, "I must go home."

"You cannot go alone."

"I do not care to accept your escort."

"Then—you send me away?"

"No," she said, in a hard voice. "You can come if you like." So I humbly
attended her to the Hotel St. Antoine.

# III.

As we reached the Place Verte and turned into the court of the hotel, the
sound of the midnight bells swept over the city, and a horse-car jingled
slowly by on its last trip to the railroad station.

We passed the fountain, bubbling and splashing in the moonlit court,
and, crossing the square, entered the southern wing of the hotel. At the
foot of the stairway she leaned for an instant against the banisters.

"I am afraid we have walked too fast," I said.

She turned to me coldly. "No,—conventionalities must be observed. You
were quite right in escaping as soon as possible."

"But," I protested, "I assure you—"

She gave a little movement of impatience. "Don't," she said, "you tire
me—conventionalities tire me. Be satisfied,—nobody has seen you."

"You are cruel," I said, in a low voice—"what do you think I care for conventionalities—"

"You care everything,—you care what people think, and you try to do
what they say is good form. You never did such an original thing in your
life as you have just done."

"You read my thoughts," I exclaimed, bitterly—"it is not fair—"

"Fair or not, I know what you consider me,—ill-bred, common, pleased
with any sort of attention. Oh! Why should I waste one word—one

thought on you!"

"Miss Wyeth,—" I began, but she interrupted me.

"Would you dare tell me what you think of me?—Would you dare tell me what you think of my father?"

I was silent. She turned and mounted two steps of the stairway, then faced me again.

"Do you think it was for my own pleasure that I permitted myself to be left alone with you? Do you imagine that I am flattered by your attention—do you venture to think I ever could be? How dare you think what you did think there on the sea-wall?"

"I cannot help my thoughts!" I replied.

"You turned on me like a tiger when you awoke from your trance. Do you really suppose that you mewed? Are you not aware that my father hypnotized you?"

"No—I did not know it," I said. The hot blood tingled in my finger tips, and I looked angrily at her.

"Why do you imagine that I waste my time on you?" she said. "Your vanity has answered that question,—now let your intelligence answer it. I am a Pythagorean; I have been chosen to bring in a convert, and you were the convert selected for me by the Mahatmas of the Consolidated Trust Company. I have followed you from New York to Antwerp, as I was bidden, but now my courage fails, and I shrink from fulfilling my mission, knowing you to be the type of man you are. If I could give it up—if I could only go away,—never, never again to see you! Ah, I fear they will not permit it!—until my mission is accomplished. Why was I chosen,—I, with a woman's heart and a woman's pride. I—I hate you!"

"I love you," I said, slowly.

She paled and looked away.

"Answer me," I said.

Her wide blue eyes turned back again, and I held them with mine. At last she slowly drew a long-stemmed rose from the bunch at her belt, turned, and mounted the shadowy staircase. For a moment I thought. I saw her pause on the landing above, but the moonlight was uncertain. After waiting for a long time in vain, I moved away, and in going raised my hand to my face, but I stopped short, and my heart stopped too, for a moment. In my hand I held a long-stemmed rose.

With my brain in a whirl I crept across the court and mounted the stairs to my room. Hour after hour I walked the floor, slowly at first, then more rapidly, but it brought no calm to the fierce tumult of my thoughts, and at last I dropped into a chair before the empty fireplace, burying my head in my hands.

Uncertain, shocked, and deadly weary, I tried to think,—I strove to bring order out of the chaos in my brain, but I only sat staring at the long-stemmed rose. Slowly I began to take a vague pleasure in its heavy perfume, and once I crushed a leaf between my palms, and, bending over, drank in the fragrance.

Twice my lamp flickered and went out, and twice, treading softly, I crossed the room to relight it. Twice I threw open the door, thinking that I heard some sound without. How close the air was,—how heavy and hot! And what was that strange, subtle odour which had insensibly filled the room? It grew stronger and more penetrating, and I began to dislike it, and to escape it I buried my nose in the half-opened rose. Horror! The odour came from the rose,—and the rose itself was no longer a rose—not even a flower now,—it was only a bunch of catnip; and I dashed it to the floor and ground it under my heel.

"Mountebank!" I cried in a rage. My anger grew cold—and I shivered, drawn perforce to the curtained window. Something was there—outside. I could not hear it, for it made no sound, but I knew it was there, watching me. What was it? The damp hair stirred on my head. I touched the heavy curtains. Whatever was outside them sprang up, tore at the window, and then rushed away.

Feeling very shaky, I crept to the window, opened it, and leaned out. The night was calm. I heard the fountain splashing in the moonlight and the sea winds soughing through the palms. Then I closed the window and turned back into the room; and as I stood there a sudden breeze, which could not have come from without, blew sharply in my face, extinguishing the candle and sending the long curtains bellying out into the room. The lamp on the table flashed and smoked and sputtered; the room was littered with flying papers and catnip leaves. Then the strange wind died away, and somewhere in the night a cat snarled.

I turned desperately to my trunk and flung it open. Into it I threw everything I owned, pell-mell, closed the lid, locked it, and seizing my mackintosh and travelling bag, ran down the stairs, crossed the court and entered the night office of the hotel. There I called up the sleepy clerk, settled my reckoning, and sent a porter for a cab.

"Now," I said, "what time does the next train leave?"

"The next train for where?"

"Anywhere!"

The clerk locked the safe, and carefully keeping the desk between himself and me, motioned the office boy to look at the time-tables.

"Next train, 2.10. Brussels—Paris," read the boy.

At that moment the cab rattled up by the curbstone, and I sprang in while the porter tossed my traps on top. Away we bumped over the stony pavement, past street after street lighted dimly by tall gas-lamps, and alley after alley brilliant with the glare of villainous all-night café-concerts, and then, turning, we rumbled past the Circus and the Eldorado, and at last stopped with a jolt before the Brussels Station.

I had not a moment to lose. "Paris!" I cried,—"first-class!" and, pocketing the book of coupons, hurried across the platform to where the Brussels train lay. A guard came running up, flung open the door of a first-class carriage, slammed and locked it, after I had jumped in, and the long train glided from the arched station out into the starlit morning.

I was all alone in the compartment. The wretched lamp in the roof flickered dimly, scarcely lighting the stuffy box. I could not see to read my time-table, so I wrapped my legs in the travelling rug and lay back, staring out into the misty morning. Trees, walls, telegraph poles, flashed past, and the cinders drove in showers against the rattling windows. I slept at times, fitfully, and once, springing up, peered sharply at the opposite seat, possessed with the idea that somebody was there.

When the train reached Brussels, I was sound asleep, and the guard awoke me with difficulty.

"Breakfast, sir?" he asked.

"Anything," I sighed, and stepped out to the platform, rubbing my legs and shivering. The other passengers were already breakfasting in the station café, and I joined them and managed to swallow a cup of coffee and a roll.

The morning broke, grey and cloudy, and I bundled myself into my mackintosh for a tramp along the platform. Up and down I stamped, puffing a cigar, and digging my hands deep in my pockets, while the other passengers huddled into the warmer compartments of the train or stood watching the luggage being lifted into the forward mail carriage. The wait was very long; the hands of the great clock pointed to six, and still the train lay motionless along the platform. I approached a guard, and asked him whether anything was wrong.

"Accident on the line," he replied; "Monsieur had better go to his compartment and try to sleep, for we may be delayed until noon."

I followed the guard's advice, and crawling into my corner, wrapped myself in the rug and lay back watching the rain-drops spattering along the window-sill. At noon, the train had not moved, and I lunched in the compartment. At four o'clock in the afternoon the station-master came hurrying along the platform, crying "montez! montez! Messieurs—Dames, s'il vous plait,"—and the train steamed out of the station and whirled away through the flat, treeless Belgian plains. At times I dozed, but the shaking of the car always awoke me, and I would sit blinking out at the endless stretch of plain, until a sudden flurry of rain blotted the landscape from my eyes. At last, a long, shrill whistle from the engine, a jolt, a series of bumps, and an apparition of red trousers and bayonets warned me that we had arrived at the French frontier. I turned out with the others, and opened my valise for inspection, but the customs officials merely chalked it without examination, and I hurried back to my compartment amid the shouting of guards and the clanging of station bells. Again I found that I was alone in the compartment, so I smoked a cigarette, thanked Heaven, and fell into a dreamless sleep.

How long I slept I do not know, but when I awoke, the train was roaring through a tunnel. When again it flashed out into the open country, I peered through the grimy rain-stained window and saw that the storm had ceased and stars were twinkling in the sky. I stretched my legs, yawned, pushed my travelling cap back from my forehead, and stumbling to my feet, walked up and down the compartment until my cramped muscles were relieved. Then I sat down again, and, lighting a cigar, puffed great rings and clouds of fragrant smoke across the aisle.

The train was flying; the cars lurched and shook, and the windows rattled accompaniment to the creaking panels. The smoke from my cigar dimmed the lamp in the ceiling and hid the opposite seat from view. How it curled and writhed in the corners, now eddying upward, now floating across the aisle like a veil. I lounged back in my cushioned seat watching it with interest. What queer shapes it took. How thick it was becoming—how strangely luminous! Now it had filled the whole compartment, puff after puff crowding upward, waving, wavering, clouding the windows, and blotting the lamp from sight. It was most interesting. I had never before smoked such a cigar. What an extraordinary brand! I examined the end, flicking the ashes away. The cigar was out. Fumbling for a match to relight it, my eyes fell on the drifting smoke curtain, which swayed across the corner opposite. It seemed almost tangible. How like a real curtain it hung, grey, impenetrable. A man might hide behind it. Then an idea came into my head, and it persisted until my uneasiness amounted to a vague terror. I tried to fight it off—I strove to resist—but the conviction slowly settled upon me that something was behind that smoke veil,—something which had entered the compartment while I slept.

"It can't be," I muttered, my eyes fixed on the misty drapery, "the train has not stopped." The car creaked and trembled. I sprang to my feet, and swept my arm through the veil of smoke. Then my hair slowly rose on my head. For my hand touched another hand, and my eyes had met two other eyes.

My senses reeled. I heard a voice in the gloom, low and sweet, calling me by name; I saw the eyes again, tender and blue; soft fingers touched my own.

"Are you afraid?" she said.

My heart began to beat again, and my face warmed with returning blood.
"It is only I," she said, gently.

I seemed to hear my own voice speaking as if at a great distance; "you here—alone?"

"How cruel of you," she faltered, "I am not alone." At the same instant my eyes fell upon the Professor, calmly seated by the further window. His hands were thrust into the folds of a corded and tasselled dressing-gown, from beneath which peeped two enormous feet encased in carpet slippers. Upon his head towered a yellow night cap. He did not pay the slightest attention to either me or his daughter, and, except for the lighted cigar which he kept shifting between his lips, he might have been taken for a wax dummy.

Then I began to speak, feebly, hesitating like a child.

"How did you come into this compartment? You—you do not possess wings, I suppose. You could not have been here all the time. Will you explain—explain to me? See, I ask you very humbly, for I do not understand. This is the 19th century, and these things don't fit in. I'm wearing a Dunlap hat—I've got a copy of the *New York Herald* in my bag,—President Cleveland is alive and everything is so very commonplace in the world! Is this real magic? Perhaps I'm filled with hallucinations. Perhaps I'm asleep and dreaming. Perhaps you are not really here—nor I—nor anybody, nor anything!"—

The train plunged into a tunnel, and when again it dashed out from the other end, the cold wind blew furiously in my face from the further window. It was wide open; the Professor was gone.

"Papa has changed to another compartment," she said, quietly; "I think perhaps you were beginning to bore him."

Her eyes met mine and she smiled faintly. "Are you very much bewildered?"

I looked at her in silence. She sat very quietly, her white hands clasped above her knee, her curly hair glittering to her girdle. A long robe, almost silvery in the twilight, clung to her young figure; her bare feet were thrust deep into a pair of shimmering eastern slippers.

"When you fled," she sighed, "I was asleep and there was no time to lose. I barely had a moment to go to Bombay, to find Papa, and return in time to join you. This is an East Indian costume."

Still I was silent.

"Are you shocked?" she asked simply

"No," I replied in a dull voice, "I'm past that."

"You are very rude," she said, with the tears starting to her eyes.

"I do not mean to be. I only wish to go away—away somewhere and find out what my name is."

"Your name is Harold Kensett."

"Are you sure?" I asked, eagerly.

"Yes,—what troubles you?"

"Is everything plain to you? Are you a sort of prophet and second sight medium? Is nothing hidden from you?" I asked.

"Nothing,"—she faltered. My head ached and I clasped it in my hand.

A sudden change came over her. "I am human,—believe me!"—she said with piteous eagerness; "indeed I do not seem strange to those who understand. You wonder, because you left me at midnight in Antwerp and you wake to find me here. If, because I find myself reincarnated, endowed with senses and capabilities which few at present possess;—if I am so made, why should it seem strange? It is all so natural to me. If I appear to you—"

"Appear!!!"

"Yes—"

"Elsie!" I cried, "can you vanish?"

"Yes," she murmured,—"does it seem to you unwomanly?"

"Great Heaven!" I groaned.

"Don't," she cried, with tears in her voice, "oh, please don't! Help me to bear it! If you only knew how awful it is to be different from other girls,—how mortifying it is to me to be able to vanish,—oh, how I hate and detest it all!"

"Don't cry," I said, looking at her pityingly.

"Oh dear me!" she sobbed. "You shudder at the sight of me because I can vanish."

"I don't!" I cried.

"Yes you do! You abhor me,—you shrink away! Oh why did I ever see you,—why did you ever come into my life,—what have I done in ages past, that now, reborn, I suffer cruelly—cruelly!"

"What do you mean!" I whispered. My voice trembled with happiness.

"I?—nothing—but you think me a fabled monster."

"Elsie,—my sweet Elsie," I said, "I don't think you a fabled monster;—I love you,— see—see—I am at your feet,—listen to me, my darling."

She turned her blue eyes to mine. I saw tears sparkling on the curved lashes.

"Elsie, I love you," I said again.

Slowly she raised her white hands to my head and held it a moment, looking at me strangely. Then her face grew nearer to my own, her glittering hair fell over my shoulders, her lips rested on mine.

In that long sweet kiss, the beating of her heart answered mine, and I learned a thousand truths, wonderful, mysterious, splendid,—but when our lips fell apart,—the memory of what I learned departed also.

"It was so very simple and beautiful," she sighed, "and I—I never saw it. But the Mahatmas knew—ah, they knew that my mission could only be accomplished through love."

"And it is," I whispered, "for you shall teach me,—me your husband."

"And—and you will not be impatient? You will try to believe?"

"I will believe what you tell me, my sweetheart."

"Even about—cats?"

Before I could reply the further window opened and a yellow nightcap, followed by the Professor, entered from somewhere without. Elsie sank back on her sofa, but the Professor needed not to be told, and we both knew he was already busily reading our thoughts.

For a moment there was dead silence,—long enough for the Professor to grasp the full significance of what had passed. Then he uttered a single exclamation; "Oh!"

After a while, however, he looked at me for the first time that evening, saying; "Congratulate you, Mr. Kensett, I'm sure;"—tied several knots in the cord of his dressing-gown, lighted a cigar, and paid no further attention to either of us. Some moments later he opened the window again and disappeared. I looked across the aisle at Elsie.

"You may come over beside me," she said, shyly.

# IV.

It was nearly ten o'clock and our train was rapidly approaching Paris. We passed village after village wrapped in mist, station after station hung with twinkling red and blue and yellow lanterns, then sped on again with the echo of the switch bells ringing in our ears.

When at length the train slowed up and stopped, I opened the window and looked out upon a long wet platform, shining under the electric lights.

A guard came running by, throwing open the doors of each compartment, and crying, "Paris next! Tickets, if you please."

I handed him my book of coupons from which he tore several and handed it back. Then he lifted his lantern and peered into the compartment saying: "Is Monsieur alone?"

I turned to Elsie.

"He wants your ticket—give it to me."

"What's that?" demanded the guard.

I looked anxiously at Elsie.

"If your father has the tickets—" I began, but was interrupted by the guard who snapped, "Monsieur will give himself the trouble to remember that I do not understand English."

"Keep quiet!" I said sharply in French, "I am not speaking to you."

The guard stared stupidly at me, then at my luggage, and finally, entering the car, knelt down and peered under the seats. Presently he got up, very red in the face, and went out slamming the door. He had not paid the slightest attention to Elsie, but I distinctly heard him say, "Only Englishmen and idiots talk to themselves!"

"Elsie," I faltered, "do you mean to say that guard could not see you?"

She began to look so serious again that I merely added, "Never mind, I don't care whether you are invisible or not, dearest."

"I am not invisible to you," she said; "why should you care?"

A great noise of bells and whistles drowned our voices, and amid the whirring of switch bells, the hissing of steam, and the cries of "Paris! All out!" our train glided into the station.

It was the Professor who opened the door of our carriage. There he stood, calmly adjusting his yellow nightcap and drawing his dressing-gown closer with the corded tassels.

"Where have you been?" I asked.

"On the engine."

"*In* the engine I suppose you mean," I said.

"No I don't; I mean *on* the engine,—on the pilot. It was very refreshing. Where are we going now?"

"Do you know Paris?" asked Elsie, turning to me.

"Yes. I think your father had better take you to the Hotel Normandie on the rue de l'Echelle—"

"But you must stay there too!"

"Of course—if you wish—"

She laughed nervously.

"Don't you see that my father and I could not take rooms—now? You must engage three rooms for yourself."

"Why?" I asked stupidly.

"Oh dear—why, because we are invisible."

I tried to repress a shudder. The Professor gave Elsie his arm and, as I studied his ensemble, I thanked Heaven that he was invisible.

At the gate of the station I hailed a four-seated cab, and we rattled away through the stony streets, brilliant with gas jets, and in a few moments rolled smoothly across the Avenue de l'Opera, turned into the rue de l'Echelle, and stopped. A bright little page, all over buttons, came out, took my luggage, and preceded us into the hallway.

I, with Elsie on my arm and the Professor shuffling along beside me, walked over to the desk.

"Room?" said the clerk, "we have a very desirable room on the second fronting the rue St. Honoré—"

"But we—that is I want three rooms—three separate rooms!" I said.

The clerk scratched his chin. "Monsieur is expecting friends?"

"Say yes," whispered Elsie, with a suspicion of laughter in her voice.

"Yes," I repeated feebly.

"Gentlemen of course?" said the clerk looking at me narrowly.

"One lady."

"Married, of course?"

"What's that to you?" I said sharply, "what do you mean by speaking to us—"

"Us!"

"I mean to me," I said, badly rattled; "give me the rooms and let me get to bed, will you?"

"Monsieur will remember," said the clerk coldly, "that this is an old and respectable hotel."

"I know it," I said, smothering my rage.

The clerk eyed me suspiciously.

"Front!" he called with irritating deliberation, "show this gentleman to apartment ten."

"How many rooms are there!" I demanded.

"Three sleeping rooms and a parlor."

"I will take it," I said with composure.

"On probation," muttered the clerk insolently.

Swallowing the insult I followed the bell-boy up the stairs, keeping between him and Elsie, for I dreaded to see him walk through her as if she were thin air. A trim maid rose to meet us and conducted us through a hallway into a large apartment. She threw open all the bed-room doors and said, "Will Monsieur have the goodness to choose?"

"Which will you take," I began, turning to Elsie.

"I! Monsieur!" cried the startled maid.

That completely upset me. "Here," I muttered, slipping some silver into her hand, "now for the love of Heaven run away!"

When she had vanished with a doubtful "Merci, Monsieur," I handed the Professor the keys and asked him to settle the thing with Elsie.

Elsie took the corner room, the Professor rambled into the next one, and I said good night and crept wearily into my own chamber. I sat down and tried to think. A great feeling of fatigue weighted my spirits.

"I can think better with my clothes off," I said, and slipped the coat from my shoulders. How tired I was. "I can think better in bed," I muttered, flinging my cravat on the dresser and tossing my shirt studs after it. I was certainly very tired. "Now," I yawned, grasping the pillow and drawing it under my head, "now, I can think a bit," but before my head fell on the pillow, sleep closed my eyes.

I began to dream at once. It seemed as though my eyes were wide open and the Professor was standing beside my bed.

"Young man," he said, "you've won my daughter and you must pay the piper!"

"What piper?" I said.

"The pied piper of Hamlin, I don't think," replied the Professor vulgarly, and before I could realize what he was doing he had drawn a reed pipe from his dressing-gown and was playing a strangely annoying air. Then an awful thing occurred. Cats began to troop into the room, cats by the hundred, toms and tabbys, grey, yellow, Maltese, Persian, Manx, all purring and all marching round and round, rubbing against the furniture, the Professor, and even against me. I struggled with the nightmare.

"Take them away!" I tried to gasp.

"Nonsense," he said, "here is an old friend." I saw the white tabby cat of the Hotel St. Antoine.

"An old friend," he repeated, and played a dismal melody on his reed.

I saw Elsie enter the room, lift the white tabby in her arms and bring her to my side.

"Shake hands with him," she commanded. To my horror the tabby deliberately extended a paw and tapped me on the knuckles.

"Oh!" I cried in agony, "this is a horrible dream! Why, oh, why can't I wake!"

"Yes," she said, dropping the cat, "it is partly a dream but some of it is real. Remember what I say, my darling; you are to go to-morrow morning and meet the twelve o'clock train from Antwerp at the Gare du Nord. Papa and I are coming to Paris on that train. Don't you know that we are not really here now, you silly boy? Good night then. I shall be very glad to see you."

I saw her glide from the room, followed by the Professor, playing a gay quick-step, to which the cats danced two and two.

"Good night sir," said each cat, as it passed my bed; and I dreamed no more.

When I awoke, the room, the bed had vanished; I was in the street, walking rapidly; the sun shone down on the broad white pavements of Paris, and the streams of busy life flowed past me on either side. How swiftly I was walking! Where the devil was I going? Surely I had business somewhere that needed immediate attention. I tried to remember when I had awakened, but I could not. I wondered where I had dressed myself; I had apparently taken great pains with my toilet, for I was immaculate, monocle and all, even down to a long-stemmed rose nestling in my button-hole. I knew Paris and recognized the streets through which I was hurrying. Where could I be going? What was my hurry? I glanced at my watch and found I had not a moment to lose. Then as the bells of the city rang out mid-day, I hastened into the railroad station on the Rue Lafayette and walked out to the platform. And as I looked down the glittering track, around the distant curve shot a locomotive followed by a long line of cars. Nearer and nearer it came while the station gongs sounded and the switch-bells began ringing all along the track.

"Antwerp express!" cried the Sous-Chef de Gare, and as the train slipped along the tiled platform I sprang upon the steps of a first-class carriage and threw open the door.

"How do you do, Mr. Kensett," said Elsie Wyeth, springing lightly to the platform. "Really it is very nice of you to come to the train." At the same moment a bald, mild-eyed gentleman emerged from the depths of the same compartment carrying a large covered basket.

"How are you, Kensett?" he said. "Glad to see you again. Rather warm in that compartment—no I will not trust this basket to an expressman; give Miss Wyeth your arm and I'll follow. We go to the 'Normandie' I believe?"

All the morning I had Elsie to myself, and at dinner I sat beside her with the Professor opposite. The latter was cheerful enough, but he nearly ruined my dinner for he smelled strongly of catnip. After dinner he became restless and fidgeted about in his chair until coffee was brought, and we went up to the parlour of our apartment. Here his restlessness increased to such an extent that I ventured to ask him if he was in good health.

"It's that basket—the covered basket which I have in the next room," he said.

"What's the trouble with the basket?" I asked.

"The basket's all right—but the contents worry me."

"May I inquire what the contents are?" I ventured.

The Professor rose.

"Yes," he said, "you may inquire of my daughter." He left the room but reappeared shortly, carrying a saucer of milk.

I watched him enter the next room which was mine.

"What on earth is he taking that into my room for?" I asked Elsie. "I don't keep cats."

"But you will," she said.

"I? never!"

"You will if I ask you to."

"But—but you won't ask me."

"But I do."

"Elsie!"

"Harold!"

"I detest cats."

"You must not."

"I can't help it."

"You will when I ask it. Have I not given myself to you? Will you not make a little sacrifice for me?"

"I don't understand—"

"Would you refuse my first request?"

"No," I said miserably, "I will keep dozens of cats—"

"I do not ask that; I only wish you to keep one."

"Was that what your father had in that basket?" I asked suspiciously.

"Yes, the basket came from Antwerp."

"What! The white Antwerp cat " I cried.

"Yes."

"And you ask me to keep that cat? Oh Elsie!"

"Listen!" she said, "I have a long story to tell you; come nearer, close to me. You say you love me?"

I bent and kissed her.

"Then I shall put you to the proof," she murmured.

"Prove me!"

"Listen. That cat is the same cat that ran out of the apartment in the Waldorf when your great-aunt ceased to exist—in human shape. My father and myself, having received word from the Mahatmas of the Trust Company, sheltered and cherished the cat. We were ordered by the Mahatmas to convert you. The task was appalling—but there is no such thing as refusing a command, and we laid our plans. That man with a white spot in his hair was my father—"

"What! Your father is bald."

"He wore a wig then. The white spot came from dropping chemicals on the wig while experimenting with a substance which you could not comprehend."

"Then—then that clue was useless; but who could have taken the Crimson Diamond? And who was the man with the white spot on his head who tried to sell the stone in Paris?"

"That was my father."

"He—he—st—took the Crimson Diamond?!" I cried aghast.

"Yes and no. That was only a paste stone that he had in Paris. It was to draw you over here. He had the real Crimson Diamond also."

"Your father?"

"Yes. He has it in the next room now. Can you not see how it disappeared, Harold? Why, the cat swallowed it!"

"Do you mean to say that the white tabby swallowed the Crimson Diamond?"

"By mistake. She tried to get it out of the velvet bag, and, as the bag was also full of catnip, she could not resist a mouthful, and unfortunately just then you broke in the door and so startled the cat that she swallowed the Crimson Diamond."

There was a painful pause. At last I said; "Elsie, as you are able to vanish, I suppose you also are able to converse with cats."

"I am," she replied, trying to keep back the tears of mortification.

"And that cat told you this?"

"She did."

"And my Crimson Diamond is inside that cat?"

"It is."

"Then," said I firmly, "I am going to chloroform the cat."

"Harold!" she cried in terror, "that cat is your great-aunt!"

I don't know to this day how I stood the shock of that announcement, or how I managed to listen, while Elsie tried to explain the transmigration theory, but it was all Chinese to me. I only knew that I was a blood relation of a cat, and the thought nearly drove me mad.

"Try, my darling, try to love her," whispered Elsie, "she must be very precious to you—"

"Yes, with my diamond inside her," I replied faintly.

"You must not neglect her," said Elsie.

"Oh no, I'll always have my eye on her—I mean I will surround her with luxury—er, milk and bones and catnip and books—er—does she read?"

"Not the books that human beings read. Now go and speak to your aunt, Harold."

"Eh! How the deuce—"

"Go, for my sake try to be cordial."

She rose and led me unresistingly to the door of my room.

"Good Heavens!" I groaned, "this is awful."

"Courage, my darling!" she whispered, "be brave for love of me."

I drew her to me and kissed her. Beads of cold perspiration started in the roots of my hair, but I clenched my teeth and entered the room alone. The room was dark and I stood silent, not knowing where to turn, fearful lest I step on the cat, my aunt! Then through the dreary silence I called; "Aunty!"

A faint noise broke upon my ear, and my heart grew sick, but I strode into the darkness calling hoarsely:—

"Aunt Tabby! it is your nephew!"

Again the faint sound. Something was stirring there among the shadows,—a shape moving softly along the wall, a shade which glided by me, paused, wavered, and darted under the bed. Then I threw myself on the floor, profoundly moved, begging, imploring my aunt to come to me.

"Aunty! Aunty!" I murmured, "your nephew is waiting to take you to his heart!"

And at last I saw my great-aunt's eyes, shining in the dark.

———

Close the door. That meeting is not for the eyes of the world! Close the door upon that sacred scene where great-aunt and nephew are united at last.

THE END

# ROBERT W. CHAMBERS
# BIBLIOGRAPHY

FICTION

In the Quarter (1894)
The King in Yellow (1895; stories)
The Red Republic (1895)
With the Band (1896)
A King and a Few Dukes (1896)
The Maker of Moons (1896; stories)
The Mystery of Choice (1897; stories)
The Haunts of Men (1898; stories)
Ashes of Empire (1898)
Lorraine (1898)
Outsiders (1899)
Cambric Mask (1899)
The Conspirators (1900)
Cardigan (1901)
The Maid-at-Arms (1902)
The Maids of Paradise (1903)
In Search of the Unknown (1904)
A Young Man in a Hurry and Other Short Stories (1904)
The Reckoning (1905)
Iole (1905)
The Tracer of Lost Persons (1906)
The Fighting Chance (1906)
The Tree of Heaven (1907; stories)
The Younger Set (1907)
The Firing Line (1908)
Some Ladies in Haste (1908)

Special Messenger (1909)
The Danger Mark (1909)
Ailsa Paige (1910)
The Green Mouse (1910)
Adventures of a Modest Man (1911)
The Common Law (1911)
The Streets of Ascalon (1912)
Japonette (1912)
The Gay Rebellion (1913)
The Business of Life (1913)
Blue-Bird Weather (1913)
Quick Action (1914)
The Hidden Children (1914)
Anne's Bridge (1914)
Between Friends (1914; stories)
Who Goes There! (1915)
Athalie (1915)
Police!!! (1915; stories)
The Better Man (1916; stories)
The Girl Philippa (1916)
Barbarians (1917)
The Dark Star (1917)
The Restless Sex (1918)
The Laughing Girl (1918)
In Secret (1919)
The Moonlight Way (1919)
The Crimson Tide (1919)
The Slayer of Souls (1920)
A Story of Primitive Love (1920; story)
The Little Red Foot (1921)
Eris (1922)
The Flaming Jewel (1922)
The Talkers (1923)

The Hi-Jackers (1923)
America, or the Sacrifice (1924)
The Mystery Lady (1925)
The Man They Hanged (1926)
The Drums of Aulone (1927)
The Gold Chase (1927)
The Rogue's Moon (1928)
The Sun Hawk (1928)
The Happy Parrot (1929)
Painted Minx (1930)
The Rake and the Hussy (1930)
War Paint and Rouge (1931)
Gitana (1931)
The Whistling Cat (1932)
Whatever Love Is (1933)
The Young Man's Girl (1934)
Secret Service Operator 13 (1934)
Love and the Lieutenant (1935)
Beating Wings (1936)
The Girl in Golden Rags (1936)
Marie Halkett (1937)
The Fifth Horseman (1937)
Smoke of Battle (1938)

PLAYS

The Witch of Ellangowan (1897)
Iole (1913; musical comedy based
  on the novel)

ART

Washington: or The Revolution
  (1895) [text by Ethan Allen]
Halifax in Wartime (1943) [text
  by Frank W. Doyle]

ESSAY

ALS (1921)

CHILDREN'S BOOKS

Outdoorland (1903)
Orchard-Land (1903)
River-Land (1904)
Forest-Land (1905)
Mountain-Land (1906)
Garden-Land (1907)

Lightning Source UK Ltd.
Milton Keynes UK
UKHW02f2051200418

321420UK00004B/212/P

9 781933 586489